THE LAST ENGINEER

THE LAST ENGINEER

Darrk World: Book One

Russell E. Van Dyke

MILL CITY PRESS

Mill City Press, Inc.
2301 Lucien Way #415
Maitland, FL 32751
407.339.4217
www.millcitypress.net

This is a work of fiction. Although historical places and people are mentioned, as well as actual cities, places, structures, and institutions, the characters and their actions are entirely fictional. Any similarities to anyone living or dead are purely coincidental.

Printed in the United States of America.

Paperback ISBN-13: 978-1-6322-1190-3
eBook ISBN-13: 978-1-6322-1191-0

For Donna, who put up with my crazy hours and crazy ideas.

And for Marge Eakins, the greatest English teacher I ever had,
who put an idea in my head I never got to thank her for.

And for Cal and Marie, who I never got to thank for their
friendship.

There were over sixty ships at the start of the battle. Orbiting a red dwarf now, there were nine. Eight of them were Borm ships, oblong and grey in color, most with the burn holes and blaster marks from the Darrk ships. Of the Darrk ships, there was only one left, black and pyramid-shaped, covered with burns and holes from the Borm ships' weapons. Large pieces of both types of ships were floating in space along with the corpses of Darrks and Borms. Except for the lighter furred ones, the Darrks' corpses were almost lost in the deep, permanent night of space while the thin limbed, pale Borm stood out in the dark void. The last pyramid-shaped Darrk ship was under attack. Holes marked the hull of the ship, and the last Borm ship with working weapons was getting ready to fire on it again. Soon it would be over. With the weapons down on the Darrk ship, this battle was as good as over; soon as their pulse cannons charged, the last Borm ship would finish the Darrk ship.

Commander Nantes was in middle age for a Darrk. Silver fur ran down his back to his stubby tail, his face silver around the eyes and muzzle and up his long ears. The bridge around him was littered with the bodies of Darrks, he was standing there alone, the only Darrk still with breath in him on the bridge. He was yelling, or one might say barking and howling, at the last engineer in the engine room who was still alive.

First Engineer Rahm was wrapping up his left paw with the right one, one of its seven digits was missing, but he didn't know where it went. It was probably mixed somewhere into the pieces of his fellow engineers now scattered about the engine room, those who'd lost their lives when one of their four engines exploded from the Borm ships' blaster fire. He tried not to think about or look at his shipmates or what was left of them, at least. The commander yelling at him was a great help refocusing his attention, that, and the blue-green blood he had to keep blinking out of his bright blue eyes. "We need to engage the stardrive! We have no weapons or shields, and the drive system is damaged!" The commander's howl roared from the speaker, "If we're here when they have charged up enough to fire, we will die!"

"But, sir," Rahm answered, "the computer is gone! We don't know where we will end up. We could come out in the middle of a star, or on the other side of the galaxy!"

"Do it or we will all die for sure!" the commander shouted. He could see the glow of the blasters on the other ship start to come up, and he knew he only had seconds left.

Rahm grabbed the lever of the stardrive, and thrusting it down and away from him, engaged the drive. *God, don't let us end up in a black hole,* he thought. Light seemed to stretch, sound became muffled, and there was a queasy feeling in both his stomachs. Then he fell, unconscious. After all, you shouldn't engage the stardrive while standing, and the chair *was* missing . . . along with half the computer and the *whole* watch stander.

Rahm came around in Sick Bay. *Well, at least we aren't in a gas giant,* he thought, *but where in the name of the four planets are we?* Looking around, he saw the medical personnel running on all fours from one patient to the next; some they were treating while some they were just making as comfortable as they could. Some, Rahm could tell, were already dead. He whispered a prayer to the god of the underworld and sat up. He had to get back to

Engineering. One of the doctors, a female named Hathor, rushed up, "You need to lie back down, you have radiation poisoning, and have lost much blood."

"Then, who is in Engineering? I was about the only functioning one before we jumped."

"Two of the junior officers are in there with part of the service crew, cleaning up," she said. "We have shut down the engines until we figure out where we are and can make repairs. After you engaged the drive, you fell unconscious and struck your head on something."

"I struck my head on something before then." He replied sarcastically, "How long have I been here, and how are the others? Have you seen the chief or the second engineer?"

"You have been here since yesterday," the doctor replied, and as she moved off, she said, "And sir, you are the only engineer left."

Rahm was shocked, *there had to be someone,* he thought. He got up anyway, his head felt as if it would explode. In the loud, confusing room, he was surprised the doctor even had noticed him. He had to get back to engineering. He needed to know how much damage had been done to the engines. Straightening his tunic, which was spattered with the blue-green blood of the Darrks and had a dozen burn holes in it, was a futile gesture. He stumbled to the door.

The door opened and he weaved out into the passageway. He looked around and found they'd cleaned up the passageway as best they could, but he could still see the blood stains on the bulkheads, the holes in the hull temporally fixed with spraluminum. He had started down the passageway toward engineering when he looked out of one of the ports into space. They were in orbit around a large planet with multi-colored rings. He did not recognize it or what he could see of the system. *Hopefully, the commander knows where we are,* he thought. *I just hope we didn't end up on the other side of the galaxy,* but he had a feeling that his hope wasn't going to be fulfilled.

TABLE OF CONTENTS

Chapter One

ERICK

She was calling him. He felt her call more than heard it, a gentle tug on his consciousness. How long had it been? Not long, he knew, but how many years? "Grandpa, I need you!" He could feel Eileen calling to him.

"Coming, Granddaughter . . . I will be with you soon." He could feel her weakness stronger than his own; he must hurry.

At a crypt, in a once secluded cemetery in Virginia, there was a scraping sound that came from the vents in the top of the granite structure. If one were inside, they would see the top of one of the four granite sarcophagi inside starting to move. Side by side, they were aligned in a row across the floor. Devoid of any ornamentation or carving, no names appeared on their surfaces.

A dark thin hand curled around the edge when the crack appeared, scattering debris that was resting on its surface as it was lifted away. A black rat, its eyes red in the glow from the vents set high in the walls, ran for the dark corners of the crypt. As soon as the top was half open, a dark skeletal figure sat up. As he looked at his rotting clothes, he figured he had been asleep for around twenty years, but no matter, he had slept longer before. The first thing to overcome was his weakness, then his appearance. He felt that itch in his head, the one that told him he had to feed. He stopped to regain control, calming himself. Standing up on strong but shaky legs, he moved toward the entrance, his vision seeing clearly in the almost completely dark room. Opening the door to the crypt, he looked across the hillside. He was surprised at all the lights at the edge of the cemetery. When he had first lain here, it had been much darker, more on the edge of town. It seemed much closer now, almost in the city; perhaps it was now. The town and cemetery he had chosen had apparently been growing much larger with the passing of time, the flat markers of metal, stone, and concrete spreading out; while the older section of the cemetery where his crypt stood, with its granite, limestone, and marble markers and crypts, looked much more comfortable to him. When did this happen? There was still snow on the ground in patches where he was and the night was cold, mid-March, he guessed, that would be about right for this area. His musing of this was short-lived, however, as he heard a familiar sound, a heartbeat, close, *food*.

The drug addict was just getting ready to fix, pulling the works out of his coat: lighter, spoon, candle, syringe, a short piece of rubber tubing. When he heard the noise behind him, he spun around. He saw nothing. "Fuckin' nerves!" the young man spat. He needed to fix *now!* He hunched down behind a large headstone and set the candle on top of a flat granite marker, jamming the end in the cut granite at the top of the "T" in the name of someone unknown to him. He never had the time to light the candle or even to take the small, black balloon out of his pocket.

When the shadow grabbed him, the man's past flooded through him. The violence this man had brought on others was seen by him just as clearly as if he'd looked through the man's own eyes. In his hunger, he wouldn't take just a little of this one's blood; no, he'd take it *all*. Tearing at the man's throat, the addict couldn't even scream as he struggled, he had looked into a face that brought him pure terror. Hair in patches hung on its head, eyes just two ice blue orbs in a skeletal face with half dried skin stretched over it. And the teeth, those fucking teeth! He found the strength of whatever had a hold of him too great—even a weakened Darrk is formidable.

As he drained the addict, then dropped the corpse at his feet, he could feel the strength returning to him, feel his shrunken body heal itself and his powers rejuvenate. He would have to feed again this night, perhaps twice, to return to full strength, but he knew he would be able to take care in choosing whom and control his hunger. He didn't like hurting the innocent, it was one of the reasons he had been able to live all these millennia. He looked down at the body of the young man lying on the grass and patchy snow at his feet. The man had wasted his life, yet even knowing this and being responsible for his demise, he felt pity for him. He must move quickly.

Picking up the man as if picking up a sack of flour and throwing him over one shoulder, he headed back to the crypt. Taking the addict's coat to cover his tattered clothes, he tossed the man in the coffin. Reaching into the man's coat pockets, he found a glass pipe, a black balloon filled with what must be drugs, and an envelope. Looking at the postmark, he found the year, nodded, and threw them in the coffin with the man, then gently closed it. Sliding the heavy granite sarcophagus lid closed, he walked out of the crypt and closed the door, throwing the bolts on the locks with a wave of his hand.

The man had gotten better than he deserved really, a nice, *permanent*, resting place. He knew no one would look for the man, just one more faceless one lost, and he went on his way. He would find another like him that should restore him to almost full strength. Otherwise, he would have to feed several times to achieve the same result, which would be much more time consuming. He would find another criminal, then, to Eileen.

Calling on powers he mastered over millennia, the shadow moved on. They might be able to find him now. Some might know he was awake, even follow his scent. He wasn't strong enough yet to confront them, so he wanted to be far away until his strength was restored. If anyone had been watching, he would have seemed to vanish in the foggy night air.

Chapter Two

JOHNATHAN

Two hours later, a dark figure seemed to just materialize in a dirty alleyway. The man was four inches over six feet with black hair graying at the temples, pale skin, and bright blue eyes. If one were to guess his age, they would think it close to fifty or fifty-five, and they would be wrong. He'd appeared near a large brick home toward the center of the city. Built just before the Civil War, it was the first house built on this block and the oldest. The original old farmhouse that stood down the street had been torn down years ago as the city got larger, only to be replaced by an apartment building. Feeling fully restored, he had landed in an alley around the corner from this home because he wished to not be seen by prying eyes, and it seemed there were several at this hour—strange. There was a place he could have landed on the top of the house, but he needed to know the condition of it first, and know if another building had been placed in sight of it.

The home was one of many scattered across the world. When one thinks of life in terms of centuries rather than decades or years, learning to think ahead becomes a must; it's what keeps you alive. This home and others were maintained by an old law firm in Washington D.C. Cleaning people came once a month, dusted, ironed, and pressed clothing in the closets that no one had worn, changed bedding on beds no one had slept in, collected, and threw away the junk mail no one would read. It piled up on the floor behind the mail slot, like a small hill, making it hard to open the door after a while.

The law firm generally maintained the home, calling whatever maintenance people were necessary from plumbers to carpenters. Depending on what was needed, they would make sure the home was left alone and in good repair. They were paid well to deflect any questions asked of them about the house and to keep it secure. It took up the entire lot and didn't have a yard, its walls coming to twenty-four inches of the sidewalk.

The man was careful, not wanting to run into anyone. He still wore the half-rotted clothes and knew he smelled of decay. He would have to dispose of these clothes soon, but he was in the right place to do so. He loved this house, the brickwork, high vaulted ceilings, beautiful moldings, and doors. They were typical of the architecture of the early to mid-1800s. It seemed the longer he lived, the more impersonal and plain buildings became. Man was removing the beauty in his work, in the name of progress. He hoped the time would come when builders would realize their error.

Coming around the corner of the house, he noticed many of the other homes had fallen into disrepair and the street needed attention. There were several potholes and one of the streetlamps was out. Trash littered the street and a large beer can in the gutter caught his eye. There were bars on the windows and doors of the homes as well as on his house. The people that were out this hour, about 11:00 P.M., looked around in either fear, suspicion, or plain hatred. What had happened here?

The sound of an engine caught his attention, and a few seconds later he saw a limousine pulling around the corner, swerving up to the curb. As it halted, the driver got out smartly, and coming around the car, opened the back door. An older gentleman got out of the back, leaning heavily on a cane. The man recognized him immediately, even though he had advanced in years. Johnathan Marks was a short pudgy man when he last saw him, but now had given way to fat. He had always told Marks he needed to get out from behind that desk. A partner with Lee and Marks, Attorneys at Law, he was personally in charge of his holdings. He was the fourth Marks to do so, beginning with his great grandfather during the Civil War.

Three young men across the street leaned against the building, looking bored. They watched the limousine pull up and saw the man who stopped and talked to that lawyer when he got out. The lawyer they'd see before, not this new guy. The one in the middle said, "That's him. That's him I tell you," he whispered.

The one on his right shifted so the gun in the back of his pants would stop digging into his back. "You sure?"

"Fuck yeah, I'm sure!"

"Call him."

"Erick, my good friend, you haven't aged a day!" Johnathan Marks exclaimed jovially. "Me on the other hand, I look like the old dinosaur I am. Shall we go inside, the air out here is cold and damp, and these old bones don't like it." Turning back to the car, he addressed the driver, "Howard, stay with the car please." The man nodded slowly and seemed to come to attention next to the car. Erick realized the man was going to stand next to the car in the cold and thought the action somewhat odd, he would have to question Johnathan about this. The sheer size of the man, well over six feet tall with broad shoulders, carrying a gun under the black leather vest on the right side, told Erick the man was left-handed. Something about this one was familiar, but he couldn't place it. His powers hadn't fully been restored, that would take time.

Johnathan broke him of his musing and turned, going up the steps. Then another thought crossed Erick's mind: how did Johnathan know he was awake?

He waved his hand out of sight of the driver and felt, more than heard, all the locks disengage. Opening the steel gate, then turning the knob, he opened the door, letting the lawyer in before him. Johnathan headed straight across the entry and stopped at a little box on the wall, where a blinking red light was and began tapping on a keyboard, but the box hadn't been there the last time Erick had been in the house. Before Erick could ask, Johnathan began to speak while not looking at him, keeping his attention on the box, until the red light became a solid green. "It's an alarm system; we had it installed about fifteen years ago when the neighborhood began to deteriorate. I'll give you the code, although, with your talents, you may not need it." He was rubbing his hands together as he spoke. Although he wasn't cold, Erick realized it was chilly in the house.

Turning left, Erick walked to the double doors of the library, throwing the doors open wide, he entered, followed by Johnathan. Waving his hand at the fireplace, the wood sprang to life, large flames dancing above it and quickly warmed the room. He crossed to the liquor cart and poured a brandy for Johnathan, handing it to him, he spoke softly. "I am sorry to leave you as I have many questions, as I'm sure you do, but I must bathe. I will be back downstairs in thirty minutes." Although Johnathan hadn't said anything, Erick knew he smelled of dirt and rot. Twenty years lying in a coffin does not leave one with any other smell but of the dead.

"Take your time, I don't sleep much anymore, and besides, your brandy is always the best I've ever tasted, and I see the decanter is full. But rest assured, I do know time is of the essence."

Thirty minutes later, Erick was coming down the stairs. Dressed in a black wool suit with vest, dark gray silk shirt, and black tie.

The suit coat over one arm, he was busy fastening the cufflink on his right wrist. As he entered the library, he saw Johnathan in an armchair next to the fire, the now half-full decanter on the end table next to him. Erick poured himself a glass and setting it on the other end table, put on the suit coat and sat in the armchair across from Johnathan. "Well now, my friend," he said, taking a sip of brandy and savoring its flavor. "What has happened in my absence these last twenty years and what happened to my neighborhood?"

Nodding and looking at Erick through glassy eyes, Johnathan began, "In plain English," there was no hint of slurring in his voice, even after half a quart of brandy, "the city got larger and they made low-income housing out of the apartments down the street. After that, the neighborhood fell into decline, people moved out, and the other homes were turned into apartments. Yours is about the only single-family dwelling in the whole neighborhood. More low-income tenants moved in, and now your home stands in one of the worst neighborhoods in the city. I've had to have an alarm system installed, gates put on the doors, and bars on the windows. I've had cameras installed outside that are monitored by a private security firm, but the home is secure as you requested. The private security comes by several times a day completely unscheduled, so the crooks leave the house alone. Seems that when everyone who has tried to break in gets arrested and prosecuted word got around that this place is 'off-limits.' Nobody who has tried to break in has even gotten inside, and all have been arrested and jailed. There hasn't even been an attempt in months."

Taking a sip of his brandy, Johnathan continued, "I know the expense would have been approved by you anyway." Erick nodded agreeably. "Now in other business, your personal wealth has increased by over two hundred million, corporate wealth even more, and I have funneled it into the various necessary companies. All taxes are up to date, and, lately, you have been listed as 'traveling'." Reaching inside his coat, he pulled out a large envelope, "Here is your passport, all stamped and updated, as well as your wallet, one thousand in cash, all the proper identification and credit cards. The code to the alarm is on the back of my business card if you need of it."

"Your timing is perfect as usual. You arrived back in the United States yesterday evening on the flight from Paris. You were at an auction in Paris this last week and purchased several antiques. They have been shipped to your warehouse in New York and should arrive there in two weeks. Gary will be happy you are back because being you keeps him far too busy. He is getting on in years and it may be time for another double. He has already stated he would rather stay in New York and just run the shop and retire to it. Being a double for you isn't all it's cracked up to be, I guess."

"I have already notified the pilot, and your plane is fueled, and has put in a flight plan to Seattle. I have informed the new Seattle office you will be in residence tomorrow morning, so everything should be ready for your arrival. I assumed you would be making the trip after our meeting and would need the plane."

"And before you ask, I had a motion detector installed in the crypt on one of the vents looking in. When you started moving, I got ready to come here. I'm glad I got here when I did, as it would be hard to explain how a man who lives at a house wouldn't know it had an alarm. Another thing," reaching into his coat pocket, he pulled out a cell phone and handed it to Erick, "you'll need this, it's a new cell phone. Don't ask me to explain it, just ask any child."

"Lastly, your account is being turned over to a firm in Seattle as I am retiring. As I have no children, I am turning over the firm to a capable young man here in D.C. who would think I was insane if I told him my client has known my family for almost one hundred and fifty years. I think you will approve of this firm in Seattle, after all, its name is Raven-Hawk." Erick's eyebrows rose. "They are a legal and security company who mostly deal with management of exclusive clients and personal security, bodyguards, and the like. Have I done something wrong?"

"No," Erick said, "my grand-niece and nephew?" he shook his head, "No, I'll get back to that." Johnathan nodded as he continued. "As to the cell phone, I had one of these before I slept, not very large is it?" Erick mused, turning it over in his hands, and thinking of the one he had before he entered the crypt. "What happened to the one I had?"

"Outdated. Your old one was analog; they are all digital now. Don't ask me to explain it to you, I ask my neighbor's grandson to explain something to me all the time. But I will say this, it has more storage space on it than your old computer did. Raven, Hawk, and Eileen's numbers are already in it, as well as mine. The tech is growing so fast they become outdated before they even hit the market."

"Technology has advanced that much in twenty years? And Hawk and Raven, how are they?" A look of concern crossed his face, Johnathan could tell, although that face rarely showed any emotion, it always did when it came to family. "They were in high school when I left, and Eileen, she is ill?"

"They were seniors, in fact. Seems there was a great deal of money set aside for their education by someone." He had an impish grin on his face that Erick knew well. "They put it to good use. Hawk went to Annapolis after he was accepted; Raven went to Harvard. Both graduated with honors, and Hawk stayed in the Navy for about ten years. Raven interned for me, then came to work, and after a time, I suggested she move to Seattle as Eileen had fallen ill. In truth, Eileen has just gotten old. I don't look that good now; Eileen at 250 years old looks amazing. Anyhow, Raven went to work for me in a small office in Seattle, so she could be near Eileen. I started sending her your holdings there. She was helping me with all your holdings at the office in D.C. anyway. When Hawk left the Navy, they started their own firm, Raven-Hawk, with my blessing and the money you left them in trust. I have been slowly turning your things over to Raven for about the last five years, she has it all now. They are particularly good and very capable attorneys."

"How much do they know?"

"Next to nothing, other than what they were told as children. Here, on paper, you just looked like a wealthy client; there were no names on what she saw. When she moved to Seattle and started on your holdings there, that's when she saw your name. I got a call from her awhile back and she asked, mad and point-blank, I might add, if this was her 'granddad's' stuff. She wasn't happy about me not telling her, but she understood. The only other thing she said was, 'where is he?' All I told her was abroad. She seemed to let it go at that. But knowing her and that inquisitive mind, I'm sure she has been studying you for some time now. As for Hawk, he runs the security side of the company, I doubt she has even discussed it with him." Johnathan stopped and drained his glass, "that covers everything necessary, I think. I believe you wish to get going to Seattle, and I need to be on my way to bed for all the good it will do me. I'll have Howard drop me at home then come back to run you to the airport." He stood up slowly and stretched, "I'll be on my way then."

"We have to get together when I return from Seattle," Erick said as they left the library. "There are so many questions to ask, although I don't know how long I'll be there, as I can't see the condition of Eileen. I'm not strong enough yet. I'll call you from Seattle when I know for sure what's happening, and we'll set the time to get together."

"You might be able to get your questions answered by Raven. You'll have to tell her eventually. That is, if she hasn't figured it out already. Not that I want to not see you. You know more about history than any book or university professor or historian I've ever heard of. As I seem to recall, when I was in high school, a certain friend of my father's gave me an account of the Civil War that was so accurate, when I took finals I almost got expelled for cheating. The teacher had never covered the details like that in class!" They both shared a laugh. "I do enjoy our conversations, but the questions you might really need to ask you should ask Raven. You will find her articulate and very well read, and up on all your finances as well. So, I bid you adieu, my friend, call me and tell me how Eileen is doing, would you, and give her my love." Erick helped him into his coat, handed him his cane, then opened the door. They shook hands and Johnathan started down the steps, "I'll call Raven tomorrow and tell her to take it easy on you," he said as he climbed in the car with Howard holding the door, "be careful my friend, Dianna has been looking for you." He waved before Howard shut the door.

Then, as Howard walked around the car to get in the driver's seat, he gave Erick a nod and glanced at three teenagers across the street, as if warning him of something. Erick had already noticed them, but was glad the man felt it needed his attention. Johnathan was in good hands. Howard shut the door, started the car, and pulled away from the curb.

Chapter Three

MAC

He had taken notice of the three when he opened the door, his senses had warned him of the possible danger, although he hadn't shown it. The three teens were staring straight at him, not even trying to hide their gaze. What they were doing on the street at this hour he didn't know, *they should be in bed,* he thought, there is school tomorrow and none of them looked old enough to have finished. He made like he didn't notice and shut the door without even so much as a glance at them they could notice. *Curious,* he thought, *twenty years was not that long, but it seems centuries ago from the way the world was when I went to sleep.* Looking at his new cell phone, he thought, *technology has advanced as well, it won't be long now; it'll be time to go. That's why Dianna has been looking for me.*

He turned around in the entrance, and looking across the floor, he saw a portrait on the wall there, an olive-skinned woman in a plain green dress, her raven-colored hair laying across her right shoulder. Her green eyes seemed to sparkle in the painting, and her soft smile was turned up in the corners just a little, as if there was a secret in her mouth and she dared not open it. Erick had paid the painter twice as much as he wanted for it. The artist had caught her so well in the painting it almost looked like a photograph long before there was such a thing. When Erick had commissioned the painting, he never guessed the man would capture her so well. It was in Delft, while he was there on business, that he met the man at a dinner. The man seemed so captivated by Erick's wife he had asked Erick if he could paint a portrait of her. Erick told him he would pay him for his work if it was of good quality and the man agreed. So, while Erick was away during the day, Johannes worked on the portrait in the hotel sitting room with his wife. "Because of the light," the painter had said, but in those days, you didn't put yourself in a hotel room alone with another man's wife. When Erick saw the finished work, he almost wept. He had two more done before her death by different artists, and none was as good as the one done by Johannes Vermeer. This house was a fortress and always had been, because of this painting. Not because the painting was valuable, but to Erick, the person in it was. He missed her love every day, at least for the last 400 years, it was almost as if God had made her just for him. It was time to go to Seattle, just one more thing to attend to.

With a last look at the painting, he started down the hall, went through the kitchen, and opening the door past the stove, took the stairs to the basement. At the bottom, he turned the light on, more out of habit than need, he knew where he was going, and he could see quite well in the dark. He went to a spot in the wall where the bricks showed through the concrete falling away from the wall, odd in such a well-maintained home. With fingers stronger than iron and fingernails sharper than knives, he pried a brick from the wall and pulled the necklace out from behind. On the end of it was a round amulet. Smiling, he put the chain over his head and around his neck, tucking the amulet inside the gray silk shirt. Looking around the basement after replacing the brick, he saw many things that should probably be in a museum. Uniforms from the Civil War, one of the first repeating rifles ever used in battle, a pair of revolvers, a couple of muskets and uniforms from the Revolutionary War, a Blunderbuss, a favorite rocking chair of

Maria's from the 1600s, numerous other furnishings, candle sticks, and kerosene lamps filled the large basement, and in the corner, a large chest. Remembering a promise from some time ago, he walked over to the chest and lifted the lid. He removed the tray at the top that was filled with various paper currencies from different periods in the nation's history. Inside the bottom were hundreds of silver coins and gold pieces from the Civil War era and earlier; pocketing five of the coins, he replaced the tray, closed the lid, and turned to leave.

A feeling of danger washed over him and the hairs on the back of his neck stood up. His hearing became more acute, and his vision sharpened. Someone had just entered the house, no, three someone's. *Ah, our friends from across the street,* he thought. Moving silently to the stairs, and with a wave, the lights dimmed and went out, he would wait in the darkness; he wanted to make sure of their intentions. He could hear three hearts beating quickly. They may not live to regret this night, their choice.

The three young men stood in the entry by the front door, one held a small semi-automatic in his right hand, one had a bat, while the third was large but unarmed—his arms almost too large for his coat. "Is he upstairs?" the biggest one whispered, "I'm telling you, this house is bad news, it's been nothing but trouble to anyone who ever tried to get in it."

"Yeah, but that was when nobody was here, and the alarms were set," said the one with the gun. "I can't believe the old bastard left the front door unlocked! Look, we search and find it and get paid." He moved quietly further into the house. "Billy," he said quietly to the one with the bat, "go upstairs and see if he's up there, we'll check down here and go through this place."

"Old bastard?" Erick thought, then he noticed it, a fourth heartbeat. Who was this? This heartbeat was smooth and even, not

stressed; Howard, he realized. *Why in the world did he come back?* He felt the two young men coming down the hall and a floorboard creaked, confirming what he already knew, they were headed for the kitchen. He felt Howard move to the stairs and start creeping up to the second floor. He must have thought Erick was upstairs and might need help; he doubted his intentions were malicious. He would be there to stop these young men, not help them. The other two were in the kitchen now, he heard one of the kitchen knives slide out of the wood block on the counter, probably the large chef's knife, which would be about the mentality of this group Erick surmised. There was a thump from upstairs, then another, then silence.

The two were standing in the kitchen looking at each other, "Go see if Billy's okay," said the one with the gun, "I'll make sure he's not down here." He wasn't even trying to be quiet now. As the large one turned to go with a large chef's knife in his hand, the pistol holder was headed for the basement door, and the biggest shock he had ever had in his short seventeen years of life

He opened the door to the basement and flipped the light switch, nothing, then he flipped it again, still nothing. He tried to peer down into the darkness, but it seemed even darker than it should. The old fucker was hiding down there for sure, he thought, taking a step down. Then suddenly, two blue lights were hanging in the air. He stared for a moment, then it struck him; they weren't lights at all, they were *eyes*. He brought up the gun immediately and fired twice and screamed as Erick grabbed him and threw him down the stairs, hearing the young man's neck break when he hit the hard concrete floor below.

The bullets had torn through Erick's chest, going completely through him on the left side, but his heart was on the right, so it didn't even slow him down. It was almost healed when he caught up with the large one with the knife in the hall. The large one took one look at the man coming toward him and knew he was going to die. It seemed the man was floating a half a foot off the floor, *impossible!* The only thing that saved his life was he dropped the knife. Erick's fist caught him squarely on the cheekbone under the left eye, if the young man's bones hadn't been so thick, the impact would have crushed it. As it was, the blow knocked him off his feet, making a crack from the eye socket to the top of his mouth and knocking out two teeth. All the big boy saw was a bright flash before his eyes, and he went crashing to the floor, unconscious.

"Christ!" Erick spun around to see Howard standing at the end of the hall. "I hope you never hit me!" Then he started to laugh, "I heard the shots and thought I made a mistake, but Johnathan was right," looking down at the youth, "you can take care of yourself." Then he noticed the bullet holes in Erick's coat, "Have you been hit?" He hurried over, then stopped and stared, there was no blood, a dark stain on the side of the coat, but no blood.

"No," Erick replied. "I wasn't wearing the coat, this must be from whatever the coat was over," he said, indicating the stain.

"Oh," but he looked curiously, nonetheless. Erick was saved by Johnathan, as he came through the front door.

"I see Howard's instincts are as good as his work," he exclaimed. "Are you alright?" He knew the answer Erick would give, but he felt he should ask anyway. Howard looked suspicious enough as it was.

"Where's the third one?" Erick asked, trying to change the subject.

"Oh, he's taking a nap upstairs. Where's the first one?" Howard asked inquisitively. He was looking extremely hard at Erick.

"At the bottom of the basement stairs," he replied. "Seems he fell down the stairs in the dark. I think he broke his neck."

"I'll go make sure," Howard said gruffly, and started for the kitchen.

"And I'll call the police," Johnathan ventured, "and I think you need to change your suit before they get here," he whispered to Erick.

Howard, or Mac, as his friends called him, reached the top of the stairs, and looked down. "It's blacker than a whore's heart down there," he muttered, but he could clearly see a body on the floor at the bottom of the stairs. *Why didn't he turn on the light?* He saw the switch to the left of the doorway and snapped it upwards, the bright bulb illuminating the stairs from above and saw the young man at the bottom. He was still breathing, gasping more like it.

Howard hurried down the stairs and saw a beat-up 9mm on the floor next to the young man's body. It was out of his reach, so Howard left it where it was, careful not to touch it. He also noticed two shell casings, one on the last step, one on the floor next to him. The boy was trying to say something, Howard bent down holding his ear just above his lips. "Not human . . . not real . . . not human . . . not real . . ." he repeated this several more times, then he stopped breathing altogether and died.

Looking around, Howard noticed it was very dusty down here; the cleaning service obviously didn't include the basement on its monthly tasks. There was nothing he could see that would have caused the stain on Erick's jacket. *So, where did it come from?* He saw a set of footprints in the dust, going to the wall under the stairs, where he saw some pieces of cement on the floor; he went over and found a loose brick. From there, the prints went to the corner by that trunk. Then back to the stairs. Something was wrong, but what? Then it hit him, there were two sets of footprints in the dust coming down the stairs, a third set that only went down the first two steps, but there were none *going up* the steps!

Ten minutes later, Erick was coming down from changing and saw Howard talking to Johnathan. "He's dead now, but he was alive when I found him. Couldn't say anything, just gasped for air. He must have fallen pretty hard." He turned to Erick, "Johnathan and I think it best we do not inform the police you changed, I'll explain later. Our boy upstairs still sleeping it off?"

"Yes, handcuffing him around the leg of the bathtub was a nice touch. He would have to be pretty strong to lift a hundred fifty-year-old claw foot tub." Erick said agreeably. "Where are the police?" He glanced over at the big one, blood was coming out of his nose and mouth and a large bruise had formed under his eye, but he showed no signs of coming around soon. "Should we be doing anything for him?"

"Hell no, he doesn't belong here anyway," Howard spat. "I'll be out front."

"You have a good man working for you, Johnathan," Erick replied.

"Oh, he doesn't work for me, he works for Raven-Hawk."

In the fifteen minutes more they waited, Johnathan explained how Howard came to be there. Several months before, Johnathan had had someone break into his office, which was no small feat as the alarm system was almost as good as the one here in the house. They didn't take anything that could be determined, but they'd gone through all the files. Whatever they were looking for must not have been found as every drawer in the office had been overturned, including the ones in all the desks.

When Raven heard of this, she dispatched Howard to Washington and wouldn't take no for an answer from Johnathan. Howard was now Johnathan's personal bodyguard. He was relieved by a man named Thomas every two weeks. They were trying to find a replacement for Howard, but, as of now, there was no one Raven and Hawk would entrust his safety with more than Howard and Thomas. They would be around until whomever broke into the office was caught. Howard was a friend of Hawk's. They had met while Hawk was in the Navy and had served together in Iraq, Afghanistan, and other places he wouldn't mention, although Johnathan couldn't get out of either one what they had done there. Howard was a man of few words but many funny but tasteless jokes, and while Johnathan thought he saw danger on every corner on the street, he couldn't find fault in the fact the man was very good at his job and had the instincts of a cat. After the next incident, Hawk and Raven decided to make the position permanent, Howard was to stay until relieved or told otherwise.

He was at the office when Dianna, Erick's sister, came by just two weeks ago, demanding to know where Erick was. She started toward Johnathan when he told her he didn't know and asked her to leave. Howard had gotten between her and Johnathan when she stepped toward him and ran straight into him, from the look on her face, she'd run into a brick wall. She had stopped, somewhat shocked, looked him in the eye, then said she must have been wasting her time, and strode from the room. And while this may have impressed Johnathan, he had no idea how much more impressed Erick was. If his sister had left, there was something about Howard that scared her, or at best, made her feel ill at ease. They both knew Dianna was able to go right through Howard and could any human, but for some reason did not. It made Erick wonder what the reason for her withdrawal was. There was something about Howard that Erick had noticed as well when he just came to attention next to the car. But he couldn't put his finger on it, even after all these centuries. The most disturbing part, he *should* be able to. But he wasn't fully rejuvenated yet, so his powers weren't close to peak.

He was pondering this when the blue and red lights of the police cars came and stopped in front of the house. They walked in behind Howard, who was waiting on the porch for them. Two of the officers and a man in a suit, a detective Erick assumed, went past them with Howard and headed for the basement. One man in a rumpled suit that looked slept in and another uniformed officer stopped in front of Erick and Johnathan. "I'm Detective Wallace," he said, producing a badge and identification, "which of you is the homeowner?" When Erick stated he was, the detective looked at him and replied, "Mind telling me why there is a dead man in your basement?"

Johnathan started to interject when Erick held up a hand to silence him. Erick started to tell him about the meeting with Johnathan and how after he left, he neglected to lock the front door. While he was making that account the other detective and Howard came in from the hall, and Detective Wallace took Howard and Johnathan over under the portrait, with Johnathan arguing how he needed to stay with his client. The questions went on for an hour, with Erick getting more irritated with every moment but not showing it. This was mostly due to the fact the detective would ask the same questions he had already asked over again, until finally the detective stopped asking. About that time, the other detective came over and started asking the same questions over again, while Detective Wallace started asking questions of Howard and Johnathan.

While they were being questioned, ambulance personnel took the large one, placed him on a gurney and the police cuffed him to it; he still had not regained consciousness. The one upstairs was brought down kicking and screaming for the officers to "get off me!" and was half-carried toward the door followed by another covered gurney being pushed out by two men wearing coveralls that said, "Coroner" on the back. When the one kicking and screaming saw the covered gurney, his eyes grew wide and he suddenly stopped struggling. "You killed him," he screamed, "why did you kill him?"

"Because he had a gun, dirt bag!" said one of the officers holding him.

"He didn't have no gun! The fucker just killed him! We'll sue! Fuckers, we'll sue!"

"He fell down the stairs, dipshit! Get him out of here!" yelled the detective. As they watched the youth being pushed out the front door, the detective turned to Erick, "And by the way, I found two shell casings on the floor at the bottom of the stairs, 9-millimeter, but no bullets. Do you know where they went? What direction was the gun pointed?"

"I'm not sure, Detective, I was hiding under the stairs, heard two shots, then the one started down the stairs and slipped in the dark."

"He didn't turn the light on? It was on when I went downstairs."

"I turned it on," said Howard, walking up. "It was off when I went downstairs to check on him." His cell phone started to ring, "Excuse me."

The two detectives were looking at Erick, "I don't know, I turned it off when I heard them coming down the hall." He said quietly.

"Looks pretty cut and dried to me, Tim," said the other detective in the rumpled suit walking up, "looks as if they just tried to invade the wrong house. Say, is that really a Vermeer?" He pointed at the portrait.

"You know your art. Yes. It's been in my family since it was done."

"Then the one over there is really a Picasso?" He pointed to the painting across from the doors to the library.

"Yes."

"Beautiful painting. And the other paintings in the house, originals?" Erick nodded. "Why would someone live in a neighborhood like this one with something like those on the walls?" he asked, "Shouldn't they be in a museum, or shouldn't you be living on the other side of town, not here."

"You should wait until you see the basement," the detective he called Tim said.

The detective with the rumpled suit shot him a hard look. "Question still stands, why haven't you moved?"

"My family built this house. It's been here and in my family for over a hundred and fifty years." Erick said coolly, "And I'm not letting myself get pushed out, by anyone."

"That a fact?" was the reply. "Don't go anywhere, Mr. Scott, we may need to speak to you again." His hands pressed the arms of his suit coat as if trying to iron out some of the wrinkles.

"I have to go to Seattle, Detective, my aunt is gravely ill. I'll leave an address and phone number with my attorney," he indicated Johnathan, "you can reach me there through him."

"I'll be in Seattle as well," Howard said, walking up and slipping his cell phone in his pocket. "The home office wants me to come back and explain what has happened to them. Here is my card, which is where I can be reached." He handed the detective a card.

"I could tell both of you to stay here," he stated.

"You could if you charged them with something," Johnathan replied. "Are you?"

"No, not yet. Leave access to the house, Mr. Scott, my team still has to find the slugs from those shots."

"Johnathan has access, you may ask him for entry."

"Very well, goodnight." And with that, the police left. It was almost 4:00 A.M.

After they had closed the door and were out of earshot, Erick turned to Howard, "You said you would tell me why we shouldn't tell the police of my changing."

Howard looked at him squarely, "The holes in the jacket and the stain on it; I didn't see anything like that there in the basement, much less where you could hang a jacket, except a nail on a post. Both bullets are in the post, by the way, and I know the detective saw them; he wanted an excuse to get back in the house obviously. Having to explain would have taken more time and resulted in your being charged with manslaughter. I don't think there is time for that right now. We both have to get to Seattle."

"My plane is ready to go at the airport. I'll meet you there in an hour."

"I was told to not let you leave my sight," Howard explained.

"Then it will take longer as you have to wait for me, then I you."

Howard figured he was right and knew he couldn't waste the time. All he needed at his flat was his notebook, but he did need it and they would have to double back to go to the private airport where Erick's plane was waiting. He knew that Erick had to get to Seattle, and his personal plane was about the fastest thing available, so he made a judgment call he would regret later. "Okay, I'll meet you at the plane in one hour," or so he thought.

EILEEN

After Johnathan and Howard left, with Johnathan smiling, Erick went straight to the closet next to the front door. Removing a black wool overcoat, he turned and started up the stairs while waving his hand to lock the door. The upstairs was furnished like the downstairs, not one piece of furniture was less than a hundred years old. There was none of the wall to wall carpeting that Erick detested, but rather a beautiful hall rug that went from the rooms to the left of the stairs, down to the door to the master bedroom on the right at the end of the hall. There were ten doors leading off the hall, he went to the one second from the stairs across the hall and opened it, a set of stairs led up to the attic.

That's when he remembered the alarm system, he would have to go down and set it unless . . . he concentrated on the little box on the wall next to the Picasso. In his mind, he could clearly see the buttons next to the keypad, one said "ARM." In his mind, he saw himself pressing the button, a light came on flashing yellow, and on the little screen at the top, digital numbers started counting down from 0:05:00. *Plenty of time.* He started up the steps to the attic.

At the top, he looked around him. If the basement was cluttered, the attic was stuffed. From floor to roof, boxes, trunks, and crates were stacked. Furniture and paintings were mixed throughout, and various racks had different clothing from another century hung on them. It was almost as if one had stepped back in time or into a movie studio's costume and prop department. Weaving between the stacks, he came to a set of narrow stairs leading up to a door. This door led to the roof. A telescope lay in the dust at the top of the stairs, covered by a sheet. Careful not to topple it, he stepped out on the roof.

A small ten by ten foot landing was up there on the roof, unseen from the street. Blocked by the chimneys on the right and left and the peaks of the house on front and back, the landing was in darkness. Perfect. He pulled out his cell phone to call the pilot. He told him that Howard would be there within the hour, but he was taking something faster than the old '79 Cessna. He would meet him in Seattle. Although he knew Howard would be mad, he also knew he would only be able to get away with this once.

He started the spell; distance made this one much harder. He should have been stronger before trying this, but the strength would come in time. Picturing where he wished to go and concentrating, he saw a door in his mind. As he turned the knob and looked through it, he saw a ferry moving through water toward an island. As he stepped over the threshold, he shut the door behind him. If anyone had been watching, they would have seen him appear to vanish.

Erick seemed to appear out of the mist in the backyard of a large mansion in the Magnolia district of Seattle. Bordering Discovery Park at the end of the street, there were no neighbors on one side and Elliot Bay off Puget Sound bordered the rear. With Bainbridge Island more than a few miles across the water, it kept the home away from prying eyes. The house was well sheltered in trees and on an exceptionally large lot, the closest neighbor being at least fifty yards away. Being on the water, he could smell the salt air, hear the ships' horns blaring into the fog out on Puget Sound, and hear the bells clanging in the buoys marking the channel. A ferry was moving to Bainbridge Island in the distance, otherwise all was quiet. It was 2:30 A.M. in Seattle.

The night was overcast and dark; he stood in the light rain and listened to the sound of the water dripping off the trees for a few minutes. He had learned many centuries ago that sometimes you needed to enjoy the moment. He knew he needed to see Eileen, but he wanted the time to collect his thoughts. He had been alive so long it seemed to him time was an illusion. It came and went with the passing of those around you as the passing of the stars in the sky. Who you remembered and who you forgot was dependent on how much they took the time to etch themselves into your orbit, and fill your mind, body, and soul, if he in fact still had one. He did hope so. He then became aware of two sounds, heartbeats, one extraordinarily strong, one weak and failing, Eileen; also, a third person, sleeping. Female. Raven. He turned and walked toward the house.

He entered through the greenhouse at the back of the home, taking note of the numerous trays with growing flowers and herbs. He came to a sliding glass door in the rear of the greenhouse, and opening it silently, he turned into a dark room. He would know it, even if he couldn't see it clearly in the blackness of the early morning and headed for the stairs to the right. There were various herbs and flowers dried or drying in the room; most, hanging from twine, while some were in jars lining the shelves on the walls. Potted plants filled the space, and he stepped around these deftly and silently approached to the stairs. He climbed up them sound-lessly to the third floor, skipping the second, not even touching the hardwood steps, and let his feet come to rest on the oak at the top of the stairs. This staircase only went to the third floor. He would have to cross the living room to take the main stairs to the fourth floor.

From here, he looked across the living room, seeing the same artworks in the same places he had left them, the furnishings the same as if he had left this morning, not twenty years ago. This was his house after all, and although it had a woman's touch to it, it was decorated to his liking. He walked across the oak floor of the living room, headed for the entry and the staircase going up. Upon arriving in the entry, he noticed a change. A lift had been installed in his absence next to the staircase. In the classic style to match the home, it was made of cast iron and very much looked a hundred years old, but he could see the motor and cables were quite new. Large enough for five people and built in the curve of the staircase, it stopped up on the fourth floor, not going to the fifth or office level as he always thought of it. It went down as well, and apparently opened into the recreation room next to the greenhouse and the pool.

The house was huge by any standard and considered one of the oldest mansions in Seattle. While it had been remodeled several times and added to, it still held the character of the original mansion. Built on a hillside of brick and stone, from the front driveway, it looked three stories tall, from the rear, five floors were visible and with it being built in a T shape, the leg of the T jutted out of the rear of the home then across the lawn toward the sandstone cliff called Magnolia Bluff, fifty feet above the waters of Puget Sound. The ground floor in the rear had a large roofed patio that filled the space on one side, and the pool and the greenhouse were side by side on the other side of the T. On the third floor at the main entrance, you could walk right out onto the front of the house to the circular driveway. Like the house in Virginia, it had an upper deck on the roof for his telescopes. The home had five offices and featured eleven bedrooms, each with its own bath and walk-in closets. It also had eight half baths, an indoor pool with sauna, hot tub and steam room, an exercise room, showers, two locker rooms, a library, two sitting rooms, a recreation room, a theatre, two living rooms, a formal dining room off the main kitchen, and a second large family kitchen with a small dining room off of it. A small dining table was next to the center kitchen, which had a small two-burner wood stove next to the ovens. On chilly mornings, it was the perfect place to sit and read the paper with your morning coffee and listen to the wood crackling in the stove.

The main kitchen on the third floor was capable of handling exceptionally large parties, with four ovens, an open gas broiler and grill, under a commercial hood, with a six-burner gas stove. There were two large commercial refrigerators, one at the end of the island by the prep sink and another by a door leading to the stairs going down to the walk-in cooler and freezer on the ground floor served by a dumbwaiter. Just past that was a door going out the side of the house. French doors off the kitchen opened to an outdoor brick barbecue and outdoor kitchen, with pizza oven and a full wet bar on the third-floor patio. A long set of folding glass doors opened to the formal dining room and could be opened to the patio in good weather. There was a recreation room with another full bar on the ground floor as well. The main entrance was on the third floor and another was on the ground floor garage level. With the home built on a hill, its driveway split, one curving around past the main entrance while another went down a hill into the garage. The guesthouse past the garage entrance had at one time been the old carriage house.

While he might call it his house, it had really belonged to Eileen and her sister Rose. She was the mother of Hawk and Raven. When she was over 100 years old, she found she was pregnant. After Erick had told her that her own mother was almost 200 when she came along, he didn't think she would have any problems. She was healthy and looked to be about thirty at the time. She was ecstatic. The twins came early in the morning on a warm October night and were welcomed into the loving arms of their mother, their aunt, and a great-great-grandfather who couldn't be happier.

When Rose died in a boating accident when the children were four, they immediately began to be taken care of by their aunt, Eileen. She raised the two children in the house that she and her sister loved so much. But sadly, the large parties had stopped when Rose died. It had been such a lively place while she was alive.

As the twins grew older, Erick had retreated to the guesthouse on the property. Making it a point to be around at Christmas and birthdays and such, but otherwise, he left Eileen to raise them. He didn't want them tainted by his presence. He had found his shear age had made him someone who, while not living in the past, had habits and mannerisms that dated him somewhat as someone much older than he seemed. He had his own problems to deal with anyway, at the time, and they had been mounting rapidly mostly due to his age. He looked much younger than he should have, and questions were beginning to be asked at the office. At best guess, his age was eighty-five. Then why did he look fifty? Hadn't he been running the place for sixty years? He began to wonder if he had made a wise decision to hang on so long. So, he had decided it was time to die. He and Johnathan made out a will leaving most everything to his son, Erick Scott IV, and he went and lay in a coffin for twenty years. Shorter than he wished, but it should have been enough.

He slowly went up the stairs, making sure to make enough noise so the attendant would hear him and he wouldn't startle her. He knocked softly on the door to Eileen's room, then turned the knob and entered. A nurse sitting in the corner set her book down and stood, "It's alright, Amanda, I've been waiting for him. Could you leave us, please?" Eileen's voice was cracked and dry. The nurse nodded and quietly left the room. After the door closed, she let out a breath and said, "Grandfather, thank God you're here." Erick removed his coat, then draped it over a chair by the door. He walked up to the bed, pulled up the chair that was next to it, and sat down, taking up her hand. She had an oxygen tube around her ears with the two ends in her nostrils; she looked very pale. "Look old, don't I," she smiled.

"You look as lovely as ever, Grand-daughter. Especially for a woman who's over 250 years old," he smiled, "I am so sorry for not being here to help you with the children. But it was not safe for them if I stayed. They could have been used as a weapon against me."

"I know, they may still be yet." A coughing fit followed for a few moments, then she laid her head back and sighed. "My spells were weakening, Dianna hasn't yet been in the house, but I've seen her on the property, the wards I have on the doors and windows won't keep her out, but they do keep out her minions, which have been increasing in number, and I wonder if they are all hers. But I don't think they work anymore; she has found a way around them and I'm worried. For me, it won't be long now, and the twins will need your help. Raven studied as a young girl, but stopped when she left for college. I'm hoping with you here she will take it up again. She is so good with potions. Although she tells me what she thinks I want to hear, she doesn't genuinely believe anymore, I don't think she will be of much good to you. You are the strongest wizard I have ever seen, but they will be too much for even you."

"Don't worry about that, I still have a few tricks up my sleeve." Erick smiled at her and then he just sat there, holding her hand, like he had done for so many of his children and grandchildren; and his lovely Maria. After Eileen was asleep, he started the spell.

The sun was coming up, peering through the clouds. Eileen was asleep and had been for some time. Erick gently released her hand and stood. There was a buzzing in his head, and he felt drained, *good then, it should work.* Walking over to the window, he pulled the curtains aside, letting the sun in the room. With the house sitting at an angle on the lot, her bedroom on the fourth floor was on the crossbar of the T of the house and faced northeast. He loved watching the sunrise; while bright, he still loved it. All the humans that were turned, the Nightwalkers, they called them, couldn't be in the sun, while he and all his kind could be out in it and just receive a sunburn at best, like any human. It also did something else he found over the years, although it took some time for him to notice. Right now, he needed the sun, at least to take some of the paleness out of his skin. He heard the knob turning and stayed looking out the window. He knew who it was.

Raven entered slowly, keeping her eyes on the back of the man at the window. The nurse had told her when she saw her this morning that a man was in Eileen's room, that she knew him and told her to step out. When she described the man Raven couldn't understand how he had gotten here already. When a very pissed off Mac had called and told her Erick had taken a quicker flight, she was skeptical, but now, seeing him at the window, she was dumbfounded. The only way he could have gotten here so fast was on a rocket. He slowly turned around. *He hasn't aged a day since I saw him last!*

Now it was Erick who had his breath caught in his throat, Maria? No, Raven. It was almost if her ancestor had been reincarnated in her, right down to her green eyes. Her hair was long and black, and she carried it in a braid over the right shoulder. Her slender form hid a strong and lithe body, and the eyes themselves contained an intelligence that was easy to spot and must be married to a quick mind. It was Maria, maybe not her, but her mirror image in mind and body. It visibly shook him. This wasn't the girl that he last saw in high school who resembled her, but like Maria, this was an incredibly beautiful woman. He then realized something else the second she spoke, like Maria, he couldn't lie to her, she would know.

"Oh," she said simply. She looked at Eileen, then beckoned him into the hall. "We'll let her sleep," she whispered, then backed into the hall, never taking her eyes off him. *Why hasn't he aged?* "Shall we go downstairs for coffee?" She held her hand out toward the stairs, then shook her head, "I'm sorry, but Aunt Eileen always referred to you as 'Grandfather', and you don't even look old enough to be my uncle."

"You may call me that if you wish, or you can just call me Erick," Erick smiled and said softly, "and coffee sounds perfect."

They went down the stairs where Amanda the nurse was sitting on a loveseat in the third-floor entry, reading. When she saw them coming down, she stood and went back upstairs to the fourth floor, smiling as she passed, to be with Eileen. They went through the living room, into the formal dining room, then down the stairs to the family kitchen on the next floor down. There was a pot of fresh brewed coffee on the counter. Raven opened the cupboard above it, took out two coffee mugs, and began to fill them. "You really pissed off Mac." She said, her eyes were smiling, "That is very hard to do, almost as hard as tricking him." She cast him a sideways glance, but there was laughter in her eyes, and laugh lines around those eyes. She looked to be in her mid-twenties not her late-thirties. This was someone who laughed, not cried, and not one to complain either he would bet. As they went to sit at the small table at the end of the island, he held her chair for her, she had never had anyone do that before and it felt a little strange, but nice. "I'd swear you look as if you haven't aged a day."

Avoiding that remark for now Erick asked, "I'm sorry, Mac?"

"Oh, you probably know him as what Uncle Johnathan calls him, Howard."

"Ah, yes. How has Eileen been doing? Has she been like this long?" The concern was clear and genuine on his face, and she knew he spoke the truth, he was concerned, but she also caught the evasion about his age.

"She has only been bedridden for about two weeks now. A few years ago, she fell ill, but after I moved home from D.C. she got better, but she seemed to suddenly start growing old. You know Uncle Johnathan gave me your accounts? I was given them when I came here from D.C. I never knew you owned this house. I had always assumed it belonged to Aunt Eileen. When I saw the records, I was surprised. You have a whole lot of money shoveled into accounts that don't trace back to you easily. When Aunt Eileen said you would be home soon, I didn't know what to expect." Her brow furrowed, "I certainly didn't expect a man who looks almost as young as my brother. Take away the gray hair at the temples and you could pass for thirty."

"So I've been told." Not knowing how to get around the subject, he decided to try a different approach. "I've aged well," was the simple reply.

"I would say so, for a man that is at my worst guess, supposed to be 120."

"My passport says I'm fifty-three."

"And in your records, there are documents signed by you that are over a hundred years old." She looked him squarely in the eye, "Who are you." It was a statement, not a question. "When I was a girl, Aunt Eileen said you have always been here but that was as far as she would go." He was saved by the shutting of the side door on the kitchen, and Hawk strode in the room. Strode was the right term, the last time Erick had seen him he was a tall, thin teenager of seventeen. Now, as an adult at thirty-seven, the change was remarkable. Hawk Scott was six feet four inches tall and a stout man, with black hair and blue eyes that looked at the world with suspicion. He carried himself well for someone Erick guessed was pushing 215 pounds and pushing it well. Light on his feet, Erick figured there wasn't enough body fat on this man to grease a frying pan. *The only way your knocking this man down is with a truck!* He walked up to his sister and kissed her on the forehead. He had only glanced at Erick as if it hadn't connected yet. This was not being rude; he was trying to keep Erick off guard.

"Good morning, Sis. How's Aunt Eileen doing?" His voice was low and one that commanded attention without being arrogant or bossy.

"As well as to be expected, I guess, at her age. The good doctor will be along later this morning. I'm going to stay for that, then head to the office."

"Doc did say he was stopping here before he locked himself in his lab and went to work." He turned to Erick, "Have we met?"

The realization had come to him, but he was playing it as if he didn't know him, Erick knew, so Erick reached in his suit coat pocket and pulled out the five Confederate gold coins he had taken from the trunk, laying them on the table. "I know you said you only needed one for your collection, but I brought you a few."

His blue eyes looked at Erick suspiciously, "While you do bear an uncanny resemblance to Erick Scott, you are far too young." He had recognized him, he just didn't show it, or perhaps, believe it.

Erick knew the time had come. "Oh, it's me alright, all more than 8600 years of me." Erick said this as if he didn't believe it himself and the color drained out of Raven's face. He's telling the truth, *impossible!* My God, it was all true. Raven was speechless. Hawk noticed the change in his sister and was looking back and forth between them. "As I said, dear Granddaughter," Erick looked Raven in the eye, "I've aged well."

Chapter Five

RAVEN

To say Mac was mad would be putting it lightly, he was furious. When he arrived at the airport to meet Erick, he was informed by the pilot that he had taken an earlier, faster plane. He does it all the time was the captain's casual comment. The Cessna Citation was an older model but quite comfortable and would make good time to Seattle. There would be a refueling stop the pilot informed him, but breakfast was in the galley as well as coffee, and if he would like to have a drink, there were various liquors in the cabinet and a good selection of micro brews in the refrigerator. He had called Johnathan and told him what had happened and was politely informed that next time, "Don't tell Erick you were not to leave his sight. Relax Howard, have a drink. It's going to be a long flight. Get some sleep, read a book." Easy for Johnathan to say, the skipper was going to kill him or at least keelhaul him.

About an hour into the flight, he got bored and went up to see the pilot. After some talk and proving he was more than qualified, the pilot let him take the controls for a little while. The last thing he had piloted was a helicopter, so it felt good to have the yoke of the Citation in his hands. Howard could fly just about anything, but jets were his favorite. The pilot watched him for about a half-hour, then told him he was going to use the head and get some coffee and would be back in a few minutes, he knew the plane was in good hands.

Mac began to think about the incident at the manor. Erick seemed not even bothered by the fact the young man in the basement had died, and it disturbed him for some reason. It's as if he took it casually, not like a sociopath, more like it happened all the time and he had grown *used* to it. And the fact there were no footprints going up the stairs, just down, was odd. He had covered the footsteps by going up and down a few times, but that was as far as he would go. He would not interfere with a police investigation any more than he had to, and he felt it might have done too much already.

And the police, let's not forget them. The bullets obviously were in a thick post at the bottom of the stairs, the grouping of the would-be killer, tight. He had looked at both, without touching them, and saw the same stain around the outside of the holes. Taking a handkerchief out of his pocket, he took a little of the substance and folded the handkerchief, putting it in his pocket until he could have Doc analyze it at the office. His mother had always told him to carry one, and these last few years working for Raven-Hawk, the habit had come in handy.

He wished he had been able to reach his mother, but she had been "unavailable" now for about three months, telling him she was going to South America on a dig and wouldn't be able to be contacted. She was an archaeologist and a university professor, so this was common. But when it came to things like this, she was always interested and always seemed to have the answers. He knew how, but she had studied people so much she had insight that was uncanny. And the sticky blue-green fluid on Erick's jacket, Mac had seen that before—on his mother. Then the answer came to him, and he felt as if someone had just kicked him. *No, it can't be!* He needed his mother now more than ever.

"Please," Erick pulled out the chair on the vacant side of the table, "Hawk, sit down." With the fourth side against the side of the island, the table only had three chairs. With them being alone in the kitchen and the nurse upstairs with Eileen, Erick, knowing without needing a doctor to tell him her time was short, had to bring these two up to speed much faster than he wished.

"What I am going to tell you will seem impossible, but it will be the truth. Raven will know if it isn't." Raven felt uncomfortable having him know that, she had never told anyone but Hawk her secret, and Hawk had told no one. *How did he know this?*

Erick continued, "There was once a group of witches centuries ago. I am one of the original twelve and was the only one not from," he seemed to wait, deciding what word to use, "around there at the time. Several millennia earlier, a number of my kind out of a crew of 900 became stranded here when our ship became damaged and we couldn't return home. The technology was too far away for anyone on this planet to help with what we needed to repair. So I, being the last engineer, was tasked with building a power plant so we could begin manufacturing the parts we needed. Against my wishes, our second commander thought it best to make ourselves appear like gods to get the population to help us as workers. Some of us were dispatched to what is now known as China, some were dispatched to South America, Europe, and so on. I was dispatched to what is now known as Egypt and the Middle East to find the site for the power plant. The others were to find sites to build receivers in their respective areas. This was when things started to go wrong."

"You see, our food stores had been destroyed. We had machines onboard that created a synthetic liquid we would drink to provide the certain minerals, and particularly an enzyme we couldn't live without. Even on the home world, our population had grown to the point that it was these machines that kept us alive. As we used up the resources that made this liquid, we became a warrior world that set out to conquer the systems around us. It was in a battle against another race that our ship had become damaged. The only escape we had was to engage the stardrive. Not knowing where we would end up, as the computer for navigation had been destroyed, I engaged it anyway under orders, and one of my greatest fears was realized, and we ended up on the opposite side of the galaxy. We were so many light-years from home, that there was no way to contact anyone with our damaged systems, and not enough spare parts onboard to fix damage as extensive as ours. We were trapped. Without stores and machines to create food, we began to starve. We could eat what little stores that were left, but without that necessary enzyme, we were slowly starving to death."

"To make the synthetic derivative, we needed the machines and a set of extremely specific chemicals. Most of the machines had been destroyed, and the chemicals and minerals were lost. We decided to, under system drive, head for a planet in the system that supported life. The trip would take several earth months. I remained awake while the rest of the crew went in stasis. I couldn't as the ship was so severely damaged it wouldn't make it without me to keep it running and keeping the stasis chambers powered. If I didn't and the chambers lost power, the crew would die. I've often wondered if I did the right thing."

"The ship itself, set in the right direction, would move toward the planet until caught in its gravitational pull, then it would fall into a weak orbit. Then, setting a time before they entered the chambers, the crew would wake, reassess our situation and place the ship in stable orbit. I was never supposed to be awake for the transit. I was going to set up two probes and follow the crew into the chambers after a boost around Jupiter to pick up speed, but an accident before I finished the probes made me see that someone had to stay awake, and I was the only one on board who could. You see, I was the last engineer."

"Over the next nineteen earth months, it was all I could do to keep the generators and engines running, and finish converting two of the three fighters we had left onboard into probes—one for mining and one for research. I was eating emergency stores on the ship but weakening, unnoticed to me. I just thought that being alone was making me a little space crazy. While the enzyme was in the emergency rations, it degrades rapidly. By the time the ship arrived here, my condition had deteriorated further, to the point where I wasn't thinking clearly. I had become paranoid, selfish, and was in a fit of rage. Getting in the last fighter, I left for the surface."

"I touched down in North America, on the edge of the Great Plains. When I stepped out of the fighter there were three natives to greet me, with about ten behind them on a low hill. As soon as I opened the door and the smells of the Earth hit me, my sanity broke completely and drove me into a fit that, to my undying shame, caused me to kill the three men there to greet me. As I started to come to my senses, feeling the sun on me, I could feel my strength return, but the men on the hill were running toward me, rightfully trying to kill me. The first arrow went in my thigh, the second in my chest. I grabbed them both and tore them from my body with a strength I had never known, and to my amazement watched as the wounds closed and then began to heal. Turning, I ran toward the men, and I slaughtered every single one. The next day, two of the crew arrived in our escape shuttle and saw the bodies of the thirteen men scattered around, torn to pieces. They found me in the same place I had fallen after the battle, if one could call it that, in the tall grass, covered in the blood of the men who had just come to greet me. We had found part of what we were looking for, and it was horrifying to me. But in time, I began to change my mind. Leaving the fighter, they loaded me in the shuttle and took me back to the ship."

"What happened next should not have surprised me thinking back on it, and God knows I have thought about it. We tried to start construction on the various projects but still had problems of keeping ourselves away from the populace. Some of us went rogue, making the populations near us treat us as gods and bring our food to us, taking care of our every whim."

"Others, like myself, tried to keep quiet about our arrival on earth and work on our projects, keeping away from the masses, only using the word of 'the gods' to keep them away. Still, others set themselves as kings and emperors over the populace to disguise their activities. But all of us had the same problem, and it drove some of us crazy as we became insatiably hungry for power over the people. The people began to rebel. They attacked and killed several of us in South America; then a few months later, several others were killed in China. While making their escape from Asia, we found out something completely by accident. If a human died in a certain way, we could bring them *back to life;* or at least a resemblance of it. Totally subservient, strong, and tireless, these reanimated humans became our watchers, our sentries, our soldiers, but they had a major problem. While we only needed to feed once every five to ten days, depending on how much energy we had to expend, they needed to feed daily, sometimes even twice. While we tried to keep this 'security' force in check, they would go insane after a time and break away. When they did, they were easy to follow—we followed the corpses. The other problem is they could only be out at night; the sun would kill them. We called them Nightwalkers."

"In the end, Egypt had become our last stronghold. All the other outposts were gone. I had almost finished the power plant, in what is now known as Egypt. It had taken me centuries with the crude tools I had to work with. That's when they came to me. They wanted me to turn a dying young pharaoh into a Nightwalker; I refused. I told them he would be a dark soul, going insane as he got older and would not even resemble their beloved pharaoh. They pleaded with me to help their boy king as he was dying, and I did not. After his death, they became angry, but after placing him in his tomb, it seemed forgotten. I thought that was the end of it when three months later, they came in the daylight and killed all but three of us in the Egyptian plant, including my wife and children."

"They had waited until we were separated and in small groups working each on a different section of the plant, too far apart to help each other. They did this during the day when the Nightwalkers would be asleep and couldn't help. We are hard to kill and how they succeeded where others had not is, they removed the head and buried it separately; then buried the bodies in a location far from the heads. Some of the Nightwalkers we had left behind were sealed in the tombs with royal family and pharaohs, a watcher alive but not alive; to kill any grave robber who tried to loot the tombs."

"With no communication with any of the others, our grand plan to repair the ship died with my wife and children. While making my escape from Egypt, I searched for them. When they were found, all I found was a grave. I heard later my sister and one other had escaped, but I didn't find her for over a thousand years. I began to wander the whole of the Middle East, Africa, Asia, and Europe. I didn't even know my sister had made it out of Egypt until later and didn't run across her until centuries later. I never stayed long anywhere as to not arouse suspicion. When I heard of a young general from Macedonia who was going to make a move at conquering Egypt, I signed on. Helping one of the greatest generals and rulers I had ever known conquer Egypt gave me the vengeance I felt I so rightly deserved, but in this process, I had lost a piece of myself and realized I was alone."

"I started occasionally running into Nightwalkers. Not knowing where they came from, I had assumed it was the work of another of my kind but didn't know who. When I was chased out of Egypt, some had been left behind, and this too may have been an answer. But with the Nightwalkers came something new, Hunters. I began to have to start avoiding them. They couldn't tell the difference between us and the Nightwalkers, and in truth, they didn't care. Luckily, Nightwalkers couldn't be out in the day and in the sun. I didn't have this problem. I was caught by them once, and to test me to see if I was a Nightwalker, they staked me out in the sand. As I lived when the sun came up, they cut me loose, but the one staked out next to me, the one that I had been hunting for, became a pile of ash. While the sun makes us stronger yet uncomfortable, we come from a twilit world in perpetual half-light, it literally burns the Nightwalkers into ash. To get rid of these Nightwalkers, staking them in the sun was an efficient way to dispose of them."

"We had also made another discovery after we came here— we weren't aging. At least not like we were supposed to. You see, my race is what humans would consider long-lived anyway. Our life span would be about four to five hundred of earth's years on our home world comparatively. But it would seem there is something about your sun that rejuvenates us. We store its energy up like a battery. It enables us to heal impossibly fast, and in some it heightens an already high ability for telekinesis and other more supernatural powers. There are those of us who have the ability to move at tremendous speeds, and the energy we draw from sunlight lets us all heal after extended periods of sleep lasting decades. When we wake, we feed, and our bodies repair themselves."

Erick stopped his recounting and drained his coffee cup, "One last thing about it is this: each of us in my race has a born ability, like knowing when someone is lying, or being able to make your-self float and seem to fly, being a math savant, or being of insane strength, and many others. These are natural abilities on my world in the populace, and it is generally the case that we have only one of these abilities on home world, while some of us here have many. But whatever that ability was on home world, it is *ten times stronger here*." Erick looked at the two of them, "Something is going to happen soon. The two of you are going to be right in the middle of it, and there is nothing I can do about that. You will be used as weapons for them to get what they want. You may be used to bend me to their will."

"I've heard enough." Hawk looked disgusted, "I can't listen to any more of this crap. Relative or not, this guy is lying and I'm not listening to him." He stood, glaring at Erick.

"Hawk," Raven began, "he's telling us what he believes is the truth."

"Great, that makes him crazy, not a liar. Either way, I'm not lis-tening to this bullshit," he replied as he headed for the door.

"Hawk," Erick called, he stopped with his hand on the knob, "remember in battle, you knew something was wrong; changed direction only to find out later you would have died staying on the original path. You ever have a time that you knew you were in danger, without a doubt, if you stayed where you were you would die. Have you ever just known where the person you were seeking was, even if you had never met that person?" Erick asked softly, knowing Hawk would leave anyway, but he needed him to have something to think about. Hawk turned the knob and left.

Raven looked at him, staring into his blue eyes. Very few people would or could do that; it seemed staring into his eyes made something in them become unhinged, yet Raven held his gaze. "I know you believe what you told me is the truth, but I do find it hard to believe."

"I thought you might," came a soft reply, then before her eyes, he *vanished*.

Raven stood up suddenly, almost knocking over her chair with her eyes darting around; *he was just here!* "Granddaughter?" She spun around to see him standing by the sink. Then she began to feel light-headed and plopped back down in her chair. *It was true, all true.* She found herself staring at him in bewilderment, he continued. "What you just witnessed was not a vanishing act," he smiled, "it was really me moving faster than you could see. One of the abilities I have ended up with, and over the centuries practiced, is speed. I also can step into another dimension and step out where I want to be, like entering a door and then stepping out another. Another I have practiced, and mastered, is levitation." He lifted off the floor several inches then came back down. "Another, fire," he brought up his hand and a ball of flames sat in it. As she watched, it got larger, then smaller, and with the closing of his hand went out altogether. "There are several others I know, which brings me back to where I started, at the twelve."

Raven had a question she was reluctant to ask, but did anyway, "How many of you are left?"

"I don't really know. It's the Hunters. As I mentioned, we can create soldiers to help protect us. Some of us have gone to extremes and made too many. Those are the ones the Hunters are truly after. They are what you would call vampires; but as to seeing others of my race? I haven't seen any except my sister in centuries."

Raven stared at him. "What do you mean those myths are because of your people? Why would they be like that?"

"You see, you, and I mean humans, are our *food*. Whatever the enzyme or chemical my kind needs, is only found here in *human blood*."

Raven suddenly felt sick.

Raven said she needed air and the two of them found themselves walking slowly down the hill toward the guesthouse, Erick's old residence. The rain had stopped before dawn and a beautiful, crisp sunny morning had taken its place. Erick was silent as they walked the path, its sides filled with rose bushes and rhododendrons. In several weeks they would bloom with colors of red, pink, and white, but right now they looked like what they were a sparse stick with a few leaves on it or an evergreen with wide leaves, half dormant through the mild coastal winter. The borders of the property were covered with cedar and alder trees; the alders, barren and waiting for spring, while the evergreen of the cedars standing out in the chilly air. Erick could see the guesthouse through the trees. Its condition, while maintained, looked drab. There was moss growing on the cedar shake roof. One of the gutters was loose and hung down a little, with leaves and other debris spilling over the top. The walks around the guesthouse were covered in leaves long dead from the fall and were in need of sweeping, with moss growing in patches on the walkways as well as on the slab of concrete by the entry. Wire and steel yard furniture was piled instead of carefully stacked in one corner of the patio.

As he had already told her of his powers, he felt no reason to disguise it. She needed to learn there was good in it as well. The breeze picked up and the leaves seemed to suddenly dry and began to blow off the cement, the gutter seemed caught by a gust of wind and lifted itself back in place. The yard furniture was blown out of the corner and tumbled into their places on the patio. Then the wind disappeared as quickly as it came, leaving a surface that was swept clean. He stopped and pulled a chair out for her. She looked surprised, then sat. Erick took a seat next to her looking toward the water. They sat silently for a time, just looking at the water. He knew she would speak when she had time to process it all, and Erick had time on his side.

Chapter Six

DOC

The silence was broken about thirty minutes later. "Raven!" came a voice from the house.

"Over here, Doc!" Raven called to him. Erick heard him trotting down the path. Listening to his heart, Erick realized the man was in great shape, the heart didn't even double in its beating. He was even more surprised when he came around the corner by the rhododendrons. He saw Doc was about sixty years old.

Dr. John Bradley M.D., Ph.D., was sixty-three, balding, and what one would call a "health nut." He had gotten on that wagon in med school and stayed aboard. Born in the small town of Forsythe in Montana, he seemed slow and too relaxed to most people to be a doctor. His slow manner of speech, casual tone, and blunt manner caught most people off guard. If he had something to say, he'd say it. If he didn't, he wouldn't. But what most caught people off guard, was his wicked, yet dark, sense of humor. But what everyone always missed was an extremely sharp and busy mind that was always two steps ahead of you. When given a problem to tackle, he would work at it doggedly until it was solved to the best of his ability; which was another trait of his, he knew when to quit.

A shorter man, only five feet five inches tall, he was slender and in extremely good shape. He ran at least two miles before breakfast and showered before he allowed himself one cup of coffee, two cups of fresh fruit, a bagel, and a large glass of orange juice for breakfast. He then wouldn't eat again until 3:30 in the afternoon, when he would have dinner with one glass of wine. Oftentimes a vegetarian, he did eat seafood and range-fed eggs, but his meals were generally high in protein and fiber, low in fat, and as Hawk would say, "cardboard would taste better." Then it was back to work until 7:30 in the evening, a short workout of free weights and cardio until 8:30, then he would shower, read for an hour, and go to bed by 11:00 P.M. Getting up at 4:00 A.M., he would start the whole cycle again until the weekend; which were always filled with bike riding, kayaking, cross country skiing, backpacking, fishing, or a combination of all. Rare was the occasion that broke that regimen.

Doc had never married and yet had a steady parade of women seemingly wishing to marry him over the years; none had caught him. Retiring as a captain, surgeon, researcher, and specialist in internal medicine from the U.S. Navy four years previously. He had treated Hawk when he was in for a broken arm and minor injuries when something incredible happened. Hawk had healed the bone in two weeks, and in six, you couldn't find where the break had been in an X-ray unless you knew just where to look. The cuts had healed in just two days *after* rejecting the stitches he had put in, and in a month, they had barely left a scar. He decided he needed to find out why and had been working on it ever since with Hawk's blessing.

Hawk had worked hard to get him here, or so he thought. The fact he was living in a city surrounded by forests and water was the clencher. Hawk really didn't have to give him the hard sell; he had made his mind up after he had been stationed in Bremerton ten years previously. He was Raven-Hawk's company doctor, coroner, forensic pathologist, and self-proclaimed "general pain in the ass." He was also the private physician for the Scott family, which he took very seriously, and his position was about to get much more serious.

"Ah, Raven, my dear, you get lovelier every day!" He turned and looked at Erick, "And who might you be, sir? I am Dr. Bradley to some, hack to others, but you can call me Doc," he held out his hand smiling. Erick stood and grabbed a hand much smaller than his, but the grip was firm and confident, the interest genuine, and as Doc's life filtered through his mind, he knew that with Doc, what you see is what you get—no walls, no barriers, and no bullshit.

"I am Erick Scott, Doctor, a pleasure to meet you."

John's brow furrowed, "I pictured you as much older." He looked a little confused.

"You must be thinking of my father, we have the same name."

"Oh, for a moment I was wondering if you were friends of Ponce De Leon and had found the Fountain of Youth. If you are and know where it is you can tell me, I won't tell a soul. I hadn't heard your father had had a son." He chuckled. Erick didn't answer, just smiled.

"How is Aunt Eileen?" Raven inquired, turning the subject from Erick.

He sobered immediately, "Much better it seems," he replied, taking a seat. "I'm afraid there isn't much more I can do for her, but the difference between yesterday and today is remarkable. I hope when I'm one hundred plus years old, I'm doing as well. She won't take the prescriptions I have given her and instead drinks that tea concoction you make for her; which is delicious, I might add."

"How long do you think she has, Doctor?" Erick felt a knot in the pits of his stomachs.

"Hard to say, her mind is strong, clear, and sharp, it's just that the body is worn out. Yesterday, I would have said could be a couple of weeks, at best a month. Today, I would almost say a couple of years. She's resting right now and said she would like to see the both of you later." He seemed bothered by her condition. Like all doctors that truly get to know their patients, he would grieve her passing and was doing all he could. There was no fault that could even be considered his, but he would shoulder some anyway.

"Thank you, Doctor. I know you are doing all you can," Erick said comfortingly.

"Call me Doc, please," he replied, looking down, "I never quite got used to being called Doctor."

"Doc it is."

"And I must be off, there are physicals on new employees to perform and old employees to piss off as I do their annuals." He stood, "Nice to meet you, Erick, if I may be familiar, and you do need to do something about your circulation; your hands seem a bit cold." He turned to Raven, "Oh, my dear, parting is such sweet sorrow." He gently kissed the back of her hand.

"Get out of here, you old reprobate!" she laughed. Seriously, she said, "Do me a favor and tell Hawk I won't be in until later."

"Your wish is my command." She playfully slapped him on the arm as he turned to leave. "Have a good day, you all." He trotted off up the path.

Erick knew his circulation was fine; it was his body temperature that was cooler, five degrees cooler than a human on average. "He won't have to give him that message," Erick said.

"Why?"

"Because he's behind us about thirty feet." Erick almost missed him, he wasn't a danger, so the part of him that warned him of such, didn't alert him to Hawk's presence. What had given Hawk away was when Erick opened his hearing to listen for the doctor's entrance he heard his heartbeat. Rare was the person that could sneak up on Erick, exceedingly rare.

Chapter Seven

H Λ W K

When Hawk had left them in the kitchen, he didn't leave the property. He walked down to bluff and stared at the water. *How had he known?* He knew better than to think Mac had said anything, *so how did he know?* His mind drifted back to a time that was another life, a time when he could only describe himself as one thing, a killer.

"But, Skipper, we are supposed to go that way!" First Class Petty Officer Gary Wallace was right; they were supposed to go down the alley, coming out in the square. But somehow, he knew it was wrong, all wrong, and he didn't know why he felt that way. And the dark night with no moon made it worse.

"I'm with you, Commander," Chief Petty Officer Howard McGregor whispered, "it doesn't feel good to me either, I don't know why, it's just . . . *wrong*."

That was it, Mac confirmed the way he felt and that was good enough for him. "God, this is Bird Brain, you see anything?" He asked the question to a member of the team who was up high, overlooking the scene, on a tall building's roof about two blocks away. A qualified sniper, the man was looking at the area through a night vision scope.

First Class Petty Officer Albert Riggs' answer was a few seconds in coming as he looked through the high-powered scope scanning the area yet again, "No, Skip, I don't see a damn thing," came the reply in a thick Southern drawl.

"God, be advised, we are changing direction to target."

"Copy that."

"Wallace, you and White go left and circle around. Be careful, this is White's first trip. We want his cherry broken, not shot off. Mac and I will go right; see you in the square."

"Yes, sir," Wallace responded. Then he and a wide-eyed Lt. Robert White started to creep slowly to the left.

"God, be advised we are two by two Romeo Lima, not down center."

"Copy that."

Mac and he began their slow move to the right. Intelligence had said to take the alley, as it would be quick and clear. Hawk didn't think so, he didn't know why, but he didn't think so. It reminded him of shooting gallery; if nothing else, no exits, one way in, one out. His feeling saved their lives. About five minutes later, as he came around the last corner and could overlook the square, God spoke.

"Bird Brain, this is God, be advised there is movement next to your location in the alley. Say again, movement in the alley."

As the man stood to toss a grenade in the direction of White and Wallace, God removed the top of his head with a .50-caliber bullet, the grenade dropped to his feet and blew four other men to meet Allah. Then all hell broke loose.

The firefight lasted less than a minute. To the men on the ground it seemed much longer. Such is the way of battle; everything seemed to move so slowly. When the last of the enemy was quieted forever, Hawk quickly moved away from the building, ran up to a burned-out truck, and surveyed the square; he was joined by Mac. "He's moved, he's in that building." Hawk pointed to a half-collapsed building.

"With you, sir," came the quick reply. Hawk stood and hustled over to the side of the building, flattening himself against the wall, then he watched for any sign of movement while the rest of the team flattened themselves against the wall, one by one, the last to arrive was Wallace.

"There you are, being right again, sir. My mama would have been real pissed at me for dying."

"No problem, my sister would have been pissed at me too. Ready?" As he pulled a flashbang off his web gear, he knew that was as close to a "thank you" as he was ever going to get from Wallace and smiled. He threw the flashbang in the doorway and went back to work.

At the debrief the next morning, a captain in khakis was staring at him. "Why did you deviate from the plan?" A man in a suit leaned silently against the bulkhead across the room. He could feel the carrier moving and was starting to feel seasick Hawk knew.

"It felt wrong," Hawk replied.

"It felt wrong. And why did you go in the building across the street instead of entering the one you were given by intelligence?" the captain asked harshly.

"I just knew he was there and not where we were told."

"You just knew." The captain stared at him for a few moments, then smiled. "Congratulations, Commander, you all came home with not even a scratch, and you got the bad guy to the extraction point and back here safe and sound." He shook Hawk's hand. "Now go get some chow, a shower, and some sleep. You got a busy week ahead of you."

If Hawk had known how busy, he would have jumped overboard. As he left, he overheard the captain telling the guy in the suit, "That man has instincts from where I don't know. That's the third time in a month he's changed a plan on the fly, and he's been right every time."

The memories brought tears to his eyes, all brave men, some he took to their deaths. He didn't get them all through it, White, Harrison, Moore, Ridgeway, and Wallace, he would never forget their names. He reached in his pocket, pulling out the five coins he was given; did he really think he could have avoided all that shit just on instinct? No, *he knew*, and that was different.

He had seen Raven and Erick headed for the guesthouse and held back, watching from a distance. Then he saw the wind pick up, saw it sweep the concrete and place the table and chairs. When he saw it fix the gutter, he was speechless, he decided to creep up and just listen. He watched for a time through Doc's visit, until Erick had told Raven he was there. *How did he know?*

When Hawk heard Erick, he stood up, brushed the leaves and cedar twigs off his damp clothes, and started in. *Thirty feet,* thought Erick, in street clothes, *very* impressive.

"I still don't know what to believe, but I'm ready to listen," Hawk said.

"That's all I ask." Erick held out his hand and Hawk grabbed to shake it. Their handshake was like an electric shock and neither could let go. Erick's entire life was laid open to Hawk, all of it, as Hawk's was laid open to Erick, but Hawk was overloading. Erick, knowing he couldn't let go, had to soften the blow of almost 9000 years of life, and the best way to do it was the way he did it 400 years ago. So, he drove himself and Hawk deeper into the trance. When Hawk went into an apparent coma, they fell to the ground, hands still locked together. What he had done was turn off Hawk's mind, while leaving himself in a state of sleep, like he was in the coffin. He had successfully turned off both his and Hawk's conscious minds. Now he could walk him through it, instead of having him torn through it. He wondered how long it would take this time, and what *he* would show him.

Raven watched in terror as she saw both men shaking, she didn't know what to do, she reached out to pull them apart and a blast of energy blew her across the patio, unconscious. What she didn't understand was what had happened. "Raven," came a voice so sweet she turned toward it in her mind and ran toward the sound in a dream. "Raven," it repeated. She started coming into a lit room with walls made of stone, no not stone walls; a cave. She realized it was lit from several torches in holes in the rock. In front of her stood a man, or rather part man. He had the head of an eagle or a hawk and was wearing a long golden robe. The bird-like head seemed to melt away and was replaced by a wolf's or a jackal's head with long ears. Soon, it too melted away and there stood Erick, with long, tightly braided, black hair and those bright blue eyes. He looked much younger, she noticed. "It will be alright, Raven, this will take some time, but we will be alright. Have the good doctor start an IV on Hawk; he will need nourishment. I require nothing. Nothing but time." Raven seemed to be pulled away from the light and Erick. She tried to fight her way back but didn't seem to have the strength. "Nothing but time." She still lay where she was after the shock, unconscious.

That was the way Mac found them later.

He had been over the grounds twice when he decided to go down the hill and check the guesthouse. Raven's car was still parked in the drive at the front of the house, so she had to be here somewhere. As he walked around the corner of the path to the guesthouse, what he saw first was Raven, and as he ran the rest of the way over, that was when he saw Hawk and Erick, their hands locked together. He knew what that was. After a check to make sure nothing was broken, he picked Raven up, kicked open the door to the guesthouse, and placed her carefully on the couch.

Running back outside, he reached out and checked for a pulse at Hawk's neck. The pulse was awfully slow, under fifteen beats a minute by his watch, but he was alive. When he checked Erick's pulse, he felt nothing, he repositioned his finger on his neck and checked again. He was just about to give up when he felt it, very faint. He pulled his cell phone out of his pocket and was ready to start dialing 911 when Raven, at the door, said, "Stop!"

He turned and saw her standing in the doorway; hurrying over, he saw a strange look in her eyes; all he could seem to ask was, "Why?"

"They are alive, I saw some of what was happening, we are going to have to let this run its course. A transfer of sorts is going on, I'm not sure, but I don't think Erick meant it to happen. I do think he started Hawk's condition, almost like a coma." *He did it to save Hawk's mind?* "If they are separated, they may both die."

"Yes, that is possible. But more than likely, it will just be Hawk," said Eileen. She was standing in bare feet and nightgown on the path to the house. "Grandfather has to try and save his mind before this is done, or he will wake up insane."

"Aunt Eileen, how did you get here? You should be in bed; where's the nurse!" Raven hissed. Then she noticed she was looking through her. Mac had already noticed this, Eileen wasn't here, at least her body wasn't.

He was able to grasp that better than Raven, he had seen ghosts before, mostly as a child. His mother had told him there was nothing wrong with that, just don't tell anyone except her. "They can't hurt you, and others will think you're crazy because they can't see them. That doesn't mean they aren't real; it just means they believe in the physical and have discounted the spiritual."

Almost like she could read his mind, Eileen said, "Mac, you can reach your mother now, I suggest you do so, and Doc." Eileen then began to fade, then she disappeared.

"Go check on Eileen," Mac told her. "I'll take care of them and call Doc." Raven kissed him on the cheek and ran for the house. When she was out of sight, Mac bent down, and as carefully as he could, picked up both men as easily as one would pick up a stack of firewood and carried them inside. He went straight to the bedroom, after all, he knew the guesthouse well. He placed both men on their side, facing each other, on the bed. Looking at his friend, said, "You been through worse, Bird Brain." Then turning to Erick, he said, "Old one, please don't fuck this up."

He pulled out his cell phone, pushed the icon for the Doc's number, told him he was needed at the house. Without saying another word, he hung up. *What am I going to say? Mom, I think I found an old one.* He had told Raven about his past, but not all of it, and why he had become a friend of her brother. She believed him. She had always known as Eileen had told her that she and Hawk had alien blood in them, and though she thought Eileen believed it, she had passed it off as a strange story by an old family member until she met Mac. Even then she wasn't sure until now. He framed what he needed to say carefully in his mind, then dialed his mother.

When Raven arrived upstairs, Eileen had woken up, and the nurse Donna was there, helping her sit up; Amanda had gone home. "Miss Raven! I don't know what happened, she just woke up and said she needed to sit up now." Donna looked at Raven with concern, "I've never seen her like this!"

"It's okay, it's okay," Raven assured her, "you may go downstairs and have a cup of coffee while I take care my aunt."

"Yes, thank you . . . I think I will," the look of concern giving way to puzzlement. She hurried out of the room.

Raven turned back to Eileen, "How did you do that? You scared me, I thought you had died!" Although Raven had always believed in ghosts and astral projection, she just had never witnessed it.

"No, my dear niece, I will die when it's time. And I feel better today, my bones don't hurt as much, and I feel stronger. The tea you made me is lovely."

Raven always had a knack for the potions and other remedies that could be made from the gardens and greenhouse, better than anyone in Eileen's memory, even her mother, who was the second-best she'd ever seen. Her mother had acquired the centuries-old book at an estate auction before her death, leaving it to Eileen. The large leather-bound book in the greenhouse made better sense to Raven than even herself. She had taken to it so well, even being able to read some of the old potions that had been written in Latin and other, even older languages. Raven, in fact, was *adding* to it. She had surpassed Eileen's knowledge early in life.

By the time she was fourteen, it seemed Raven had gotten bored with it somewhat, although no one in the house ever had a cold that lasted more than a day around her or a sore muscle that bothered them for more than an hour. Even Doc would ask her for her "liniment" when he overdid one of his weekend jaunts, or for a cup of tea when he had the sniffles. She would make you a "pot of tea" and your cold, headache, or any other ailment would seem to miraculously disappear. Eileen's aging was the one thing Raven couldn't fix, and it irritated her.

"I projected myself out there before I woke. Erick had come to me in a dream and warned me. I felt Grandfather lead Hawk into his memories. They are in a dark, dangerous place to be for the uninitiated." She spoke, as only someone who has seen knows. "I've seen a limited amount of them that he has shown me, and some have terrified me. He has been here a long time, fought many battles and wars, killed many men, also women and children."

"But it has only been the last 2000 years he has had a conscience about such matters. Ask him to show you the memory that changed him, and you will understand why the change in him has been so permanent and complete. I don't think it will ever leave. Like the many scars on his life and body, he doubts it, but his mind is fully changed, he's converted to it. Human life has more meaning to him than his own, and he treasures it now. He does nothing that won't serve as a penance to that first 7000 years."

"He was not expecting the connection like the one with Hawk. That has happened spontaneously only four times in his life, and those were the first in 26 AD, and the second in 544, the third in 1065, and the last in 1642 when he met a human he married. She was your ancestor and my grandmother. It seems they come about in times of great change in his, or the people around him, lives."

"Your grandmother? Aunt Eileen," Raven had to point out the obvious. "That was almost 400 years ago."

"Yes, and I am over 250 years old. I was born in Boston in 1757, your mother was born in 1879; we had five other siblings. My father was killed in the Revolutionary War, and she remarried twice, once in 1792 and again in 1866 after the Civil War; that's when she had my sister, your mother."

It was too much for Raven to process in one day. She sat down on the chair next to Eileen's bed, and began to cry. Eileen wrapped her arms around her, not saying anything, just holding her. When Doc walked in ten minutes later, she was almost cried out. Looking into Eileen's eyes, he felt he understood; it wasn't her or Eileen. It was something else; he sat down to wait.

Mac had just hung up after talking to his mother; his concern had grown after finding out it had happened five times in her life, with a bad result on one of them that resulted in death, was disturbing. She had seen it eight times in other Darrks. To find out two of the humans were forever changed afterwards, that scared him. She told him she would be there as soon as she could.

He never told her he had found an old one, she already knew when he informed her of the condition of his friend and the man whose mind he was in a struggle with. When he told her that Hawk was in a trancelike state caused by the other man, she eased his mind by saying the old one had obviously been through this before. He had slowed down the transfer, so he could, in a way, walk him through it. What was happening to Hawk would forever change who he was, but not in a bad way. If he came out of this sane, he would have the experience of over 8000 years. Without the old one he called Erick to help him through what he was seeing, the experience would drive his human mind past the breaking point, and he would die or wake up hopelessly insane. When Mac asked why that was, she simply stated the human mind cannot conceive living that long. That's why the Nightwalkers go insane after a time, but with them, it happens faster, as the brain begins a deterioration of sorts almost immediately, destroying all beliefs, morals, and compassion. Now and again, there would be a Nightwalker who stayed sane. They would keep their beliefs and individuality. Generally, this was because of love, but it was exceedingly rare.

Knowing she was coming was at least comforting; she would know what to do. Howard, or Mac, as Hawk, Doc, and Raven called him, sat down to wait. And pray.

Chapter Eight

LAUREN

In Caracas, a tall, pretty, long-haired golden blond put her phone on the nightstand. Looking down at the street in front of the hotel, there was a protest going on against the socialist government. Shaking out her wet hair as much as shaking her head, she had to get it to dry before she could leave. She began to run a comb and a towel through it, forcing out the excess water. After putting a comb attachment on her blow dryer, she began to dry her hair.

The phone call from her son disturbed her. She had done the best she could to ease his mind but tell him the truth. She had never lied to him and wasn't starting now. So, he had found an old one. He had told her about finding Hawk when he was in the Navy, but Howard was sure Hawk didn't know he had blood from an old one in him. While it was rare, she only knew of some, one of them being Howard. She was thinking about the name, Erick Scott, no known middle name. Was he from the party that was set down in Iceland that had disappeared? She didn't know, she had been trying to piece together where the other eighty-five went for the last 800 years with mixed results. She had found a trace of her love in Alexander's army, then in the Roman army, then in Jerusalem about the time of the Crucifixion, after that, nothing. But she would never stop looking for him, dead or alive, she had to find him. The trails laid out over millennia were hard to follow sometimes, but she had an edge, she knew they had existed. Most of the evidence of the eighty-five was not good, she had confirmed several deaths and still wasn't any closer to finding the key. And she needed that key—needed it to stop them.

Ten were alive that she knew of. Two in China, two in Russia, one in Canada, one in Scotland, and one in Australia. England had sent him there in 1850 because he was "touched" along with his entire cellblock from the sanatorium. The government gave them all a one-way ticket to colonize the continent. There were also three of the original group left in Australia, they were with the Aborigines who they had taken to living with after communication broke down between the groups as all battery power faded about 7500 years ago. She had heard there were more than her in the United States, but after eighty-five years, she still hadn't found them. Wherever they were, they kept an extremely low profile. But now, thanks to Howard, she may have found not only one of her shipmates, but his offspring as well, and to judge by what Howard had told her, they were well-adjusted and contributing well to their community and country.

This is what she wanted to see. Most of the ones she'd found that were dead were the ones that hid in the shadows until found by the Hunters, normally with a small army of Nightwalkers. Most had committed suicide. There were still many unaccounted for, along with sixteen children born on this planet that were full-bloods—at least those were the ones she knew of. Of the children, four were unaccounted for, six were dead, including three of her own. One was with its parent in Australia, and the other five were with their parents in the Aborigine tribes in Australia. It still hurt to think about it, even after 3000 years the deaths of her cubs, boys, hurt deeply. She had to find the rest of the children as well. Of mixed blood, she didn't know. She knew of at least eighty, and that number was growing. But with the mixed bloods, every generation had less of the blood of the Darrk species. And here was what she found the most interesting, *none* of them required the enzyme while seventy percent roughly, exhibited some of the powers of her race and all had much longer lifespans than a human.

Lauren McGregor looked to be about forty-five. Long golden hair hung to her waist and had two streaks of white; one starting at her left temple and the other on the peak of her forehead on the left side. She was wearing a worn, long-sleeved denim shirt with the sleeves rolled up over her elbows. She had long slender fingers and a petite waist but was full breasted and wore an athletic bra. In matching jeans, she was narrow of hips, had long muscular legs, strong ankles, and feet that had been walking in boots less than two hours before. She never could wear heels, at least tall ones, they were far too uncomfortable, and at six feet, impossible. She was tall for a woman, which was bad in the United States, but more so especially here in Venezuela. Wearing heels was out of the question. They made her tower over men, and here she attracted too much attention as it was anyway. Besides, it was too hard to get funding for digs if you towered over the university board and alumni at dinners. And although she didn't need the money, it was better to look the starving professor-archaeologist. She slipped on a pair of beat up Sketchers about the time there was a knock at the door.

"Come in, Carlos!" She smiled as he opened the door. "May bags are by the television."

"Yes, Señora Lauren." As he gathered them up, she reached into the pocket of her jeans pulling out a stack of bills, taking five $100 bills off it, she handed it to Carlos.

"Now Carlos, this is very important, ship my bags to the address on the name tags." She closed her hand around his fist. "Make sure they get there."

"Si." In his best English, he said, "Yes, UCLA."

"Right, Carlos. I gave you enough to cover it, but here's my phone number if you have any problems and I will help you."

"Si, no problem! No problem."

She knew he would get them there, even if he had to take them all the way there by himself. "Thank you, Carlos." There were advantages to always staying in the same hotel, even if it did make her easy to follow.

Carlos smiled and went out the door. He would not disappoint the most powerful witch he had ever known, he had seen her disappear once! He had never told her or anyone he knew. This might not be good for his health.

After he left, she went to the window and looked down at the street below. The man was still there, leaning against the post. He and another followed her here from the pyramid in the jungles of Brazil; one of them would be in the back, watching the rear. She was about to get them in a whole lot of trouble. She closed the curtains.

Her hair was dry and there was no reason to delay any longer. She took a denim jacket off the bed and slipped it on, putting her cell phone in the waist pocket. A patch on the lower right front of the jacket read, "My mother wears Army boots." Leaving the key and an American twenty-dollar bill on the dresser of a room in which all she had done was take a shower; then, she closed her eyes and vanished.

Chapter Nine

DIANNA

D r. John Bradley sat in the chair next to Eileen's bed, stunned. At first, he thought it a joke or the ramblings of dementia. So, he asked a few questions, got a few answers, asked a few more questions, got a few more answers. By this time, he was baffled, then Eileen did something that he couldn't believe, she rose two feet off the bed. He had laughed defensively, then started to look for wires, or anything that would prove this was just some trick, a joke being played on him, and couldn't find any. More puzzling was when she brought the wheelchair over without touching it, glided away from the bed, and gently lowered herself into the chair. That's when Donna showed up at the door, and promptly fainted. Doc looked at her on the floor for a minute then thought, *I think I might join her, I prefer being shot at!*

Fifteen minutes later, he was feeling a little better but was having a hard time overriding fifty years of science. Raven had Donna on the couch with a cold washcloth on her forehead, repeatedly telling her she must have imagined it. Donna wasn't so sure but allowed herself to be walked out the door to her car. She was given the rest of the day off to relax. When she got home, she loaded a pipe with some Shirley Temple and some Warble Blade, then smoked the whole bowl. When her husband got home to a house filled with the skunky odor, he found his wife in her recliner, so stoned she couldn't watch "Wheel of Fortune."

After Donna had been gone about twenty minutes, Doc snapped out of it. "How long have you been able to do that?" he asked Eileen with a soft look.

"Since I was a little girl," she replied, "Erick taught me the spell."

"Erick or his father?"

"They're the same person." Raven watched him closely after her answer, she was afraid he might go into that strange daze again. He took it better than expected and instead asked another question.

"And when did Hawk and Erick fall into this 'trance'?"

"About 9:30 this morning."

Doc noticed Eileen seemed to be more agile than she had been in weeks and much more, with no other word for it, *together*. Maybe a crisis was just what she needed. He knew some older people just give up because they don't feel useful anymore. "I think it's time I saw my patients." He stood up grabbing his bag. "Ladies." He held his arm out to the door.

Still a little shaky, Raven thought with relief, *but the old Doc is back.*

As Doc loaded up Eileen and her wheelchair in the lift, Raven ran before them to take some blankets out of the closet in the downstairs hall. Meeting the two on them at the back door, she covered Eileen's legs with one blanket and draped another, a quilt, over her shoulders. Eileen protested the attention but tightened the quilt around her shoulders, then they started out into the misty afternoon for the guesthouse.

When they entered the guesthouse, Mac stood up from the chair; he had been facing the door. Raven ran over and he wrapped his arms around her, kissing the top of her head. Eileen watched the exchange with a smile. She had known all along. The meetings in the guesthouse, telling the housekeeper she didn't have to take care of it over the winter, and the gardener. But she was concerned how Hawk would take it. She knew it could go either way, he would either accept his best friend and his twin were very much in love or feel betrayed; but one problem at a time.

Doc noticed the exchange as well, "Looks like I'm going to have to be nicer to him," he looked at Eileen and whispered, "I think she's off the market!" Then he headed for the bedroom. Eileen chuckled and just shook her head. The two hadn't even noticed them in their embrace. Then she slowly started moving the wheelchair in the direction of the bedroom, keeping her hands in her lap.

Around dusk, Doc was pushing Eileen back into the living room. Mac and Raven were asleep on the couch with Raven in Mac's arms, or so they thought. Mac's right eye opened and he gently laid Raven on the couch and covered her with a quilt. "How are they, Doc?" He had spoken so softly Doc almost didn't hear him. He waved Mac into the kitchen and pushed Eileen's chair that way. When they were in the kitchen with the door half-closed, he began.

"To start off with, I'd like to say I'm way out of my element here. Hawk appears to be in a coma, but his blood pressure is almost unregistrable, which is clinically impossible in someone who isn't dead. Yet his pulse is ten and hasn't changed while his temperature has gone down to 94.6. Respiration is two breaths a minute. This is unheard of, and dangerous normally, but in this case, what's normal? It gets worse when you look at Erick. His blood pressure doesn't register at all, his pulse is less than one beat in five minutes; his temperature is 66.0, which is the room temperature. If the room were 70 degrees, I have a feeling his would be too. His respiration is nonexistent. If I hadn't heard his heart beat twice in the ten minutes as I listened for it and seen him breathe once in the thirty minutes while I was paying attention, I would have declared him dead. I really don't know what to do. I did start an IV on Hawk and am giving him a saline drip right now to keep him hydrated, but I'm going to have to get some nutrients in him at some point if this lasts longer than a couple of days." He stopped to take a breath to continue, but Mac raised a hand and stopped him.

"Mom's here."

Lauren appeared on the lawn ten feet from the chairs Raven and Erick had been sitting in. Immediately her mind was screaming, *Danger!* She caught a familiar scent and breathed deeper, not recognizing it at first, then an awful scent made her nostrils flare, *Nightwalkers!* She calmly walked toward the guesthouse, and without knocking, walked in, locking the door behind her. It would only give them an extra second, but it was a second more than they had a minute ago. Again, the familiar scent she couldn't place, stronger in here. There was a woman on the couch asleep, *one-eighth Darrk.* Howard came through the door from the kitchen. "Mom!" he gave her a hug and she held him so tight he couldn't breathe. "Mom, you're doing it again," he wheezed.

"It hasn't killed you yet," she said softly. "Oh, my beautiful boy." Raven sat up and Lauren immediately picked up Howard's scent on the girl, a twinge of jealousy went through her head briefly, but only briefly. *He has finally found someone, and a beauty at that! Not to mention someone he will be able to grow old with!* She couldn't have been happier. Before anyone could say anything else, she looked at Howard and mouthed, "Nightwalkers." She could tell by his reaction he understood but recovered well.

"Mom, this is Raven, Doc, and Raven's aunt, Eileen." She could tell, as he turned, he was looking at windows, doors, anywhere Nightwalkers might use to enter as he indicated each of them. *Good boy!* Their chances of survival with the Nightwalkers just went up.

"Where are the two affected?" she asked casually, almost clinically. Doc was having a hard time believing she was referring to Hawk and Erick.

She already knew they were through that door on the right side of the living room, she could hear the faint heartbeat of the Darrk and the heartbeat of the human, no, one-eighth Darrk, Hawk's heart. Then she understood, he was the twin to this one, Raven. That's why she was tired. *There's a connection! Rare! Strong apart, but extraordinarily strong together. A true find indeed! And one will soon have the knowledge of an old one! She doesn't know how lucky she is, she can help with this and save her brother!*

Doc broke her out of her thoughts. "They are through here," he held out his hand, walked over, and opened the door. When the door opened, the scent she had found so familiar but couldn't place, flooded the room . . . and she recognized it immediately. It had changed a little, why she didn't know, but it had.

Mac saw the change in her, saw her face suddenly go slack and her mouth drop open, *something's wrong*. Then he saw the tears start to roll down her face, "*Darrk women don't cry and shed tears on Darrk, we howl, but Howard, pain, anger, sadness, mostly we only howl, but Darrks here on earth cry and shed tears when their emotions are strong. Emotion like this is unheard of on Darrk. We have stronger emotions here on earth or have emotions we didn't before. I think when we changed into human form, the emotion of love came with it. We don't have that on Darrk.*" He remembered her saying that at his high school graduation. She was incredibly happy, she had said, with tears rolling down her face. She was taking a picture of him with his certificate.

She looked at him briefly, then started, on shaky legs he noticed, to enter the room. "Thank you, my son, thank you for finding him after all these centuries, all this time, all these years! I thought he was lost to me forever, my love . . . my . . . mate . . . Rahm!" They all watched her fall to her knees because she couldn't walk anymore, she crawled the last few feet, burying her face in his side and wrapping her arms around him. She began to howl.

Standing in the dark corner of the house by a large cedar, Dianna heard that howl clearly and knew its meaning. When she did, tears began to roll down her face and she lowered her head respectfully. There would be no getting him now, not this night. *The unknown Darrk that had appeared*, she thought, *had to be*. Dianna had not seen the Darrk that entered, but Brandon had told her of the female that had materialized on the lawn and quickly entered the house. *Brother, you are indeed a blessed and lucky man. Hathor has found you, will protect you in your condition till her last breath, just like she would her cubs. I am happy for you, Brother, your mate has finally found you. Mine was lost long ago.* With a thought, she sent the Nightwalkers away; some were very puzzled but did as she commanded. They wouldn't consider disobeying their master. With that, she let out one long exultant howl, just like she had at their pairing ceremony.

Mac couldn't believe it. The man she had been looking for all these years was named Rahm. Mac should have figured sometime over the last three thousand years he would have changed it. Then he heard the howl coming from outside. He knew the howl of a Darrk in anger or defense, but this was different, it sounded . . . happy.

Lauren heard that howl and knew who it was. She lifted her head and listened to the joyful cry of Isisi, Rahm's sister, but why was she not in the house? Why was she out with the Night . . . ah . . . Lauren realized then that her timing was perfect, she had gotten here just in time. Was Isisi about to kill her brother and his family? But she wouldn't know where the key was any more than Lauren did. Without the key, and Rahm had the only one, the ship wouldn't run. Without Rahm, the repairs, even with the parts, could not be completed. No, they weren't here to kill him, they were here to *enslave* him, and to do that they needed his *family*. The desperation was obvious, she didn't think Rahm would want them to go home any more than she did and for the same reasons, at least he didn't when they had last seen each other. But that was thousands of years ago, but the promise had been made. No, they would bring the fleet back and decimate this world. But Isisi wouldn't have brought all the Nightwalkers unless she was taking the key by force and taking Rahm with her, he was just as much a key as the one he held.

Lauren had dedicated her life to not letting that happen. She had searched for the key, knowing when she found it, she would find Rahm or find he was truly dead. Looking down at him, she only prayed Rahm still felt the same. If he didn't, why would Isisi come after him? It would be easy enough to find out, she could enter his mind, find wherever he was with *(Bird Brain? Where did that come from!)* Hawk; that was his name, interesting name for a human, and talk to him. To do that, it was safer taking another with her.

They had left her alone with Rahm and Hawk, gave her some time with him, and for that she was profoundly grateful, but they were on borrowed time. She sat with her mate for several more minutes, lovingly looking down at his face not wanting to leave his side. A face she could never forget, even after 3000 years. But she had to make sure they all survived this and had to make sure all was ready before the coming of the night tomorrow. She breathed in his scent, how could she have not recognized that, but why had it changed? And changed it had. But Isisi wouldn't wait forever. She stood, kissed him tenderly on his head, nibbled his nose a little, and started to walk out into the living room. She stopped, looking at the back of her hands, and giggled. She had better put the fur away; she didn't know them *that* well.

They had dimmed the lights and she (as well as Raven and Howard) could see better than with them on. Doc had nodded off in a recliner, and Howard was watching the security cameras in the corner of the dining room. She had to remind herself to think of him as Mac, like the others, if that was what he wished to be called. She felt Odmen would approve. Raven's head was on the arm of the couch, asleep. She saw Eileen over in a corner, looking out a window, *ah, a quarter.* As Raven was asleep, so she let her be for a moment.

"Hi," she said simply, as she walked up to Eileen as to not startle her in the gloom.

Eileen looked over at her, "I saw you coming over, my vision is still quite good in the dark. I didn't know Darrks mate for life until Mac told me; Grandfather never mentioned it. It must have been quite a shock finding out you were this close to him all these years and never saw him. That must have been horrible without him all those centuries, not knowing if he lived or died."

"In truth," Lauren took a breath, "I knew he was alive, and I would find him someday. I just wasn't ever close enough to pick up his scent."

"How close would you have to be?"

"Depending on the wind? Fifty miles."

"Wow!" She looked genuinely surprised; just one more in a day of them. But the day wasn't over yet. "So, who is Mac's father?" She looked at her with a puzzled gaze.

She giggled, "I don't know, he was a boy when I found him."

"*Found* him?" Eileen looked at her incredulously.

"Yes, in an orphanage in Germany, in 1946."

"You mean he's over sixty years old?"

"'Over seventy, actually." They couldn't contain their laughter and woke Raven up.

"What's so funny?" she asked, stretching.

"They are talking about how old I am," Mac grumbled.

"Seventy-six. He told me two years ago when we started . . . dating. What of it?"

"She knows! I see his timing is off as usual. That's good, at least he didn't try to pass himself off as forty, even if he doesn't look that. If I didn't figure you for about forty," she began, "even if you do look like you're twenty-five, I'd say he was robbing the cradle!" Raven could tell Lauren was joking with her. She smiled.

"You already know we have been together for some time, don't you?" Raven was looking at Lauren when Eileen spoke.

"Raven, honey, I have known for three years. You can't hide your glowing face after a night in the guesthouse. You have taken this too well. Yesterday, you'd claimed you didn't even truly know that Darrks existed, but you can't hide love from me. I had always known there was something different about Mac, I couldn't figure what, but it was right in front of me the whole time. I had always thought we were the only ones by some trick of nature; I'm glad we aren't. I like knowing there are more, knowing you won't grow older unchanging, and see the man you love getting older, and dying in front of you, while you still look so young is comforting in a way. Knowing you won't have to live with that broken heart . . . but you can't hide love. Not from a 250-year-old woman who has outlived three husbands, eight lovers, two children, and her siblings." Raven's cheeks turned a bright red, and Eileen and Lauren laughed.

"You're what?" Doc said incredulously. They hadn't even realized he had woken up. Then they all began to laugh except Doc. He grinned and knew the joke was on him.

Hours later, Lauren looked at Raven, she had been going over everything that could happen once they connected with Rahm and Hawk. "Do you understand what I'm asking you to do?" She wanted to make sure Raven was aware of the danger. "If you get off track, I may not be able to pull you back, you may have to do that yourself with or without Hawk's help pulling him along. He may seem to look through and not even see you. But it's the best way to get this over quickly or they may be here several days, and we just don't have that kind of time. Isisi will be back tonight with even more of the Nightwalkers. We got lucky when I came in. She respected Rahm's and my pairing and our being reunited, that's the only reason she didn't strike last night. But without Rahm … Erick, we don't stand much of a chance against that many Nightwalkers. You are not strong enough and … Mac, while strong, well-trained, and knowledgeable in the ways of Nightwalkers, just isn't enough by himself."

Mac, who'd been staring at the floor, looked up. He knew she wasn't being cruel—most Darrks didn't know how—just truthful. "You don't have to do this, hon. Although Mom has been present at several of these, she has only done this once before, and she didn't know the Darrk very well. The human died."

"Much to my shame," Lauren then spoke in the Darrk tongue, which sounded more like a growl, "Much to my shame." While Howard knew what she'd said, he was glad his mother used the Darrk term. It was imperative Raven understood that what they were about to do was against Darrk laws. One was not to invade the privacy between the host and subject, which was considered sacred. Lauren had explained this to her as well.

"I understand." Raven's reply sealed it. They were going to try.

Lauren turned and looked at Doc, "When the sun fully rises, I want you to take Eileen and go to the offices you have downtown, you should be safe there."

"Now just a cotton-picking minute. Any of you may need medical attention in a fight, and I'm no greenhorn at being under fire and in battle. My cherry was broken long ago. Maybe not as long as one of your kind, but long enough for me. Physically, you aren't much different than us, I'd say you got your heart in the right place, but there, I'm not sure."

"Same here," said Eileen, "while my spells may not be as good anymore because I don't have the strength I used to, they do still work. And if anyone can be expendable, it's my old tired ass!" In fact, Doc had never seen her this strong, and finding how old she really was had impressed him greatly. He may not ever get that old, but he hoped he would take growing old with the grace she had.

"This will be a fight like no other you have ever seen," Lauren spoke the truth and Raven and Eileen both knew it. "I can't abandon my mate now that I have found him. We have been apart for over 3000 years. Moving the two of them right now is out of the question, it would more than likely kill Hawk and maybe even Rahm. That risk is too much. I couldn't bear it. Even what we are attempting is dangerous, but more so to Hawk, R . . . Erick will snap out of it, feeling like the worst hangover in the world is knocking in his head, but he'll pull through."

"It's settled then," came Doc's reply. "You two better start shaking that old spook, or it's going to be a long night without him."

Lauren and Mac suddenly stiffened, and she sat up straight like she was listening to something far away, then they all heard, "Hathor!" It came from outside; the voice was crisp and even. Then in Darrk that only Lauren and Mac could understand, it said, "Come speak with me my sister, the time is nigh! I grant you Free Right! No harm will come to you, no trickery, I follow the old word!" It was Isisi.

Chapter Ten

ISISI'S DILEMMA

Lauren knew she spoke the truth; there was something about the Darrk language that didn't permit lies when one used the old terms. She stood.

"Mom! You're not going out there! Even without Nightwalkers, she is dangerous!"

She needed to start thinking of him as Mac. "Yes, I will be fine. She used the term 'Free Right.' Trickery of any kind will not be allowed."

"That's on your home world, Darrk. In case you haven't noticed, you aren't on Darrk and haven't been for some time!" Mac was obviously worried.

"We started from here, we are always here." Lauren said this, speaking in Darrk; to the others it sounded like a dog yipping and growling. Mac knew he had lost. "She will do nothing, my son. One must respect their upbringing. If one doesn't, they are no better than the lowest animal. If she didn't have that respect, she would have attacked last night." She walked to the door and went outside into the dawn.

She saw Dianna standing on the lawn by a rosebush. It was just starting to bloom, her powers tricking it. As its beautiful red flowers opened, she picked one with a long stem and held it out for Lauren. "Good to see you, Sister." She looked at Lauren with what only could be described as love.

"And you, Sister," Lauren replied. With a tear starting to roll down her cheek, she graciously accepted the flower, "Thank you." Dianna was in a long red dress the same color as the flower. The sleeves were long and wide, as she held the flower out, they had hung down half the length to the ground. Her golden-brown eyes glimmered in the early morning light, and her dark red shining hair hung to her waist, typical of Darrk females on earth. The same height as Lauren, her long slender fingers had the nails painted to match the dress. Her feet could not be seen, but Lauren knew they would have sandals on them, the sandals of the Egyptian. Her beauty was stunning and had lured more than one to their deaths. "Shall we sit?" Lauren indicated the chairs on the patio.

"Thank you," she said as she moved over to the table and sat in one of the chairs with her back to the water. Lauren sat in front of her across the table, with her back to the door. Then it became formal, and Isisi started speaking in Darrk, "Peace in our speech."

"Peace in our speech."

"It is always good to find one's mate again," Isisi said.

"Yes, thank you for the respect," Hathor replied.

"With grace," she said, using the old term. "I have come before you to discuss terms."

"For what I might ask, do I need terms for?" Hathor asked. Old term Darrk was at times hard to follow, especially not being able to see the body language of the natural form, and human throats weren't designed to speak it. Lauren hadn't the opportunity to use it for several centuries, but Isisi was coming straight to the point.

"I seek a key, a key of great importance."

"You believe I have this key?" Hathor asked.

"I believe your mate does."

"I cannot speak for another."

"You can speak for your mate." Isisi stated.

"Only if he can't."

"He can't."

"He can, in three days," Hathor murmured.

"That is not certain," Isisi returned.

"I know not where the key is," Hathor stated formally.

"I do."

"Where then."

"It is around his neck." Isisi replied. That surprised Hathor, and it showed before she could hide it.

"I cannot give you what is not mine."

"It belongs to all."

"He was entrusted this by Commander," Hathor said pointedly.

"Commander is long gone." A look of sorrow briefly crossed her face, then looking at Lauren, she announced, "I am the Sub-Commander," Isisi pressed.

"He cannot betray Oath and Trust."

"I invoke Health of All." Isisi replied sternly. She was well prepared. Health of All was from the early history of Darrk, where it was found in the High Council that when the good of the many, or the people of Darrk in that case, was interfered with by Oath and Trust, it was considered void. But in this case, Hathor believed, the good of the many, humans, was held secure by Oath and Trust. Specifically, the oath taken by Rahm from the commander when he was given the key, the oath Rahm was given by the commander, was *to protect the humans and their world!* Even if it meant stranding the remaining crew on the water planet (earth).

He had given Rahm the key *because* of his failure at first contact. They had approached Rahm in a peaceful way, *not to harm, but to learn.* Commander had determined early on that humans were a sentient race of beings and therefore needed protection, not exploitation. He felt there was too much of that going on already in the galaxy; exploitation was what was keeping Darrk in a perpetual state of war. When the others disagreed with him, the commander had pulled Rahm aside and had him give his solemn oath in front of Hathor and another Darrk—Odmen, the captain of the ship's guard—to protect the human world.

The commander was assassinated three days later. They could not find out who was responsible, but the oath stood as far as Rahm, Hathor, and Odmen were concerned. When they disembarked, Rahm hid the key in his bags and took it with him. Odmen told them if they ever needed him to just call. That he would uphold his end of the oath as he thought the commander was right. Then he went to a small volcanic island between what is now Europe and North America, and they went to the northern part of Africa—now Iceland and Egypt. By the time it was noticed the key was missing, it was already on earth with Rahm.

"I cannot accept this. Only Rahm can break an oath he has made before his death." Hathor said pointedly.

"You are making this difficult. He is incapacitated. You, as his mate, can break his oath with Health of All."

"But he is only temporary this way."

"It may become permanent," Isisi snapped.

"I think not. And you have no other to repair the ship but Rahm."

"We have one trained," Isisi replied with more confidence than she felt.

"You know that only an engineer can teach an apprentice."

Again, she said, "His condition may become permanent." Isisi was becoming frustrated, she realized Hathor wouldn't budge on this until Rahm died.

"But as of now, it has not."

"I see an impassable block to a conclusion. We leave Free Right then." Isisi said, the frustration showing in her voice.

"I see the same. We conclude Free Right upon the completion of going." Hathor replied.

"Agreed."

Dianna looked at Lauren, speaking in English now, "I'm sorry, Sister. I will not stop until I have what I want."

"I am sorry too, Sister. But I cannot let you take the key, and I cannot let you take Rahm."

Dianna nodded, then closed her eyes and said softly, "I'm glad you found him. We lead such a lonely life on this planet. Especially those of us that had a mate."

Lauren sat at the table for a moment; looking at the water, she answered slowly. "Yes, without him, my life has been empty. I looked until I found something to fill the empty space in my heart until I found him again." She looked over at Dianna, "What have you been doing, Sister? How have you been spending the centuries?"

Dianna looked across the table at her, "Sleeping mostly. Dreaming of home. Dreaming of the soft light on my face, of the den of my birth, and the smells of the forests."

"You could make this home; the humans are a good people in all. There are some that are bad, but most are good." Lauren was watching Dianna's face as she spoke, looking for any emotion at all. She didn't see any.

"No, Sister, this will never be my home, and the humans are beneath us with their constant squabbling and petty wars. They are a stupid race, and they wouldn't last against a superior Darrk army, just like all the other worlds. We should be ruling them, not hiding from them."

"Are our wars much different? We kill a world and do it in the name of our survival, when in fact, we do it because we have grown to like it." Lauren continued, "We don't even know if Darrk is still there, after all this time and all our wars, who is to say we didn't find someone who could defeat us."

"Never," Dianna spat in a voice of steel. "We would never be beaten, never fail."

"Are we so sure?" Lauren replied softly. "We don't have to hide, even I work in plain sight." She knew her words were useless.

Dianna looked at her and said softly, "You do that work as a human in their form. On this world, there is no room for our form."

Lauren looked at her in sadness, then in Darrk she said, "Peace run with you, Sister."

"And with you." Dianna then closed her eyes and vanished into the morning's soft light. The rose she had in her hands was sitting on the table.

Lauren sat for a moment, looking out to Elliot Bay. Watching a ferry cross the water, it came to her that Dianna would never give up until she was on her way home.

When Lauren entered the guesthouse, Mac and the others were over at the security desk in the corner of the dining room. They were listening to a playback of their conversation. Mac was translating it for Doc, Eileen, and Raven. "How did . . ." Lauren began.

"I reversed the speakers on the patio so I could listen, you taught me much of Darrk language, but I'm missing a few things here." Mac was intent on listening.

"Basically, we are right where we started." Lauren breathed. "Mac, take Doc and go get supplies—you know what we need—and food. You pick, if what I hear about Doc is true, I don't want to have to live on soy burgers."

"They are good for you," Doc, smiling, said defensively, then added. "I'm going to need medical supplies as well."

"Yeah? Well, I'm on not turning vegan after 9000 years of meat." Lauren said playfully.

Mac was skeptical, "If I leave, that will leave you defenseless."

"What am I, chopped liver?" Eileen grinned.

"Isisi will not start anything until after dark when she can use the Nightwalkers. I'm surprised, but she's following the rules."

"Yeah, but for how long? And by the way, Mom, they didn't have Nightwalkers to fight for them when they made those rules." Mac started for the door. "Let's go, Doc."

Chapter Eleven

MARIA

They were sitting on the sides of the bed: Lauren next to Erick, Raven next to Hawk. Raven was trembling a little, Lauren noticed. She was a little afraid. That was good. Eileen was sitting and watching Raven, a knot in her stomach.

"Now we will begin," Lauren said softly. "As I said, you will begin to feel like you are floating, then, everything will become darker. You will see me walking toward you, I may not look the same, but I'll be calling your name. When I hold out my hand, take it, then we will go find them. Now take my hand and Hawk's free one." Raven did so. "Now close your eyes and we shall begin." Lauren reached out and picked up Erick's free hand. Closing her eyes, she began what could only be described as self-hypnosis, but it was much more complicated, and much more dangerous. When she was far enough into the trance, she spoke, "Raven, my dear girl, where are you?"

Raven was floating in the gloom of a fog, its wisps encircling her. "Raven, Raven, my dear girl, where are you?" It was Lauren's voice.

"Here, in the fog." It started getting darker, "Over here." She saw something moving in the fog, then a large animal appeared, but not like one she had ever seen. It looked like a wolf, but its ears were much longer. Its fur was sleeker and golden; it was the color of Lauren's hair. She thought it looked like it was walking on its hind legs. For some reason, she was not afraid of it. As it drew closer, it held out its paw, she grasped it in her hand, noticing it had six toes and what looked like a thumb.

"Raven, it's me, Hathor . . . Lauren. We will look for them now. Close your eyes if you have to. We must go through Rahm's life as he has already shown Hawk, but it will be like watching a movie on fast forward. I won't let go of your hand until I tell you, have no fear, what you will see can't hurt you, it will be a memory. Alright?" Raven nodded. "Okay. Rahm, Rahm, my love, where are you?"

Raven noticed they were coming out of the fog into a shadowed place. The plants growing looked strange, but it wasn't much different than the rain forest out on the peninsula. Then she saw about fifteen wolf pups running through the trees, they were yipping and . . . laughing? The scene faded, became a building with round doors, four of the wolves were biting and snapping at one in the corner, blue-green fluid was all around it, blood? Then it too faded. A large room came into focus, one wolf was (talking?) to another group, pointing to large machines behind him. They were all wearing coats of some kind with a green stripe, then, it too, began to fade.

Then an explosion went off nearby, she saw pieces of the wolves all over the room. There was one, with a rag on its paw that was soaked in the green fluid; he also had it running down the front of his head. It was blinking the fluid out of its eyes over by a square machine of some sort. It was being howled at by someone through a speaker, and it was howling back. Then it reached to a lever, pushed it away from itself, then pushed it down. The vision faded.

They were in the same room she thought, but the pieces of the wolves were gone, and things looked much cleaner. There she saw the wolf with the rag on its paw and another. The one with the rag on its paw was behind the other one, then she realized they were mating. He had some of the golden fur of the other one in his mouth as he had bitten down on its neck, like he was trying to hold on. Lauren stiffened and her paw tightened on Raven's hand. Raven saw that the one under him was the one who had her hand. How could she not have noticed; it was Erick and Lauren! Then, with mercy for Lauren, the vision faded. She then saw Erick the wolf taking a small clear crystal triangle from a silver-headed wolf, then placing his paw across his chest and repeating what the other said.

The visions seemed to pick up speed after that, and they became disjointed and ran together. Raven could tell the difference now between the two and saw them together several times. A glimpse of Erick and Lauren playing with three puppies in the sand at night, a man looking at a naked Lauren in human form, and when he turned, it was Erick; Erick looking at a diagram and pointing to a pyramid that looked half done; Erick with a sword fighting another man amongst many others doing the same; Erick, the wolf, taking three cubs, running in the sand at night. Many visions of Erick and Lauren in human form coupling, playing with three children, sitting at a table with three young men, laughing. These visions were coming so fast now. Then Erick, standing over a woman with her throat ripped out, eyes staring up at him, the blood running down his cheeks and chest not his own. After that, thankfully, Raven took Lauren's advice and closed her eyes. She could still hear but couldn't see; voices speaking in languages she didn't know, all running together, sounds of metal crashing together, screams of battle, and screams of terror; then, one long and lonely howl.

She didn't know how long she'd kept her eyes closed, but after a time, she heard Lauren's voice, cracking, "Open your eyes, Raven."

She was now holding the hand of Lauren; the wolf was gone. Before her, she saw a younger Erick sitting on the ground, looking up at a man who was on top of a hill, sitting on a rock. He was speaking to the people gathered below. She noticed Erick was in a Roman soldier's uniform. Listening to the man speak, his face was calm, no longer with the cruel gleam it had. It looked . . . peaceful. She couldn't understand the words the man was saying but the effect on Erick was unmistakable. A tear rolled down his cheek, and he smiled. He was looking at the man . . . with love.

When she looked at Lauren, there were tears rolling down her cheeks, the speaker had her listening as well, and whatever he was saying she obviously understood. Then she saw them, Hawk and Erick, standing there watching the man on the top of the hill, tears running down their faces. She turned her head and looked up the hill, and although she couldn't understand him, she suddenly understood the message and where she was. She stood and watched with them in awe. The shock plain on her face, *it can't be*, she thought, *it can't be*.

Lauren saw Erick and Hawk standing to the side of her, this was what he needed Hawk to see. He needed to see what it was that had caused such a profound change in him. So profound, *it changed his scent!* She had felt that change when she first touched him. She couldn't believe it, but this was what Hawk, what *she* needed to see. She reached over and gently took Rahm's hand. She knew this was where a change had taken place in Rahm. This was why she could never find him in the last 2000 years. His scent had changed. He had become . . . *human*. The scene began to fade, Erick, not Rahm, looked at her lovingly, and the *four* moved on.

The area around them began to clear, and color came back to daylight. Lauren saw three crosses on the hill, and fear stole her heart. There were three men on the crosses, the one in the center was dying in great pain. She saw Erick standing at the base of the cross, in the uniform of a Roman soldier. The man on the cross was saying something to him she couldn't hear. He was shaking his head. The man on the cross said something more to him. He looked down, then back up at the face of the man he had grown to love. With a sadness in his eyes she found unbearable, he stood up straight, and drove his spear into the side of the man on the cross, killing him.

Thunder roared in the sky, rain as strong as she had ever seen began to come down, and a river of blood came running down the hill. Erick was kneeling now at the base of the cross, howling in agony with blood from the man dripping down on him. She had never seen him in such pain, even when she saw him grieving over her and the children's loss coming out of Egypt. This man on the cross, this man had changed him, forever.

The next thing she saw was Erick listening to another man on a hill, overlooking a crowd of people, speaking to them. Erick was watching in the clothing of a man from the desert. He looked calmly up the hill, listening, but didn't have the expression he did before, this one was more, well, for lack of a better term, studious. The banners of Islam surrounded the crowd, the people were watching with an expression of rapture on their faces, except Erick. This too, began to fade.

Then, she saw him in a robe, with eleven others dressed the same in a circle. Pagans. As she watched, she saw a man touch Erick on the back of his hand, then both fell to the ground. A transfer, each to the other, had started to take place. Things seemed to speed up then. She saw both men wake up, saw the human look at Erick in terror, and tell him he needed to leave the moors now, or he would have to have him hunted down and killed. Fade once again.

When her vision cleared once more, she saw Erick stacking corpses like cordwood, the marks of plague on the bodies. It wrenched her emotions; she knew this sight. This was Europe, in the latter part of the fifth or sixth century, she guessed. It faded to Erick pouring oil on the corpses and lighting them aflame.

Next, when her vision cleared, she saw a familiar place, Angkor Wat, but it looked new. The stone was smooth, not weathered. Erick was dressed in the garb of a monk, sitting with others in a circle, listening to an old man. He was talking of peace and of loving everything that lived, of never taking more than you need, and giving back as much as you could. The vision faded.

Again, she saw plague, Erick doing as before, collecting the dead, then burning them in a field. His face filled with sorrow. This looked to be in the twelfth century by the clothing. Many visions followed, all with Erick helping when others wouldn't or couldn't: tending to wounds during what appeared to be a war, helping someone fix the wheel on a cart. More tending of wounded. It tore her heart; every time there was suffering, every time there was death, Erick would be there, ready, and willing to help. She knew of these events, but like most Darrks, she'd avoided them. In plague, the blood was tainted, and would make them ill if taken, and it could also be fatal. Yet here was Erick, always in the middle of the suffering, doing what he could. Blood, tainted with plague, could have killed him if consumed, yet, here he was. Again, this vision faded.

When it cleared, it was night. Erick was standing alone on a shoreline looking to sea, leaning heavily on a staff of wood. The almost full moon hung over it, shining its light on the water. Yet Erick didn't see it, in fact she didn't think he saw anything, such was his stare. She could see the loneliness etched in his face, feel it. A voice came from behind him, from the darkness, speaking in Italian, "Why so lonely? I've watched you from my father's house, up there on the hill. You have been here all day, just looking out to sea. I know it is loneliness. I feel it like I once felt my own. You don't drink, you don't eat, you just stare. Please, please, come with me. Do not stand here so alone, come be with others, do not let your heart be so empty."

A beautiful woman stepped from the darkness. Lauren heard Raven take a sharp breath inward. The woman was wearing a simple green dress and white blouse, and catching the moonlight, her eyes sparkled an emerald green. She had shining black hair, braided; it lay over her right shoulder, her hands were rough from work. *Oh my God,* Lauren thought, *it's Raven!* She knew it couldn't be, but the woman before her was a mirror image of her. She walked up to one of the most dangerous beings she could have ever come across, not knowing, just as she would walk up to anyone she saw in such pain, and gently took his hand. "Come, come with me, do not stand here like this. Come, I will make you something to eat." Without a word, Erick allowed himself to be led from the beach. She, holding his hand, led him away from the beach and up the hill.

They entered a small house with a dirt floor. A man, perhaps in his forties was at a table repairing a basket. He saw her walk in with the stranger he had seen on the beach all day and stood. "Good, my daughter, I thought you might have gone to speak to him. Please sir, sit," he indicated the chair he had just vacated, "are you thirsty?" He walked over to a shelf and came back with a ceramic jug and a cup and poured some wine for Erick.

Erick was awestruck by the charity of these people. They obviously didn't have much, but what they had they gave to a total stranger without any thought for themselves. He looked down at himself and realized he had been wearing the same clothes for several weeks; they were dirty and had several tears in them. In his depression, he hadn't even washed, he looked terrible, and yet, they took him in. Why?

"Praise God you are still of good health." The man offered him a bowl of olives; "Maria will have your food soon, wash if you wish." He pointed toward a washbasin and a pitcher of water next to it.

"Why am I here?" Erick muttered.

The man looked at him and smiled. "God told her to help you," he said simply. Then turned and went back to his basket.

"Wait! What do you mean, God told her to help me?" Erick looked at him strangely.

"He told her you did not wish to live anymore but He needed you, needed you to finish something for Him," said the old man. "I know not what. But when God speaks, we listen."

The look on Erick's face told Lauren that it was the truth, he was going to kill himself, and Maria's intervention was the only thing that stopped it. Lauren knew that a great number of the Darrks that were dead had committed suicide. How did she know Erick wanted to die? The vision began to fade as Maria brought a plate and smiled at him, then he buried his face in her apron, and as she wrapped her arms around his head, he began to cry.

The next vision they saw was Erick, clean-shaven, and in Italian peasant clothing. Maria and the old man were in a shop at the market. There were baskets of all sizes and shapes stacked against the walls. Erick was helping load several in a wagon when he saw three men, pushing their way through the crowd of villagers, then they turned and came into the shop. They began to threaten the old man, telling him he'd missed his payment to the Don; that his payment was now doubled, and he would pay this today. The old man said he couldn't pay, he had just sold enough baskets to make the past-required payment, he could not make twice that now. They laughed and slapped him. As he was lying on the floor, the biggest one said, "Then we take her," pointing to Maria, "she will do well on the waterfront with the sailors!" They laughed again, and one turned to grab Maria.

That was when Erick, who had listened to the exchange from outside, entered. "I cannot allow that," he said simply.

"Ah, she found another to marry, eh, basket weaver. You know what happened to the first one. You know this is not allowed; she belongs to our Don. Without your payment, she goes back to the brothel!"

"No, in God's name, I will make the payment, just give me more time!"

"No. I have my orders, basket weaver," and he turned and quickly thrust a knife into Erick's abdomen. There was confusion on his face, as Erick did not fall. He thrust again and again with the knife, and Erick smiled. To Lauren, a well-known gleam came to his eyes. She knew the man wouldn't live long enough to realize his mistake. Erick restrained himself somewhat. Grabbing the hand with the knife thrust into his belly, he pulled it out, holding the man's hand around the handle, the unmistakable blue-green of Darrk blood on the knife. Erick's strength easily overpowered him, and turning the knife upwards, Erick thrust it into the chest of the man; staring in his terror-filled eyes as he died.

Erick watched as the corpse fell from his hands to the floor, the knife sticking out of his chest. Then he calmly stated to the remaining two men, "You will return to your Don, you will tell him this is over. He will leave these people alone; not just Diego, but all the merchants here. He does not wish to anger me, that would be very, very, bad; I am the protector of these people. Or I will bring hell to his front door and eternity with me. This I will do to him and any who stand in my way. Now pick up this dog and be on your way." Erick knew this was not over, you could see it in his eyes. As he went over to help Diego to his feet, the other two men dragged the body of the third between them out the door. The other merchants in the square had gone silent as they watched the exchange, but Lauren was surprised at the looks on their faces, it wasn't fear, it was awe.

The old man looked at him. "I knew God sent you here, I knew it."

"Perhaps not God, my friend. Perhaps not God." He picked the man up and placed him on his feet. Turning, he reached into his vest and removing a heavy leather pouch, handed it to Maria. "I want you to go to the other merchants, buy a wagon, horses, provisions. We have little time." She looked inside the heavy pouch and her eyes widened, inside was more gold than she had ever seen. The vision began to fade like the others, but not completely.

As things came back into focus, Lauren saw it was dusk. Erick was loading a basket into a wagon. He turned to Diego, "Go out on the road north, I will catch up to you there. Do not stop; do not look back. I will come to you." Diego nodded and climbed up next to Maria.

"God be with you," Diego said. The wagon moved off with Maria looking back at Erick over her shoulder, tears streaming down her face. Erick then looked the other way, across the village, seeing more than twenty men moving from a large house on the hill, moving toward the village.

"So, it begins," he whispered. The vision faded.

Clearing, Lauren noticed it was night, the moon shining full over the harbor. The house on the hill was in flames, dancing like demons up into the night sky. Rahm was walking down the hill, in Darrk form, blood soaking his black fur. As he walked the fur began to disappear and he became shorter, leaving a tall man walking naked down from the house, covered in blood. Mutilated bodies were strewn to either side of the road, some with arms torn off, almost all with the throats torn open and terror in their sightless eyes, they went all the way to the gates of the big house, which now sent billows of smoke and flames into the sky. Hell had come, and with the promise of eternity, the devil had collected.

The villagers stood with fire buckets at the bottom of the hill, staring at the demon coming down the road. Some had witnessed Erick's battle to those gates, witnessed his change. It was something they would never forget, but no legends or tales would be told of this, the story was not even passed down, for they knew that the devil had come to their village, and if one spoke of him, he might come back.

As he reached the people, they parted in front of him like the sea before a ship, then something Lauren had not expected happened. One of the villagers walked up and poured a bucket of clean water over his head. This was followed by others as he walked, until after going several feet, he was clean. Someone offered him a cloth to dry himself.

He seemed to snap out of the trance he had been in, coming down the hill, and was surprised at the reaction of the people. He took the cloth and began drying himself while he kept walking. Next, someone gave him pants, then a shirt, shoes, vest, and coat. When he reached the end of the villagers, the blacksmith held a saddled horse for him. Without saying a word, he swung into the saddle, with a look of gratitude to the villagers; he spun the horse and left, going north.

As he looked behind him, the villagers, instead of throwing water on the fire, they were throwing in the bodies. He trotted north, hurrying to catch up with Diego and his daughter. He had done this and thought the villagers would kill him when he was done, Lauren realized, instead, they helped him get away. The vision began to fade.

It came back into view with Erick and Maria sitting by a fireplace. She looked to be about six months pregnant. As Erick reached out to hold Maria's hand, a shock went through them and she saw Erick do probably the same thing he did with Hawk, he seemed to be shutting down her mind. She would have to ask him how that was done. He was the only one she had ever seen do it. The vision began to fade.

They came to a room, Erick was pacing back and forth, Diego sat in a chair with a pleased smile on his face. "Relax my son, this has been going on since Adam and Eve left the garden!" Concern was on Erick's face, but for what, Lauren didn't know, then she heard a baby cry. Erick's eyes brightened, then another cry came, and he smiled.

A few minutes later, the door opened, and the midwife beckoned them inside. Maria lay in a bed with a tired smile on her face, in her arms were two beautiful babies. "My husband," she said, "we have two lovely girls!"

"What shall we name them?" Erick asked, smiling.

"This one we will name Rose, after my favorite flower. This one, we will name after your favorite bird, Raven."

The vision faded.

When she could see again, Erick was kneeling next to a bed, holding an old woman's hand, Lauren knew it was Maria, and a great sadness overcame her. Two women, who looked to be in their teens, were kneeling on the other side, crying. "I am so sorry I have to go, my dear Erick." Maria had spoken these words in English, not Italian.

"It is I who am; sorry, my love; sorry I couldn't grow old with you, sorry I cannot accompany you to the hereafter you so much deserve. You saved my life, dear one, and in return, I watch you leave me."

"It has been a good life, my husband. Promise me this, you will watch over our children and grandchildren on into the years, without hiding from them who you are and help them to understand the magic that flows through you, and them. Do not abandon them; keep them safe; they will not understand living as long as they do without you to tell them. Promise me."

"I promise, my love. And I also promise never to forget you and the gifts you have given me." And with that, the old woman let out her last breath and died. Erick buried his head on the side of the bed and began to cry.

"I have more to show you, Hawk," Erick said. "But we must return now; take your sister's hand, she will show you the way." He turned to Lauren, "I don't know where you have been all these centuries, I had thought you lost when I found the boys, but I'm glad you are here now and have seen this. I have to go somewhere now, alone; we will talk when I return," he gently touched her cheek, "my beautiful Hathor." He began to fade from view, then Lauren opened her eyes and found herself sitting on the bed, with Raven looking at her with tears in her eyes.

What had seemed minutes in Erick's memories had been hours. Doc was back with Mac and he was taking Hawk's blood pressure. "His blood pressure, heart rate, temperature, and respiration are coming up. I think he's coming out of it."

Erick had released Hawk's hand, but he was still. His breathing had started increasing as had Hawk's, but he still had farther to go. Lauren thought it would be close to dark before he awoke, while Hawk seemed to be coming out of it . . . too fast. She just hoped it would be in time for Erick. As for Hawk, she had never seen this, and only time would tell.

Erick walked in the fog for a while. Soon, he came upon a light dancing in the fog. "You wished to speak to me."

A voice softly came from the light in the fog, "Yes, Rahm. I'm glad you came."

THE LESSON

As she walked out into the living room, Lauren saw that Mac had picked up a trunk from his apartment, a trunk she recognized. "Still have that old thing, I see."

"You did tell me not to get rid of it as I might need it someday. I'm glad I didn't, although at the time I thought you were being a bit melodramatic." It was open and she looked inside.

Several very sharp Samurai Katana swords were in the top tray, scabbards covering their edges. With them were the shorter Wakizashi swords that accompanied them. With the tray removed, she knew one would see four crossbows in two levels of two, one facing one way opposite of the other with four full bolt quivers.

He had also stopped by a hardware store and had gotten the materials to make several pipe bombs, which were lined up on the coffee table, and something else she didn't recognize in a plastic water bottle, he had caught her eye on them. "Homemade napalm with a charge on them. And those," he pointed to another group next to them, "are claymores of a sort. They just don't have a good side and it doesn't matter which side is toward the enemy, good for us, bad for them. They have monofilament line as trigger wires. I'm hoping they won't be seen. Every one of the bombs has an extra surprise I added myself." He smiled and picked up an empty paper dime wrapper, then added, "There are also twenty Molotov cocktails in the kitchen. The ten with gasoline are in green glass bottles, the other ten in clear glass are kerosene." He looked as if he was enjoying this, she would have to talk to him later, she thought.

"Any flares?" Hawk's voice coming from behind her made her turn around. Hawk and Doc appeared from the bedroom, and Hawk looked visibly tired but appeared to be in good condition.

"No, I hadn't thought of that, why?" Mac looked at Hawk for his answer.

"It was something I saw in Grandfather Erick's memories. Flares are bright enough to temporarily blind them for several minutes, their eyes don't recover fast as ours." He explained, then he and Mac went to the garage under the house.

Raven looked at Lauren after they left, "Something has happened to him, he seems . . . older."

"He is, as are you. He, though, has looked at almost 8000 years of life, and it has forever changed who he is. And more will come to him as time passes."

"And me?"

"The languages will come first. I feel that is so you understand and can interpret what you see. The rest you will just suddenly see a little at a time without really knowing where it comes from." She didn't add that insanity, if it were going to happen, would happen in a few days as the memories that filled her unconscious mind bled over to the conscious.

"You speak as if there was something in control of this."

"There is, I think. As we have been on this planet and go past what would be considered a normal life span even to us, this 'transfer' has begun. I have found that those of us who have been involved in it are the only ones that stay completely sane. I think it's a way for us to deal with the years, to help our minds stay healthy. Unfortunately, all the humans it gets transferred to, those who have no Darrk blood in them, go insane or die." Lauren stopped for a moment, gathering her thoughts, then continued. "On Darrk, we transfer things, one to another, a lot. It's a way to show the inquisitor what happened after an accident, or a youngling how to do something. But we were not meant to live this long, I believe. Many of us, who have been stranded here, have committed suicide over the years or have been killed by Hunters. None has died of natural causes that I know of."

"Whatever it is that selects who this transfer goes to I haven't found, but it is there, and it is selective. It almost never selects anyone anymore who is all-human. Maria is the only one I have ever seen who came through it intact, and in the vision we saw, she looked pregnant at the time, at least I think so. I'll have to wait to talk to Rahm first. The first transfers started by trying to transfer to humans. As the humans died or went insane, suddenly, some of the males among us started having children with humans. Which at first, we thought was impossible. For every female Darrk stranded here, there were about fourteen males. In the whole ship of over 900 Darrks, there were only ninety females on board, or one in ten at the beginning. Then, the battle left only sixteen of us out of eighty-seven. Rahm's pairing to me after we arrived was significant, it only left fifteen females, one being his sister, who was already paired to another." She stopped, thought a moment, and went on.

"I think that whatever is in us that drives our will to survive, works independently of our consciousness. Our minds know only one thing, survival. When that is threatened, or our sanity starts to slip, there is a part of our mind that makes a correction in some of us as it refuses to die. Then there is another portion of that mind and it wants not only the individual to survive, but our race and its collective intelligence. So, it changed the body of the male of our species so it *could* have children with a human. But to my knowledge, only girls are first generation, males are not born until a generation has gotten between the Darrk blood and human. Howard

. . . Mac, is the only one I have ever seen. Born to a human mother who died giving birth to him, after escaping from a concentration camp to a convent. The Nuns hid him until after the war and put him in the orphanage where I found him."

"His mother was Jewish?" Raven looked puzzled.

"No. She was a Gypsy."

On the way to the garage, Mac asked how Hawk felt. His concern for his friend was obvious.

"I'm not sure," he stared at the water as he walked, like he was seeing it for the first time. What Mac didn't know was Hawk was looking at a memory that wasn't his. Erick had stood on this bluff many years ago, staking his claim to the property that on the original deed was titled Osprey Hill. "I feel different somehow, like I'm looking through an old pair of binoculars, the vision a little blurred, changing what I see, and yet, somehow making it look more beautiful."

Mac was also having a hard time thinking about how he was going to tell Hawk about Raven. Both of them thought at the time the relationship started it was best not to tell him. And the longer the relationship went on, the harder it was to tell his friend. He was startled when Hawk spoke, "Do you love her?" Mac looked at him incredulously.

"You know?"

"Have for about the last couple years. My sister stopped dating and you stopped dating about the same time. Then both of you would disappear at the same time. It wasn't hard to figure out. And having one of our guys follow her for a few days confirmed it and brought the answer I already had for myself. I knew better than to have you followed." Hawk was looking at his feet, a rare but sure sign he was embarrassed or uneasy. Then he picked his head back up as always and smiled. "Just take good care of her. I know she's the toughest broad in the world to most, but she sees the world as something she needs to take care of or fix, and she needs someone who will take care of her. Can you do that, Chief?"

Mac thought he knew this man better than most, but every time he thought he knew him, Hawk surprised him. "Yes. Yes I will, Skipper." Mac shook his head, "So, we weren't fooling anyone." He paused, then looked at Hawk, "You had her followed?"

"Hey, not my finest hour." Then they both started to laugh.

In the garage, Hawk had pointed over to the corner, "There's a box of road flares over there on the bench with a box of marine flares as well; the flare pistol should be in the box with the flares." Hawk had stopped and was looking at a '56 Ford pickup, one of seven vehicles in the garage. It had a late model Cadillac Escalade, a '61 Ford Falcon station wagon, a '69 Cutlass Supreme, a '57 Thunderbird, a '69 Mustang convertible, and an old Ford Model A. They all had battery tenders running to them, except the Model A and the Cadillac, neither of which needed one. All the vehicles looked as they did when they were new, but the real prize was the Thunderbird. The '57 was the only year the car came with round, porthole windows, which made it worth more than the Model A to some. Hawk spent many days polishing the car so he would be allowed to use it on dates. He knew now that the car had been a birthday gift, from Grandfather Erick to Hawk's mother, Rose. He understood now why he had told him to be careful with it, yet never refused to let the sixteen-year-old drive it. Erick actually felt the car was his anyway. He also knew now that he also considered the Mustang Raven's car. Their mother had ordered the car herself, and it was her favorite. He'll have to tell her that, as Raven loved driving it as much as their mother had. The only ding in any of them was a small dent on the right side of the front bumper of the '56 Ford truck.

He remembered Grandfather Erick taking him out to get a Christmas tree one year. When they had stopped for gas, Hawk had slid behind the wheel and was pretending to drive like any other six-year-old when he kicked his foot out and knocked the four-speed out of gear. Erick had gone in to pay for the fuel and Hawk panicked as the truck rolled down the slight incline. Slowly picking up speed, it ran into a pole about twenty feet away, breaking the headlight, denting the bumper, and denting the right fender. He thought his grandfather was going to kill him. But when Erick ran up to the truck, *or was it suddenly he was there*, after asking if he was all right, he walked around to the front of the truck. He stood there for a little while; Hawk felt worse and worse, then started to cry. Lifting his hand, Erick had beckoned with his finger for him to come out to the front of the truck. Hawk thought for sure he was going to get it but walked around to the front with his head down, ready to take his punishment. Hawk could see the memory clearly, but suddenly he was seeing it from his grandfather's eyes.

"Pick your head up," Erick said softly. The boy in front of him sniffed, wiped his eyes and his nose on the back of his sleeve, and looked up. "You know what you did." He nodded. "Should you have been behind the wheel?"

"No, sir," he had been told many times not to get behind the wheel, and he started to look down again.

"Head up!" The boy's head shot up. "You broke a couple of things but there wasn't anyone hurt, thank heaven. That's the main thing. The truck is just a piece of steel, iron, and glass; it can be fixed, but if you would have hurt someone, that would bother you for your whole life. And sometimes we don't really know how long that is. Now remember this, you were wrong and you admitted it, that's good. But always hold your head up. We are not perfect; we make mistakes. Always admit when you are wrong, and always hold your head up. Don't let someone shame you into not being proud of who you are, even when you are wrong. Do you understand?"

"Yes, sir."

"Now get back in the truck while I clean up this glass. And I think it best we keep this just between us and not tell your aunt; we'll both be in trouble."

Hawk never forgot the lesson he was taught: no matter what he did in his life—right or wrong—admit it. But most of all, take whatever consequences there were for your actions gracefully, and always hold your head up.

Mac walked up, "I hate to break up a trip down memory lane but we need to get back to the guesthouse." Hawk nodded, and with one last look at the truck, they left for the guesthouse. Upon reaching it, they went straight to the kitchen and went to work, making a few more surprises for their unwanted guests.

Raven sat for about an hour afterward, thinking. Hawk and Mac came back from the garage carrying a large box and went straight to the kitchen without saying a word to her. Soon she got up and went over to Eileen. She had just woken up from a nap and looked in good spirits, and there was something she saw in the visions from Grandfather Erick she had to ask her about. She smiled to herself as she walked up, and Eileen caught it. "Something is turning in that pretty little head, share," she had an impish smile on her face.

"It's just that as I was walking over here, in my mind it was the first time I truly thought of him as Grandfather Erick." She laughed, then looked down at the floor when Eileen's broad smile came across her face. "What I saw was amazing, and I still can't believe it."

"There will be more," Eileen said, then she tried a little experiment; in perfect German she said, "Mac means a lot to you, doesn't he?"

"Yes, I have finally found the man I want to spend my life with." Raven hadn't even noticed Eileen speaking in German and she had answered her in perfect German. *She understood her!*

Again, in German, "Has he asked you to marry him?" Eileen was smiling at Lauren, who had noticed the exchange.

Raven sighed, "Not yet, but I'm hoping."

Lauren walked over and in Greek said, "He hasn't asked you? Do you want me to ask him?" She smiled as Raven answered,

"No, I can wait. I've waited thirty-seven years, I can wait a few more months." She noticed the two women looking at her with concealed laughter.

"What's so funny?"

Both women burst out laughing, Doc woke up on the couch looking confused, and thought that he was in an asylum. Every time he woke up around here someone was laughing. They all might die and yet they are laughing. He was in a loony bin, but it wasn't a bad idea. He stood up and went to the bedroom to check on Erick, closing the door.

"I've been speaking to you in German."

"And I, Greek."

"But I don't know German or Greek."

"You do now, girl, you do now." Eileen smiled. And they again broke up in a fit of laughter.

"Oh." Was all she could come up with.

Lauren left after the laughter calmed down and said she was going to see what the boys were up to. Raven turned to Eileen, "Was your mother Rose or Raven?"

"Raven. She named your mother Rose after her sister. I was actually named after my father's mother."

"How come you didn't have children?"

Eileen cast her eyes down looking very sad and Raven immediately wished she hadn't asked the question. "I did. I had two boys with my second husband."

"Where did they go?" She had to ask, she was this far in, she had to finish.

"They both died in the Civil War. They were good boys, following their hearts, your Grandfather Erick went with them, but he couldn't protect them from what happened, they split the three of them up. One, he died at Antietam, the other at Gettysburg. They fought for the Union and for what they believed in."

"What happened to Grandpa Erick?"

"He was assigned to a hospital. When they found out how much he knew about medicine, he was placed in a Union hospital." Eileen said.

"He was a doctor?" Raven seemed confused, "He isn't one now. When did he stop being a doctor?

"He actually never was, but I know they thought he was one. He was good at it."

"After the First World War," Erick said from behind her. She spun around, and he was standing by the door to the bedroom with Doc standing behind him. Her great-great-grandfather looked very tired.

Lauren burst through the door of the kitchen, ran up to him and literally jumped into his arms.

"Why didn't you attack last night while you had the upper hand, they were vulnerable!" The man spat on the floor, "I think you may not be the right one to lead this attack, you've become soft."

"And you forget your place and upbringing!" Dianna snapped. They were in a large house, standing in a living room with heavy curtains over the windows, blocking out the daylight. "We are not animals! Remember, we need Rahm; without him, we can't fix the ship. He is the only one that understands all the systems."

"There is another," said the man.

"No, there is not. He has studied the information, but he has never done it in practice. The equipment is sensitive, and it hasn't been started in almost 9000 years. Do you really wish to turn it over to a Darrk that when we got here was nothing more than a paw slide away from not existing? He's never even been to space, he was born on this planet!"

"We just make a transfer."

"It's not the same, and you know this. Rahm would have to start the transfer, and he isn't going to do that. Having the memory and doing it the way the other did it is not exact, and this must be exact or we will be dead or stuck here forever."

"But we can get him to do it if he doesn't wish to, Hades can start it himself."

"Rahm can block it, you know this, and Rahm's magic is far stronger than any of ours! We don't even know where he got it! And his *is* magic, not just trickery masquerading as magic! We would not even know how to use the planet's magnetism and winds to move objects, open a door through dimensions to travel, or to slow down or speed up personal time if it wasn't for Rahm."

"He doesn't want to leave this planet, he's gone native. We have known this for many years!"

"How many times must I go over this? We will get him to fix the ship under the ruse we will not take him with us and we will not take the armies of Darrk back here." Dianna was trying to keep her brother alive and trying to not hurt his family. But if she couldn't get him to fix the ship or give them that damned key . . . she had to do whatever was necessary to return the others home. She was disappointed she couldn't convince Hathor to give her the key. She might even have let that idiot Hades have a shot at fixing the ship. She was even sure she knew where the escape shuttle was, but she knew she needed Rahm. Only he could modify the parts and make suitable replacements. Without him, they would surely fail.

If she had gotten the key, she may have been able to get Rahm's help. Although she hated it, she may have to fight her own brother, force him into repairing the ship and giving her the key, and telling her where, for sure, the escape shuttle was hidden. Maybe she'd have to take his precious offspring as hostages. She'd tell him they would release them after the ship was fixed. She might even have to, depending on how good his truth reading abilities were now. They hadn't spoken but twice in the last hundred years, and only seven times in the last 800, and she was unsure how much his powers had grown, but grown they had. She knew they had because she'd felt it, but not seen it. He exuded a power that was greater than any she had seen, even her own. He was strong enough to beat her, but she knew he couldn't kill her. She didn't have that problem. Wherever he had found it, his self-righteousness would prevent it; it had made him soft.

She could hear stirrings coming from the basement, it would soon be time to go, after they went out and fed. That was becoming a problem, there were too many in this area and they needed to spread out to avoid alerting the authorities. The homeless were their first choice for prey, but taking too many of them would be noticeable, and an obvious population of homeless was necessary. The police on patrol would notice a sudden decline of them, but some had to be left, so street walkers and drug dealers were next, two types of people that would be noticed if gone, but would not be looked for very hard. Although she hated it, she would have to fight her own brother and force him into repairing the ship, or all this was for nothing.

She heard the noise behind her, but before she could turn around, her arms were grabbed from behind and pinched to her sides, and a hood was thrown over her head. She began to fight them, but at least four of them must have had a hold on her, and she really didn't try that hard anyway. Soon she was bound at wrists and ankles, growling and screaming in anger. "Throw her in on my bed! We'll take care of this, she had her chance!" Thorm yelled. "Tonight we get the key and the engineer! I've had enough of these excuses!"

"You fool! They'll kill you all!" Dianna spat.

"If she says another word, gag her. We can't lose control over the Nightwalkers! When they return, we will end this!" Thorm shouted, "Hurry, we need to prepare before the Nightwalkers return."

Dianna felt herself carried down the hall where the two that were carrying her threw her on the bed. "Don't do this," she pleaded, "Rahm is too strong, he's been preparing for this for a thousand years; you will fail."

They never said a word, she heard them cross the floor, and shut the door. *Damn,* she thought, *he just took the bait sooner than I thought! But they can't hurt Rahm!* She felt cornered and did the only thing she thought she could do. *"Brandon. Brandon my love, come to me!"* She called for him, then again, *"Brandon, come to me, my love. Hurry, we are in danger!"*

What appeared to be a young man was standing in a dim corner off Pioneer Square. It was early, but he was supposed to return back to the house on Queen Ann Hill as soon as he fed. The sun had gone down less than an hour ago and the street was still full of people. He was watching a drug dealer waiting for someone. As soon as he was done with him, he would make his move. He had been watching this one for a couple of weeks, and soon he would walk over and get him to step into the alley for what the dealer would assume was a quick purchase. It would be the last transaction he would make. *"Brandon, Brandon my love, come to me!"* He knew it was his mistress, but this wouldn't take long. *"Brandon, come to, me my love. Hurry, we are in danger!"*

"Coming, Mistress!" He left immediately for the house on Queen Anne.

He was notified of the failure from the night before and found himself concerned with her resolve. Staring out the thirtieth floor window toward the pyramid, he began to dream of home, it was so close! The man in the three-piece suit turned from the window and ran a hand through his long black hair, not even seeing the Native American artifacts that filled the office on every table and shelf, some thousands of years old. His reddish skin was smooth with no trace of beard on his chin, brown eyes glinting in anger, he picked up his cell phone and began to dial. Answering on the first ring, a voice said, "Yes, sir."

"You have secured her?"

"Yes, sir," the voice on the other end repeated.

"Then it falls to you. Don't disappoint me." He said this and abruptly hung up, not waiting for an answer.

Now that Erick was awake, the focus was getting out of the guesthouse and into the mansion. The guesthouse was too small. Although it was a good defensible position with few points of entry, it was made of old wood framing with cedar siding and roof, and it would burn hot and fast. Erick was afraid they would set it alight. A fire wouldn't damage the key, and he confirmed to Lauren and the others that it was around his neck. Reaching in his shirt, he pulled out the amulet on the chain around his neck.

The amulet was a gold circle with two silver dollar-sized triangular crystals; one blue and one clear, forming a six-pointed star in the middle. There was some engraving or carving on the sides of the gold ring that looked familiar, but otherwise it looked plain. Doc pointed out that other than looking incredibly old it didn't look like much. Erick surprised him when he said, "I had the chain and the gold ring made 6000 years ago in Egypt. While I've repaired it several times over the centuries, this is pretty much the way it was made. The clear crystal belongs to the ship, the blue to the shuttle."

"No offense," Doc began, "but I don't see how these two crystals are a key."

"Think of them more like a computer chip," Lauren said, "with the startup instructions loaded on them."

"Why don't you just destroy them?" Mac started, "Crystals shatter pretty easy."

Erick looked at him seriously, "If I did, it would be an Extinction Level Event." Mac paled. "That's why they are in the gold frame. It made them easier to carry and protect them."

"Extinction Level Event? I'm not familiar with that one," Hawk said curiously.

"Let's say you took the blue one and struck it hard with a hammer, it would create a blast that would knock a hole in the earth's crust about a quarter mile deep and fifty miles wide." Hawk could see that Erick was serious when he said it. "The clear one would likely do three to four times that much damage. Nothing on earth would survive. The dust it would blast into the atmosphere alone would darken the sky and not let the sun in for years, not to mention what it would do to the planet itself. Earthquakes never seen before and a large volcano would form where it was done. It would be at least twice the power of the blast that killed the dinosaurs. You see, these are Horus crystals; we use them to power our ships. But ones that are clear and faceted like a diamond, whatever their color, are used to store information like a computer chip. The startup sequence of the shuttle and the ship are on these two crystals and trust me, that's a whole lot of information. They can't be destroyed on earth or it would kill everything on the planet. It would be an Extinction Level Event. We know this because Darrk has destroyed many planets with them."

"My God!" Doc felt a shiver running up his spine, "Then I guess you better put it back inside your shirt!"

Chapter Thirteen

THE VISITORS

An hour later, Erick had changed into jeans and a black wool sweater, and was busy trying to explain the various ways to kill a Nightwalker to Raven. The others gathered things together for the trip to the house. "The old legends are not far off, a wooden stake through the heart is a common one that you hear as well as silver. Both are true, but silver will begin to burn whatever point it touches the flesh, but above all, it's very painful and will distract them. Even a little will keep spreading until they turn to ash, or if it is on a limb, say an arm, the arm is removed."

"A wooden stake works well but is only temporary as all it really does is stop the healing process, remove the stake, and the wound will heal. Holy water does nothing. You pour any of that on them and they will laugh at you. Garlic is another, they could eat it for breakfast if they wanted, but solid food makes them sick. Unlike Lauren and I, who can eat just about anything, their bodies, once turned, can no longer process food. They can only exist on blood, and it doesn't have to be human, but human blood provides the most nourishment."

"You must decapitate them to truly kill them or make sure they burn to ash. Silver will make them start to burn wherever it touches, and that burning will spread. And don't bury the head with the rest of them; it will grow back on if placed on or by the neck. Burn the body to destroy them for good or just leave them out until the sun hits them. Even on a cloudy day, it just works a little slower. They will turn to ash. Salt does . . ." he stopped suddenly. Raven looked across the room and saw Lauren, who was talking to Doc, stop as well. Even Mac had stopped what he was doing and was looking intently at his mother. They seemed to be listening to something nobody else could hear.

"What's wrong?" Raven was concerned they were here already; Grandfather Erick had said they wouldn't be until after they'd fed.

"I think we have a visitor. He is alone," Erick whispered. The feeling of danger had come to him, and the hair on his neck was standing. He could even hear the slow beating of its heart; necessary to move the nutrients through the body, but much, much slower than a living human. Although the tissue needed oxygen, it could go for hours without it. The heart rate was about ten beats a minute; it could only be a Nightwalker. He went over to Lauren. "What do you think?"

"At first, I had thought they had arrived much earlier than we thought, but he's alone. I think a scout, perhaps? Have they ever done that?" Lauren looked as puzzled as he felt.

"I don't think so, he's approaching the door." Erick, still listening, could feel more than hear it. But this one was casually strolling up to the door. A soft knock came at the door. "I think I better go see what our guest wants."

"Careful," Lauren warned. "I don't like this."

"Neither do I."

Erick walked over to the door and as casually as if a neighbor had come over, yelled, "Who is it?"

"I don't want to come in, all I want to do is deliver a message and get the hell out of here before I'm caught." The voice sounded young, but strong. "I have my orders not to hurt anyone and do not plan to disobey them." With a wave, Erick unlocked the door and opened it, still eight feet away. Standing on the porch was what appeared to be a young man in black jeans and hoodie, he was smiling, and something about his smile reminded Erick of a cat just before it pounced. He walked over and out the doorway, closing it behind him and locking it. The porch light was off so he could see clearly, and the young vampire seemed unworried about being in his presence. Knowing Erick could tear one of his kind apart, his arrogance irritated Erick.

"The great Rahm, you don't look like much." He grinned, then continued, "I bring a message from my mistress, Dianna."

"Looks can be deceiving newborn." Erick used the slur to knock this one off guard; it didn't work. "Deliver your message and leave then."

"With pleasure, Your Highness," he used a slur of his own easily. This was not a newborn; he had been around awhile. "My name is Brandon, bound to my mistress Dianna. She sends word you will be attacked tonight, though not by her, but by ones who don't care about your welfare. They just want the key—within the hour I would say—she wants you to know this is not her doing. The attack will be from twenty-five Walkers and six old ones. She will not be here."

"Why tell me this, why aren't you with them?"

"I serve my mistress and do not reside at that pigsty with the others. My mistress and I live . . . elsewhere." He smiled and continued, "I am not under their control; I follow only my mistress. Although I will miss the festivities tonight, I was looking forward to it really, it would have been so much fun." The smile left his face, "I only tell you this because my mistress commands it!"

"Where is she?"

"To be frank, a little tied up right now; in a house on Queen Anne. She wouldn't let me untie her," he said.

"Tied up?" Erick brow furrowed.

"Yup. They took the attack away from her as they said she was going soft; yeah, right." He turned to leave.

"What makes you think I should let you leave here?"

Looking over his shoulder he sneered, "Honor." He walked away up the path.

"You are much older than you seem," Erick said under his breath.

"I heard that!" Brandon called, not turning around, and throwing up his arm, pointing his middle finger at the sky.

Erick entered the house, closing the door behind him, and setting the locks. He looked thoughtful, staring at nothing for a moment. The others waited patiently for him to speak; they had all heard the conversation on the porch. He looked up. "We're moving now—everyone to the mansion. Take what you can and go now or as soon as your group is ready. Lauren, stay with Hawk and Doc, you'll go up with them. Mac, you are with me. Raven and Eileen, leave when you can. Go! We'll meet in the library. We have less than an hour. We'll go this way."

"Why the sudden change?" Hawk asked, as they went to their various tasks.

Lauren answered, "Because Dianna would have followed the rules; these other six, if they took command from her and tied her up, won't. They'll burn this guesthouse down right around our heads and hit us from every angle all at once. With so many coming, it's best if we spread them out, so it makes it more critical if they don't catch any of us here. The more possible entrances, the more spread out they will be. Dianna wouldn't have killed Erick or burned the guesthouse down on us, but these old ones might. The mansion is mostly stone and brick. All they want from us is the key. If they do want him alive, they will want someone as a hostage to make Erick work. The rest of us are a nuisance they can't leave behind." Before he could ask, she stated simply, "If they leave me alive, I'll hunt down and kill every one of them." By the look in her eyes, she meant every word.

As she spoke, Erick walked over to the bookcase, pulled out a book, reached into the open space, and there was an audible click, and the bookcase swung out. "Through here."

"I wish I had known that was there two years ago." Raven reached to grab her things.

Erick reached inside a closet, opened a panel in the back and pulled out a sword. Mac thought to himself it was the most beautiful, and the oldest, he had ever seen. The leather handle had a dull metal guard and pommel that Mac knew was silver that had tarnished in the closet. He guessed without looking at it closely that the sword was at least 500 years old. Mac was a collector of swords but even he couldn't place this one. When Erick pulled back the scabbard to check the blade, He saw a slightly curved, single-edged, thin but wide, blade like the one on a Samurai sword in thickness, but wider. Out of place, the blade looked Japanese in what had first appeared to be a European medieval sword. "You think you could show that to me if we live through this?" Mac asked.

"I think we can do a little better than that." Erick reached in and pulled out another, "Always have a spare." He handed the sword to Mac. It looked almost identical. "There is silver in the blades, folded in the steel by a Japanese master sword maker; these were made for Nightwalkers. Hawk, do you have a blade?"

"Yes, sir," he held up one of the swords. "One of these are perfect for me, one of those might be too heavy. I think if you have a thinner one for Raven, she could use it."

Lauren spoke up, "I've already given her a sword, lightweight; I think it will be perfect." Picking up a crossbow and quiver, she turned to Hawk, "You ready?" He nodded. They left most of the explosives behind, taking only a few; there wasn't the time. "I'll go first. Doc, I want you ten feet behind me, no more if possible, but you won't be able to see well, if at all, so don't scream if you run into me. Hawk, bring up the rear ten feet behind Doc."

"Got it." He knew experience when he saw it and was not going to argue.

There were no lights in the tunnel that he could see Doc noticed. A little uneasy, he said "I'm walking into the dark and I'm the only one of us who can't see. Great. How do I get night vision?"

Hawk shrugged his shoulders, "You could always become a vampire."

"Thanks, good advice. I think I'll take night vision goggles for a hundred, Alex." With that, he entered the tunnel, ten feet behind Lauren, as instructed.

Erick had a strange look. Raven looked at him and said, "Jeopardy."

"That still on the air? I loved that show. Ready to go," he looked at the others. "Good. Mac, you're first. Raven, you're next with Eileen. How is your night vision, everyone? Doc should be the only one of us who doesn't at least have good vision." They all nodded, "Okay, Mac." He tilted his head toward the tunnel, Mac entered, to be followed by Raven, pushing Eileen's wheelchair. She started after Mac had gone about ten feet. Erick took one last look around the room, entered, and pulled the bookcase shut.

Lauren noticed the tunnel was going up now. It had gone down at a slight angle for about thirty feet, then curved and leveled out. There were only two dim lights she saw, one at the bottom of the curve and another she could see about forty feet away, where it appeared to curve again, but this time the other way. After that, it started up, where she came to a door with no knob. Looking at the surface, she saw a hole about the size of a quarter. Putting her finger in the hole, she heard a soft click, and she gave the door a gentle push.

It opened to the library. With all the lights in the room off, it had an eerie gloom. She silently moved into the room, giving the others enough room to enter. Doc banged his shin on an end table, and to his credit, didn't cry out. Hawk came after him with a smile on his face. "I don't care who you are, that is still a painful way to arrive."

"Well, I can't see shit!" Doc was whispering.

"Doc, they aren't here yet," Hawk grinned. "You don't have to whisper."

"Then, can we turn some lights on before I ruin my other shin, shithead?"

A few moments later, Mac came out of the tunnel. He was followed by Raven and Eileen, then Erick. With a wave of his hand, the lights in the room came on.

"Finally!" Doc said with a sigh of relief. "I'll never get tired of that trick."

"I'll have to show you how it's done," Erick said, turning around.

"What? You mean . . ." Doc started.

"Okay, here's where we split up. Lauren, you take Raven, Eileen, and Doc to the fourth floor. Go to her bedroom. It has two ways in and one is the window, but it's on the back of the house and that's four floors up. They still may use it, so be watchful. Then, you take up a position in the hall. Raven, you will be in the room with Doc and Eileen."

"I hate to interrupt, but she would be better fighting with the rest of us. Doc and Aunt Eileen can hold off any of them until she can get back there," Hawk said.

"Oh? Is there something I don't know?" Erick asked.

"Yes, sir." Then Hawk said simply, "She's an expert with the sword, holds black belts in four different disciplines; she also happens to be the self-defense instructor for the firm. This is to a bunch of people who think they don't need any further training, until they meet her, my skinny sister." He was smiling at Mac.

"Yeah," Mac said, looking at Raven, while he winced and instinctively covered his crotch after thinking of their first painful meeting.

"At least I never had to worry about her dating. All those martial arts classes you paid for when she was young made most boys scared of her." Eileen said this with a smile while Raven turned beet red.

Erick raised his eyebrows, looking at Raven; he hadn't gotten any kind of a read on her yet, he hadn't really tried. He nodded and went on, "Then the two of you take the fourth floor," looking at Raven and Lauren. "Mac, Hawk, I want you two on the roof at the start of this. Use the crossbows; pick off as many as you can with them. When they begin to close on the house, use the cocktails, the flares, and then the pipe bombs. That should slow them down. But use the bombs as a last resort if you can, the neighbors are just through the trees and may call the police when they hear them."

"We got a break on that," Raven advised. "They are in Arizona for the winter and aren't home. The house will block a lot of the sound, and it will take the other neighbors some time to figure it out with the sound bouncing off the water. It should be as loud as if it was coming from across the water."

Mac looked at Erick, "We can set most of them off by remote. When we get to the roof, we can throw them in areas we think they will do the most good. When we see a good effective time to detonate one, we can. The pipe bombs may do more than just slow them down too." He grinned and added, "They are each filled with half a roll of silver dimes."

"I think you guys may have a better handle on this than I do." Erick just shook his head.

When they were ready to split up, Erick got an idea, thanks to Mac. Going to the painting behind the desk, he pulled it out of the way, exposing a safe behind it.

"I never even knew that was there," Raven laughed.

"Probably a lot of things you didn't know were here," Eileen said. "When your grandfather built this place, he paid a great deal of money to the craftsmen that worked on it. There are passages and little hidey-holes all over this place. I knew of this safe but have no idea what the combination is, and every now and then, I ran into a passage or a closet that didn't look like it was there."

"When I built this place, I had just brought Eileen and Rose from back east. I put in the passages as escape routes for no other reason than my own peace of mind. The 'hidey-holes' as she calls them were for smuggled goods. I haven't always agreed with what the law said you could and couldn't have; and the combination to the safe? Simple really," Erick said, spinning the dial and looking at Eileen, "it's your sister's birthdate." Throwing the handle, he unlocked the door opening the safe. He reached inside and pulled out an old heavy cashbox and set it on the desk. When he opened it, everyone saw it was full of rolls of quarters. "Take these," he said, handing them out. "These are all silver, I put them in the safe in 1955. They will all be ninety percent silver from '55 and the years before. You may need to improvise. And start turning on lights, we will do better than them in bright light."

"Thank you!" Doc said, looking up.

Erick could think of nothing else, "Be careful and smart with these Nightwalkers. Most seem to lose intelligence when turned, while some do not. Do not take it for granted they will be dim-witted; some are not, like that Brandon. Above all, take no risks, let them come to you."

"Where will you be?" Mac asked.

Erick smiled, "I'm taking the ground floor by the pool, I'll make them come by me first and give them a chance to talk if they are so inclined."

"Be careful." Lauren knew she didn't have to say it, but she had to.

Erick nodded and headed for the door.

Erick was standing by the pool; the only light he had turned on was the pool light. The glow off the water turned the room a pale blue. Breaking open several rolls of quarters, he threw them in the pool. *Homemade acid bath*, he thought, *might work.* He saw something hit the ground in the yard in a dense clump of bushes, one of Mac's pipe bombs he guessed. Lauren had taught him well. He shared some of Hawk's memories now and knew of the battles he and Mac had been through, making the bond between them stronger and much closer than friends. Putting them together in this would make them better, and he knew it. They would protect each other, and if necessary, fight back-to-back with no thought of losing. Having been through so many battles together, they would work together without even needing to talk.

He would have to learn more about Raven, but he felt her strength. He tried not to look inside a person's mind, as one's thoughts are his own, but sometimes he had too. Something like shaking someone's hand would transfer more information than he wished sometimes. But she would not have accepted being kept out of the way when others were in danger. Moving to the side, he lifted the sword and began to practice and loosen up. After over 8000 years, it was all muscle memory and reflexes. If nothing else, it calmed his nerves and yes, he was nervous. His other powers had not fully woken up yet; he was more vulnerable now than he would be in a couple more days.

It was another hour before the first of the Walkers arrived; he felt them. All of them arrived within just a few minutes, and they scattered themselves all over the grounds. There were only Nightwalkers at this point, but then, the heartbeat of a Darrk arriving was unmistakable. Seconds later, two more arrived. The last three arrived at once, one at the front of the house, one on the east side, one on the west. The other three were together in the backyard.

A few minutes went by when one of the Darrks called out, "Rahm, I wish to speak to you!" It was Thorm, from the group that had been placed in Iceland.

"Then come in by the pool. I promise you a safe return." *More than he would promise me.* "I know you're right outside, so come in." He could smell Thorm's fear.

There came some voices from outside, then a figure showed at the glass door.

"Come in. We can talk in here."

Thorm looked about suspiciously, then slid the door open and lightly stepped inside. He saw the sword about ten feet away from Rahm, not far enough from this one. He stayed by the door. "I wanted to give you a chance, a chance to come to your senses."

"On what? My enslavement? I will not repair the ship to allow you to go back to Darrk and bring the fleet back with you." Erick had no illusions of what would happen, his greatest hope was that the armies of Darrk had been defeated by another planet over the years, but he couldn't guarantee that. "The earth in its current state would be no match for it and would be enslaved and destroyed. They don't have the weapons to protect themselves."

"What do you care?" Thorm spat angrily, "They are nothing to us, nothing! All they are is food! You are helping them live while our own planet is dying! Do you hate your own race so much? They are an inferior race, fit to be controlled, not worshipped! To help and hold them above your own is to be nothing but a traitor!"

"How do you know our own planet is still alive? It has been over 8000 years here on earth and almost 7000 on Darrk. We have lived longer than any Darrks in our history. How do you feel knowing you are one of the oldest beings in the universe? Should we at least let this planet and its people learn what it's like to explore the stars? To let them learn and allow them to get to their fullest potential?"

"Fine! Just give me the key, and I will leave."

"I cannot do that anymore than I can tell you where the escape shuttle is."

"Then we have nothing more to talk about." Thorm raised his arms, and as he did, four Nightwalkers came through the glass on either side of him, scattering broken pieces in their paths.

The sword flew across the room into Erick's hand. The first one to make it to him he cut in half at the waist, and on the return stroke, cleanly took his head off before the vampire had even begun to burn. A second, he kicked into the pool, where it suddenly began to scream and spasm uncontrollably. *I'll be damned, it worked!* The third he ran through with the sword, kicking him off the blade, even as his body burst into flames and began to turn into burning coals. He swung around and decapitated him before the fire had spread to the head. The fourth had gotten around him and was trying to take him from behind, but in one smooth motion he spun and watched the Walker's head fall, bounce off the deck and roll into the pool in a cloud of steam. When Erick looked over by the door, Thorm was gone.

Mac and Hawk heard the glass breaking on the roof. The second it did, Mac fired a silver tipped bolt from his crossbow into the chest of a Nightwalker under a tree across the front yard. He watched with satisfaction as the intruder turned into a ball of flame and ash. On the other side of the roof, Hawk fired a bolt into another one by a line of rose bushes. Without even glancing at the one he shot, he then dropped one of the Molotov cocktails on the cement at the edge of the patio leading to the pool, putting a wall of flame between the enemy and Erick by the pool. Several were crossing the yard, so he picked up the remote and detonated two of the bombs in a flower bed in the middle of the yard; he saw four of them burst into flames and turn to ash in seconds. He didn't have time to be amazed at how well Mac's improvised bomb worked, as one came over the edge of the roof and headed straight for them. He fired another crossbow bolt into the attacker's right eye, where the silver tip began to work like an acid on its head and spread down the body. By the time it fell at his feet, nothing but ash remained. Mac had taken his sword and removed the right arm of another, and swinging around, took its head off. As it began to burn, he shouted, "It's getting crowded, we need to get back into the house; hit the napalm!" Hawk grabbed the remote, turned the dial to the right number, and pressed the button.

Erick saw the crossbow bolt hit the one in the yard and saw it start to burn from the center out. Seconds later, flames came between him and the Nightwalkers he saw in the yard heading his way. Then there was a blast, and all the windows in the poolroom and several on the greenhouse shattered, as silver dimes and pieces of pipe rained down, shredding four of the Walkers as they burst into flames. One was stumbling around on fire, and came through the broken glass door of the poolroom, and fell into the pool. Smoke and the smell of burnt flesh filled the room. Then, a line of flames started across the yard; three of the Walkers were flailing around on fire when Erick saw two more headed for the door into the recreation room. He ran that direction, and coming from the poolroom into the recreation room, he leaped over one of the pool tables, picking up one of the balls on the way. He threw it with such force that when it hit one of the two that had come through the door from outside, the top of its skull came off, spilling its brain all over the wall behind it, followed by the pool ball, which buried itself deeply into the lathe and plaster wall. When he landed on the other side of the table, he realized the one in front of him wasn't a Walker, but one of the Darrks. A large Darrk with an eye patch was standing in front of him. Aries.

Aries stood, looking at Rahm with his sword in hand, and a smile crossed his face as he thought the traitor was his. Bringing his sword up, he taunted Erick. "I see you have decided to come to your death instead of hiding, Traitor. Good. I don't want you alive. I'd rather see you dead. You have forgotten how to be a Darrk and forsaken your power. You instead have become a weak human and hid from the dark like they do. We will have to see if you die well or die groveling like a human, begging for life."

Of all the Darrks, Aries was one of the strongest. As the leader of the assault force on the ship, he was a veteran of many battles before coming to earth. He loved war and battle, thrived on its misery, and had spent the last 8600 years pursuing it wherever he could find it. His body was scarred, one eye was missing, lost in the Battle of the Four Worlds, and the socket covered by a patch. Tattoos covered his arms over the many scars, some over the tops of others. Erick knew this would not be easy; Aries would make him pay for any mistake. They had served in Alexander's army together after Egypt drove him out, killing his sons, and he thought for the longest time, his mate. Alexander conquered Egypt and while he did it, Aries bathed himself in the blood of humans and reveled in misery and death. In the end, Aries left to find more battles, more wars, and Erick thankfully never saw him again. He had never seen one so cruel. This Darrk had become even more cruel after landing on earth, if that was possible. Erick had once seen a photograph he thought Aries was in. It was of a group picture of Nazi SS officers during WWII, and Erick had been sure it was him, right down to the eye patch. With some checking, he found the officer's name was Carl Richter, and he'd died in an explosion at the end of the war. Just the kind of thing a Darrk could walk out of. He wished he had. He had only one chance, "Ah, Carl, isn't it?" Erick refused to call him by his Darrk name. "I see you did escape the rope at the end of the war."

"Yes, I did. After I killed and raped my way through these humans across Africa and Europe." He laughed, but Erick saw a familiar look in his eye.

He pressed further. "Nothing like losing, is there, Carl? Pretty name for a loser, Carl. How many other losing sides did you get on over the centuries? How many other loser names? A big, cruel one, such as you? I bet a lot, eh? You would have loved the side you could be the cruelest on. Is that what you will be here, Carl? A cruel loser again?" Erick was seeing the anger in his eye, *yes!* He wanted him mad, just as mad as he could get him. "You going to lose to a bunch of humans? Show how great and strong you are against a people a fraction of your strength, age, and experience? Did you do in Germany what you did in Egypt, take little girls to scare them before you beat, raped, and killed them like a pervert?" That did it.

Aries howled and lunged, swinging his sword. Erick deflected it but felt the power in the blow shaking his shoulders. "You will die, Traitor!" Three more quick blows followed, then a thrust, then a swing that Erick sidestepped as Aries sword shattered a chair. Bringing it up he struck Erick with the heavy end of the pommel, but luckily, Erick was pulling his head away when the blow came. It glanced off, not as hard as it should have been, gashing open his forehead, but still making his ears ring. "You'll be on your knees, begging for life, Traitor! I'll see you in the underworld below God's back paw!" Erick then went on the offensive and dealt four quick blows before he stepped back to assess his attack. *This might take a while,* he thought.

Lauren and Raven were on the fourth floor, each about ten feet from Eileen's room on either side in the hall. Lauren heard the howl but there was nothing she could do. Back-to-back they had four more Nightwalkers come into the hall; they had already killed two when these came through the windows at each end. One of the Walkers laughed at Lauren, "You know, I never learned how to use a sword." He pulled a large revolver from under his coat, as he was starting to level it, a fireball rushed up the hall, engulfing him. Screaming, he fell over the banister, landing on the tile floor below. Lauren was surprised. *Eileen can throw fireballs?*

"That's cheating!" Eileen shouted, and threw another one down the other end of the hall by Raven, the flames wrapping firmly around one, and he screamed. Lauren removed the head of the one closest to her while Raven took the right arm off another. Suddenly, four more were in the hall. Eileen yelled, "Quick, in here!" backing into her bedroom.

Doc leaned around the corner and fired two blasts of a 12-gauge shotgun down the hall both ways, hitting three. All it did was slow them down. He slammed the door shut, leaning against it as the wood above his head splintered. Four sharp claws on the end of strong fingers poked through the wood. Then they heard a blast and a couple of dimes came through the top of the door. The hand above Doc's head began to burn, then it disintegrated, dropping burning ashes on his head. Beating the top of his head with his hand, he knocked the still smoking embers off, saying, "I think the boys are having way too much fun." His furrowed brows locked odd with the crooked smile, then there was a knock at the door.

"Room service!" Mac's voice was unmistakable. "Who ordered the right arm?"

Erick was tiring. Aries' blows were hard, and he pressed them rapid fire down on Erick, pushing him back toward the entrance to the elevator. Erick knew he had one last chance and took it. Closing his left hand in a fist as tightly as he could, he cast the spell, Aries heard the words and it puzzled him, *Latin?* Erick then opened his fist, fingers spread, palm toward Aries. The blast caught Aries off guard and threw him across the room, he struck what was left of the window off the back patio and flew through it. Erick watched the window for a moment and then collapsed on the floor, trying to catch his breath.

A howl rang out in the night. The Nightwalker that was left and Darrks went away, their heartbeats fading. Then all was silent.

"Erick!" Lauren was calling out to him as she ran. Coming into the recreation room, she saw him on the floor by the elevator. "Are you alright?" She was followed by Mac and Raven.

"Never better, only tired; I ran into an old friend, it seems." His arm had been slashed but had already healed, as well as the cut on his forehead.

She helped him sit up, "Who?"

"Aries. Son of a bitch is still as strong as ever, and this damn planet doesn't help. Makes him twice as strong as us. I had hoped he'd died in the war; no such luck."

"Aries is alive?" She glanced at Mac, who was in the doorway looking at the pool.

"I think we better change the water in the pool." The remark was casual, but by the slump in his shoulders, Erick knew he wasn't the only one that was tired. "We also better get a blind contractor; I don't know how we're going to explain this. Sorry about the glass, Erick."

"No problem. I know just the guy if he's still in business, that is." He noticed the way Lauren looked at Mac, and then he realized what it was that he couldn't put his finger on about Mac; he looked just like Aries. The eye patch threw him off. "I think we need to talk," he whispered to Lauren.

"Yes, I think we do," she whispered back.

"Is everyone else alright? Hawk? Eileen? Doc?" Erick asked.

"Fine. Everyone's fine." Lauren was looking at Erick, "Do you think anyone called the police?"

"We'll know in about five minutes." Raven was looking at the damage to the greenhouse with her back to the pool table and the back door. Something stood behind her across the pool table. Before anyone could say anything, she leaped from the floor flipping over and landed on the pool table facing the Walker that Erick had struck with the pool ball. It's head still half missing but its brain had healed somewhat and was intact enough that its basic instincts were working, and it was hungry. The first thing it saw was Raven, and the last thing it saw was Raven as her blade cut his head off cleanly. "If they are coming, we will hear them soon." She continued as if nothing had happened. "We should hide the body parts somewhere, what little there are, but I have no idea where. There isn't much left of them but blood and an arm. Oh, and this one," she said indicating him with the sword. "I guess the blade doesn't have enough silver in it."

"My fault, I tried to give you a lighter blade," Lauren said apologetically, then started to giggle. She was joined by Erick just as Mac came back in from the pool with a baffled look on his face.

"What gives? Delayed reaction to my jokes?" He had just come back from the pool and had missed the whole beheading of the vampire.

"No," said Erick, "we just realized we are all alright."

Mac looked at Raven. "What are you standing on the pool table for?"

The other three looked at him and broke up in an even worse bout of laughter. Raven said between giggles, "Will you help me move this one?"

"I can get it myself, no problem," he replied, with a puzzled look on his face, looking back and forth from Raven to the others. "But where do I put it?"

"In the pool." Erick looked at Mac for a moment as he grabbed the body of the vampire in one hand and the head in the other and started to the pool, but Erick stopped him, "Let's see if Doc wants to take a look at that one first." Mac dropped both parts with a thud.

"Well, make up your minds," Mac said, rolling his eyes.

Erick thought, *yes, he was Aries' child, but did he know it?* His strength gave him away. A half Darrk is normally not that strong, at least none in his family were. But then, Hawk was the first male born to his line, and he didn't know any other part-Darrk people.

They went to get the others.

None of them wanted to tell Dianna, much less untie her, knowing their failure. Aries was the only one who disagreed with pulling back, but even he, the only one of the Darrks who actively fought in the battle, had been injured. Erick's blast had blinded his one good eye after losing the other in the Battle of the Four Worlds. The other would at least grow back on this planet. But even he wanted nothing to do with untying her after this. Twenty-four Walkers lost. Only one came back with them, and he was going to be in his coffin healing from burns for a month. She would be furious. They had been told the three of them and the old witch wouldn't be too much to overcome, but when they arrived, there were six. In the end, they all blamed Thorm for talking them into it, and made him go untie her.

Dianna looked furious. But she very calmly got off the bed, glared at Thorm, and walked out the door toward the others without saying a word. As she entered, she surveyed the room. Aries was injured with a bandage over his good eye. An eye, which will take about a week to heal she figured, then he would be able to see completely again. The other five, including Thorm, weren't even dirty. Aries was the only one to join the fight she assumed, that idiot Thorm talked them into overtaking her, then he watched the others fight while he cowered in the brush. But she knew who really was responsible.

"Well, well. How many Walkers were lost?" Nobody answered. "How many?" she snapped.

"Twenty-four." It was Beli that answered, staring at the floor. "And one is going to have to heal. He's in his coffin and will have to stay there for a few days."

"Twenty-four? You lost all of them?" she said calmly. "All twenty-five?"

"We won't need much time to make more, and your servants Brandon and the others didn't even show up!" Thorm was raising his voice as he had just before he had the others tie her up.

She smiled, Ajax knew Thorm had overstepped, and he would have to get him to calm down. Ajax had been around Isisi for several centuries now on this planet, and that smile was deadly. "Thorm, now don't get pushy, you know they're not yours to command and only do Isisi's bidding. She wasn't there, and they would have known that."

"Why would that matter? We all had our Walkers there! They were supposed to be there!"

"They weren't there because they only follow my command. But you were there, I was not. I was tied up on a filthy bed in this filthy house you filthy bastards don't know how to keep clean because you are den bugs." Dianna-Isisi used the offensive Darrk term.

Then she looked at them all coolly, "So who answers for this, eh? Who has the eggs to stand up for the disaster you have caused?" They were all silent, looking at the floor. She remembered what her father had taught both her and Rahm before they left for school, "Hold your head up." It was said so softly the others weren't sure what she'd said. "Who will take responsibility? Thorm? Beli? *Ajax? Aries?*" She looked at each in turn, and looking at the last two, she was so disgusted she wouldn't even say their names. She walked over the end table where she had left her sword earlier; it was right where she left it.

Before any of them could stop her, even before they realized the blade was in her hand, Thorm's head was severed and flying into the corner as his body buckled to the floor. Blue-green blood gushed out the neck, spraying the ceiling, the furniture, the floor . . . them! Dianna walked calmly over to the head and picking it up, licked the blood off her lips. She held it faced towards her, watching Thorm's eye's blink in disbelief. "Apology accepted," she addressed the head, looking into its eyes until the last glimmer of life left them. Then she tossed it carelessly back into the corner, where it landed with a hollow thud. "Does anyone else want to take over?" Silence answered her. "Does anyone have anything else to say?" Silence. "All of you owe me a digit. I will be back in a week and I'll collect them then. In the meantime, I want this place cleaned up. If I walk in that door and this place still smells like a Basilisk den, I'll take two heads!" She spun on her heel and left out the front door into the dawn, leaving it open.

Looking at the number on the ringing phone before he answered it, he opened it on the third ring. "Did you get it?"

"No, it seems that someone wasn't listening when I told them taking it by force was a mistake. So, I was overstepped, tied up, and left on a filthy bed."

"Isisi!"

"Who else? Did you really think you could have Thorm take it?" Dianna let that sink in a moment. "That spineless tree bat couldn't take a whelp to task. I know it was you who let them. You really thought they could pull it off without me? They can't even control their own Walkers, which by the way, they no longer have. And now one of them is injured and can't do anything, but wait a week until he can see well enough to not piss on himself when he has to go."

"I had no choice, you failed!"

"I didn't fail! I showed respect and you know our laws! Have you been here so long you have forgotten what we are? We are not savages! Approach the council if you must when we do get home but let me do my job and do not interfere. We will go home if you let me work. Now we will have to wait a week before we will be able to talk to them again. They will think they have the better hand now and will be in that damn tower, and we will have no option but to let them relax before we can negotiate again. Hathor's return will only strengthen his resolve."

"He is your littermate; you are too close to this. What you do by negotiating with him is prove to him he is too important. You should order him to give you the key!"

"The key is no good without him! Do you really think the youngling can repair the ship with no formal training? We need him. Even if he weren't my brother, I would be doing this the same way. We can't repair and run the ship without him! I have told you this, many times. He *is* the only way we are getting home!" With that, she hung up.

They cleaned up what they could, throwing everything in the pool. It worked well at disposing of what was left of the Walkers. Mac, at Doc's request, had put the one that Raven had beheaded on the patio table, and was fascinated by the changes in the physical structures. "Look at the teeth," he pointed, "the canines have grown a good inch top and bottom." He had performed a Y incision and had looked inside the vampire as well, making note of the shriveling of the intestines and the atrophy of the muscles that supported the structures and the digestive system. The stomach and the duodenum were the only organs that appeared to be in use. The liver was shriveled, as was the pancreas. The lungs were smaller as well, but still functional. Erick told him the only thing they needed them for was to oxygenate the tissue, the brain, and the eyes. Everything else could almost get enough oxygen from the transfer at the skin level. He had seen them buried for long periods of time and reanimate once uncovered and exposed to the air and moisture, not unlike what you see in the old horror movies.

Erick then told Doc that Darrks could sleep for years, but it had to be in a dark place without too much moisture; most generally set Nightwalkers as guards of a sort while they slept. Coffins and tombs were good as they were generally left alone, except by criminals, which served their own purpose as far as he was concerned; the basement of a house or the dungeon of a castle, not so good. You were found eventually, generally by someone innocent of wrongdoing. You see, a Darrk woke up hungry. The longer they slept, the hungrier they were when awakened. Sometimes, when sleeping for a long period of time, this was uncontrollable. This was because time would dry them out and they became more shriveled and dehydrated. While the brain was protected, it would shrivel as well. So, they would need even more blood to return to normal and the nutrients in that blood was a must for them. Even he couldn't stop himself from satisfying that hunger when he awoke. After a long sleep, Darrks literally woke up starving.

A grave robber opening a coffin on a Darrk that had been asleep for a hundred years or more was doomed before he started breaking in the door to the tomb. Nightwalkers were worse. The Egyptians sealed some in tombs with the rich and royalty. When grave robbers opened the tomb, they would release the Walker and be killed. The problem was, once released, they became free vampires, unencumbered by a master and operating under their own free will until their death, or until the Darrk that made them found them and took control again. This had started many legends about mummies, or a corpse from a Pharaoh's tomb, or a tomb of the rich being cursed and walking the land. When in truth, the vampire was normally wrapped like a mummy when sealed in the tomb. So, it appeared that a mummy was walking the land, when, in fact, it was a vampire. When Doc finished with his examination of the body and the head, they joined the others in the pool.

Raven came out of the greenhouse with a bottle of silver nitrate, "Will this do any good? If I remember my chemistry, it will probably do a better job than a handful of quarters."

"Couldn't hurt." Doc was looking at the body foaming and steaming in the water, the head bobbing like an apple. "I'd say the faster we get them to go away, the better."

As the sun came up, the blood and body parts they hadn't been able to clean up outside, looking like rust colored paint with cereal in it, had been thrown all over the yard and greenhouse. This was because of the blasts of the pipe bombs. The explosives had dispersed the intruders' bodies all over the yard and the greenhouse and had been highly effective. This debris started to smoke, then it seemed to turn into dust or a cigarette-like ash, and then it was gone in the morning breeze. What they couldn't do anything about was the burnt patches in the yard and patio. They cleaned up what they could, but Erick said they would have to pour more concrete and replant the grass and flowerbeds. He had a contractor in mind who he knew was very discreet when paid well and asked no questions, and his people were meticulous. Erick had used him a couple of times before. No one asked where he found him. As the sun came around to the pool and shone into it, the parts and bits remaining in it fizzed, leaving a pool full of dirty water.

After making a phone call, Erick found out the contractor was still in business although he had retired, and his son was running it now. If it were an emergency, they could be there in an hour. Erick said it was and after a few more words, hung up. It would be well worth the cost. Raven said she would call the nurses and the housekeepers and tell them they wouldn't be needed at the mansion today. She'd tell the housekeepers they were off with pay until further notice but at least for two weeks, and the nurses were told Eileen would be at her condo downtown.

"I think I need to put that contractor's number in my Rolodex." Hawk wasn't joking, although Doc laughed. They were all very tired. Erick told them to get their things together and they would go to a hotel. "We can just go to the office." Hawk added, "We occupy ten floors of the building, and the top two floors are penthouses. Raven, Mac, Doc, and I are in one each and there is one for Aunt Eileen set up already. There is one on thirty and two on twenty-nine. Twenty-eight has two we use as safe houses, and our offices are on that floor as well. You can have your pick of any of the three of them on thirty and twenty-nine. Aunt Eileen already has one across from Doc. I've wanted her to move in there anyway. We can send out one of the girls and have them get Lauren some clothes and whatever other items you need."

"That sounds fantastic," Lauren said, then stiffened. She looked at Erick, and he nodded. She added, "You guys go on, I'll have Mac take us in a few minutes."

"What is it?" Raven questioned.

"Dianna," Erick replied.

Dianna waited for the others to leave, then walked out of the trees slowly. She did not wish to make them think she was here to do anything but talk to them. And she truly did wish to see Erick. After all, he was her brother. As she got closer to Erick and Lauren, she called out, "Good morning, my brother, and good to see you again, Hathor." Lauren bowed her head slightly in response.

"Good morning, Sister. You catch me at a disadvantage." Erick noticed spots of the blue-green blood of a Darrk on her dress. It seemed she must have had a "conversation" with whoever was responsible for her being tied up. He spread his arms out, indicating his torn, dirty clothes. "Seems we were kept a little busy in the night."

"That is unfortunate, and not what I wanted to have happen. A show of force, yes, but I was hoping for a negotiation. There are some, hot tempered ones I might add, who want you destroyed, but I prefer another conclusion." She looked at the missing glass in the greenhouse and pool and noticed the ash blown into the corners of the patio. *Such a waste.* "The more radical one has been removed for now, one might say. All you will have to deal with is me from now on. I'm thinking we can come to some sort of agreement."

Mac, standing in the corner behind his mother and Erick, thought, *this woman would eat her own young. Nothing she says can be trusted!*

As if she knew what Mac was thinking, she looked at him, noticing the resemblance to Aries again, like she had in that damned lawyer's office. She would stay away from this one. He had no idea how strong he was or what he was capable of. After what Aries had done during the Second World War here, she wouldn't be surprised if he had bastard children all over this planet. Interesting to note, to her knowledge, this one was the only half-breed *male* born. She wondered what chance of that happening again was. Maybe there was another. She looked back at Erick.

"Brother, as I said, I didn't want this to happen. Shall we call a truce for now? Just think of this, you don't have to answer right now, I'll give you one week. All I want you to do is fix the ship and give me the key so I can run it. I'll even let you wipe earth's coordinates from the drive computer before we leave. That way we can't get back to earth easily, but you have my word *I won't try to return.* We both know you are the only one left who knows where the ship and the escape shuttle were hidden, and I know you are the only one who knows where the fighter was abandoned. We use the shuttle to get everyone else aboard, and you use the fighter to come back to earth after you repair the ship. Then we leave, and you can stay here with your precious humans."

"I have figured out where the key to the ship is but am guessing on the shuttle. The key to the ship I'm sure you keep around your neck. That amulet you have is too obvious. It took me centuries to figure out that you'd hidden it in plain sight. But I still haven't figured out where the shuttle key is unless you keep it with the ship's key, which I would think might perhaps be a little dangerous. The ship's key is useless if I can't get to it." She paused for a moment, if it were to catch her breath or let what she said sink in, they didn't know. She looked around the yard, with her eyes stopping on the burnt rose bushes, "What a waste of Walkers, and what a waste of such beautiful flowers. They are the only thing I'll miss from this planet, except you and Hathor." She turned back. "I'll give you one week." Closing her eyes, she vanished.

"Not much for letting others speak, is she?" Mac said dryly.

Chapter Fourteen

SECOND AVENUE

The offices of Raven-Hawk were in downtown Seattle of Second Avenue, a few blocks from the Pike Place Market. Mac pointed out the top ten floors were theirs with the penthouses on the top two. Two more penthouses were on the third floor down from them, but they were strictly safe houses with his, Raven, Doc, and Hawk's offices on that floor as well. His office was sort of next to Doc's, which was also the medical offices for Raven-Hawk, and more of a lab than an office, and took up more than half the floor. The company moved in here when they rapidly outgrew their other offices a few blocks away. Those offices were kept as storage now.

"I left suddenly for Washington D.C., so I'll have to look in my refrigerator and see how my science experiments are going." Erick parked the Cadillac in the underground garage beneath the building in a spot marked "Reserved." Hawk's Chevy truck, Doc's Land Rover, and Raven's Camaro were already parked in the row with Mac's Suburban just past them on the first level. On the other side of them were several black sedans and SUVs belonging to Raven-Hawk. They had taken their own cars, which had been parked in the driveway by the third-floor entrance at the mansion.

"The elevators with the card readers and no buttons on the outside are the express elevators to the twentieth floor and up. The company offices are on twenty through twenty-eight with Hawk's office on twenty-eight. The penthouses are on twenty-nine and thirty. You can move between twenty and twenty-seven with the buttons marked as such, but to get to twenty-eight or the penthouses, you must use the card. I'll get you one after I take your picture. I'll just run down to the office and make them. Investigations and background checks are my main job, but you'll find I fill in wherever Hawk or Raven need me. The gym is on twenty-six and you will need your card to access it. They'll be the regular company cards that will get you through the security check on the ground floor entrance as well."

"There are a hundred restaurants around here, you could eat at a different place every meal and not get back to the first place where you ate for a month. There is a café-bar on the third floor. They make a great breakfast and have a great salad bar for lunch. There is a full-service restaurant on the nineteenth floor, which has a great view of the Sound. The food is tremendous and the wine list even better. They will also do room service to the penthouses, but you will have to buzz them up."

"Take your card with you everywhere in here. Security's job is to do just that, keep it secure. There are four guards on roving patrol 24/7. Don't be offended if you get stopped in one of the halls and asked for your ID card, even if the guard knows you. There's a random number generator each guard carries with a card reader. When it tells them to stop someone, he'll take your card and swipe it through the reader. Shows the system he did his check. It's random and they will check anyone, even Raven and Hawk."

"The safe houses are on twenty-eight. I think we will let you stay on thirty, next to Hawk's place. They are all furnished, but the two on twenty-eight are only used for safe houses. They have bulletproof glass in all the exterior windows and most interior spaces have cameras. They have bunkrooms in them that can sleep up to eight guards. Depending on who is occupying the room, they may have guards rotate after a few days instead of doing their normal shifts. The doors are armored. We are contracted by several agencies for their use so don't be surprised if you see guards you don't recognize standing outside the doors. But if you have any suspicions at all, contact Security. If you see something you think you can deal with yourself, don't . . . until you contact Security."

"When you step out of the elevators on twenty-eight, a left to the safe houses, a right to Doc's lab on the right. Across the hall to your left is Raven's office, mine is across from Hawk's who is next to Raven's. Just stop at the reception desk when you get out of the elevators, but after they get to know you, you'll be able to just go where you need to with no trouble unless you go left, and I wouldn't recommend it if the safe rooms are in use. It's one way in, one way out. There is a stairwell between Hawk and Raven's offices, but the alarm will go off if you open the door, and you probably won't be able to hear for a week afterward if you do." He stopped for a moment, then asked, "Did I miss anything?"

"Yeah," Lauren said, "what was it you said after the card reader for the elevator?"

"Smartass." Mac looked at Lauren with his face scrunched up. Erick knew where he got it.

The penthouse on the thirtieth floor next to Hawk's had a stunning view overlooking the Pike Place Market and the waterfront. Mac took their pictures on the computer in the small office and said he would be back in a few minutes. Lauren was standing in the living room, looking out over the water. Erick walked over, putting his arm around her. "This view is beautiful," Lauren said. "I can see why Hawk moved here from the mansion."

"When I built that place, the water was open all the way across to downtown," Erick sighed. "The guesthouse used to be the carriage house. There were no homes on the hill. Mine was one of the first. It's been remodeled several times as the years went by. The view when I first moved Eileen and Rose there was fabulous. Now, it's all crowded."

"It's hard to imagine this is the same planet we first came too," Lauren said, "Remember how it looked from space? The night side all dark, only in the sun was it lit. No cities or light on the night side, just darkness. Even Darrk had cities you could see at night from space. But this planet, nothing. I think that's when I knew we were truly stranded."

"I do remember, but it was lifetimes ago." Erick wrapped his arms around her and kissed her neck gently.

"How long do you think it will take Mac?" Lauren asked.

"Do we care? I think we are way past the age of consent," Erick said with a smile. She pulled away, not letting go of his hand, guiding him toward the bedroom.

Erick woke to the sound of the shower running, he had only dosed off for about an hour. Looking across the bedroom, he saw the bathroom door was open and could see Lauren in the shower through the glass doors. Had it really been that long? They both had acted like it was the first time, at least in human form. They had learned years ago they preferred sex in human form as it wasn't as violent and was much more intimate. In Darrk, it was for pro-creation mostly, and there were times one or the other partner would be hurt. Not so they wouldn't heal, but it was common for it to take a while. Although the Darrk was a mix of the three main species on their planet, they were all the same now. Millions of years ago, there had been three different and distinct animals. But evolution had other things in mind and started to mix them, and the combination it chose was almost if it had a mind of its own.

If you believed Darrk mythology, the god of sky, the god of the water, and the god of the soil grew tired of hearing their greatest works fight and bicker with the other two over who was better. So, they decided that Arcas, god of the earth, would take his oldest boy, the god Lycaon, and put a spell on him to make him mate with the god of the sky's daughter, Siren, under the same spell. Her father, Rahme, cast the spell over her and Otus, the son of the water god, Posdian. The mating of the three would bring the twins, Castom and Polyduce, the first Darrks. Siren then had three daughters, Phobe, Hilera, and Leda. Leda, in a fit of jealousy, tried to kill Hilera and in return was killed by Rahme. It was then decided Castom and Pollum would each take a female for life, and once mated, they would never take another until their death. Thus, all Darrks mated for life from then on.

Erick watched her through the cloudy glass for a few moments when an idea came into his head. He got up and went to join Lauren in the shower. As he entered, she turned around, pink from the hot water. Smiling, she pulled the door closed.

It was well after dark when they woke up. It had been so long they just enjoyed being together again. They would make love, then lay on the bed and talk, catching up on all the years apart. Finally, Erick just had to say it, it had been bothering him for hours, and he had to get it out of his system. "Are you upset I married Maria and had children?"

She gently wrapped her arms around him, laying her head against his chest. "God no! We were apart for so long, each not knowing about the other, not even knowing if the other was alive. We have been alive for so long; we've seen this world grow up. You, being a part of that makes me proud of you. I saw how your life was, so lonely it tore my heart. I'm happy you found someone to take that loneliness away, if only for a brief time. You were a good Darrk, Rahm, but as Erick, you are a much better man." She smiled and then added, "And the children you have had are strong, smart, and devoted to this world and this country. They also keep you from being lonely, just like Mac keeps me from being lonely. You never asked what I did all those years apart from you either, I do want you to know."

"We have spent so much time apart, I don't think we can hold the past against the other," Erick said simply.

She changed the subject, "You missed going to a university in the '60s, didn't you?" Lauren teased, "You would have done well with some of what I found. You know that plant we used to eat on Darrk? They found a way to make its effects here; it's called LSD. That and marijuana were all over campus back then."

"I knew of that and LSD," Erick laughed. "Eileen and Rose used to smoke pot, I never could see the point in it myself, but LSD? Sounds like a great way to lose most of your mind, to me."

"Actually, it can be relaxing and fun in the right place," Lauren said, with a small smile, as memories of her sitting in a room with a black light on listening to the Chicago Transit Authority, the Grateful Dead, and Jefferson Airplane came to mind. The memory was strong enough that Erick picked up on some of it and was surprised—Lauren had always been very practical, and it didn't seem to suit her. They would have to learn so much about each other that they had missed. But in that, he realized his powers were coming back.

"Right now, I was wondering when you fed last."

She knew what he meant, "In Caracas, so I'm beginning to feel spent after last night's escapades. What about you?"

"Outside D.C. several hours before coming here and I feel the same. I burned up a good share of my strength last night and have no reserves. I had been sleeping for twenty years and my body hasn't caught up yet."

"I was wondering how you almost lost to Aries, it seemed unusual that he bested you so soon," she didn't say it with any malice, but it still stung a little. She knew that, while Aries was stronger, Erick was a much better swordsman. Aries was just a bull. She saw Erick wince and knew she had better add the rest of what she was thinking, "He is as strong as any of us I have ever seen and with you just awakened and in a weakened condition? You're lucky you're still alive. You have more tricks than he, but he's just a bull in a china shop."

"The thought crossed my mind," Erick said dryly.

"That brings me to something else, remember when I told you Mac was found at an orphanage at the end of the war?" Lauren began. She didn't need to go further; to Erick, he looked too familiar. He was the spitting image of a young Aries, and his strength proved it in his mind.

"Does he know?"

"I don't think so, although he does wonder where he came from. I have told him he is half Darrk and he accepted that. All we know for sure was his mother was in a concentration camp when she became pregnant. She'd escaped but died giving birth to him." Lauren stopped for a moment to gather her thoughts and went on. "From what the nurs at the orphanage told me, he was an exceptionally large baby. I have a theory that is why when we intermix with humans, there isn't a boy until the next generation or more. The child is just too large. Darrk males are born to us at almost sixteen pounds for a small male, and we normally have more than one, but bearing one male that size would kill a human female. In our natural form we are at least seven feet tall and our bodies are much denser as you know. In recent years I've had to be careful at the airport and some other places as my weight is almost 250 pounds here on earth, even though I look like I weigh one forty dripping wet at six feet. Technology has gotten to where you pass over scales in security checkpoints, and if you don't see it, you can't lighten the load on the scale. I had to teach Mac how to levitate a little before I could even let him go to school, I was terrified they would put him on a scale." As if she was reading his mind, she said, "He weighs over 300 pounds."

Erick let out a small whistle. "He weighs as much as a Darrk?"

"Yes. His bones are dense like ours as well, and he's just as strong as one."

Erick let out another small whistle, "Damn." Was all he could say for a moment. After a few seconds, he went on, "Okay, so you're pretty sure Aries is his father, how do we confirm this?"

"You don't have to," came Mac's voice from the living room.

After they got over their surprise and had dressed, Erick out of his suitcase and Lauren grabbing a robe, they went out into the living room to find Mac was stretched out on the couch with his feet hanging over one end. When he saw them, he sat up. "After I dropped your IDs off, I went back to my place and showered and took a long nap. I just came back in and heard you talking, so thought I'd wait to see if you wanted to go to dinner."

"You heard what we were talking about?" Erick's ears were good, and they were down a hall and had the door shut; he never even heard Mac come in, but in truth, he wasn't listening either; also, he wasn't a danger. Mac's hearing must be as good as a Darrk's, along with his strength.

"A little; what got my attention was when you started talking about the orphanage and my birth. You can correct me if I'm wrong, Mom, but I think I've figured out who my father was."

The genuine look of surprise on Lauren's face made it obvious to Erick that she had never told Mac about her theories. "How did you come up with this?" Lauren was genuinely curious. She had never discussed it with him in-depth, just when he was a boy and curious as to who his father was, and she had told him at the time she didn't know. Even now, she didn't really; she just thought she did. Although, Erick seeing Aries still alive after all these centuries last night had cemented the idea in her mind that Aries was Mac's father.

Some of Mac's quirks were like the Aries she remembered. He, too, was stubborn and single-minded at times. Refusing to see failure, especially in the failure of his body, Mac would run until he dropped, then pick himself up and run some more. He would swim five miles, lay on his back in the water to catch his breath, then swim five more. His dogged determination at times was frustrating, as was his blindness to see failure until it hit him over the head. But he had some good traits that must have come from his birth mother. He was good at figuring things out with few clues, and his mind was an impossible computer, able to notice and remember even little things most others carelessly overlooked and forgot. He was caring and gentle with others, and cute things like puppies or kittens would turn him to mush. As a warrior, he was unbeatable; many had tried. When she had heard he had become a Navy SEAL, all she felt was pride; she wasn't worried about him a bit, especially after she met his commanding officer, a young man by the name of Hawk Scott, that she knew had Darrk blood in him, but wondered if he did.

But his ability to be compassionate, gentle, and genuinely care for another must have come from his mother, as that was not a trait in Aries at all. In fact, from what she remembered of Aries, there were times when he could be very cruel and vicious, and she had never seen that in her son; and yes, she did believe Mac was her son. She may not have borne him, but she had raised and loved him very much just the same. All she had ever seen from Mac was a boy who would stick up for the one that was bullied and get in front of others in a time of danger. She remembered the boy that cried when his dog was hit by a car, or when he pushed the kid out of the way of a bus only to be hit himself. No, there was no compassion in Aries, but there was in her son. She wished several times she had been able to meet his mother, but from what she found out, by all accounts, you could never have met a more loving and compassionate human being. The other Gypsies she had been with who had survived the camp had nothing bad to say about her. He may be a little of Aries, but he was a lot his mother.

The emotion was strong enough Erick felt it, and some of the memories going through her mind he read clearly. He found his feelings for Mac going up a notch or two as well. Mac went on, not wanting to make this drag on any further.

"I am the lead investigator here and have access to many things most of the staff don't. You had an old photograph years ago, which had a man circled on it. It was of the SS officers at a concentration camp used at the Nuremberg trials at the end of the war. The officer circled was not there and was tried in absentia. By looking around a little I found he'd died in an explosion at the end of the war but was tried anyway. The court wanted to make sure that if he popped up, he wouldn't get away with what he had done. I looked a little more and found out he was at the concentration camp my mother was a prisoner, and he was a cruel son of a bitch. The man was in many battles during the war. He was used whenever they wanted someone who could just destroy someone or something. The Germans were even afraid of him. His name was Carl Richter. I'm assuming you thought that was my father and he was really a Darrk."

"I tried to find out more about him but all record of him ran cold shortly before the Nazi's came into power. His records said he was from a small village in Austria, but there is nothing on him there. It's like he just moved to Berlin in 1935 and joined the Nazi party. He just came out of nowhere. His cruelty was unmatched on the battlefield, and he rose in the ranks of the SS quickly after the Germans invaded Czechoslovakia in 1939. His interrogation methods were nothing less than medieval, and by all acccunts, he enjoyed it. If he is my father, I would rather be his executioner."

Lauren was surprised, but not much. The man Mac was would not have tolerated someone like that, and he had spent many years trying to root out such men. She was proud of him. He had taken it very well, she thought, but she would have to talk to him later and make sure that was how he really felt. He was good at hiding struggles internally and she wanted to make sure this one was laid to rest.

Erick knew Aries' cruelty and had seen it firsthand. Mac's reaction to him was not surprising. Most recoiled away from Aries instinctively, even Darrks. But something about Mac not being any more curious about him puzzled Erick. He would talk to Lauren about it later. Then he caught a strong memory from Mac; it was of a little boy running into the arms of a man, yelling, "Uncle Duncan!" The boy looked to be ten or so, and he couldn't quite see the face of the man, but one thing was sure, this was the man who had the most influence on Mac. This was a man Mac would have been proud to call "Dad." Even though he called him "Uncle," this was Mac's father. He was proud of him. Whatever his past, Mac had grown to truly be a man.

Mac looked at them as if he hadn't said anything and said, "So what about dinner? I'm starving. There's a great Italian place in Pioneer Square."

"I think I still need to get some clothes first," Lauren said, looking at herself in the refection of the window.

"I think you look great." Erick had to say it because she did; the thought of what was under that robe was what he really was thinking of, though.

"I somehow don't think the restaurant would agree with you." She gave him a look he remembered that told him she knew he wasn't talking about the robe. It was a "Hey, my eyes are up here, look."

"Too much information," Mac began, then he said, "problem solved, there is a bunch of packages and garment bags in the hall by the door, seems Hawk had his secretary and her husband do some shopping for you. He was more than happy to help her; it was his day in the rotation to sit at the desk at the main entrance." Mac then said, "I have already talked to Raven, but I'll see if I can pry Hawk away from his desk and we will join you in a bit. I'll help you get them and carry the stuff in. Doc says he's too busy, and we stay out too late for him anyway."

"Then it looks like we are eating Italian," Erick said simply.

The clothes they'd purchased for Lauren were perfect, at least Erick thought so, although she kept mumbling about them being "a bit too fancy" for her. Erick had packed two suitcases before he left Magnolia. He settled on a black suit, which was more evening than business wear. When he started to grab a tie, Lauren looked at him and said, "We are going to dinner. Not a funeral. I think you can do without that."

"But I always wear a tie when I go out."

"Who are you and what did you do with Erick? You got stuck in the '50s somewhere, didn't you," she laughed, while Erick gave her a puzzled look. "You're going to look like an undertaker."

He put the tie on anyway as it was his custom and looked at Lauren. She had put on a white silk blouse and black pants that fit her legs well and had braided her hair and coiled it on the back of her head. Erick could get used to that as he thought she looked stunning. He gave her a kiss as he heard the front door open and Mac call out, "You decent?"

They went out to the living room to find Mac, Raven, and Hawk by the bar where Mac was pouring wine for the three of them. Upon seeing his mother, he whistled and grabbed two more glasses. Hawk looked over and saw the two of them, and said to Lauren, "I see they got your sizes right. I told her you were tall."

"Yes, thank you," Lauren said. "I'll have to do some shopping on my own tomorrow as all my things are in California and not really appropriate for this climate anyway. I think I'll drag this one with me," hooking a thumb at Erick, "his sense of style is stuck on undertaker."

Raven walked over to Erick, loosened, and removed his tie. "You are not going to a funeral."

"That's what I said," Lauren quipped.

"Aunt Eileen will be along in a minute, and I have the driver ready when we are," Hawk said. He was dressed in brown slacks, a while turtleneck sweater, and a brown leather sport jacket. While Raven was wearing a blue blouse and pants, Mac was in black jeans, a dress shirt open at the neck, and Erick was starting to think, the ever-present, black leather vest; of all of them, Erick realized he was a bit overdressed.

When Eileen showed up ten minutes later in a new wheelchair, really a three-wheeled, battery powered scooter. She was dressed as casually as the others. Erick thought maybe he did need a little fashion advice. Hawk called the driver, and they left for the elevator.

As they went through the lobby, the uniformed security guard behind the desk stood up and greeted Hawk, Raven, and Mac by name, calling them Mr. and Miss Scott, and Mac, Mr. McGregor. Hawk smiled at him and said, "Hey, Roger, how are the boys?"

"Keeping Carol and I busy as ever. Going to dinner?"

"Yes, and could you sign us out please?" Then, indicating Erick and Lauren, "This is my Aunt Lauren and my Uncle Erick, they will be staying in 3002 for a while."

"I'll make a note of that sir, pleased to meet you. Miss Eileen, pleasure to see you again." Roger bowed his head.

"And you, I'm back in 2904 again for a spell." Eileen smiled, "And you can just call me Eileen."

"Yes, ma'am." She knew he never would, Erick realized that from the start. The men they had serving as guards at the front desk would be very polite, he would guess, also are very capable of handling anything that walked in the door. Roger was about six feet tall and weighed a little over two hundred pounds he guessed, and something else he noticed, although the normal person couldn't know it. This man's heartbeat was slower than a normal person's was at rest, and it was extraordinarily strong. This man was extremely fit. He began to think that anyone who worked this desk would be a copy of Roger. Hawk and Raven weren't ones to leave much to chance he was learning. They had come an exceptionally long way in the last twenty years.

There was a van with a lift in it out front that looked more a small bus than a van. The driver greeted them and began to help Eileen as they all got in and took their seats, while Mac made a comment about being on the "short bus," again. A light rain had started and there was a great deal of traffic and people on the street. Erick noticed what appeared to be several homeless people. He asked Hawk about this. "I think a lot of it is the winters, it's pretty mild here in Seattle this time of year, and it rarely freezes compared to other cities this far north; there just aren't enough homeless shelters around, and some of the homeless wouldn't go to one if they could. We support one over in the University District, but sometimes it's hard to get them inside unless it's freezing cold. Most of these people want to stay off the grid."

Erick looked at them passing by in the crowd. *It would also give the other Darrks a perfect place to find enough bodies to build an army,* he thought.

Chapter Fifteen

CHANCE MEETINGS

Dianna was sitting behind a desk in her office, writing something when Brandon walked in. He hadn't knocked as the door was open but would have if it were shut. Because the door was open, as was his custom, he took a chair across from the desk and waited for her to finish what she was doing. One did not interrupt her if they had a brain in their head.

"I see you gave the message exactly as I told you."

"Yes, Mistress. If I may, why did you want them to know you were tied up and not taking part?"

"I need Rahm to think I don't have full control. I need him to think I answer to the others." She spoke calmly and looked up from her paperwork, there seemed more of it every day they drew closer to being able to leave. Most of them were invoices for parts that could be modified and electronics. She had taken the specifications out of the same manuals Hades had used to learn from.

"Do you have control again, Mistress?" He had put the *Mistress* on the end to soften the blow of what he said. The last thing he wanted to do was to make her think he was questioning her about her abilities to control the others. He was sure their even being able to tie her up and throw her in a room was allowed by her. He didn't believe for one second that she would have allowed it otherwise.

"I had never completely lost it." She held his gaze until he looked away.

"I didn't think you had," he began. "I just was curious why you let what happened to you happen at all."

"I needed to remove a thorn in my side and put the others back in line, while I also pacified someone so he would, see things my way . . . if it works. There is a prize at the end of this, and I don't need the others messing up my plans with their constant bickering, backstabbing, and questions. And I don't need someone telling me what to do long distance if they aren't here. My plan will work if it can play out as I planned it. I know my brother, and after the death of the commander," she paused like she sometimes did when she thought of him, then continued, "I am the one in command, and I don't rule by committee." She looked at him and added, "You are hungry, you need to feed. Be careful though, they are downtown now at the building on Second. Rahm and Hathor will know when you are close to them, it is not time yet to crowd them. Keep an eye out for prospects as well, it's time to build our numbers again." She squinted, "Why do you dress like that now?"

"As you taught me years ago, Mistress. 'Blend in' you always said, 'look like everyone else, you will live longer.' You began telling me that when you first made me on that battlefield. As I look forever twenty-one, I need to dress like I'm twenty-one."

"Very well. Come see me before you sleep in the morning."

"Yes, Mistress." He closed the door as he left, and that was normal for him, as he seemed to do it automatically. Now she had other things on her mind, like how to keep her head with the ass in Mexico.

He had been upset at her not attacking that first night and leaving the others out of it, then furious at the answer. Then, why did she give him a week? She had more than enough Walkers to do the job on her own, so why wait?

She then had to explain to him that it was best if they had his cooperation. Forced labor because they had one or both twins might prove costly. He could sabotage the ship just as easily as he could fix it, and if he thought Darrk would bring the fleet back, he would sacrifice himself to prevent it. No, they would have to be careful; they needed him. Then she was told they had another to do the repairs and she found herself explaining to him how complex the systems were, just like she had told him the last time they spoke.

"Very well, we'll try it your way. But I'm not going to wait forever, we have spent enough time here!" Then he abruptly hung up. He was getting impatient. If they weren't careful, this whole thing would blow up in their faces, literally. She really didn't want to hurt her brother, but she was getting backed into a corner to the point she just might have to. For an educated Darrk, that bastard didn't think things through; he always wanted to be on the offensive. He had no idea and wouldn't listen to the fact that over the centuries, Rahm had learned a thing or two, you couldn't push him too much, or you would hit one hell of a defense.

He set his cell phone down and ended the conversation. His face displayed no emotion on it, but inside, the man was angry. He was beginning to think she didn't have the resolve to finish this, that she was too close to it, and him. He knew her plan to get the others in line without exposing him was good, but the cost might have been too high. Even losing one of them would not be acceptable to him, and if he lost the engineer, he did have the youngling. He stood, straightening the gray three-piece suit unconsciously, to think. He had always thought better on his feet. His gaze out the window looked toward the pyramid outside the city, and he found himself longing to be there and not up here, high in this sterile room.

She was second, now first in command, so he had to trust her, somewhat; until the time for trusting her was past, and he was beginning to think so. Her failure to find where he was sleeping was understandable. He had four of his best search the offices of his lawyer, and they couldn't find where he had gone either. Then she went to ask that damn lawyer directly; again, a dead end. They searched records and found four homes in the United States alone and several pieces of property, but all led nowhere. Even after each was searched, one he couldn't, but observation proved he wasn't there. Then he decided to have his contact there watch it, paying him a sum up front and a monthly allowance to watch it. One could always find corrupt police. And that was almost screwed up.

He was hiding various properties, that was obvious from the records, but there were too many holes in the records. Those were the things he had needed to find, and those records were not at that lawyer's office anymore; *where did they go?* As he knew Rahm was sleeping, a search of cemeteries was made, turning up nothing.

Then simple fate stepped in. His precious granddaughter fell ill, her time had run out, and suddenly he had shown up in Virginia. When he got to Seattle, she was informed. And that was when she had changed. The very first night, she could have taken the key easily. But the respect of her office, pounded and beaten into her as an incredibly young officer of their race, combined with a natural caring for a sibling, made her make a mistake. Or at least he thought so. She would need to be watched carefully, from a distance, by someone who she wouldn't know was there.

He walked over and punched the button on the intercom, without waiting for someone to answer, said, "Get me the Frenchman."

"Si, Señor."

Dinner was terrific. The waiter knew Hawk, Raven, and Mac and immediately sat them at a table in the rear of the restaurant. While relatively small, the place was spotlessly clean, packed with customers, and decorated in such a way that with the smell of the kitchen lingering in the air, Erick was transported back to Italy.

Approvingly, Erick noticed it was in full sight of both entrances. The veal was tremendous, the breadsticks delicious, and the home-made pasta perfect. Service was more than excellent, and Erick could not remember when he had last enjoyed a meal this much.

He found out their waiter was the owner's son, and the owner came out wearing a chef's uniform and wiping his hands on a towel to ask them how the meal was. After introductions, he greeted Lauren and Erick, and then Erick in flawless Italian, told him he hadn't had a meal this good since he was last in Italy. The owner beamed with pride, and then came a conversation between the two men in Italian that was so fast the owner's son had a hard time keeping up with it. He told Erick to come back anytime; it had been years since he met anyone in America who could speak so well, and he complemented Erick on the fact that he didn't even have an accent. Erick told him he would.

Before the man said his goodbyes, he had his son bring out a bottle of wine he thought was perfect for the occasion. He opened it himself and poured a little in a small clean glass, handing it to Erick, which he properly tasted. He was not wrong; the wine was perfect. Smiling, the owner poured a glass for all, as well as small one for himself, and after a toast and setting the remainder on the table, retreated to the kitchen. Mac started telling jokes shortly thereafter, and soon the whole restaurant was laughing as people around them began to overhear his jokes.

They all turned down dessert and relaxed with a glass of wine as the meal settled. Erick said he was calling the contractor the next morning without saying anything else to see how the repair of the mansion was going, although he admitted that the penthouse was perfect. Hawk told him to take his time. After all, he did own the building. When Erick's eyes opened wide, Raven laughed and said, "It's one of your holdings." Lauren then realized why he dressed the way he did. While they were apart, Erick had made himself into a businessman, and an extraordinarily successful one. As an engineer, he delegated the work well, that would work in business just as well. That's why he had a guesthouse closet full of dark pinstriped suits and not much else. He had turned into a stuffed shirt. She began to giggle, then broke out in laughter.

"What's wrong?" Erick looked at her questioningly.

"I never pictured you as a banker," then she broke out in another fit of laughter.

But, at one time, he was.

It was getting late and they could tell it was nearly closing time. Erick intercepted the check before Hawk could get a hold of it and left a sizable tip. He hadn't had this much fun in an awfully long time. After the check was taken care of, he stood and helped Lauren with her coat, still thinking of how beautiful she looked and of how beautiful she'd looked in the flowing gowns of the Egyptians. He'd almost forgotten how she looked as a Darrk, but he remembered he'd thought that form of her was beautiful too. He began to realize his own Darrk form was almost forgotten to him. He couldn't remember the last time he allowed himself to change to it, then he did remember. It was before a mansion on a hill, centuries ago, just before he burned it to the ground, killing everyone in it—all to save a village and a human woman he had loved.

Lauren sensed some of what was going through his mind and began to realize something about him now, over the centuries he had become tortured. He had become the man he was now to protect his family here on earth, and he wasn't going to lose another one. The realization made her love him more, but he needed very badly to become comfortable with himself, both the Darrk and the human. By rejecting one, he had put a terrible burden on the other. If they didn't figure it out soon, she would lose both. Lauren then realized something else, she refused to lose him, she had just found him, and didn't want to live the rest of her life without him.

As they walked out of the restaurant, Mac saw his mother stiffen, then noticed Erick glancing around as well. "What's wrong?"

"Nightwalker, and close," came Lauren's whisper.

"You guys go on," Erick said loudly, "I think we'll walk off dinner." Then he whispered to Mac, "Get them back safe."

"Yes, sir." He said quietly, then in a normal tone, "They say they are going to walk, so let's go. I need to catch up on some sleep."

As Lauren and Erick fended off the protests of leaving them, the others got in the van while Lauren and Erick waited. Hawk asked them if they had brought their IDs, and they assured him they had. Then the driver closed the doors of the van and started its journey back the mile or so to the office and the apartments. Lauren and Erick casually turned in the direction of their building and started off. When they got to the end of the block, they turned the corner out of sight of the restaurant. Lauren asked, "Did you see where he was?"

"Yes, he was across the street in the side of the alley. It's Brandon, the one that came with the message last night. I don't think he planned on seeing us as he was just as startled as us, he tried to pull back when we came out of the restaurant."

"He wasn't following us?"

"I don't think so." Erick was thinking it was a chance encounter but wanted to make sure. "Remember trapping on Darrk?"

"Oh yes."

"Ready?"

"Anytime, old man," she giggled. They both vanished.

Brandon was relieved they had left; it would not do to report to Dianna that he had run into them in Pioneer Square. When they had turned the corner at the end of the block, he let out a sigh of relief. Then he went back to watching the addicts and dealers work. He had already fed and disposed of the body, but he was watching to see what the patterns of the dealers were and looking for possible soldiers for Dianna. He felt their presence at the same time Erick came around the corner of the alley. As he turned to run away, he found Lauren right behind him. Throwing up his hands, he gave up. "I'm telling you I didn't mean to run into you, okay?"

"You weren't following us?" Erick's eyes burned red in the dark and Lauren noticed an edge to Erick's voice she had never heard, it was protective.

"No, man. I swear. My mistress told me to stay away from you. I didn't know you would come to Pioneer Square! If she finds out about this, my balls won't heal for a month!"

Again, Erick got the feeling that this one was older than he seemed, "So you just happened to be across the street when we came out?"

"I swear."

"Then I'll make you a deal. We will forget about this little encounter if you answer a couple of questions."

"I can't do that, and you know it! My mistress will know if I gave away any information."

"These will be personal questions, so you won't be breaking your oath. So, unless you tell her, she won't know." Erick knew he had him cornered and there was no way he could slip away from the two of them.

"Alright, what are the questions?" Brandon couldn't say anything about Dianna, or she would know, pick it out of his brain just as surely as one picked an apple from a tree.

"When were you made?"

"That's what you want to know?" As he looked at Erick, he could see his patience was wearing thin. "In 1864. After a battle with the Union, my mistress found me with the wounded who couldn't be saved and had been left to die."

"During the Civil War?"

"Yes. I was barely twenty-one."

"Must have been Johnny Reb. We didn't leave men behind."

"Yeah, right. Union, huh? You guys were just as fucked up as we were."

"I patched up several of you over the course of the war, the ones you left behind." That was new to Lauren, she didn't even know Erick was in the Civil War, much less that he'd been a medic of some sort.

"Well, you didn't find me, motherfucker! But your sister sure as shit did! I've been stuck in this miserable body for over a hundred and fifty years! Doing the bidding of your sister!"

"Interesting. How long have you been in the Seattle area?" Erick asked him, overlooking his outburst.

"I came here a little after the war. We had found out you moved here."

"She's been following me, keeping tabs on me?"

"I can't answer that!" He looked down at a piece of trash in the alley and kept his gaze there.

"Then maybe you would prefer to be torn to shreds."

"Go ahead! Look, all I know is she needed to keep tabs on you after she found you; something to do with some last engineer bullshit. Look, can we conclude this little session, this really makes me uncomfortable." As he looked up, they were gone. "Oh shit!"

Lauren and Erick materialized where they started, on the side street off the square. It was getting late, and there were few people, and there wasn't anyone there when they started. Now there was a homeless man in a doorway close by who saw them just suddenly materialize. The man looked at them, looked down at the bottle in the brown bag, looked at them again, then threw his bottle into the trash can by the curb. Shaking his head, he stumbled off into the drizzling rain.

"Think we got him to swear off the booze?"

"I don't know," answered Erick, "but I'll bet he won't drink any more tonight." They let out a small laugh, and arm in arm, started for their building. Erick noticed this area of downtown had fallen into disrepair somewhat. He could see young men selling drugs here and there, as well as a few with a kind of blank stare in the doorways. This area may be dangerous. Perfect! He didn't have long to wait.

They hadn't even got one block when the two young men came out from a doorway they were passing, "Got a match?"

"No, I don't smoke," Erick replied, knowing what was next.

"Then I'll take your wallet!" The youth was curious about the couple, they didn't seem worried at all, it could be the last thing he would ever be curious about as Erick reached out and grabbed him so fast, he didn't even see him move. There was a sharp pain in his neck and then he just drifted off into nothingness as his knife clattered on the sidewalk.

Lauren and Erick put the two in the alley and walked away. The two men didn't bother them at all, Erick had a glance into their past and found the lives they had destroyed, mostly their own—all for drugs and money. But they were not guilty of any major crimes; that was the only reason they were still alive. They had taken the pint or two of blood they needed and stopped. The two men would wake in a few hours and not remember a thing about what had happened, wouldn't even remember seeing Erick and Lauren. They came back out of the alley and headed for Second Avenue, not speaking for a few moments until they had cleared the area. "Did you see any cameras?" Lauren asked.

"No, was I supposed to be looking?"

"I didn't see any in the alley, I did when we came out on the street." Lauren remembered that Erick had been sleeping for twenty years, so she tried to enlighten him on the subject. "They are everywhere now, you can't do anything almost without being caught on one. You will have to look around before you do anything that might be considered . . . negatively. I think we were alright on that last one; not all the cameras are monitored or checked unless something happens, but one does need to be careful. The last thing you need is to have to answer a lot of questions. I don't think anyone will be looking for those two until they wake."

"Are there really that many cameras now?" Erick remembered the cameras around his house outside D.C.

"There are getting to be more of them. You can't walk down the street without being seen by one anymore, at least in the cities." Lauren thought of the ones on the campus in California. She had been questioned once by campus security as her image had been caught on camera the night one of the sorority girls had disappeared. She had nothing to do with it, but it made you think of them more—especially when you had something to hide. "The resolution is getting better now too. They aren't as grainy anymore." It made her glad she never did anything around the campus. She related the story to Erick.

"Man, that's going to make things tougher." Erick mentioned the cameras that had been installed at his house in Virginia while he had slept. "Seems we don't have to worry about just drunks anymore." He began noticing the cameras. Lauren was right, they were all over.

Lauren looked at him, "You have a house in Virginia?"

The conversation went on all the way back to Second Avenue. Erick had seen the silhouette of the building on the skyline, but it was further than he thought, the buildings reaching to the sky threw off his perception somewhat. The light rain had them wet by the time they got there. He held the door for Lauren, and they entered the foyer. There was a different guard behind the desk now, and he stood smiling.

"May I help you?" he asked them politely, and Erick saw his guess earlier had been correct. This man and Roger could have shared uniforms.

"Yes, I'm Erick Scott and this is Lauren, we are staying in 3002." He presented his ID card as Lauren fished hers out of her coat pocket. He noticed as she held it, waiting to give it to the guard, it said Dr. Lauren McGregor-Scott. Mac was a tricky one.

"Yes, sir, I've been expecting you. Did you have a nice walk?" He asked this while he ran the card through a reader, compared the picture on the card with Erick, handed it back and took Lauren's. He then repeated the process, all just taking a few seconds.

"A little damp, but good, nonetheless," Erick answered, as the guard handed Lauren's card back.

"Well, have a good evening. The direct elevators are around the corner," he pointed in the general direction, "if you have any problems, don't hesitate to call; pick up any phone, press zero, and you will get this desk. My name is Garrett."

"Thank you, Garrett. You have a quiet evening as well." Erick had removed his overcoat and draped it over his arm, it was warm inside the building, and the brisk walk after dinner, dessert, had warmed him up.

"I truly hope so, sir," Garret replied with a smile.

As they entered the apartment, they realized neither was tired. Darrks didn't sleep that much anyway unless you counted the occasional hundred-year nap. Lauren set about making a pot of tea, and they sat down at the kitchen table and began to talk. Three pots of tea later and the dawn coming in the living room windows, Erick got up and stretched. They had talked the night away it seemed, it had been so long they had spent the night telling stories and filling in the other on what they had been doing. Erick was not surprised to find that Lauren held three Ph.Ds. in archaeology, anthropology, and psychiatry, and a fourth much older one in medicine that she had gotten after the war but couldn't use now. He joked with her about being the only being in the universe with medicine, anthropology, and psychiatry degrees from two planets, and if Darrk had archaeology, she would have that one too. Her position in medicine was from Darrk, and she had been the third doctor onboard the ship. She said it wasn't until the Second World War that she could even go to a university on earth.

She was not too surprised to find Erick had been a mercenary for part of the time they were apart after losing her and the boys. Even after all this time, she couldn't stop thinking of them as their boys, even though all three were fully grown and over 5000 years old at the time of their deaths, but it still broke her heart. Erick said the same as well. When the Egyptians came, it had taken them totally by surprise. They had tried to collapse a tunnel Erick was working in that was to be a tomb for one of the Pharaoh's court, and although it took him several weeks to dig himself out while the humans with him died, dig himself out he did. They had guards posted at the entrance to the tunnel, but as it had been several months, they'd grew bored of the duty and weren't paying the attention they should have. When he finally broke the surface one night, they weren't looking at the entrance, but looking out of

the Valley of Kings, not into it. And Erick came out dehydrated
. . . and hungry.

He'd searched for Lauren and the boys for several weeks, and
eventually had come across a soldier who told him, with a little
persuasion, they were buried outside the village of Khery-Aha,
by the Nile River. That they, the Pharaoh's soldiers, had come
into where the boys were working and said they were looking for
their father. They told the soldiers he would be back in a few days.
When the boys were put at ease and went back to work, they were
slain from behind, along with the woman with them. Erick had
assumed the woman was Lauren. After killing the man who said
he had helped move and bury them, Erick set off to find the grave.

He found it right where the soldier had told him it was,
unmarked at the edge of the village where they buried criminals.
He dug down to where the bodies were. They had decomposed to
such a state he couldn't recognize them, but he knew they were
the boys. Larger than an Egyptian, they had been buried in the
same grave with another body wearing an Egyptian gown piled
on top of one another, their heads missing. In misery, he covered
them back up and then searched for their heads, which he never
found. He then left Egypt, thinking about nothing but revenge.

After that, he had become a mercenary and fought many wars
and many battles until he came across Alexander's army. When
he found out Alexander's objective was Egypt, he signed on for
free. In Alexander's army, he ran into Aries and was not happy
about it. Aries loved battle, and all the others were so afraid of
him, he literally got away with murder. After Alexander conquered
Egypt, Erick went his own way. He eventually ended up in the
Roman army.

Lauren told him she was on the other side of the village when
she had heard the boys and a girl one of the boys was seeing had
been killed. The villagers working with her told her there was

nothing she could do right now and to live and avenge them later. She was smuggled out of Egypt, and along the way was told Erick had been killed while working in the Valley of the Kings. She was devastated. She wandered around for many years, killing every Egyptian soldier she could get her hands on, but she knew it would do no good. Her family was gone. She wanted to die, but couldn't do it herself, her mind wouldn't allow it. A single widowed woman in those times was fair game to many of the thieves and men who ran the brothels, and she began to use this to her advantage by hanging around where such men were, killing and robbing them when they tried to enslave her. After a time, she began to run alehouses and inns in Europe, always moving north.

About 600, she came to the shores of Northern Europe and had a stroke of luck. She came across a group of men on a ship, armored raiders, they tried to catch and enslave her. She killed one and wounded another. The rest of the men backed off and began trying to communicate with her. Then one of the parties said something to her in Germanic, which she understood, and she answered him. The man seemed relieved and began to speak to her in broken Germanic. The gist of which was she was worth twice as much as a warrior than a whore.

It was a Viking raiding party. They took her in, and she fought by their side and stayed with them for many years, when again, her age became an issue. When one of the leaders asked if she was a god, she didn't dispute it, and thought the matter was dropped. Then one day, he said she had to go with his men to the next kingdom, there was someone there who wanted to meet her. When she got there, she had the shock of her life. Standing there was Odmen, one of the Darrks sent to what is now Iceland. He was so happy to see her he almost crushed her when he hugged her.

They began laughing and speaking to each other in Darrk so fast it was obvious to the others they knew each other. So, she had to be a god after all, Odin was and he knew her personally, and she spoke the language of the gods. Then there was a great feast and Odmen / Odin told her what happened to the others.

About 1300, she found herself in Central Europe when the famine came, followed not long thereafter by plague. She remembered all the dead and began to try and think of a way to get to what became North and South America. She had been in North America on raiding parties there with the Vikings years before. The Vikings had settlements there at one time but abandoned them in favor of the European coast. She knew they had put other Darrks there and couldn't find any in Europe anymore, other than Odmen, and at that point she hadn't seen him in years. But without Darrk technology, she was just as stranded in Europe as the Darrks in North and South America were. It would be another 300 plus years before she made it. She was unable to carry herself the distances Erick could by then, and she asked when he learned he could and how far he could go.

"I don't know how far. But I found I could go from London to Boston about 1750. It was the furthest I tried to go at the time. I went from Seattle to Hong Kong in 1909. I had been going from what are now England, Ireland, and Scotland, to North Africa, and from there to India since about 500 AD. And I went from India to Cambodia in 1150 or so." Lauren just shook her head. She hadn't been able to go more than a couple of hundred kilometers until the 1800s. It took two stops for her to go from Caracas to Seattle when she came and found him. It surprised her to find out he had been in Boston while she had been in New York.

Then she got curious, "Hawk said you own this building, didn't you know that?"

"No, but there are a lot of things I own and don't know what they all are."

"How is that?" She was genuinely curious. She couldn't see how he couldn't know. She understood that as long as they had lived, you would know a few things and forget a few things. Where a certain artifact was, where a chest of gold or silver had been stashed, where a ship had sunk, but to not know what you owned, she couldn't wrap her mind around that; especially something as large as a thirty-story building. She could kind of give him that one though, he was asleep as it was built, but it had to be in the planning stages, unless it was purchased after it was built and *while* he slept. But that would require a team of people taking care of your finances and doing investments for you. But Raven had mentioned she watched his holdings and did the legal work on it. So, he obviously had people doing investments for him. Erick had been a busy man the last few centuries.

He tried to explain it to her. He had gotten to a point where it was all a big machine and several companies, independent of each other, pretty much ran on their own now, he just got the dividends of it. While he still had the parent company, which was now a bank and had been since the late 1800s when he went to sleep, he had decided he wouldn't run it anymore. He had run it for over 300 years. It came about like this.

After he married Maria, it wasn't long before her father's hands got to where he couldn't weave the baskets anymore. As Erick didn't have the patience to weave a basket after repairing advanced equipment, he found a few people to do the work of weaving for him. He then concentrated on the selling and delivering of them. Maria would accompany him on some of these trips and enjoyed seeing new places and people. While at home, her father would oversee the making of the baskets.

Erick found out he was a good salesman, and began to sell other goods as well, but after the birth of his two daughters, Maria stayed home to raise them. As he was so busy overseeing the operation, he opened an office in the town she wanted to live in so he could run the investments.

His traveling became a rarity and he stayed at home more. Business trips were lessened so he could be home with his family. Most turned into day trips. It was good communication was difficult. It would have been hard to explain his being in one place a thousand miles away yet being home that night. He invented "brothers" to explain his being in two places miles apart on the same day. Giving them their own names and signing contracts with them.

It was at that time that he had realized the name he had been using his whole life would not work in the modern world. He took the name Erick Scott mostly on a whim. The brothers became Markus, Rhys, Raymond, and Edwin; each with their own area. Not long after, he started a shipping company, Scott Shipping and Management Company, which he moved to Boston in the late 1600s, after the death of Maria's father. By the late 1800s, he moved the family west and again changed the name of the company to West Wide Bank, with its offices and main branch in Seattle. In the Seattle fire of 1889, he lost the original building and built another of stone. As none of the working capital was in paper money, which was not in much use out west, the fire did nothing to the gold in the safes, so he picked up when he could and went on. Working as a banker and buying and shipping lumber, and after a time coal to San Francisco and other points south by rail and using his ships to carry goods to San Francisco and Seattle from elsewhere. He had made quite a fortune until the economic problems of the 1890s. The bank was still named that to this day; he just didn't run it anymore.

Before moving to America, Erick began to invest in several other companies, and soon owned everything, from shipbuilding to gunpowder manufacturing; and owned the company that built his ships. He began to have his hands in a great deal of shipping and began to build ships for other companies. But the British began to say only British ships could move cargo to and from the Colonies. That was when his frustration with them started.

Maria knew he couldn't stand the sight of Europe anymore, so after a long talk, she said the best they could do for their daughters was move to America. Erick had agreed as he knew there was much more opportunity there, and wood for building the ships was getting awfully expensive and hard to find where he was. He felt the decision to move the shipbuilding operation to America with them was the best idea. The girls were twelve at the time, and they started helping their mother start to pack, while he took care of choosing the best ship and captain to take them across the Atlantic. He wasn't going to leave that to chance. Also, on the ship were his two best shipbuilders and their families, on another, the best craftsmen. Two weeks after their decision to move to America, they were loaded and on their way. It was 1661.

They arrived in Boston and were greeted by his warehouse master. He said his wife had found them a house where Erick and his family could stay until they found or built a suitable place of their own. After they moved into the loaned house, Maria loved the house so much that he had one built like it, and she lived the rest of her life in it. The shipbuilding and shipping companies flourished, and upon her death, she was buried at Old South Church. Her marker was there to this day, just a few plots away from Paul Revere's, though she'd been buried there more than fifty years before him.

When the businessmen in Boston found that Erick and his family were fluent in almost any language, they were often called upon as interpreters. His daughters, Rose and Raven, acted as secretaries in his company. Back then, they were the first women at "paying jobs" in Boston who didn't work in a dancehall or brothel.

The shipping business kept getting better, but Erick found he had to go around the British somewhat. He financed several privateers and his luck held out. People moving elsewhere made it easy for him to stay in one place for a time, no one noticed his age or that his daughters were aging more slowly than they should—except for an old sea captain who said once he was the "spitting image of your father" and Erick said nothing to dispute this.

There were problems with England wanting to control shipping, and around 1663, England had passed the Navigation Act, which cut into Erick's shipping business. It stated all imports to the colonies had to use English ships, and exports of sugar and tobacco around that time had to use English ships. Erick began to pay a large tax to haul goods and register his ships in England. He soon found the better way was smuggling and running the black market. He began to get wealthy. By the time the Revolutionary War broke out and independence was declared, half his profits were already dumped into the coffers of the young country. When war ended, almost all of his wealth was invested in the new country.

As time passed, both of Erick's daughters got older but still looked young. Not having children yet, Maria felt she would be gone by the time they could marry and have children. They all four knew there wasn't anything to be done; they were aging slower than normal. He had problems with the girls, as they were upset that they couldn't marry and have grandchildren for their mother. Although she never voiced it to the girls or to Erick, Maria wanted grandchildren, and he knew she was worried she would never meet them.

Then, there was a chance occurrence that Erick took advantage of in a way, which he never did. He was known for his fairness and honesty. There was a man who worked for him who had two children. His wife died when his daughter was born. After quickly talking to the girls, a decision was made. He was one of the mates in Erick's fleet, and Erick offered to take care of them until he returned, and something worked out. The boy was about three at the time and the daughter, newborn and without a mother, would die soon without proper care. When Erick showed up at the house with the children, he told Maria about what he had done.

He thought she would be a little mad at him, but he felt it would take her mind off the girls staying young and not marrying yet. He couldn't have been more wrong.

She started taking care of the two like they were her own. When their father saw how well they were cared for, he was incredibly grateful. After a couple of years, the two men had a long talk one sunny afternoon, and over a couple bottles of wine it was determined that the children were much better off at his home with Maria than being moved back and forth when the ship's mate was home. Pierre and Margret came into the house permanently. Erick and Maria raised them like they were their own. Pierre married when he was seventeen and had three children in the first three years, and three more over the next five years. Margret married at fifteen, and over the next nine years, had eight children. After a while, there were so many children and laughter running around the house, you'd have thought Erick and Maria were running a school.

When Maria passed away at ninety-seven in 1717, half of Boston came to her funeral, and Erick was amazed at all the people who said his "aunt" was responsible for them knowing how to read. Pierre gave the eulogy, and Erick felt more alone than he had in centuries. But Maria had lived a long life, and he had cherished every moment of it. So, with great sadness, he laid to rest the woman who'd saved his life. Shortly thereafter, the girls had children and he began to keep his promise to Maria. They would always know who he was and where they came from. Maria made him understand that they came from love.

ELLIOT

After he had showered and changed, Erick called Raven while he waited for Lauren. She was in her office and said he could come down anytime. Erick said they would be down in a few minutes and waited for Lauren. He needed to find what had happened to his finances while he slept. Lauren was right about one thing: he should know what he had. He went over to the large window overlooking the market and Puget Sound. Although the view was perfect, he was thinking of something else.

Not for the first time, he found himself wondering what Dianna was up to. With her, there were always plans within plans. He ran through what he considered she was doing and came up with extraordinarily little, except one thing—she wasn't acting alone. He knew damn well she wouldn't give up if he just gave her the key. Unless . . . Aries wasn't interested in his being alive, why? So, it seemed as though they had trained someone in the ship's engineering, but who? It took a certain amount of aptitude to grasp some of the concepts. Even on Darrk, there was a battery of tests before you even saw any part of the engines.

On Darrk, pups were given tests at an early age, and the outcome of those tests determined which school you ended up in. There were five schools and five vocational centers. The schools were engineering, medicine and psychiatry, sociology and politics, administration and management, and military. If you graded too low, you were sent to a general vocational center and taught the basics of math, reading and writing, and vocational training fitting many of Darrk's more planet-bound jobs; farming and husbandry, sanitation, construction, service and housekeeping, and industry. Of those five, industry was the best and of the first five, military was the highest, followed by engineering. Military commanded the ships; engineering kept them running.

Erick was engineering; Lauren, medicine and psychiatry. To be an engineering officer, you had to have extremely high marks and the ability to solve complex problems. Dianna was military. From what Erick knew, to go to the officer's portion of that school you had to have high marks in being resourceful, ruthless, and have restraint or discipline. In the language of the Darrks, there was only one word for this. In any earth language, it took at least two. Dianna, being second in command of the ship, was a sky officer and would have had to grade very highly. While ground officers, like Aries, would have scored much, much lower but still high enough to keep himself out of the rank and file. These weren't written tests, but rather, once taken to be in the military program, you started in basic training and worked up from there, being continually graded by superiors. Many Darrks died in basic training, about six percent, and only one percent of those left made it to officers' training. This was determined in basic; no Darrk was ever guaranteed officers' school. It was something awarded at the end of basic.

When they were broken up after basic into the various fields to be learned, like ground troops, small arms, infantry, or artillery, the officer candidates were pulled from the rest and sent to the officers' school. There, after a basic training of several weeks, they were divided further into sky or ground, and sent to the respective school. In officers' basic, there was another four percent that died and only five percent of those left were sent to sky school, while the rest were sent to ground. After that, it was unknown how many died in school, but they say it was worse than any of the others. About one-third washed out of ground officers' school and were sent down to the regular ranks, but none ever came out of the sky officers' school. It was rumored there was only two ways out of sky school, and one was death.

Erick knew one thing for sure; his sister was about the most devious person he had ever met in human or Darrk form. She wasn't like that when they were pups. She was smart, but never devious and sometimes cruel. He had no idea other than thinking there was a plan being made to capture one of his grandchildren to force him to work and give them the key. But when Aries tried to kill him, that reset his thinking. He was no longer in a position of strength. Now he wondered what was she really thinking? What was the one pulling the strings thinking? Try as he might, he couldn't grasp who it was, he couldn't see them. His mind would see Dianna. Maybe she was acting alone? Doubtful, there were too many holes for him to fill.

That's how Lauren found him when she walked out of the hall, staring unseeing out the window, and six inches off the floor with what she could only explain as a glow around him. She realized he had done this unconsciously; this made her think of the night before. It was when they had surprised Brandon; Erick transported himself quickly, almost not thinking about it, while she had to think about doing it, *except* when she was near him. Last night, she had only begun to think of leaving Brandon when suddenly she appeared on the other street, she just thought, *that was fast,* but the more she thought about it, Erick had transported *both* of them, and she had been standing ten feet away from him. She didn't know how he did it, especially with Brandon *between* them!

Something else came to mind, she was so relieved to see him at the guesthouse she hadn't thought it through; how did he drive

Hawk into a coma? How did he wake so fast after the transfer, most Darrks wouldn't have come around for several more hours after completing a transfer, and how did *Hawk wake first?* The one being transferred to always wakes after the one it came from wakes. It's like Hawk was put on speed dial first he came out of it so fast. And in the transfer, she was moving through his memories in the order he had *shown* Hawk until she found them, faster yes, but in order. Erick was only letting Hawk see what he wanted him to see. After he had connected to Raven and her, they saw what he *wanted* them to see, like he was selecting home movies to show and only picked certain ones while leaving others out. *No,* she thought, *that couldn't be true. I doubt he would have allowed Hawk and them to see him with the spear by the cross.* Something else came to her; the man on the cross was saying something to him when he thrust the spear. Then he stood *with the blood rushing over him* in the storm. She recalled Diego saying God sent him, now she began to think he had.

Erick noticed her and turned around, "I would like to stop by Raven's office before we go shopping," he said.

Lauren snapped out of her thoughts, "Oh, yes. I'm sorry, I was thinking of something else."

"I've wondered many times myself if he really had sent me." He said this softly, with reverence, it seemed.

Lauren was stunned. Her legs suddenly felt wobbly, and she was having a hard time standing. Erick caught her just before she collapsed and set her on the couch. "What . . ." She couldn't speak. Erick had read her *mind.*

"I'm sorry. When thoughts are strong, I hear them, even when I try not to," he explained. "With you it seems even easier. Though I can read anyone's thoughts if I try."

After a minute, Lauren could speak again, "How . . . how long have you been . . ." She couldn't say it. Some Darrks could feel strong emotions or tell when one was lying, but none she knew of could read minds, which was a myth . . . or so she'd thought.

"After the transfer with the high priest of the twelve and many other things, as well."

Lauren recovered quickly after that. "The twelve?" She was puzzled.

"The man who told me to leave the moors."

"That would have been a thousand years ago."

"No, it was more like 900 years ago."

"Close enough," Lauren said, with a lopsided grin.

"Yeah, I guess so. A hundred years or so to us anyway, what's the difference?"

Lauren knew something was bothering him and asked what it was. "Dianna. I don't know what she's up to and she is always up to something. If she were around me long enough, I could get it from her, but she's smart enough not to be. Everything she does is a feint for another move—like chess here or Daggers and Caves on Darrk. But I feel there is someone else pulling the strings. Even as my powers get stronger the longer I am awake, I'm blind to whoever this is, and I don't know why." Erick then changed the subject, "I told Raven we would be down in a few minutes. I wanted to see her before we went shopping."

"Then we better not make her wait. Mac tells me she's always busy, so we had better not hold her up." Lauren wanted to talk more with Erick about the powers he had "picked up" from his connection with the man in the robe, but Erick was distracted. He'd tell her more in time. She just hoped her patience held out. She desperately wanted to find out what the man on the cross said to him. Another thing stuck in her mind, does Erick know where the Spear of Destiny was, the spear that killed Jesus Christ? Wasn't it in Vienna or something? Was he truly the one that killed him? The story said he was dead when the spear pierced him. The thought sent chills up her spine.

Raven was busy on Erick's holdings, so this was the perfect time for him to come by. She even had the most current printout from the investment company. She was wondering if he knew that if he added all of it together, put under one name instead of several names and companies, he was worth over two and a half billion dollars? It was not earned illegally either as he consistently paid the taxes and fees on it in whatever country it was in, and even paid income tax on any money transferred to the United States. Really, only $200 million in cash could be found to personally be his, and even that was kept in a bank he owned. The rest belonged to four other different names. Johnathan had told her she had a surprise coming, and she thought she knew what it was.

In truth, she found herself distracted today. She hadn't talked to anyone really about what she had seen with Lauren in his memories. The dreams she had last night seemed, well . . . disjointed. They were like movie clips from everywhere and every time; some in Rome, Asia, England, but most from Egypt. She found she could understand whatever language was being spoken as well. There were perks to this. Testing herself, she found she knew Chinese, Russian, Greek, Japanese, Arabic, Swahili, German, several Native American languages, and God knows what else. Hawk hadn't come in yet, which was unusual for him, he normally was the first one at work. She really needed to talk to him, because he knew what she was seeing.

The phone buzzed and the voice of her assistant, Elliot, came over the intercom, "Mac on his way in." Elliot always tried to give her warning as to who was coming in the door, but Mac came in so fast and never knocked, so he barely had a chance to say anything.

The door burst open, "Good morning, my lovely! Have you seen Hawk?" he asked her.

"I was going to ask you the same thing. He isn't in his office. Amanda said she'd tried to call him and got his voicemail." Mac started to look concerned, and that made Raven worried, just as the outer door opened, and Lauren and Erick came in.

As Elliot looked up at them, Raven said, "It's okay, Elliot, that's my . . . Uncle Erick and his wife."

"And my mom," Mac added.

As Elliot greeted Erick and Lauren, he thought she looked almost the same age as Mac; she must have been incredibly young when she'd had him. He began to wonder if he had taken a job at an asylum instead of a lawyer's office. He had been here just two months and it just seemed every day got weirder. He was a paralegal and the job was paralegal, assistant, and secretary. It was just the two of them; Hawk Scott's work was all with the security side and had a large legal staff on the twenty-fifth floor doing most of the work for it. While Raven seemed to take care of the personal legal work for the whole family, except for one.

Elliot had noticed almost all the files were connected to one client and a very wealthy one at that. While she did help Hawk with corporate legal matters, he knew Hawk had a law degree of his own and it hung in his office. But that one client consumed eighty percent of her time. Then he went back to his work on the computer, it was a property purchase in Brazil, and he was going over the contract Raven had drawn up for any errors. In truth, he should normally do the drawing up of the contract as the paralegal and she should be checking his work. At least that was the way it worked for his old boss. But he knew even though the name wasn't on it yet, this was for that one client. Weird.

His partner Jerry had told him to stick it out, "There aren't many places that will hire a fifty-seven-year-old queen, especially for the money she's giving you," he had said. Elliot had worked for a lawyer, just a few blocks away from here, for over twenty years. When he died of a heart attack, the firm had given Elliot his full retirement and six months' severance pay, which was more than fair, but he wanted to keep working. He missed his old boss, they were friends he felt, and he was not just an employee.

A friend at the old firm told him of a lawyer who had gotten so busy he hadn't put the ad in the paper yet, so Elliot, armed with his resume, went straight there. He found the paralegal position was really for a woman, and the two had hit it off immediately. Raven had hired him on the spot, barely even glancing at his resume. He didn't want this job to go south as it were, it may be crazy, but it was interesting.

When the chubby well-dressed man removed his glasses and held out his hand, Erick had taken it, and he found out everything there was to know about Elliot Smalley. He and his partner had a condo up on Capitol Hill that was paid for, and he had two children, a girl twenty-nine, and a son who was thirty-one. The daughter was married and had two children, and Elliot and Jerry loved to spoil them almost as much as Lisa, the daughter, didn't want them too. His son ran a retirement home locally and had never married. His ex-wife and he saw each other often as their breakup had been mutually agreed upon. When their daughter was in her junior year at high school, Carol went to live with her partner Mary, and Elliot had Jerry move in. Both had long term affairs until one day their son pointed out to them that the only people that were being fooled was each other. Lisa had quipped from the other room that they hadn't shared a bedroom in her memory, and why don't they at least make themselves happy. The two looked at each other, then Elliot had said, "Okay." Three weeks later, they were divorced and both couples were good friends. Elliot was a very smart man and didn't miss much. He had even known about Carol's girlfriend, Mary. He was just waiting until Lisa graduated.

The other thing Erick found out was Elliot took attorney-client privilege *very* seriously. He would have to relay that to Raven. She could tell him anything or let him see anything and there wasn't a person or agency on this planet that would ever get him to say one word about it. He would talk personal finances and how work was "crazy" to Jerry, but would never tell him why, and to Jerry's credit, he would never ask or pressure him about it, and Jerry *was* an attorney. When one needed the other's help with a problem at work, they always spoke in general terms to not divulge any information about a client. It was like a free consult, and Jerry used it often. He knew how smart Elliot was and always told him he should finish law school and take the bar exam. Elliot's answer was always someday when he had the time. Jerry would always tell him "Someday, you're going to run out of time." Elliot was smart, and if he weren't told, would figure most of it out, some he already had. It was better to bring him in as soon as possible.

Erick was smiling when he walked into Raven's office without shutting the door; she looked at him curiously, "What?"

"Good man you have there," he said softly. Mac and Lauren picked up on it, but it took Raven a few seconds, "You can tell him the truth, it won't go anywhere."

"He can probably hear you," Raven glared at him.

"He's not listening."

"How do you know?"

"You haven't asked him to." Erick took a chair across from Raven's desk.

She looked at Mac, "Could you shut the door please, Elliot?" she called.

"Excuse me?" He turned in his chair, "I didn't catch that."

"Could you get the door please?" All four of them were seated.

"Certainly." Elliot stood and walked over and shut the door. It was only about seven feet from him. They were all around her desk about twenty feet away.

"He wasn't listening," Mac said.

"You sure?" Raven asked.

"One hundred percent. He responded because he heard his name, his body language suggests he was concentrating on his work." Mac shook his head, "I can't believe it, but a new employee that doesn't eavesdrop? Almost all do, it's how they learn what's going on."

Lauren agreed, "He's very well grounded. I'd say right now he indicates a little stress, but if he's a new employee, I'd say he is right where he needs to be."

Mac nodded, "A couple more weeks and you won't know what to do without him."

"You will never have to worry about him, he takes attorney-client privilege very seriously, and for that matter, employee-employer relations as well." Erick added, "You don't even have to worry about him telling his partner, Jerry."

"Jerry?" She had a puzzled look on her face.

Mac looked at her, then began to laugh. Then it dawned on Erick what he was laughing about, "You don't know?" It had popped out of her head into his about the time Mac began to laugh.

"Know what?"

Lauren looked at her and said, "You mean to tell me you didn't know the paralegal you hired is gay?"

"He is?"

All three just started laughing. Mac reached over, pushing the button on the intercom, "Elliot, could you come here for a second?"

"Be right there." He came in, leaving the door open, and crossed Raven's office "Yes?"

"You're going to have to tell her," Mac said.

"What?" Elliot looked as puzzled as Raven was. Then his eyes popped open and he covered his mouth with his hand. "Oh! She doesn't know?" Then he started laughing. After a few seconds, he looked at Raven and said, "I'm sorry, I don't advertise, but I thought you knew."

"Then you are gay?" Raven looked dumbfounded.

"Oh, yes," he laughed, "all my life."

"But you have children and grandchildren."

"My ex-wife and I got married to shut our parents up. By the time we figured out we better tell the other, we had two lovely children. We moved into separate bedrooms and stayed that way for the rest of our marriage." Elliot smiled, "It's okay really, I've got pretty thick skin and come from a time when you didn't advertise it where I was from. Unless you think you will have problems working with me. I'll go if you wish, you won't have to worry about it."

"No, no, no, it's just I didn't figure it out."

"I could see where that would be a problem," Elliot replied, choking back a laugh.

"Thank you, Elliot." Raven was beet red.

"No problem," with a chuckle, he turned to leave, feeling better about this new job than he ever had. That was the undercurrent that was bothering him, or so he thought.

"Oh, could you get me file 1263?"

"Yes, I'll be right back." He crossed the outer office, walked through a door to the records room, and went to the numbered files. He pulled the file she needed without looking at anything else but the numbers. He then backtracked to Raven's office. "1263," he said, smiling, and handed her the file.

"Thank you."

"You're welcome. Would you good people like some coffee?" Getting no answers, he said, "Okay, if you need anything else just let me know." He left, closing the door behind him.

"I feel so stupid." As smart as she was, some things Raven overlooked. Whether out of instinct or just having too many things to think about, she sometimes was blinded to what was going on around her. Raven put her head in her hands as they started laughing again.

Mac saw that they were going to do some work, so he excused himself. "I think I better find Hawk."

"He's in the gym," Erick told him. Mac figured Erick ran into him on the way down. He didn't know why he didn't answer when his secretary called, but he had done that before. To Hawk, having a conversation with someone was much more important, and he would never answer the phone, but why he didn't call back Mac didn't know. He would have to keep an eye on him; he needed *that* train to stay on the tracks.

Raven opened the file before her, "Now I know this will seem crazy, but legally, as there is no marriage license, I need to hear you say it is all right for Lauren to be here."

"I'll go out to the office and wait. Talking to Elliot sounds interesting. He can tell me where to shop," Lauren volunteered with a smile just to see Raven turn red again. It worked.

"No, I want her to stay, then she will know how complicated it is," Erick said.

"It's mainly complicated because you don't want it tracing back to you directly, it's almost like a crime family, tons of buffers between it and you, except there is nothing illegal going on."

"I'm sure there will come a day that some IRS agent or FBI investigator puts a file together on me, then the cat's out of the bag." Erick was under no illusions about it all being found out eventually, he was surprised it hadn't been done already. But he wasn't into anything illegal anymore. All the companies were legit, and all the taxes were paid, some even overpaid, simply because he didn't want it looked at too hard. It was split up into several countries, from the Cayman Islands to Zaire, under several names, and the companies themselves sometimes were founded hundreds of years apart.

Lauren was just shocked, and after sitting there an hour listening just shook her head, when Raven gave them the grand total, she thought her jaw was going to fall off. "What?"

"Two billion, five hundred and sixty-six million, or thereabouts," Raven said matter-of-factly. "Just the cash he can lay his hands on in an hour is two hundred million. In the last twenty years, personal wealth has grown two hundred twenty million and his share of the corporate wealth has grown four hundred and sixty million."

"Why did personal wealth go up so much? It wasn't set up that way." Erick asked the question due to the large sum.

"One of your holdings was confiscated by the government of the country it was in when they went socialist, and the two hundred million was a settlement, although it was more before you paid tax on it. It was for oil holdings in Venezuela. At the time of confiscation, it was worth more than four times that. You lost money, but the company was in the name of Erick Scott, so it came directly to you and the company was dissolved. Now in Venezuela, there's riots and unrest, the people are hungry, and they are upset. As with most socialists, you have those in power, and those never in power."

"My other businesses there?" He felt disappointed, as he could already guess the answer. All his companies had profit sharing for the benefit of the employees, their families, and their respective countries.

"I'm sorry, they are all gone. The oil was the only thing you got any money for at all. For that, you got cheated as much as you spent." Raven looked like she didn't want to give him the news but did it as best as one could.

"I was in Caracas two days before I came here. There was rioting and all kinds of things going on." Lauren didn't bother to say she was also about to be kidnapped. "The country is socialist now. Everything is owned by the state, and they are doing a shitty job."

"Your total worth right now would be closer to three billion if not for that. And you are lucky they compensated you for the oil. You must have been highly thought of by someone in the government," Raven added.

"So that's why Johnathan wanted me to ask you," he chuckled. "He didn't want to break the bad news." Erick had known something had happened, but he tried not to read people most of the time and didn't read Johnathan. His powers had not gone to full strength yet, but Erick had always felt it was an intrusion. A person's thoughts should be their own. He wanted Raven to give him the bad news. Johnathan had had to do it before. Erick thought he wanted to see if Raven could do it. *Mission accomplished, you sly old dog,* he thought. "Well, if that wraps it up, we have shopping to do."

"You aren't angry?" Raven was surprised, *he isn't mad!*

"Disappointed perhaps, but why be angry? It's just money and you invest it, sometimes it works out, sometimes it doesn't, and it's gotten to the point I have more money than I can spend casually."

"Is that why you left one hundred million dollars each to Hawk and me when you . . . left last time?"

"Partly, the other was in case I didn't come back. I wanted to make sure you'd be taken care of." With that, he stood to leave, "Well, now we need to go spend some of that money. I think we will start at Nordstrom's."

"It's not there anymore." Raven looked up from the desk, "I have the limo driver waiting for you, he'll know where to go."

"Thank you," Lauren said. "What are you doing for lunch?"

"You're looking at it," Raven smiled. "Elliot and I are going over my filing system a little. Seems I have it strangely set up, I still use Uncle Johnathan's and his was numeric. Elliot would like to figure it out, straighten it up, and turn it into something resembling a real filing system."

"Then we will bring lunch back for both of you, as well as Mac, Doc, Eileen, and Hawk." Lauren didn't suggest it; she said she was doing it.

"Well, watch out what you get for Doc," Raven giggled.

"Why, is he allergic?"

"No, worse," Erick began, surprising Raven, "he's a vegetarian."

"I remember my favorable assessment of him went down when I heard." Lauren said it in a profoundly serious voice with a smile on her face.

Mac entered the gym and saw Hawk running on one of the treadmills. He was wearing one of the virtual reality sets and Mac could see the treadmill was lowering like he was going down a hill. "Watch out for the mud puddle at the bottom."

"Morning, Mac, care to join me?"

"No, I did my miles this morning, running to Seattle Center and back, like I do every Wednesday. Erick told me I'd find you here, when did he see you?"

"He didn't. I would have gone with you, but for the first time in ten years, I overslept."

"Oh?" Mac wanted him to tell him how he felt without having to ask him; this might work out. He wondered; how did Erick know he was here? He noticed the universal gym had been left on its lowest position, he looked around to make sure no one else was there, then started doing one-arm curls with 500 pounds like it was 50.

"Someone leave the pin at the bottom again?" Hawk said, between lungsful of air.

"You know me. So why did you oversleep?" Mac asked the question casually, at least as casually as he could. As usual, Hawk saw right through it.

"Okay, who put you up to it? Your mom or Raven?"

"Raven. Seems she spent the night tossing and turning in dream world."

"Me too."

"Bad?"

"I find myself wondering how Grandfather Erick is still even sane after all the battles he has been in." Hawk stopped and pulled the headgear off, then looking at Mac, said, "He was at Lexington in the Revolutionary War, then, he was at Gettysburg, then France in the trenches, then Okinawa. He seems to have been in all our country's wars, except Korea and Vietnam and ours. He was a combat medic in Okinawa, a surgeon in the Civil War, and a surgeon in World War I; always as medical assistance, but he fought too, when necessary. I find I never really knew him. The man's as tough as anyone I've seen."

"But remember, Skipper, he's not a man and is about as close to bulletproof as you can get. And being a medic would have kept him away from the doctors, yet still give him access to the battlefield."

"But Mac, in all his memories, he didn't use it to have access to blood, he did it because he genuinely wanted to help. And one thing more, we haven't seen it yet, because he hides it. He's a wizard or sorcerer or something. I have seen him do things that are impossible, and Mac, I think God talks to him."

Mac thought Hawk had lost his mind, then he explained, and Mac thought *he'd* lost his own mind.

An hour after the sun had come up, Brandon walked into Dianna's office. She had changed or you'd think she had been there all night. "You're late. You need to be in your box, if the sun hits you, the tan will be painful."

"Yes, Mistress, but you wanted me to come to you before I slept." Brandon had been debating whether to tell her about the encounter with Erick and Lauren all night. Nothing had been said about her really, except general stuff Rahm would have figured out on his own easily. So Brandon wasn't compelled to say anything.

"I had told Erick I would give him one week to decide, but I never said I wouldn't watch him. I need you to take four of the others that have half a brain and starting at dark, keep a watch on him, but not so close he will know you are there."

"That may be hard, he seems to know when Nightwalkers are close, some say he knows at a mile." He could at thirty yards for sure. Brandon wondered at this new tactic.

As if reading his mind, "You're not there to be noticed, you're not there to play, just observe, there are two others that are Darrks that will relieve you in the morning."

"Is that all, Mistress?"

"Yes, Brandon, you may go to sleep now," Dianna said. When he reached the door, she added, "I know you didn't say anything to violate your oath, but next time you have a chance encounter with Rahm, tell me."

Brandon stiffened momentarily but kept walking out the door. "Yes, Mistress."

Dianna had no intention of hurting Brandon; of the fifty Walkers she had, he was the brightest, and she had affection for him. Naked and in her bed, he was more fun than she'd ever had. She also wasn't sending two Darrks in the morning; she needed to find out something. She just hoped it wouldn't be Brandon.

When Erick and Lauren returned with lunch, they all met in the conference room. Doc was pleased they'd brought him lentil soup and a salad but told them if he hung around them much longer, he would get fat. Lauren looked at his skinny frame and told him if he got fat off rabbit food and dirt beans it was okay; she would make sure he was buried in a larger shoebox.

With Eileen not in attendance as she'd said she needed some rest, the conversation was good, but avoided anything to do with the events of night before last. While Lauren didn't think that was healthy, she shouldn't have worried. When they started to clean up, Elliot excused himself and went back to the office, and Erick started the conversation. "I have been told I could move back to the mansion on Saturday. While I think I would like to, I think for the immediate future I'm going to stay on here for a while. This is much more secure, and I think we will be more comfortable here for now."

Mac quipped, "You did pay your rent in advance." After some nervous laughter, he added, "Do you think they will hit us again?"

"I don't think so, at least not for a few days, Dianna did give me a week and I think she'll hold to that, but there will be some sort of surveillance, I'm sure of that." Erick went on. "I think Eileen should stay here for a month or so, being close to Doc and being in a secure building should ease her mind. How is she doing, Doc?"

"She has gone downhill somewhat and that disturbs me, but otherwise she's fine. The energy she had shown yesterday seems to have left her, but she is still in better shape than she was a week ago." He looked right at Erick, "I would like to take some blood from you and Lauren if I may. I'd like to see if I can find out what it is you need and find a way to create a supplement for you and try to confirm that in fact it is an enzyme—with your permission of course."

"Of course, you can have some of mine," said Lauren, "and I can help you in the lab." She looked at Erick, "What do you think?"

"I think it's a great idea, but Doc, you have to assure me that only Lauren and you will look at the samples and work on the problem." Erick didn't have to tell Doc how important that was, no one else in the lab could come anywhere near it, there would be too much to explain.

"You got it," he said as he turned to Lauren, "and having a beautiful lab assistant as well is a bonus I'll take, even if she is a head taller than me. We'll work on it mostly in the evenings, after everyone goes home."

"Watch out for this old smoothie," Raven said to Lauren, then turned to Erick, "What do you think is going on here? I understand some of this but there are too many holes."

"I have been wondering about that as well," Erick began, taking note of the fact that Raven's thoughts were moving in the same direction as his own. She would be good counsel. "I think there are three camps. One is Dianna, and she wants the key and needs me to repair the ship. There's another that just wants the key and thinks they can repair the ship on their own. Good luck with that. A third camp behind both is pulling the strings, but not showing themselves yet. It took me about twenty earth years to become an engineer and another ten before they even let me in a ship other than a trainer. The systems we use are too complex. You can't just read a book and make it work. Dianna knows this, but she is getting pressure from somewhere else. I don't know where, but I don't think it's the group that attacked us, perhaps it's the third. Aries tried to kill me, not just wound me and take me captive, he wanted me dead."

Doc asked, "If it's not going to do them any good, why not just let them have it?"

"Because if, by some chance, whoever it is they found to do the repairs can fix the ship and get them back to Darrk, they will bring back a whole fleet. Earth cannot protect itself right now, they would be overrun and enslaved within days, and all the resources would be stripped from the world. That is if Darrk is still a living, populated planet and if they still have the ability for star drive. For all I know, they ran out of known worlds to take over."

"When we got here," Lauren started, "the commander realized that earth was a world just starting to come out of its primitive beginnings. He had been a commander long enough to know that Darrk would destroy this world. He had grown tired of Darrk just killing off other civilizations all in the name of its own survival, and he didn't want a planet as beautiful as this one pillaged and forgotten."

"The commander pulled the main computer chip, or key as we call it, and gave it to Rahm, telling him to do the same with the escape shuttle after he dropped everyone off. He wanted him to hide the shuttle where it would likely never be found and use the last flying suit to join me in Egypt. To this day, he is the only one who knows where that shuttle is. I don't even know. Then he made him swear an oath to protect this world, an oath taken in front of me and another Darrk named Odmen. To a Darrk, an oath is unbreakable except in exceedingly rare circumstances."

"After everyone was dropped off, Rahm and the commander hid the ship and returned with the shuttle. Rahm proceeded to drop off the others in the areas they were assigned. Before he got back, someone killed the commander while he was dropping the first group. Odmen and I were on the shuttle with him, so we knew it wasn't one of us, but we couldn't figure out who did it. Dianna led an investigation but couldn't find out who was responsible. To the best of our knowledge, no one had been told Rahm had the key."

"The three of us knew the commander was right. This world needed our protection, not exploitation, even if we were marooned here the rest of our lives. We couldn't have imagined we would still be alive now. We have lived longer than any Darrk in our recorded history. We found out why later, but it took several years to find out we weren't even aging like we should, and then there was the healing. So, we buried the commander by the river and went on."

"When we first arrived," Erick said, "I had a digit missing on my left paw, we have seven, so it wasn't that big of a deal, human form only gives us five. So, when I changed to human form, I didn't think about it. Although it had just happened before we came and hadn't healed when we first arrived, it had healed over by the time we got on the surface. Thinking about it now, I do remember it was healing strangely. When I had to change into Darrk form again, I noticed I had all seven digits on my left paw."

"In Medical," Lauren began, "we had no idea what caused the regrowth, and by this time, didn't have the battery life left in Communications to debate it, as we were split up because the commander had put at least one of the medical personnel in each group. We didn't have the facilities to work on the problem either, so the matter was dropped as a curious occurrence. As others began to experience rapid healing, I found myself wondering what was going on. Wounds would heal with barely a scar, and almost immediately. A simple cut would be gone in seconds, a larger wound in a couple minutes, and the longer we were here, the faster it happened. Then the most bizarre thing happened that changed our whole perspective, one of us was killed."

"It was in a battle with a neighboring tribe not long after we arrived," Erick continued. "I and the others, except for Dianna, had never been trained in combat, so using a sword was completely new to me, having never used a sword. In fact, none of us, not even my sister had. When we were attacked, I didn't know how to defend myself and neither did the others. So, when one of us was run through with a spear, we thought they died, or so everyone, including me, thought. As he lay next to the grave that we were digging for him, I removed the spear to bury him, then saw him start to breathe, and the wound closed. If someone had removed the spear earlier, they would have been a little shocked to see him stand up so fast. We'd left it in him all day, as no one wanted to pull it out. It only took about five minutes to heal and he stood up. The tribe came back the next day to finish us off, and when they saw him, they ran."

"I couldn't figure it out," Lauren said. "I saw him dead and then he just stood up, like nothing had happened. I wanted to see if it would happen again, but I sure wasn't going to test it. Seems I didn't have to. Two weeks later, that tribe got its courage up and came back, and this time, they killed another of our group. During the battle, he was run through with a spear, but the warrior who'd tried to kill him pulled it out himself. I'll never forget the look on his face when the Darrk didn't even fall. He screamed, the others had seen what happened, and they all ran away."

"But it was a chance encounter a couple of months later that got us accepted," Erick began. "We were on the banks of the Nile River. We had seen signs of flooding, so we placed our camp above the high-water mark, which meant we had to go down to the river to fetch water. I was down filling water jugs when a boy came by, trapped in the current. Without giving it a second thought, I jumped in the river to save him, not even thinking about the fact that I didn't know how to swim in human form. I turned into my Darrk form to keep from drowning, caught up to the boy, and brought him to shore. He was terrified of me, so I changed back to my human form. This seemed to calm him somewhat, and I found out he lived up the river and had fallen in. He was gone before anyone even noticed."

"As I walked him back to his village, I discovered by hand signals and gestures that it was the same tribe that had attacked us. I left the boy outside the village, because I didn't want to cause trouble. He said something to me I didn't understand at the time, but as I learned the language, I found it was 'thank you'."

"The next morning as the sun came up, several men from the tribe were found unarmed and sitting a short distance from the camp. Most of us worried they were going to attack us again, but I didn't think so. They were unarmed, and sitting away from the camp, which didn't seem a good attack posture to me. As Dianna had taken three of our number to scout the area for a better place to live, I had been left in charge. I decided to see if I could communicate with them."

"As I walked up, one stood and bowed toward me, then he started to speak to me, but I motioned to him I didn't understand. It took about an hour, but I figured out what he was saying. Apparently, the boy I saved was his son, and he was the leader of the tribe, and was incredibly grateful. The next part of the conversation I couldn't make sense of, but later found out he was calling me, 'The Jackal Man'."

"Within a few days, we started seeing food, weapons, clothing, and jewelry left on the edge of the camp," Lauren went on. "I realized they were giving us gifts because they thought we were gods, gods who didn't know how to defend themselves," she sat, shaking her head.

Erick went on, "Dianna saw an opportunity here, she wanted us to act like gods. She thought it would make us safe and get the locals to help us build the power plant. Many disagreed with this, including Lauren and I, and I asked her 'How do you act like a god?' She dropped it after that."

"One day, a group of children came into our camp. Running up to me laughing was the boy I had saved from the river. He grabbed my hand and started to pull me toward his village. Although Dianna, or Isisi, as she was called then, didn't think I should go, she left it up to me. Lauren, or Hathor, as she was called then, indicated to the boy she wanted to come too. After he said something to the other children, one of them, a girl of about seven, grabbed Lauren's hand and started pulling her too. We walked back to the village and found they had planned a feast for me. I was shocked to find a clay statue of me with the head in Darrk form and the body human. It was in the middle of the village and was a good likeness."

"During the feast, all the tribe sat in a circle with Lauren and I sitting next to the leader. Toward the end of the meal, he presented me with a knife, and said something that made the tribe cheer. Later, Lauren and I were shown to a hut. It was obvious they wanted us to stay, so I wrote a note on an animal skin and got across to the leader that it needed to be delivered to our camp. He gave it to another man who took off at a run in the right direction, I didn't want the rest of our group to think something bad happened to us."

"Over the next few months, Lauren and I learned their language. Once we were able to communicate, things went much more smoothly. When they asked where we came from, it seemed they couldn't grasp the idea of another planet. Every time I tried to explain it to them, it always came back that they thought I was one of the gods. They would just point up and say their name for god and add mine to it. They had learned my real name, but when they would say it, they would just say, 'Ra'. They began to educate me in the use of the spear and the bow, as well as the club and knife. They were not using swords, and there were none in the village. While training with the knife one day, one of the men cut me badly. Minor cuts were common, but this was a real deep gash in my arm, right down to the bone. I don't know if it was the blue-green blood or the fact he watched it close up and heal before his eyes, but he turned and ran. I knew they had seen the blood before in battles with us, but after talking with the leader, I found they hadn't really noticed the blood. It was the man who they saw killed who got up again that scared them; after all, you can't kill a god."

"Soon, our entire camp was moved to the village, Dianna congratulated me on the work, but was a little taken aback by the fact there was women's work and there was men's. There were some things she flat refused to do, and as a Darrk officer she didn't have to, so they laughed, saying Isisi is 'too pretty to work'. They trained all of us in the use of weapons, I think because they realized we thought of each other as equals."

"We went through a winter, and when spring came, a neighboring village attacked us. They always posted a guard at night, and we had taken to doing it for them. Our need for sleep was just a few hours a day, and our night vision unbeatable. One of the others came to my hut one night and asked me to look at something. What he saw was a large group of men creeping up on the village under cover of darkness. We didn't wake the villagers. We had learned a thing or two, and thought if we simply scared them, that would end it."

"We called to them, and they began the attack early while it was still dark. This was our element. We had grown up in the half-light of our world and we could see them clearly, so we did the one thing we knew would scare them. Right before their eyes we changed to Darrk form. Now a Darrk is anywhere between six and a half to eight and a half feet tall, when at that time the average man was about five and a half feet tall. It scared them so badly they threw down their weapons and ran. What we didn't count on was how badly it would scare the villagers. The boy had told them of our true form, but they had never seen it. When they ran out of their huts at the sound of the commotion, all they saw was ten Darrks standing on the edge of the village in the dawn light.

Screams and men shouting added to the confusion. When I finally got them calmed down and told them what had happened, they were grateful; but they were forever wary of us after that. The only one who wasn't was the boy I had saved."

"After a long talk with the leader, we decided to leave the village and work our way north down the Nile. Dianna had found a few good places where we could set up camp. We soon became known as traders up and down the Nile, trading in gold, copper, gems, and other minerals the local tribes had a hard time finding. Geology was unknown among humans at the time, and we applied it to find what we required, going all over North Africa."

"Let me get this straight," Doc began, "human is not your natural form, and the Egyptian gods were named after you?"

"It does kind of seem that way, and I think some, but not all of the gods, were named after us. And yes, this is not my natural form," Erick answered.

"Then what do you look like?"

"To compare it to something you might know, we look like werewolves with very long ears."

"Oh my," was all Doc could say.

Three days later, Erick and Lauren went down to Doc's office. Erick was surprised when he opened the door. You could call it an office, as there was a desk to the right of the door and there was a young lady sitting on a chair behind it, but from there back it was an open lab that obviously took up the whole corner of the building. The outer hall ended at Doc's door to the right, with Mac's at the end of the hall. Erick noticed that the lab went behind the wall that obviously was Mac's office on the other side and proceeded to the edge of the building on the other side. Almost half of the floor was Doc's lab. There was an examination area with a curtain that could be pulled around it for privacy right behind the desk. It was complete with scale, blood pressure, and ear examination equipment, and a countertop and cabinet with a sink across from an examination table. On the countertop were the usual jars of cotton balls and swabs. There was a row of plastic chairs next to the door to the left running along the wall bordering Mac's office.

The pretty young woman behind the desk said, "Hi, Lauren, Doc's in his office." *Everyone around here is extremely polite*, Erick thought.

"Hi, Mary, how has your day gone?"

"Ten new hires. Seems we are ramping up for the coming summer. We got the contract for all the summer concerts." She said this looking at Erick, "You must be Mr. Scott. Pleasure to meet you finally."

"Nice meeting you," Erick smiled.

"Yes, I had to drag him down here," Lauren answered.

Smiling, Mary said, "You folks have a good evening."

Coming to Doc's office, Erick knocked.

"Come in!" Doc shouted. As Erick opened the door, they found Doc behind a desk piled high with folders, he was pulling them off one stack and putting them on another after he looked at something in them. He got up and came around the desk, removing files and books from the two chairs across from the desk. "Sorry about that, I'm a little behind on my paperwork."

"Have we come at a bad time?" Lauren asked the question, while looking around the office with a smile on her face. She hadn't been in Doc's office yet, and it reminded her of her office at the university, filled with papers, folders, books, and medical magazines and journals crammed into every corner and spare space. She had a feeling though, if you asked him for a certain folder or book, he'd reach in the middle of one of the piles and hand it to you.

Doc looked up from the corner he threw the files in. "Oh no, no. I'm just trying to catch up on the personnel files and new hires after their physicals. I had been at the mansion so much with Eileen I've fallen behind. So, are you here to have your blood drawn?"

"Yes and no," Erick began. "I figure you can draw Lauren's when you start. What I need you to do for me is I need a physical, so Lauren will give me one and will instruct you in how our anatomies differ."

"Is there something wrong?" Doc had a concerned lock on his face that Lauren found charming.

"No, we don't think so," she said. "It's just I want to find out how old our bodies think we are. I need to find out how much wear and tear there is on it so I can accurately find our chronological age. Just using mine won't give me complete information, but with both of us it should."

"What do you need?" Doc asked and grabbed a pen and a pad of paper. After Lauren gave him a list, he looked up and said, "I have all of that here. When would you like to start?"

"As soon as possible."

"Mary goes home in thirty minutes anyway, and that will just leave us. We can start with the X-rays if you like. I didn't feel like working on files anyway."

An hour later, Erick and Lauren were standing in the little room in the back of the lab. Doc had sent Mary home a little early and the other two lab techs were at a seminar. Doc was preparing the films for the X-rays. Lauren wanted four shots, two with him in human form, two in Darrk. Erick knew the time to tell her had come. "I don't know how to tell you this, but I haven't changed in several centuries."

Lauren looked at him in amazement, "What?" There was a problem with this; Darrks were changelings, able to change to most forms that had the same or close to the same mass. How they fool their systems into changing was basically causing a kind of immune response. The immune system of a Darrk was extremely complicated, indisputably the most complex system in their bodies, as it seemed to have a mind of its own and was also responsible for changes in their physical and mental wellbeing. A Darrk could change form through a form of self-hypnosis, essentially fooling their immune system. But the immune system had a mind of its own and was capable of overriding the entire system if need be, including the will of the individual. The immune system was well known to have the ability to change the body of a Darrk to benefit it in extreme conditions. Lauren theorized that this was why the bodies of the males changed so they could impregnate humans and initiate the transfers. The male system did it out of self-preservation. The only thing she couldn't explain was the suicides. She also thought this "consciousness" was what gave Darrks the ability to make Nightwalkers. Their immune systems gave them the ability to protect themselves on a strange world.

This was why it was so hard to grasp how Darrks could commit suicide. Their bodies generally did not allow it. But they did know if you stayed in any form but their natural one too long, you sometimes could not change back. There was one Darrk who stayed in human form for several centuries; five, she thought, and could not change back. He eventually committed suicide. But the change was on the surface, the inside of the Darrk remained the same, just more compact, as did the body temperature, about five degrees lower than human on average.

Darrks and humans, like most sentient beings in the galaxy, were built basically the same. But Darrks had two stomachs, a larger liver and pancreas, a short duodenum between the two stomachs, a longer duodenum before entering the intestines, an appendix that worked and was more like the gizzard in a bird, a shorter intestinal tract, and two hearts. One heart was located on the right side of the chest and one-third larger than a human's and the other was located behind the bladder. This was the one that operated while they slept and was half the size of the one in the chest. In females, this second heart was the one that fed oxygenated blood to the umbilical cords for the young, leaving the one in the chest to run the body. The heart in the chest of a Darrk worked when a Darrk was awake, and both hearts would work in times of major exertion. When sleeping, the smaller heart would work, and the larger heart would shut down and repair itself, except in the female during pregnancy. Heart attacks and heart disease in a Darrk was almost unheard of because of this system.

Doc came back in and broke her out of her trance. "Here we go," he said cheerfully. After all, he was going to be the first doctor on earth to see the inside of an alien. "Four films just like you wanted."

"Umm … okay." Lauren looked distracted, Doc thought, but he didn't press. "Okay," she said, her head clearing. "First, let's do one of the head and upper chest and we will do the chest and abdomen second. Time to remove the shirt, sweetie!" She said this with her tongue hanging out the side of her mouth.

Doc thought it strange but realized what it meant when Erick said with a smile, "We got a room, we'll use it later!"

"And they say I'm lecherous!" Doc said this, looking at Lauren, who did nothing but smile from ear to ear.

Ten minutes later, at 6:00 P.M., the films were complete, apart from the ones still to be done in Darrk form, and Lauren was talking to Erick about dinner. Doc was surprised by the number of scars that crisscrossed Erick's body. Most were in the front, but his back bore the scars of being whipped at some point, like the flesh had been almost torn off. There were several scars on his body that looked as if they were fatal blows, yet here he was. Doc asked him about these. "They would have been fatal if I were human," Erick began, "but being Darrk, not so much. When I receive a blow where one expects my heart to be, they are generally surprised when it doesn't have the intended affect. As to the two bullet holes you said looked quite recent, they are; two through and throughs. The pink of the scars will go away in a couple of weeks, and the marks themselves will disappear completely in about two years. The wound must be awfully bad to leave a permanent scar. As to the scars on my back, let's just say never upset a Roman governor."

"Hey, Doc, you beat me to that one, I was going to ask where he got those," Lauren said casually, but Doc felt the concern for him in her voice. As casual as she tried to sound, when Erick's health was concerned, she took it very seriously.

Doc's cell phone started to ring, and he politely excused himself to answer it. "Yes, my dear, what may I do for you?" His face turned pale when an excited voice came from the phone. Raven yelled, "Doc, I need you in the parking garage, level two, Elliot and I have been attacked by a Nightwalker!" Erick grabbed his shirt and vanished, followed a few seconds later by Lauren.

"Damn!" was all Doc could say.

Raven saw Erick just appear out of nowhere before she even ended the call on her phone, she was kneeling next to Elliot who was bleeding quite badly from a wound on his head. Erick was still shirtless yet carrying a shirt. He started to slip it on as he ran over, looking around the parking garage. Elliot saw him just appear and if it weren't for what he saw before Erick just popping in, his appearance would have been written off to the blow on his head. There were files scattered around him on the pavement, "What the hell" was about all he could manage.

As the elevator across the garage made a dinging sound and two security guards came out, Erick asked if they were all right. Raven said, "He went off that way further into the garage, we are fine. Stop him before anyone else runs into him!" Then she looked Erick in the eye and mouthed, "Nightwalker." But she didn't have to, Erick had already found out what happened, Elliot was playing it over in his mind trying to figure out what he had done to upset the man so much that he tried to bite him. Erick had his hand on Elliot's forehead and Raven noticed the bleeding suddenly stopped.

Suddenly, Lauren appeared just like Erick had and Elliot again said, "What the hell." While the two security guards stopped in their tracks, they couldn't be sure if she came from behind the post or not. But she must have. People just don't appear out of nowhere. Erick noticed it was Roger and Garret, "Stay with them!" The two guards just stared at Lauren, "Roger, you two stay with them!" Erick shouted, indicating Raven and Elliot, which broke them out of their trance. Looking at Lauren, he said, "Let's go." When they were out of sight and hearing of the guards, Erick said, "Nightwalkers. Raven only saw one, but Elliot was looking at one standing on the ramp between one and two when the one that attacked them came out from behind the post by his car. When it lunged at them, he tried to protect Raven and struck it with his briefcase. The Walker hit him over the head and then tried to bite him, but Raven knocked it off him before it could."

"So, his wound is not caused by a bite?"

"No. Then they took off down the ramp to three."

"Going to ground you think?" Lauren asked.

"Think so, but all that will happen is they will end up cornered."

Going to ground was something Nightwalkers did when they were in trouble. They would literally go to dirt and bury themselves. They could stay that way for days if needed. Erick could see them in his mind, and they were on level four with nowhere to go. They were beginning to panic. Someone was going to be very mad at them. One told the other he should have waited; they should be back soon, then it was their turn. The other one said that he was hungry and the one in the suit wasn't one they had to watch, so he was fair game.

Lauren noticed that Erick looked as if he was listening to something far away, but she couldn't hear anything. It was just the way he *looked*, almost as if he were listening to a conversation he could hear a mile away. It gave her the chills. A Darrk had excellent hearing, but to be able to hear something that far away, he wasn't listening with his ears, he was listening with his *mind*. They were approaching the ramp down to four when Erick held up his hand for her to stop. He turned to her, "I'm going down. One of the security guards is coming down the ramp from two, keep him here and do not let him on four. I'll take care of this and be back in a minute."

"Are you sure?" One Nightwalker could be torn up by one of them easily enough, but there was safety in numbers when it came to them and fighting two Nightwalkers sometimes could be a challenge.

"Don't worry, I got it." Just the way Erick answered her told her all she needed to know—he was going to be more than fine. All worry left her, and Lauren began to wonder what those two below had in store for them.

Erick calmly walked down the ramp; he could see the two Nightwalkers arguing at the end of the parking garage. They didn't even notice him at first as he walked along, slowly buttoning his shirt and listening.

"You should have waited!"

"Fuck you, I was hungry!"

"Brandon's going to cut your balls off!"

"Who's going to tell him, you?"

"You better hope no one comes down here looking for us. We should have gone up."

"It was on the other side of you, and they didn't notice where we went."

"I'm not so sure. Why didn't you head up alone? If they do find us down here, it's because of you not going up!"

"Shut the fuck up! I'm tired of your shit!"

"Oh, I'm not, please continue," Erick said calmly as he walked further into the dim light of the garage.

"Fuck! It's one of the ones we're supposed to just watch!"

"Shut the fuck up and quit running your mouth! Hey, Mr. Rahm, we don't want to hurt you. We are not even supposed to talk to you, just watch."

"Seems you didn't follow the rules," Erick said evenly. He had his hands crossed behind his back and was looking thoughtfully at the floor of the garage. Both of the Walkers were wearing black jeans and hoodies, just like Brandon, and from a distance all three would look alike. Curious.

"So, what are you going to do? We got you outnumbered."

Erick laughed. "I see that, but if four of you can't bring me down, I doubt two of you can."

"Fuck you, old man!" the big one screamed, and lunged toward him.

Erick brought his hands from around his back, closed his eyes, and slapped his hands together, which activated the sunburst spell. A brilliant light pierced the semi-darkness of the garage, bathing the two Nightwalkers in a white-hot light as bright as the sun. The Walkers' skin disappeared into ash, then the tissue, and last the bones. All were gone in milliseconds, leaving nothing but fine ash drifting to the floor of the garage. Erick's eyes burned, even though his eyes had been closed, but he was a whole lot better off than these two were.

Lauren and Roger were standing at the top of the ramp. Lauren was trying her best to hang on to him to keep him from going down the ramp, saying, "He'll be right back after he checks it." She was trying hard not to show him how strong she was.

For his part, Roger was trying to get away without hurting her, but this woman had a grip on her like iron. "You can hear them! He's unarmed, let me go!" He didn't even get all the words go out from between his lips when a blindingly bright light came up from level four. It was so bright it temporarily blinded him the way a flashbang would.

Lauren caught the light and with her light sensitive eyes was blinded as well. Her eyes recovered more quickly than Roger's, but she had an image of the ramp burned onto her eyes that would take fifteen minutes to go away. When their vision cleared somewhat, they saw Erick standing before them, "You alright?" he asked.

"How . . .? What . . .?" Roger stammered.

"He isn't down there," Erick replied.

Roger recovered, "The hell he isn't, I heard him!"

"See for yourself, he isn't down there." Erick began to walk back up to level two, and Roger took off down the ramp.

"You're going to have to tell me about this later," Lauren whispered, starting out alongside him.

Back on level two, Doc had arrived and was treating Elliot, with Raven and Mac standing over him. The other security guard, Garret, was over on the ramp to level one, talking with Hawk. The guard nodded and walked back to the elevators, entered, and then the doors shut. Erick figured Hawk sent him back to the front desk. He also knew Roger was coming up behind him, and he was upset.

"Where did they go?"

Erick turned toward him, "Who?"

"I know what I heard, and I heard three voices, three very distinct voices. The last voice I heard said, 'Fuck you, old man.' Where did they go? There is no way out of the fourth level, except the elevators or the ramp, and we were on the ramp and locking down the elevators is standard procedure, so they couldn't have used those. Where are they? There was nothing but some ash of some sort down there on the floor. Where did they go?" Roger spoke calmly, but the event had shaken him somewhat.

Erick raised his hands, "Now, Roger," he began. But then did something Lauren thought odd. He touched the thumb and forefinger of the right hand together, while wiggling the four fingers of the left. Roger eyes had narrowed on the four that were moving the most, then his eyes glazed over. "There was no one on the fourth level when you went down there."

"No one."

"You heard no one speaking down below."

"No one."

"You stood up at the top of the ramp and waited for me with Lauren."

"Waited."

"Then you walked back up here with us."

"Walked."

Erick put his hands down. Roger looked at all of them, then said, "It looks as if they got away. It seems you must have been wrong thinking they went down there. Well, I'd better get back to the desk. If you need anything else, give me a call."

Erick looked at him, "Thank you, Roger, sorry I took you on a wild goose chase."

"No problem," he waved, and headed toward the elevators. They were all staring at Erick.

After Roger was in the elevators and the doors had shut, Erick looked at Mac, "Can you get in and erase the security tapes?"

"On my way." Mac headed for the elevators.

Erick turned around and looked at Elliot, who gazed up at him defiantly and said, "Don't you dare do that shit to me!" Raven started to giggle, then they all broke out in laughter.

Chapter Seventeen

A WARNING

Erick looked at Lauren, "Shall we?"

"Shall we what?" she asked.

"Go out to the street and scare the holy devil out of Brandon. He arrived about two minutes ago."

"Yes, most certainly," she said with a smile, as she took his hand. When they both vanished, Elliot fainted.

"Damn. I'll never get used to that!" Doc exclaimed.

This time, they both appeared in front of Brandon. When he turned around to run, he saw he was standing in a dead-end alley, "Ah, shit! Okay, okay, I'm only here to collect my boys. Yes, we are watching you, and yes, there are two guys in the parking garage and two in back."

"Well, you can forget the two in the garage, unless you've brought a dustpan with you, of course." Erick's voice was even, but the look on his face was pure anger. Lauren would have to comment on how good an actor he had become, if he was acting, she thought.

"All they were doing was watching!" Brandon spat the words and glared at Erick. His temper would get the best of him someday, Erick knew.

"Seems the big one was, 'hungry' and went after one of my people. When I confronted him, he tried to attack me, but it obviously didn't do any good. Your other Walker was just too close, so he came out extra crispy as well."

"Dianna will be upset about that," he didn't say if she would be angry about him killing the other Walker or mad about the killing of the one attacking him, but Erick didn't mind either way.

"I want you to give this message to your mistress," Erick said this in the formal language, so he would be unable to repeat it except word for word. "'Dianna, my sister, you will cease surveillance on me and mine immediately, or I will kill every single one you send, including this one'. Do you have that, Walker?"

Brandon looked at him.

"Do you understand, Walker?"

"Yes!" Brandon hated being called 'Walker'. He didn't mind Nightwalker so much, but he didn't like the slang term. It felt demeaning.

"You have ten minutes to get the others and get out of here. If I see any of you again, I will make good my word, understood?"

"Yes," Brandon said softly.

"Now, get out of here!"

Brandon let out a very high-pitched whistle. Inaudible to humans, it could only be heard by Nightwalkers, dogs, and full-blood Darrks. Erick heard two whistles come back, and then Brandon went between Erick and Lauren as they parted to let him pass. As he started down the street, he said, "This isn't over."

"Oh yes, it is," came Erick's cold reply.

When they returned to Doc's lab they went back to where they'd started, the X-ray room. Doc was helping Elliot sit on the table when they suddenly appeared out of nowhere. Doc and Elliot both jumped like they had been zapped by electricity. "Is there a way you can warn me you're coming? My heart may be in good shape, but lately, there seems to be a lot of stress on it."

"Yes, there is. Do you want me to warn you?"

Doc's eyes went wide, surprising Lauren. He looked *constipated* for lack of a better term. Doc had heard Erick's voice, but it was inside his head. Erick had never spoken. "No, I think just popping in might be a better idea."

Lauren looked at Erick curiously. She had heard him clearly and thought he spoke, but Elliot was looking at Erick with his mouth open. Darrks could only communicate with their minds to the Nightwalkers they'd made. "You didn't just . . ." The sentence trailed off; she decided she didn't want an answer to that question right now. There had been just too many surprises in the last twenty minutes. One of which was that she hadn't even thought of transporting to Brandon or back to the lab, Erick had transported both of them each time.

"Lauren, could you help me? I'm trying to set Elliot up for a full skull series. I am going to have to ask Hawk for an MRI one of these days. I just want to make sure there are no fractures, he hit his head pretty hard."

"Really, Doc? Someone, or should I say something, hit it for me," Elliot mumbled.

"Well, I need to see if you have anything up there but empty space anyway."

"Nope, nothing but gay porn and Rice Krispies Treats," Elliot said, smiling.

"Rice Krispies Treats?" Lauren asked.

"Leave it to the straight ones to ask about the treats and not say a word about the gay porn," Elliot quipped.

"Doc," Erick started, "I think he really might need his head examined. And by the way, order the MRI machine tomorrow and send me the bill."

"Are you serious? Do you know how much one costs?"

"Yes, to the first and no to the second, but it doesn't matter. Go ahead and order it."

"Go ahead," Lauren said. "He's got more than he can spend easily anyway."

Elliot sighed, "A problem we all wish we had."

They were setting up to take the next shot when Elliot asked Lauren, "What are you guys?"

Erick was in the booth with Doc, but was listening, and told her through the intercom, "You want to show him?"

"Think he can handle it?" Lauren had that lopsided grin on her face Erick found contagious.

"Very well, in fact." If Erick had read him correctly, and he was positive he had, everything would be fine. He needed Elliot to get on board soon and this was the perfect opportunity.

Doc headed for the door saying, "I've got to see this!" Erick followed him out with a smile on his face.

Right then, Raven and Mac came through the door into the X-ray room. Mac saw his mother unbuttoning her blouse, "Uh, did I catch you at a bad time?"

"Not really, remember when you asked me what I really looked like?" Lauren said.

Mac's mouth formed an "O," and turning to Raven said, "You're going to love this." Then he leaned against the wall comfortably and put his arm around Raven.

"Is she going to do what I think she is going to do?" Raven remembered what Lauren looked like in the surreal world of Erick's mind, but to see it . . .

"Yup." was all Mac would say and Elliot started looking at them strangely.

Lauren had turned her back to Elliot and removed her blouse. "You're a stripper?" he said jokingly. She then removed her bra and tossed it on the blouse, then dropped her pants. "Hey, I was kidding," Elliot said, as she pulled down her underwear.

Then, to his amazement, her blond hair began to get longer, no, *it started growing out of her skin!* She turned around then, and he saw her face stretch outward and the already tall woman began to get taller. The knees swept backwards now. Her ears became pointed and each one suddenly became almost a foot long. The pupils of her green eyes became smaller, contracting, almost to the point of not being there. They were there but had just become exceedingly small. Lauren held up her hands, or paws really, each had a thumb and six toes. Long canine teeth curled over her lower lips and white fur surrounded her eyes and muzzle. A long white streak went from the top of her head, down between her shoulders, to her waist.

As he looked at her, Elliot realized she was a werewolf. "Oh my God! Werewolves exist? Then that thing in the parking garage *was* a vampire."

Erick looked at Doc standing there speechless, with his mouth wide open. Well, that was one way to shut him up. He addressed Elliot, knowing she couldn't speak human in Darrk form, "Not really, while she resembles a werewolf, she, in fact, is not. But the vampire, yes, he was real."

"You are like this too?" Erick nodded. "Then what are you?" he asked incredulously.

"A Darrk," Erick answered. As Lauren began to change back to human form, she could speak again herself. Elliot was amazed how quickly the transformation was done.

"A what?"

"A Darrk, or that's about as close as you can get in a human language," she answered now dressing with her back to him. When she was dressed, she turned around. She knew explaining this would take a while.

In all, Elliot took it well, and by the time Lauren could say anything, Mac was deep in a conversation with Raven, "I've seen her in my dreams, but I didn't know she was so beautiful."

"That white is new from the last time I saw her change, but I would have to agree with you." Mac was looking at Lauren, "Last time I saw her do this, I was fifteen years old."

Raven looked at him, "It's been that long?"

"No, it's just the last time she allowed me to see her in Darrk form."

But Erick thought Raven was right; as a Darrk, Lauren *was* beautiful.

Elliot was firing questions at Lauren as fast as she could answer them. In the end, all he could do was shake his head and say, "I knew we couldn't be alone in the universe."

Lauren realized Erick was right. Although she hadn't doubted him, she had seen humans scream at the sight of her, even knowing she was going to change. This man didn't know what he would see; yet he accepted it calmly. He was a perfect ally to bring into the fold, and they desperately needed some help right now.

Brandon didn't want to tell her, but he knew he must. So, he decided to not put it off, and as soon as he entered, he went straight to her office. The door was closed, and he knocked. "Come in, Brandon." He entered Dianna's office fully expecting the worst.

"Please sit down."

He thought it best to start right off, "I'm sorry, but two of the Nightwalkers have been killed."

"I know. I felt their passing. Please sit down. It's alright, Brandon. You did what I told you to do." She was speaking softly, in a way he hadn't heard her speak to him in many years. "What did Erick say?"

Brandon began to tell her, word for word, just like he was compelled to.

Brandon sat in Dianna's office a little perplexed, but he admired the genius of it. If it worked as she had planned, she would get what she wanted. She wasn't even upset at losing the two Walkers that had been killed. She had needed to see what would happen in a confrontation with Erick, and she'd gotten her wish. Brandon could tell she was relieved to see him when he walked in; she put him in harm's way and knew it. The realization that she was concerned about his safety also made him take note that if she had to, she would do it again. Always the officer, collateral damage was something she couldn't avoid. He was a Nightwalker, bound to her, and he had no illusions about what that meant. She was pushing Erick in the direction she wanted him to go. Brandon would do the work for her; just knowing she really did care was enough.

He had asked her if she thought Erick would get killed, and he remembered the look she'd given him plainly—it was one of worry. No, she wasn't afraid for Erick. "Not one bit," she had said. Bullshit. She was scared to death he would be killed, that is what this confrontation had been about. She needed to know if he could defend himself. Dianna also told Brandon she couldn't tell him beforehand, because she was afraid Erick would get it out of his mind. She thought he could, and she didn't want him to. She'd needed to see what Erick's defenses were; that was the goal. She did wish Brandon or one of the others had seen it, but at least she had her answer. She still needed to see how strong his powers had become, and soon.

Dianna then said she had begun to wonder if she was on the right side of all this. His look was thoughtful, although he didn't say anything. She then did something that she never did, and it surprised him.

"Do you think I'm wrong?" Dianna's gaze was one of confusion, she was truly asking him for his advice.

Brandon was bewildered, she never asked for his advice. In thinking about it, he realized she had no one else to ask. "I can't answer that, Mistress. I am bound to you. I cannot say anything against you, and I wouldn't, even if I could." He knew he still loved her. Most of the other Nightwalkers were filled with nothing but hatred after a few months, and he didn't know why he wasn't. He felt almost as he did when she first found him dying on that battlefield, like he had seen an angel, and she saved him. He could never hurt her, no matter the reason.

Dianna sat there for a moment, staring at Brandon. She felt that feeling for him again, the one she couldn't understand. She stood, came around the desk, and took his hand. When he stood, she guided him to the door behind her desk, and going through it they went into a bedroom with no windows. It was almost black in the bedroom. The light of the day outside couldn't penetrate its walls. She released his hand and stood facing him, looking into his lovely brown eyes. She was really an inch taller than he was, but they stood looking eye to eye as their breathing increased. Brandon reached up, as he had done a thousand times over the years, and gently slid her dress down her shoulders and over her arms, letting it fall to the floor. As he stood gazing at her beautiful body, she reached out, undoing his pants and kissed him, then pushed his pants over his hips. Grabbing the hoodie from the bottom, she slipped it up over his head as they fell back onto the bed.

Chapter Eighteen

IN THE NEXT DIMENSION

Elliot had stayed the night in the second bedroom at Erick and Lauren's. He had stayed up with the two of them until Erick said that was enough for now, and he needed to get some sleep. So, Elliot reluctantly went to bed with the promise they would answer more of his questions tomorrow. Lauren talked to Erick about some of the questions Elliot had, some were very smart for someone who had just found out they weren't alone in the universe. Then she asked the one question of him she felt she needed an answer to, why Elliot?

Erick looked off into the view out the window without really seeing it and answered softly. "Raven is going to need him, especially when this is over; if she loses Hawk or Mac, even more so. Eileen is going to pass away in the next few days, which can't be helped, and I can't keep her any longer, I have to let her go, much as I don't want to."

He explained that he was propping her up, so to speak, with a life spell; one that gave her energy that at the same time took some of his. "I know it was wrong, but I did it anyway. There are some spells that you shouldn't do I have found over the years, but I wanted more time with her and I wanted her to feel useful once again. I wanted her to be able to leave happy." As she watched, a tear rolled down his cheek. Seeing Erick in that much pain tore at her heart, and tears began to roll down her cheeks as well. All they could do was hold each other while they cried.

Erick rose long before the sun. He was careful not to wake Lauren, and dressed, then slipped into the hall. He started for the elevator slowly. No matter how old he got, what had to be done never became easier. He exited the elevator on the next floor down and crossed the hall to Eileen's door. He heard the lock disengage and the door opened. The night nurse, Amanda, moved to the side to let him in, then sat back down on the chair by the door. Her eyes were glazed and unseeing, she picked the book off the table and appeared to go back to reading.

Erick crossed the room and went down the short hall to Eileen's room. He knocked lightly before opening the door. Eileen was propped up in bed. Her eyes slowly opened and she looked up at him, "Hello, Grandfather. Thank you."

"For what?"

"For letting me be useful again," she said with a smile. She looked fragile and weak, and it hurt Erick terribly, knowing there was nothing he could really do. "I know what you did and what it cost you. It's been a good life. Don't be so sad." She smiled and took his hand as he sat in the chair next to the bed, gazing lovingly at his last surviving granddaughter. He sat with her until her eyes closed and she went to sleep. About ten minutes later her breathing stopped, and in a few moments, her heart did as well. Eileen was dead. He sat holding her hand for a time, not wanting to leave, but knowing he couldn't stay. After a while, the tears stopped. He stood and gently kissed her on the forehead, and carefully laid her hand across her chest. As he said, "Goodbye, my love," the tears began anew. He then looked up toward the stars and said, "I have always done what you asked, and in return you promised to take care of them. Please take care of her. I now leave her with you." Then he went out past the still unseeing nurse into the hall, crossed to the elevator, and went back to his apartment.

When he entered, Lauren was sitting at the kitchen table. She wasn't angry with him for not telling her. She knew a dying human when she saw one. She knew that Eileen's time was much shorter than Erick had told her, and for whatever reason, he wanted the time with her alone. That wasn't deception; it was love. It was something they gained as a human. To a Darrk, love was not an emotion they truly felt. True, they mated for life, but that was an instinct, not true love. Love was an emotion that humans felt, and it guided their way in the world. When a Darrk changed into human form, there was something human that came with it, emotions not really known to a Darrk. It brought out the best in some and the worst in others.

When she and Erick had been separated all those years, Lauren found that she was feeling stronger emotions than she had ever felt before. It had taken time to realize what they were. Depression, despair, anguish, and sadness totally unknown had come over her, and it took a long time to know what they were. She had been in love. She believed it was the strongest emotion that humans possessed, the most useful, yet also the most painful. She poured him a cup of coffee, took his hand in hers, and sat with him at the table, as they watched the sky brighten in silence.

When Elliot walked in a half-hour later, they were still at the table. He knew something was wrong and had turned to leave when Erick pulled out a chair and said, "Please." Puzzled, Elliot sat. Lauren got up and poured him a cup of coffee. She refilled Erick's and her own, then she smiled at Elliot, took her coffee, and retreated from the room.

They sat in silence for perhaps ten minutes before Erick said softly, "I'll never get tired of looking out at the sea. I know this is the Sound, but to me, it's still the sea. When Raven was a little girl, I would find her out on the bench I had at the house, looking out to sea. She told me one day she finally figured out why I had the bench looking out, instead of in toward the garden. She said it was more peaceful looking to the sea."

He glanced at Elliot with glassy eyes, then turned his gaze back to the window. "You are no doubt wondering why I have told you all of this. Who I am, where I'm from, how we got here? But that is not the real reason I have told you all of this," he lifted his hand toward the sky then dropped it. "I can tell Raven really genuinely likes you. She never had many friends growing up. She knew she was different and avoided others so as to not be questioned, I think. I had always been truthful to her, so she knew where she was from. Eileen worked awfully hard so both Raven and Hawk knew the truth. I think they both thought we were a little crazy. It wasn't until quite recently she fully accepted that truth, as did Hawk, and they will need some time to adjust. I feel you understand being different. In a whole other way, true, but you understand."

"Unfortunately, time is something they do not have. What happened to you last night was the result of us being watched. We are watched by others of my kind and their minions because they will need me. I am the last engineer who survived the transit here, and being the last engineer, I am the only one who can repair the ship that will get them home. I have figured out they have one trained as an engineer, and there are some who think he can do it, but the systems are too complicated. It took me about thirty years in training to master, and this one would have never even seen such a ship if he were born here on earth. So, I don't think he can build the parts necessary to repair the ship."

"My sister believes this as well, but there is a group working against her. She was not the commander, but the sub-commander, and after all these millennia they don't feel they have to listen to her. They think that all they need is the key. Something also tells me there is someone else who has her scared and unsure of herself, but I can't see who. For the first time I cannot see past whatever it is, like a wall with not even a window to peek through."

"I have that key and I am the only one who knows where the ship and the escape shuttle are, which brings me back to you. Raven loves Mac and I know he can protect her as he loves her as well, but she will need a friend. There are going to be some very dark times ahead, and she will be separated from Mac and her brother for a time if my guess is correct. We will be fighting a battle on two fronts. Mac and Hawk fight best together, so I'm going to split Hawk and Raven. I cannot bear to lose them both or Lauren. I may have to take Mac and Hawk as things develop, but if I'm right, I'll need all of us in the first battle. I can count on my sister doing the honorable thing but not this group or the shadow I can't see. I know he's there but can't see him. So, I am going to *destroy* them! I will not allow them to make us look over our shoulders the rest of our lives, and I cannot allow them to return to Darrk."

Elliot felt a sudden chill. He had never heard anyone speak with the coldness with which Erick had just spoken. It was something that he would never forget, no matter how long he lived, and at the same time, Elliot hoped he never heard such grim resolve from Erick again. "I need you to be her friend. Eileen died this morning and Raven will be heartbroken. All I ask from all I've told you and all I will tell you in the future, is to be her friend, and hold her when the tears start to fall and the doubt creeps into her soul. I need you to let her know she is not alone. Can you do this for me, please?" Elliot saw the sadness in Erick's face and his heart went out to the man. He wished there was more he could do, and there was no way he would ever let this man or Raven down.

"I would consider it an honor."

Lauren had heard what was said from the other room and was crying. A Darrk's hearing was unmatched, and as much as she hated it, Erick was right. They needed to destroy them all, not just Dianna's group, but all who wanted to return to Darrk. That was the only way to make earth safe. What she didn't like was that he was planning to use only Hawk and Mac, not her and Raven. He needed help. Thinking quickly, Lauren went to the bedroom to retrieve her cell phone.

Eileen's funeral was four days later on a day like most others in the Seattle area that time of year—gray and wet with the rain coming down like tears from the sky. It was fitting he thought. She was to be laid to rest next to her sister in a small granite crypt in Snohomish outside of Everett. It was on a hill overlooking the Snohomish River. The night before, Erick had told Lauren and Johnathan, who had arrived that morning, that he was going out to the cemetery in the morning and would meet them there. He wanted to sit with Rose awhile.

This crypt could hold nine when the final shelves were put in place, but for now, only had two shelves in on either side of the door with the other three places along the bottom. The caretaker had already seen Erick. He came down, shook Erick's hand, and told him he was sorry for the intrusion, but he had to open the crypt and prepare for the service in a couple of hours. Erick had nodded and the caretaker opened it and noticed there were two coffins inside when there was only one person in the records. Erick explained that the one on the top right side was empty, and it was for him when his time came. The caretaker simply nodded and noticed the mahogany casket below it had a nameplate on the side that simply read "Rose." The caretaker took a cloth and began to wipe clean the outside, so it would look more presentable for the service. When he finished, he would do the one on top.

He thought it strange that this man had shown up early this morning. He was sitting on the bench when the caretaker had gotten up and looked out the window of his little home on the grounds. As best as he could tell, Erick had been dropped off, as there was no vehicle. The service wasn't until 1:00 P.M. but this man had been sitting on the bench in the rain, looking down the hill toward the river for several hours. When the caretaker came out of the crypt after wiping down the caskets, Erick stood and told him he was a member of the family and was there to watch the crypt until it was resealed. The caretaker said he was sorry, but he would need to see some identification before he could leave him there. Erick produced a driver's license with the last name "Scott." It matched the name carved on the top of the crypt in the granite, so he thought it was okay and handed it back. The caretaker told him to let him know if he needed anything, shook his hand again, and walked back up the hill to his little house, all the while thinking that some families had interesting customs. At least the burial didn't involve moving a lot of dirt in the rain.

Erick sat back down on the bench, this time, facing the door instead of the river, as he had been all morning. He sat for about an hour, then, without looking behind him called out, "Good morning, Sister."

Dianna came out of a group of trees about thirty feet away. He had started to say it before she even materialized, and it caught her a little off guard, her name echoing off the headstones. *He knew I was coming before I even arrived*, she thought, *interesting*. "Good morning, my brother. I thought it best to ask you before I attended today. I do not wish to upset your family in this human ritual," a ritual, she, even now, didn't really understand. But she did know it was a sign of respect for humans, and as a Darrk officer, respect was trained into them—respect for your own kind and respect for your adversary. She was, even after all this time, a Darrk officer. The mental conditioning required to become one was at times brutal, and often, fatal.

"Yes, of course you are welcome. You shouldn't have slept so much; you might have learned to enjoy this world and understand its customs better." It was the same argument Erick had brought up with her over the centuries. He had at least tried, but there was a roadblock there, somewhere in that sharp mind he couldn't get her past. She knew this; some of the mental conditioning was forgotten. The result wasn't, but the methods that etched it in her brain were.

Dianna quickly changed the subject. She had given him a week, and this was not the time to bring up old arguments. "I like the weather when it's like this, dark and cool. I love the feel of the light rain against the skin and in my hair. It's so much like home." She moved over and sat next to him on the bench where, uncharacteristic of her, took his hand and said, "I'm sorry, Brother." He found she truly was sorry; it wasn't just words. He could have looked in her mind, but she would know it, and this was not the time. She came out of caring truly how her brother felt, and he would not jeopardize the trust it required of her to be here. This planet was rubbing off on her no matter how hard she tried to not let it do so.

"Thank you." They sat there in the rain in silence for an hour, holding hands, just listening to the rain falling on this green and blue world. She knew he could read her thoughts if he wanted, but he'd chosen not to. She knew this, as she would have felt the intrusion, as she had before.

The caretaker up at the office looked out the window and saw the woman on the bench with the man he'd met earlier. She must have been dropped off as well, as there still were no vehicles parked anywhere. Both of them were just sitting in the rain, he in his expensive black suit and overcoat and she in a beautiful black dress, with her long red hair flowing down the back. That dress obviously cost more than he made in a month, and all she had was a light raincoat over her shoulders. She must be freezing. Some people had more money than the common sense to get out of the rain. He went to the kitchen and filled a thermos with hot black coffee and grabbed two cups and a grey wool blanket off the back of the chair by the door.

Dianna was genuinely surprised when he came up and handed the thermos and cups to Erick, and the blanket to her, saying only "Put this over you. You'll freeze out here in the rain dressed like that." Then he retreated to his office.

"I don't think he knows how tough you are," Erick grinned. Then, after wrapping the blanket around his sister, he poured the coffee. They had sat back down on the bench when Dianna looked at Erick.

"What made him do that?" She looked puzzled. She tried not to interact with humans much and had always kept her distance, except when she couldn't avoid it. She had slept for over a thousand years once and would have slept longer if it hadn't been for that fool grave robber breaking into the tomb. Why would he care? Had she really been misjudging them?

Erick laughed and said, "Concern for his fellow man, or in your case, woman." He reached into his coat and produced a large flask. Unscrewing the top, he handed it to Dianna saying, "There is a need in them to help others, some suppress it, but most do truly care."

Dianna took a small sip, brandy, an exceptionally good one. "Was Eileen like that, always wanting to help others?" She thought of Eileen as a niece in a way. She was part human, but she was Darrk too, after all, and she was her brother's granddaughter. She had watched her from afar and knew she was smart. Maybe they weren't such a bad race.

"Yes. As was Rose." He indicated the crypt, "She always thought the best of people."

"How did she die?" Dianna didn't say it with any malice. Darrks just didn't understand the pain of bringing up such things.

Erick understood this, but it was still hard to this day to speak of it. "She was out on a boat with a boyfriend, fishing in the early morning, the twins' father actually, and it was chilly that morning. He had a small propane heater down in the cabin that had gone out. The best they can figure was the cabin filled with gas and the boat exploded. They couldn't determine what the ignition source was, but the explosion blasted the boat in pieces. She was found on the shore two days later, but he was never recovered. The mix of human and Darrk is strong and heals well, but not like us. A blow can kill them just as the explosion killed Rose."

"I'm sorry." Dianna looked at Erick and he realized she genuinely was. "We will have to talk of other things tomorrow, but today, let's take care of your granddaughter."

"Thank you." They sat in silence, drinking the hot coffee and sipping from the flask.

About an hour and thirty minutes later, the hearse with Eileen in it, pulled up, followed by two limousines. Raven, Mac, Elliot, and Lauren were in one. When Raven saw Dianna sitting there with Erick, she began to worry.

"Don't worry," Lauren said. "She is here to show her respect for her brother and Eileen. That is all."

Raven realized she would never understand Dianna, she had too many sides to her and right now, Raven would settle on knowing this one.

The other limousine had Hawk, Johnathan Marks, and Doc in it, with Doc just looking miserable. During the long ride from the funeral home, Hawk had reached over and gently touched his elbow. "It's okay, Doc, quit beating yourself up. You couldn't have done any more. Her body was just worn out." Doc gave him a look of thanks, but he was still miserable. Eileen had become a friend, and not just a patient.

The six men, Hawk, Doc, Mac, Elliot, Johnathan, and Erick served as pallbearers, and took the mahogany casket into the crypt and placed it on the lower shelf on the left side. The two men from the funeral home sat in the hearse to give them some privacy. Dianna stood off to the side away from the others so as to not make them uncomfortable, but Doc walked over, opened an umbrella, and handed it to her. Then he joined Lauren under hers while Raven and Mac huddled under another. Hawk just stood in the rain staring at the door to the crypt with Johnathan standing next to him, the rain dripping off the brim of Johnathan's hat fell on his shoes unnoticed. Elliot stood next to Mac and Raven under an umbrella. He was here mainly because Raven asked him to come. He didn't really know Eileen, although he had met her, she seemed such a nice woman.

With no minister or priest, Erick stood facing them and began. They all were dressed in black, except Mac, who was dressed in his kilt and carried a set of bagpipes. "We all know life ends. Eventually we will all end up here, in a place such as this. How we live that life is how we are to be remembered. I will always remember Eileen as she was. I'll miss her laugh, her ability to find the positive in everything, and most of all, I'll miss her counsel. I know this is just a shell, an organic cocoon that she resided in; her spirit is not here. It has gone to where we will all be someday, in the stars seeing the beauty of the Universe. She's with God now. I will miss you, Granddaughter. Until we meet again in the next dimension."

"In the next dimension." Lauren, Mac, Johnathan, and Dianna spoke softly. Dianna had said it before she even realized it, and Johnathan was obviously familiar with it. Erick had given a Dark prayer. She found the short service an interesting one to give a human. He had changed it somewhat; after all, they were putting the body away for safekeeping almost. Darrks were buried in unmarked graves, burned on a pyre, or floated away on the water, sometimes with logs burning as it disappeared. Nothing covered them and they were not wrapped, they were burned to assist the body and its return to the soil, or just placed in a hole and buried.

This was the point in the ceremony when the others were invited to say something about the deceased, while some may not know this. Lauren stepped forward and said, "I didn't know you long, but I feel I knew you well. And I thank you for the caring of my mate and his grandchildren. Until we meet again in the next dimension."

"In the next dimension." This time Hawk responded with them. It had been sometime since he had attended a Darrk funeral, his mother's, but he did remember.

Mac stepped forward, "I will miss you, old woman, and I thank you for the welcome you gave me when I came to this family, and the care you have given my best friend and the woman I love. Until we meet again in the next dimension."

"In the next dimension." This was from all.

It was no surprise to Erick when Dianna stepped forward, "Granddaughter of my brother, my grandniece, I hope your God grants you rest. I did not know you well and watched from afar. I regret that now, knowing your intelligence and caring for my brother and your sister's children. You deserved more from me and did not receive it." She suddenly felt hollow, and sorrow washed over her. She'd barely knew this woman, and yet, to think of her passing, hurt. "Until we meet again in the next dimension." She barely finished.

"In the next dimension."

Johnathan stepped forward. "My dear Aunt Eileen, what does one say when they know this world has lost one of its greatest souls? God must have needed you more. Goodbye, my friend, and to a woman I was proud to call my aunt, Godspeed. Until we meet again in the next dimension."

"In the next dimension."

Doc realized the reason for a service such as this, it allowed you to say goodbye personally, in case you never got to say what you wanted to before the departed left. He stepped forward. "My oldest patient, what do I say? Your warmth and smile will follow me all my days, as will the way you cared about others, some you didn't even know, and some you raised as your own, when life and a twist of fate took your sister away from you. You cared for them well and have raised two of the finest people," he stopped, and with a quivering voice continued, "I am happy to call my friends. Until we meet again in the next dimension."

"In the next dimension."

Elliot and Raven came forward together. Raven was crying so much she couldn't speak. Hawk stepped forward and began, "My dear aunt, I'm sorry you are gone, but it is selfishness that made me want you to stay. I will miss you and the smile that used to light my day, but I feel something greater needed you more than me. I thank you for being a good mother to me and Raven. You could have turned your back on us and didn't. I know the pain of losing our mother followed you the rest of your days. Your sense of humor, your honesty, and your love will always be with me. Until we meet again in the next dimension."

"In the next dimension."

Raven looked at the coffin through the door of the crypt with tears in her eyes. "Goodbye, my aunt. You were like a mother to me and I love you. Until . . . until we . . ." her voice kept breaking and it tore at Elliot's heart, he understood and finished for her.

"Until we meet again in the next dimension," his tears running down his face.

"In the next dimension."

With that, Erick walked over and gently shut the door. Then he closed the gate and placed the locks on the gate, latching them shut. Mac walked up next to the crypt, and standing in the rain, looking down at the Snohomish River, he began to play "Amazing Grace" on the bagpipes.

With tears in his eyes, Erick listened to Mac for a moment, the mournful sound echoing off the valley floor while an eagle turned circles over the river in the distance. It was done. "Goodbye, Granddaughter," the pain in his voice was plainly heard. As he turned around to face the others, he saw Dianna standing in the back, and tears were running down her cheeks.

She finally understood.

Erick, Lauren, Johnathan, and Dianna were in the lead limousine heading back to Seattle, about forty-five minutes away. Dianna was being incredibly quiet, in fact they all were, each of them lost in their own thoughts. Erick was sitting next to Lauren, and he reached out and took her hand in his own. They sat that way for several minutes when Dianna said, "You were right all along. I knew it, but I refused to see it. It was easier to think of them as cattle you would keep on a farm instead of seeing them as beings that had thoughts, hopes, and dreams. It was easier to think of the Nightwalkers I made as guard dogs I used to protect me from them. But who is the real animal here? We look more like guard dogs ourselves," a small sardonic snort came from her, "we just happen to be very large guard dogs."

She turned her head and looked at Erick. "You could have given up on me centuries ago, why didn't you? I just tossed away everything you said as trash, yet you never gave up, why?" The look in her eyes was one he had not seen since before they left for their main schools at the end of basic training—a look of pure wonder, of caring and compassion. This was the look of his sister, he, or really it was Eileen, had finally broken through whatever barrier they had programmed in her mind.

"Because I love you. You are my sister." It may be a simple answer, but it was the truth and Dianna felt the love and warmth in the response. She turned back toward the window so he couldn't see her cry again, that would be a sign of weakness, some of that old training still there. She had to maintain control.

After a few moments she said, "What is happening to me, the feelings I don't understand, what is this feeling I have of . . . loss? It's a pain that doesn't hurt physically, it hurts . . . inside.'

"One of the benefits we get from this human form I think," Lauren began, "is the ability to feel emotions as they do. While Darrks know anger, happiness, some fear, companionship with our mates, some of the pain of loss, a need to care and protect the young and old, and the curiosity that comes with intelligence, we don't know love, forgiveness, and only have necessary compassion. We don't know pity and terrible loss. The emotion of love in a human magnifies all the others, and I feel it makes *them* stronger. The human ability to pick themselves up after terrible loss is love— love for others and love for themselves. It is the strongest emotion in them helping each person move forward after something outside of them has interrupted their lives, and I feel it is that emotion that is the most useful in them, followed by compassion for their fellow man."

Dianna thought of the caretaker making time to bring them a blanket and coffee, and he didn't even know them. After a few moments, Dianna looked at Erick with tears in her eyes, tears she refused to shed, "Will you ever forgive me?"

"Dear Sister, I already have." As she leaned against him, finding comfort in her brother as she had when they were young, he wrapped his arms around her and held her. He finally had his sister back.

Two hours later, Erick and Dianna were sitting on the bench behind the mansion, looking out at Puget Sound with the noises of an "Irish wake" coming out of the recreation room behind them. It was Johnathan's idea, he told Erick they all looked like a bunch of lost children. He thought they should do something about it and the best place he could think of was the room Eileen used to take him when he was a teenager.

His dad would come to Seattle on business, and as Johnathan's mother had died when he was young, would take Johnathan with him. When at fourteen Johnathan asked why he couldn't stay, he was told because he didn't want to leave him home alone and he "had been a teenager once." Then, leaving him with Eileen and Rose, his father and Erick went to the office downtown. At first, he thought he would be bored stiff until after Erick and his father left that first morning. Eileen looked at him across the breakfast table and said to Rose, "Someone needs to teach this boy how to play pool."

"And drink beer," Rose replied.

"Pool first, beer later." Eileen then led him to the recreation room followed by Rose. And there began the most fun he had ever had. He used to have to spend a week at a time there at the house in Seattle, sometimes three to four times a year after he turned fourteen and for the next four years. Eileen and Rose taught him how to play pool, shuffleboard, poker, darts . . . and drink beer. He had gotten to where he started asking his father when they were going to Seattle. After he graduated from law school, they had a graduation party for him at the mansion and flew all his friends to Seattle for it. To him, both ladies were his aunts and he called them that. He loved both women, and when Rose was killed, he flew to Seattle the second he hung up the phone. He left his office, ran out the door, and had to call his secretary from the airport. Nobody knew why he had rushed out of the office like that or where he had gone. He hadn't thought of it until he was sitting in the airport, ticket in his hand, with no luggage, and realized he hadn't said anything to anyone.

Erick and Dianna both had a snifter of brandy, and Dianna found it to be the most relaxed she had been since they were cubs. Her mind was at ease for the first time since arriving on this planet. They could hear the noise from the rec room. Johnathan and Doc on one pool table, Mac and Hawk on another, while Raven, Elliot and Lauren were playing darts on the other side of the room. The jukebox was playing a song from Golden Earring, "Radar Love" in the background.

"This has got to be the strangest custom yet," Dianna smiled, "two hours ago they were about the gloomiest bunch I ever saw. Now, they are laughing and playing games." She shook her head and looked back out at the Sound while Erick poured more brandy. "I have misjudged them and their resilience." She stopped for a moment, Erick knew this meant she had something important to say and waited. She made up her mind, then crossed the line.

"There is something I need for you to know that you don't, the political officer lived and made it here. He is the one behind most of what is going on right now. He has told me that if I cannot get you to fix the ship and give me the key, then he will get it. He has trained someone with the crystal the manuals are on from the ship and thinks he can repair it himself. If I fail in our negotiations tomorrow, he will take over, and he doesn't negotiate. He's the one that killed . . . the commander and he, like all political officers, is ruthless. The only reason he hasn't removed me and taken over himself is you are my brother and I keep telling him you'll come to your senses. But, Brother, I'm out of time, and he *will* kill you."

Erick knew how much talking about the commander hurt her but her training as an officer gave her strength. He saw that was the missing piece. He couldn't figure out who was pulling the strings. Now he knew, and that was why he couldn't look into the fog of his mind and see him. But even that was a problem; he had no idea how to fight a completely unknown enemy. He'd spent so much time looking at an enemy right in front of him, blinding him to the true leader. Not even knowing who he was on the ship was a problem; he couldn't track the thread. But that was also why he couldn't find him, or "read" a leader other than Dianna. He had her doing one thing and someone doing something else. It had obscured Erick's thinking because his focus was on Dianna and Thorm was blocking his way to see past them.

"I had figured you had someone else trained as engineer, but a political officer? He is really the one behind this whole mess? Who was it?"

By their very nature and orders, political officers were unknown to the rest of the crew. Taken from the military school, they were removed from the officer pool and trained separately. They were put onboard with a job and acted like any member of the crew, except they reported everything that happened on the ship to the council. The council was the only authority that could give them orders, they would follow the ships, but in conflicts they had higher orders. There were only four on board who would know who it was, the commander, the sub-commander, the chief physician, and the chief engineer; orders for the ship from the council whenever possible went through the political officer before being executed.

"It was Con."

"The mess hall keeper? You've got to be kidding me! He was dropped in South America. He's still alive?" Erick's brows furrowed and a scowl came upon his face.

"Yes. He told the others who he was after you left. The ship's doctor was with him in the group and confirmed. He's been in control of the groups from North and South America ever since."

"Damn." He could count on Dianna being reasonable, not a political officer. "Where is he?"

"I have to go to my office, he will call there soon, and I need to be there to answer the phone. I'll stall him tonight; tell him our meeting is in the morning. But we must come up with something tomorrow, something he will agree to, or he'll take over, and we don't want that. I'm out of time."

"Where is he?" Erick repeated.

"Mexico City. And he has about a hundred mercenaries."

"Mercenaries?"

"And also, Walkers; he wanted protection during the day and has made a fortune off native North, Central, and South American artifacts over the years; also, a lot of gold that was hidden from the Spanish. He's just as wealthy as you are."

"You know how wealthy I am?"

"Yes, and so does he. He figures what he can find places you at almost two billion dollars American. And he keeps track to see if any major amounts move. He knows the bank you own; he has deposits there. He figures another half again of that is stashed away in various places."

It was bad enough that Con was close to being right, but damn, he knew most of it. It was a good thing Erick had more than he thought. If he had to get money to fight this, he would get it from unknown places. He would have to start working his memory and remember where he had stashed easily converted materials so they couldn't be traced. "Did he know of the house in Virginia?"

"Yes. He was told when you got there and informed me. He has people watching there; be careful, he's dangerous in a way you don't know. He has a French Canadian merc who's ruthless. I have to go, say my goodbyes, Brother." They stood and hugged each other for a moment, then Dianna stepped back and faded away into the night. It came to him that her leaving made him feel depressed. She had finally found her true self, and she felt so much like the sister of his youth, it was hard to see her leave.

Erick entered the rec room holding two empty glasses as well as an empty decanter; no one had to ask where Dianna went. As he sat the glassware on the bar, Lauren came up and grasped his hand, "She had to go? Do you think that's safe for her?"

"It would be more dangerous if she stayed. We have a greater problem than I thought." When Lauren looked at him puzzled, he decided now was the best time to tell her. "The political officer is still alive." The color draining from her face was all the answer he needed to know she understood. "For now, let's enjoy being together at this party and save that information until tomorrow. We need to concentrate on Eileen and the twins and tackle this tomorrow when we meet with Dianna again." With that, they turned from the bar and joined the party, just as Blue Oyster Cult's "Don't Fear the Reaper" started playing on the jukebox.

An hour later, the doorbell rang, and everyone was starting to be a little intoxicated. Lauren went to the intercom by the stairs and was talking to someone on the handset for a minute. She smiled, grabbed the cash Erick had left on the end table, and started up the stairs. The pizza had shown up. Erick was just about to sink the 9 ball in the corner when he felt the familiar buzzing in his head that another full Darrk was there. He felt no danger but missed the easy shot anyway. His teammate, Johnathan, barked, "My grandmother couldn't have missed that!" Seeing that Erick was looking at the stairs made him stop.

As Erick looked toward the stairs, he saw Lauren coming down with a smile on her face and another next to her but was holding the pizza boxes high enough he couldn't see who it was. "Seems there was someone else at the door who was paying for the pizza as I opened it," she laughed. The man tossed the pizzas on the bar and turned around.

"Hiya, Brother!" came a voice with a very thick Scottish accent. "Seems you lads are ahead of me, where's the scotch?" Erick had never been happier to see someone in his life. If there was one Darrk that he knew for sure was on his side, it was Odmen.

"How in the hell did you find me?" Erick howled, giving him a hug, and then stepping back to look at someone he had not seen in 5000 years.

"I think you need to blame this lass." He hooked a thumb toward Lauren.

"Uncle Duncan!" Mac ran up and hugged Odmen, "I haven't seen you since the last time I was in Scotland, must have been twenty years ago. Who blasted you out of that castle, or did they finally get smart and throw you out!"

Odmen again hooked his thumb toward Lauren. "Nay, seems I had to come and fulfill a promise." Erick couldn't even be mad at Lauren for not telling him. Duncan looked over the bar and grabbed a bottle of Glenfiddich and poured himself a glass. "I got some real scotch coming tomorrow after it clears Customs, but this will do, I'd say."

"I have a few single malts under the bar if you need something different," Erick smiled. He now knew whom Mac had chosen as a father; he couldn't have made a better choice.

"Oh, it pains me to think of a single wasted on pizza!" He laughed. "But watch out! Now I know where it is!"

With Raven and Hawk looking more confused by the minute, Erick looked at them and said, "May I present Odmen, or as he became known to the Vikings as, Odin."

"Or as known now," Odmen began, "Duncan McGregor, Patriarch of the McGregor's, Earl of McGregor Castle, and the largest producer of fine scotch in all of Scotland and the United Kingdom."

"Really," Erick said with raised eyebrows, looking at Mac and Lauren.

"You'll be finding I'm not lying tomorrow," he grinned. Seeing Mac was wearing his kilt He asked, "So, what's the occasion?" When he saw all but Lauren and Erick look downward, he suddenly felt ill. He had no idea and felt he had just made a serious blunder. "I'm sorry, I didn't know," he began, "no one told me . . ."

"It's alright, old friend," Erick said looking at him. "How could you know, in fact this is her wake of a sorts. Her name was Eileen and she was my granddaughter."

Odmen's eyes opened wide, "You, too! Then if you don't mind, I'd like to correct my error. To Eileen!" He raised his glass, "Be happy in heaven, but remember occasionally to raise hell!" The response he got was immediate.

"To Eileen!" After raising their glasses and beers, they all drank deeply. The mood change was not as quick, but it slowly returned to more of a party atmosphere. Raven broke out a stack of paper plates, and they all began to eat, playing pool between bites or darts.

Later, Erick had found Mac in fact learned how to play the bagpipes from Duncan, and his McGregor kilt and tartan were from Duncan as well. As a child, Mac had been adopted by Duncan at a ceremony in front of the whole clan. Duncan was the father he never had, and Mac would stay with him at the castle when his mother was on digs. He had found Eileen loved the bagpipes from Raven, and one morning, he surprised her by standing in the backyard and playing. Hawk was clueless, as his playing the pipes had never come up except once at the funeral of Wallace, one of their team. There had been bagpipes there and Mac had never mentioned it, not because he was shy, the family had a whole band at the funeral, and he wasn't needed in that capacity.

Duncan laughed, "I adopted this boy when Lauren came to visit. I found he had no father that was known. It was after the war, and I knew by looking at him he had the Darrk blood. He would stay with me when his mum had digs that she had to get to and couldn't take him. He took up the pipes when he was about ten, I'd say. He's one o' the best I ever heard. And he's rather good at making whiskey to boot." He smiled, "And I like Mac, it suits him much better than Howard."

"You can thank him for that," Mac said, pointing at Hawk.

"Where's the bloody snooker table!" Duncan suddenly roared, "All I see are them small pool tables so common in this country."

"See that table with all the beer bottles on it?" Erick pointed, then continued, "It's a cover and the snooker table is under it. I haven't played in years!"

"Then I figure we better not make any bets until you get your legs back under you." Duncan laughed and started grabbing bottles.

At 3:00 A.M. Mac, Hawk, and Raven decided it was best to take the elevator to the fourth floor. As Mac put it best, "If I try to go up those damn stairs, I'm going to end up sleeping at the bottom of them!" Then it took five minutes for them to figure out how to open the door to get in it, and another five minutes to close it. "Fuck!" Mac had shut his shirt in the door. You could hear the shirt tear as the elevator door shut on it with Duncan laughing the whole time.

"It's okay," Raven slurred, "you're not going to need that shirt in five more minutes . . . that is if we can get out of the elevator when we get there." She gave him a lecherous look, and flopped butt down on the floor laughing when it jerked starting up. Hawk just looked like he was doing his best just to keep standing, his head rolling around like he was a bobblehead.

Elliot was in the corner on a sofa by the dartboard, Johnathan was asleep and snoring on one couch with Doc asleep on the loveseat, his feet over the arm and his shoes under them. Erick wobbled over to a cedar chest in the corner and produced three quilts, one he put over Doc and the other over Johnathan. Lauren took the last one from him and walked over to the other sofa where Elliot snored and covered him. After surveying their work, Erick grabbed a bottle of brandy and a glass and started for the patio, "The rest of us, to the fire pit!" Lauren grabbed a glass and Duncan took the bottle of single malt with him and started for the door, only to double back to grab a large rocks glass, with no rocks.

Erick flopped down on the sofa by the pit with Lauren sliding in next to him, and Duncan took the armchair across from them. "Some fire pit, no fire," he chuckled and started to take a swig from the bottle, until Erick waved his hand and the pit sprang to life, casting flames about two feet in the air.

"Whoa, down boy!" Lauren looked at him and started laughing as about thirty dollars of single malt came out of Duncan's nose.

"Ah, that hurts! How in the bloody hell did you do that?" He choked with his eyes wide open.

"I have many talents," Erick said with a nod of his head, pouring Lauren and himself a brandy without spilling a drop. "See. I think I'm going to hate myself in the morning."

"Why wait," said Duncan, "I'll hate you now if you don't tell me how you did that." Then they all broke up in a fit of laughter.

Dianna hung up the phone and slowly set it back in the cradle on her desk. For the first time in many years she found herself terrified, such were the threats she'd just heard. She had to come up with a plan with Erick, but for now, she had to protect Brandon and the others. *"Brandon, love, after you and the others feed, come back to the house. We are in trouble and must move! If not we will be destroyed!"* She sent that message to him first, then another to them all, including Brandon. *"My Knights! Come home as soon as you can! We must move, we are in grave danger! Be careful we may be watched!"* She began to quickly pack up her things.

Brandon ran in the door of her office ten minutes later. "Mistress!" He saw the fear in her eyes. In all the time he had been with her, this was the first time he had ever seen her afraid.

"Get the others together and get some moving trucks, I don't care how; all the coffins to the backup house in Ballard. Waste no time. I'll get things together here. And get me a headcount of those that return. Two are already gone I feel."

"Yes, Mistress!" Knowing her fear, he unquestioningly went about his duties.

She hoped they'd left in time and weren't followed.

Three hours before dawn, they were done. Everything had been moved, and she was in a room set up as her bedroom and office on the ground floor. Plywood had been put over all the windows on this floor from the outside so when the sun came up they would be safe. If they weren't followed and this place wasn't known to that damn Canadian, they would be safe for a couple of days. Only thirty-eight made it back to the house on Capitol Hill, she felt the passing of the others. She would make no more, what she had done could not be undone, but she would make no more and do her best for the ones she had left. It was not their fault they were what they were. It was hers, and she found herself unable to do it ever again. When Brandon came into the room to tell her all was ready, she walked to him, and wrapping her arms around him, held him close.

Brandon didn't know what else to do other than hold her, he had never seen her like this. What happened? What took one of the strongest he had ever met and scared her so? "I'm sorry, my love. I'm so sorry," she moaned.

"For what? What's wrong?" He found his whole being wanted to keep her safe, and not just because he had to, he wanted to.

"I'm sorry I ever took you off that battlefield. I should have left you, left you to meet your God. Now you may never be able to."

"It's alright, my mistress. I am here with you, and always will be until I am turned to ash. I will not ever give up on you." He kissed her cheek and held her close. After some time, she stopped holding him so tightly, and he led her over to the bed and had her lie down, pulling the covers over her. He held her hand until she fell asleep. He sensed a change in her, but he didn't understand it. He knew she had gone to the funeral of Rahm's Granddaughter; is that what brought this? He needed to find out. Going outside and calling on the wind, he was lifted skyward.

He arrived in Rahm's backyard by the bench. The lights were on in the room to the right of the bottom of the T of the house. Walking that way past the greenhouse, he began to smell the alcohol. Looking around the corner, he found Rahm and Hathor curled up on the couch with another Darrk he didn't know in the armchair across from them, snoring. He smiled; they were drunk! Drunk and passed out! It was a night for surprises. That's why his mistress was out of sorts perhaps; he had smelled the brandy. But that couldn't be all; there was something else. He could kill them all, but he wouldn't. He liked Rahm and Hathor. He knew that they cared about Isisi. Rahm would protect her if anything happened to him. Walking to the rec room, he saw the three men lying on the sofas and the love seat and shook his head. He looked around, where did the quilts come from? Seeing the chest next to the door, he looked inside. Taking the remaining two quilts, he went and covered Rahm and Hathor, and turning, he covered the Darrk across from them. The answer would have to wait until tomorrow it would seem. He walked out to the yard, and calling the winds, went back to Ballard.

Dianna woke as the sun was coming up. Even though she had only slept a couple of hours, she felt much better. Rising from the bed she went to shower, then she had to go to Erick.

Erick awoke in the same place he was, on the sofa with Lauren curled up next to him with a quilt over both of them. Another one lay over Duncan, who was snoring loudly in the armchair across from him. The fire was still lightly burning in the early morning. Untangling himself from Lauren, he tiptoed into the rec room to find Johnathan with a bar towel filled with ice balanced on top of his head, and Doc sitting next to him at the bar staring off into space. Elliot still snored in the corner. There was an open bottle of aspirin between Johnathan and Doc. Dianna was standing behind the bar with about the biggest smile on her face he had ever seen. "Good morning, my brother!" Her dark red hair was glowing in the morning light, which was reflecting off an Egyptian cut, knee-length, white and gold trimmed dress. She looked stunning. Her gold-brown eyes shone, and she looked as if she had gotten twenty years younger. She looked like the sister he remembered of his youth.

"Not so loud please," Doc mumbled. The last thing he remembered was playing beer pong with Hawk, Mac, Raven, and Lauren like he was back in college. "Fine thing for a sixty-three-year old man to get talked into!" His eyes looked like they had changed color to red, and he spoke so softly that Erick barely heard him.

Dianna couldn't take it anymore and broke up laughing, "You guys look like you went to war with the god of spirits! Hair of the dog?" As she held up the bottle of beer, Johnathan got up and ran to the bathroom. "Maybe not." She broke up laughing again. She needed the release; it had been a bad night.

"Morning," Erick said softly. Good thing he was wearing a black shirt, his last glass of brandy was spilled down the front of it.

"I'd start negotiations now, but I don't think they would go well," Dianna giggled.

"Are you kidding," Lauren breathed as she came in from the patio, "he'd give you anything you wanted!" She went straight to the aspirin bottle, shook several into her hand, and grabbing a beer from the night before that was sitting on the bar, swallowed them down, much to the amusement of Dianna. Lauren's face screwed up, "I think there was a cigarette butt in that." That was all it took; Doc ran for the bathroom as the three of them started laughing with Lauren holding her head.

Duncan came in off the patio, "What's so funny?" he exclaimed jovially, looking none the worse for wear.

Lauren looked at him with bloodshot eyes, "I hate you."

Ten minutes later, Raven came in humming with a tray of teacups and a large pot of tea. She began pouring cups of tea for everyone, "Don't put sugar or milk in it, it won't work as fast. I put this together sometime last night, don't ask me when, I don't remember, because I knew it would take me hours this morning. Okay everyone, down the hatch!"

"Girl, you are a godsend!" Doc grabbed his cup and swallowed it down rapidly, burning his throat, which he considered a fair trade. Dianna looked puzzled and was not the only one.

Raven looked at all of them and said, "Drink it, you'll thank me later."

Erick gingerly picked up a cup and took a taste, it was delicious, and he immediately started to feel better. He drank it down in two gulps, and suddenly, his hangover was gone. Lauren, staring down at her empty cup, said, "I know a few campuses where you could make a fortune with this after pledge night."

Johnathan looked at her, "This is the most remarkable stuff I've ever tasted."

"Makes me wish I had a hangover." Dianna was amazed in the change of the group. She had a cup herself and felt better than she had in ages. About that time, Mac and Hawk came into the room. They spied the tray and walked straight up to the three remaining teacups and each gulped down a cup just like they had done it a hundred times before, and they probably had. Then they looked at each other, both got down on their knees, quickly joined by Doc, and with arms raised in the air, started bowing to Raven. She began to laugh. "Man! What would you guys do without me?"

Mac was the first to chime in, "I don't know about anyone else, but I'd probably stay in bed all day with a hangover!"

"Not so loud!" Elliot said as he sat up on the couch. Lauren took the last cup to him. After draining the cup, he exclaimed, "My God!" He looked at everyone, "Where did this come from!"

"Your boss," Lauren smiled.

"I'm never retiring," he said.

Even Duncan said he hadn't felt that good after a night of drinking in his whole life. "Having this recipe could make a man an alcoholic . . . or rich!"

"No sale! But you can drink all booze you like if you want," Raven said, her eyes gleaming.

An hour and a half later, after everyone had showered and changed, they went out on the patio and found Elliot had, with Dianna and Raven's help, cooked a beautiful breakfast, complete with fresh fruit, eggs, bacon, sausage, bagels and lox, pancakes, and two ice-cold pitchers—one of milk and one of orange juice. They all dug in eagerly. Conversation was lively and carefree, with tons of jokes and laughter thrown in.

When they had finished, Dianna looked up and down the table, and with a sigh said, "I hate to bring a downer to this party, but we have to discuss the elephant in the room." She hated to ruin the conversation, but it was necessary. The group sobered rapidly. "My conversation with Con did not go well last night, so if we can't come up with something, he's going to come in here and take the key. Luck would have it that I was his voice to the den rather than Thorm, who can't speak right now, as his head isn't fully attached yet. We have to come up with something, even if it's just a ruse to buy more time."

"Who?" Duncan asked. He didn't have the slightest idea what she meant. After looking at the puzzled faces of the others, Erick took a deep breath and explained. The table was deathly silent when he finished. "The political officer lived." Duncan was dumbfounded. Looking at Dianna, he said, "This is a real problem. I could trust negotiations with you, but a political . . ." his voice trailed off, "with a hundred mercenaries, and more Nightwalkers?"

"I had our whole house moved to a different location last night in Ballard. Brandon understood and was a tremendous help," Dianna began. "They follow me, not Con, and not the den on Queen Anne. But the den knows I was meeting with you today, and I need to stop by for my digit. We need to neutralize that bunch, or we will be fighting on two fronts."

"Digit?" Raven looked puzzled.

"You don't want to know," Mac said; he knew what it meant. He was still trying to wrap his mind around Dianna's change of heart.

"We need to take out the den now." Erick spoke clearly but had a distance to his gaze. "Otherwise Con will add another six Darrks to his force."

"It's worse than that, Brother. I believe he already has about thirty Darrk soldiers as well."

"So that's where the rest of them went." Lauren gasped, "My God, those weren't kidnappers in Caracas, they were mercenaries!"

"Yes, and you have no idea how lucky you were. I found out last night, their orders were to kill you. I was ordered last night to finish the job. Mostly to demoralize Erick."

Johnathan's cell phone rang. He checked the number and said, "It's the office," and excused himself as several ideas as to what to do with the den were being floated around. Dianna was listening to everyone's ideas until she noticed Erick was just sitting in his chair staring out at the Sound. For someone never trained at being a military officer, she had found over the years that her brother's ability to plan, execute, and analyze battles was beyond the skills of most Darrk military officers. Yet, they had placed him in the engineering school. She had noticed, even before they came to earth, that his math skills, and especially his being able to pull something apart and put it back together again in his mind, was unmatched. He was more valuable as an engineer perhaps, but she thought they might have made a mistake. He could pull a battle apart just as he did an engine. Had he been made a Darrk military officer instead of an engineering officer, they would have found him to be a brilliant tactician.

"We need to go on the offensive. We need to take possession of the fighter, the ship, and the shuttle," Erick said this over the ideas of the others, and they suddenly quieted.

"What do you mean?" Duncan asked, his bewilderment showing on his face.

"Ever since I showed back up, we have been on the defensive." Erick stopped briefly, looking into space, then went on. "We have been reacting and not acting. We have allowed Con to make us react to external forces, which blinds us into his future moves. He wants us to destroy the den, to distract us from whatever else he is doing, but what?"

Johnathan, after taking the call from his office, came back to the table with a solemn look on his face, and announced he was flying back to D.C. in the morning. He told Erick and Mac that the police wanted them back as well. It seems the two remaining thugs told the police they were invited into the house to move something, so the cops had more questions. The thugs, prompted by a dishonest law office in D.C., had immediately filed lawsuits against Erick and Mac. The family of the thug who'd died also filed a wrongful death lawsuit and wanted charges brought up on Erick for faulty lighting on the stairs and murder and a few other things "yet to be determined." Johnathan said he would stall the police if he could delay them having to come back, but the trip was inevitable. When he noticed Erick and the others weren't listening, his mind was turning over on something else. "What did I miss?"

"About all you've missed is the rest of us being confused." Mac's look was the same as Duncan's and everyone else's at the table, except Dianna, who was sitting in her chair smiling. But then Mac realized something he hadn't before, and said, "Well I'll be damned! It's been right in front of us the whole time." Erick smiled at him.

Erick on the other hand, had been listening, and the pieces fell together. "Dianna, tell Con I will hand over the key and come down to Mexico to help start making replacement parts when I get back from a short business trip. Tell him you don't know where I've gone. Stay with him as long as you can until you think it has gotten too dangerous or until I call you." She nodded. "Hawk, do you think you and Mac can make it look like you tried to take out the Den on Queen Anne tonight?"

"Absolutely. Confused, broke, or gone?"

"Broke. You may need help, Duncan?"

"My pleasure, if you will have me," he said, looking at Hawk.

"Welcome aboard," Hawk smiled. He was still puzzled, but looking at Mac and Erick, he knew he was going to be doing something. Mac was grinning ear to ear.

"Johnathan, I am going back with you as well as Lauren, Mac, Hawk, and Raven. I think it's time to start bringing the fight to Con and I don't want him to think I know anything. I want it to look as if all we are doing is clearing up things there, which is what he wants. But I think the time to start removal of his allies has come."

"So do I!" Johnathan said he knew of the law firm and they were the type that used to chase ambulances, until they broke into the much more lucrative pastime of filing bogus lawsuits against people who "could afford it" and settling out of court. All they wanted was money, and they would drag Erick through the mud until they got it. Word had somehow gotten out that the house was full of priceless art, and they wanted a piece to shut up or they would go to the press and scream discrimination. He asked Hawk if they could put a 24/7 guard in the house or someone, alarm or not, would break in, and not knowing anything about art, would destroy more than they took. Then Johnathan thought the only way word got around was from the police. Someone there had let the law firm know about the art. The thugs that were in the house wouldn't know art if it fell on them.

Hawk looked up as he hung up his cell phone, "In the works as well as a 24/7 guard for you too." Johnathan didn't argue this time. Then Hawk added, "I could lean on them. They wouldn't go anywhere without a shadow."

"No, don't do that," Erick said. "It would look as if I've got something to hide and I don't. As if my plate wasn't already full."

"But you do have something to hide," Raven looked at him seriously, "over 8600 things to hide. You can pass normal scrutiny, but someone digging will find the real you. It's only a matter of time. I'm going to the office to get some things together. Elliot, feel like seeing Virginia?"

"Love to. Jerry is gone until next week, so the house is empty and driving me nuts!"

"I figure Elliot and I can go and run damage control. We don't need this right now, but we will have to deal with it." She turned to Hawk, "Lean on them, make them look at us instead of Erick."

"Got it, Sis," and grabbed his cell phone again.

"My firm is already going up their asses with a microscope; financial records, personal problems, arrest records, domestic violence, you name it. If any of the staff went to Woodstock, we'll know. I'll have them coordinate with you, Hawk, and Elliot," Johnathan said, looking at Raven.

"But what happens when they sue you guys?" Erick asked bluntly, "What then?"

"We pull the oldest lawyer trick in the book," Johnathan smiled, "we bury them in about a forest worth of paper. They won't see a dime without a match, or until their great-grandchildren are retired. But I don't know how deep their pockets are."

"Sucks to be you, and them!" Dianna mumbled under her breath looking at Erick, stealing a term from Brandon. "Let them at what they do best, Brother, you and I need to talk about getting ready to take care of Con."

"And Johnathan, find out what you can about the two detectives who were there at the house that night. Look for large deposits or special items bought recently. Good thing we had a great breakfast," Erick said mournfully. They all got up to go about their various tasks while Erick's mind was starting to go a million miles an hour.

253

Chapter Nineteen

BOYCE

Sitting around the patio table at the mansion, Erick, Lauren, Dianna, and Duncan were talking about what Con was up to. "Con is genuinely concerned with his position. I would be too. He's trying to stay ahead and play from both ends. If he already has a team here, then there is already surveillance. I felt I was being watched at the cemetery, but it was just a feeling. If I was being watched, it was from a distance, and it must have been human. I would have sensed a Darrk within 200 feet or more, but a human would have to be close and want to do harm to set off my defenses. I don't think just watching and taking pictures would do it. I think he's covering himself if things don't go his way, that way he can clean up. But if he has a team here and things start to go well, he has support here if nothing else. So, he's covered both bases and is leaving nothing to chance. What has to be frustrating to him if he is doing surveillance is he couldn't do it downtown, and he can't do it on the mansion easily. That's one of the reasons the mansion is where it is. About the only way to watch it is from the water. And doing that you would be seen."

Lauren looked at Duncan, "I think it's time to call the others."

"Aye. Can you still get ahold of Paul?"

"And his son, they are in Australia. Also, Chen and Mu in Taiwan, and Ramone in Italy."

"I'll gather the others from the U.K. Bobby still in Canada?"

"Yes, I'll take care of it," Lauren said.

"What's this?" Erick asked. "There are more?"

"Mate, you got twelve more on your side. We have all sworn not to let the others get back to Darrk. Lauren and I just haven't brought them in yet. Kind of keeping them out of harm's way, in reserve so to speak." Duncan smiled, "And have I a big surprise for you."

It was decided Erick and Lauren would go to D.C. with Johnathan, Mac, Elliot, Hawk, and Raven the next day to take care of that end while the others got together with Duncan. Erick had to start thinking quickly. Con seemed to be a step ahead of them, and if they wanted to survive, he had to figure a way to get ahead of him. The way he saw was the best and only way he could do maximum damage. It would be bloody, but it would be a part of his organization he thought was safe. His back door had to be shut, his escape route closed. Erick had just figured out where it was. One he would think was unknown and it would shake his foundation. It had to start in Virginia.

The plane was readied and Roger the pilot said it would be on the tarmac at 6:00 A.M. Erick and Lauren would meet them in Virginia, and Roger said he would put their names on the flight plan. Raven asked, "Why do you even have it if you don't ride in it?"

"I needed something for those who can't just pop in, so to speak."

"And the pilot never caught on?"

"He knows who I am," Erick replied. "His great-great-grandfather was raised by me. His family have been on my staff for over 200 years."

"Trusting soul aren't you," Duncan commented.

Erick smiled, "No, I'm not."

Hawk, Mac, and Duncan showed up at the mansion rec room at 9:00 P.M. They were going to hit the den on Queen Anne Hill at eight that evening while most of the Nightwalkers were out. Being at the mansion that soon made Erick wonder what went wrong, but he had a good idea what the problem was. Hawk walked up, shaking his head, "They're gone. Everything but the trash and furniture, and its trash too."

"What happened?" Lauren couldn't understand how they couldn't be there.

"They lit out," Mac sighed, "they didn't even leave an old bill. There is nothing to indicate someone was there except the filth. No old mail, no phone numbers written anywhere, they didn't even leave any toilet paper."

"I figured this might happen," Erick began, "Con's been ahead of us this whole time. I better tell Dianna not to go to the house in Ballard."

"Oh my God," Lauren breathed, "Erick, she left for there; must be over an hour ago!"

"Did she ever say where it was?"

"No," Lauren choked. The look on her face told Erick she knew what he did, Duncan too.

"What's wrong?" Raven asked.

Mac answered her. "If they packed up Queen Anne, they would destroy the place in Ballard, and if they could, Dianna with it. She's probably been followed as best they could for days now. To Con and the rest of them, she would be a traitor. They wouldn't have packed up Queen Anne unless they thought so."

"Take the Escalade to Ballard," Erick began, "pay close attention to the waterfront and any empty warehouses, I'll join you there. I'm going to try and find it and I don't know how long it will take. Go!" He spun on his heel and started up the stairs.

Hawk and Mac gave each other questioning looks until Duncan said, "Come on now, let's go, I can't drive in this bloody country!"

"We'll split up! Mom and I will take my truck!"

Brandon crawled out from under the bushes, he had to find help for her, he couldn't do anything right now to help, he was too weak. His right arm was missing from the elbow down. He had wrapped a tourniquet on it, but the many bullets that were lead had gone through him, letting out his blood and making him weak. When he had to cut his arm off, that was the end of him, he had nothing left. He had killed two when they had first shown up, putting a hail of bullets through his body, letting blood squirt out of the many holes. When one of the attackers went past him and fired a bullet that struck the back of his hand, he felt the silver start to burn. If he didn't stop the spread, it would follow right up his arm. Once it hit his torso, it would spread to his head and the rest of his body. Jumping over to one he killed, he quickly took the knife out of the sheath on his waist and cut his arm off before it spread past his elbow. He was grateful the knife was sharp; if it hadn't been, he would be gone. He realized he was now useless, then he crawled under the bushes. He removed his belt and wrapped it around his arm, tightening it. All he could do was warn her. *"Mistress! Stay away! There is danger here! We have been found! Do not come, we are all dead! Stay away!"*

"Brandon! No! Brandon! Brandon, love, answer me! Brandon!"

He wouldn't answer her; she had to stay away. He knew she would feel him but if he answered, she might come, and she must not, not right now. She would be killed. He could still hear the bullets ricocheting off the walls as the men and the silenced weapons made their march of death through the building.

Dianna popped in the hallway of the ground floor, right into automatic weapons fire. Before she could recover from the sixty rounds that had gone through her body, four men put handcuffs and shackles on her arms and legs, then wrapped wire cable around her. A man walked up to her, all she could see was his boots, so tightly she was bound. A French accented voice said, "Hello, Isisi."

Brandon had felt her arrival, he began to cry, *"Oh no, please, God, no! Why didn't you listen to me! Why are you here!"*

"Go Brandon, go, my love. I release you."

"NOOOO!"

He was looking down on the Ballard district of Seattle from several hundred feet up, looking for anything that would catch his interest. Following the Ballard Bridge and going straight up Fifteenth Avenue NW, he looked around the high school, and then drifted toward the University District and I-5 over the hill. Not seeing anything over that way, he turned his attention back toward Ballard. Following the ship canal to the Ballard Locks, he turned at the 7-11 and followed up Thirty-second Ave toward the top of the hill. When he got to Sixty-seventh Street, he found it. From the outside, everything looked fine. At one time, it had been a local museum, now it was abandoned and had been purchased by a private party. It was here.

Erick snapped out of his trance, sitting on the bedroom floor in his room at the mansion. He grabbed his cell phone and called Hawk. Soon as it was answered he said, "Go to the old school. It's off Thirty-second Avenue toward Thirtieth between Sixty-seventh and Sixty-eighth Streets. I'll meet you there."

He grabbed his coat and disappeared.

He appeared on the sidewalk on the south side of the building, next to the old playground on Sixty-seventh. He was hidden by the large maple trees on one side and a concrete retaining wall for the playground on the other. The playground was raised above street level by about five feet, the chain link fence on top of the wall was barely rusted considering its age, and there was a set of steps leading up to the playground from the sidewalk. Erick had chosen to arrive here because he would mostly be concealed from both the building and the neighbors across the street. Moving to the steps, he sat down on the fourth one and peered over the edge at the structure. It was almost eleven, and most of the lights in the houses were out, and the street was still.

It was quiet, too quiet. The building was one of the gray stone structures built around here in the early to middle of the twentieth century. All the windows on the ground floor were covered in plywood; graffiti covered the walls. Most of the buildings were either schools or libraries. This one had started life as an elementary school. Three stories high with a basement, the ceilings were high at twelve feet. The city sold it when it was found to contain asbestos by the contractor doing a refit for false ceilings in the late seventies. They found it was cheaper to build a new school and sell this one than to remove the asbestos and remodel it. For most of the next forty years it had been a museum. The organization that owned it got fewer visitors every year, and the supporters of it had died off. Eventually they decided to sell it. They just couldn't afford to keep it up anymore.

An SUV turned the corner and parked at the end of the playground down the street. Two figures got out and began to walk slowly toward Erick. As they came up to him, Hawk and Duncan crouched down with him on the steps. "It's too quiet. Where are Mac and Lauren?"

"About three blocks away now I'd say, coming from the north on Thirtieth," Hawk whispered.

Right on cue, the headlights of a Suburban came into view on Thirtieth. It passed the front of the building and made a left on Sixty-seventh and parked down the street across from the Escalade. A few moments later, Mac and Lauren came up. The steps were getting a little crowded. Erick looked at each in turn, "You guys getting anything?" They all shook their heads. "Am I wrong?"

"Nay, I don't think so," Duncan murmured, "I smell the Nightwalkers."

"Well, we aren't going to learn anything here. I'm going to check this out a little. Stay here." With that, Erick started up the steps to the playground.

As he walked away from the steps, he began to get a feeling of being watched. Whoever it was, if it was anyone at all, was too far away to hear a heartbeat. The only ones he heard were the four in the stairwell, two Darrks and two humans. The streetlamp on the edge of the playground offered little light through the bare limbs of the trees, and there was hardly any light on the playground itself. Erick walked over to the back door, and trying the knob, he found it unlocked. He gently pushed open the door. Most humans are afraid of the dark to one degree or another, but a Darrk is *raised* in it. Erick investigated the pitch-black hallway, and for the first time in his life, he felt apprehensive, not because of the lack of light— he could see clearly—it was more a feeling he wouldn't like what he found. He entered the building.

After Erick had been inside for about ten minutes, they felt they should do something. Finally, Duncan had had enough. "Hawk let's go for a walk. Mac, you, and your mum follow behind a minute after we enter the building. He said stay here, but not the whole bloody night." He stood and started up the steps, followed by Hawk. Both Hawk and Duncan started to feel uneasy when they were about ten feet from the steps, still sixty feet from the door. "We may be walking into a trap, lad. You want to keep going?" Duncan whispered.

"Safer in the building than out here in the open," Hawk whispered back.

"Aye. You see anything?"

"No. You want to warn Mac?"

"No. If we get there without trouble they should too. I bet you a bottle of my finest he'll know the danger like us anyway."

"He will." They got to the entrance and walked inside.

"I don't like this." Mac was looking all over but couldn't see anything that would make him this uneasy. It was more a feeling.

"Me either, let's go." Lauren stood and headed up the stairs.

Like the others had, about ten feet away from the steps Mac felt he was being watched, but he pushed on. If the others had made it across, they would to. As the two of them entered the building, he pulled the door shut behind them. "Did you feel that?" He looked at his mother as she nodded her head. They turned and looked down the hall, not seeing any of the others, but there was a bluish glow coming from a room five doors down and the murmur of voices was coming from the room. There was what sounded like a slapping or smacking sound as well coming from inside. Mac touched her shoulder and pointed to the ashes of Nightwalkers against the wall. The wall itself was riddled with bullet holes. As they slowly crept down the hall, Mac drew his weapon and held his .45 in front of him.

They finally reached the door and looked inside. It was an old classroom, and the chalkboard still on the wall was covered in graffiti. In the center of the room was an old steel chair with chains on the floor around the base of it, the unmistakable blue-green of Darrk blood was on the chair and chains. The light was coming from a television on a stand in the corner of the room with a DVD player on the shelf under it. A little sign on the player said, "Press ON Button." The three men were riveted to the TV screen. Lauren couldn't see it, but heard Dianna's slurred voice screaming, "GO FUCK YOURSELF!" Then there was a thud. Erick turned and walked into the hall with his face hard and unreadable. Finally seeing the TV, Lauren saw that the screen was black.

Both Duncan and Hawk turned, and with glassy eyes, Hawk looked at Mac, "Watch it," was all he said before he followed Duncan into the hall. Mac knew he didn't want to, but he also knew he had to. Mac pressed the "PLAY" button. Nothing in all his years could have prepared him for what he saw in the next five minutes. The recording started. They'd stripped Dianna naked, cutting her clothes off. There were four of them; none of their faces were visible. They were only visible from the shoulders down. In the next frame, Dianna was chained to a chair as a man walked up to her and dealt four hard, quick blows to her head with his fist. Then he spoke in a voice with a French accent, "Again, what did you tell him about Con? Did you tell him about Mexico City?"

Defiantly, she said, "Fuck you!" She then spat teeth and blue-green blood at him. This was followed by several more blows to her head and body. She was then struck on both sides of her head by at least two men in fast forward. Then the recording slowed again, and the same accented voice spoke, "Eventually, you will tell me what I want. The thing I love about your kind is this can go on all night. We ask questions, you don't answer, and we get to beat you more. We let you heal some; then we get to start over. Isn't that so much fun? But I wouldn't wait too long, you will run out of the power that makes you recuperate so well." He then took a battery-powered drill, and placing it against her thigh, he drilled a hole through her leg with a long half-inch drill bit as she screamed. The scream was muffled by a piece of her dress that was wrapped around her head and pulled tightly between her teeth by one of the men. The frame stopped, and then it started again. What Mac saw on the screen didn't resemble Dianna, her face was just a mass of torn, bleeding flesh. Her eyes couldn't be seen. Her face had swollen over them. There were holes drilled into her shoulders, arms, and legs. Her hands were taped to the chair and had been shattered so badly you couldn't see any fingers. Patches of her hair had been torn from her head and were lying on the floor around the chair. The same voice demanded, "Did you tell him about Con? Did you tell him about Mexico City?"

A croaking, gurgling sound came from the faceless thing in the chair, "Yes." Then it suddenly got stronger and louder as she continued, "And I hope when he finds you, he castrates you and stuffs your balls in your mouth just before he tears the skin off you, rips your eyes out, and fucks the holes!" A savage blow to her head made her body go slack.

The French voice spoke, "Rahm, you will give us the key. You will assist in fixing the ship. You, your friends, and family cannot hide. We will keep this one, and we will keep this up, and when or if she dies, we will take another, maybe one that will die much easier, eh? But I will be generous. I'll give you a week, just like this one did, eh? But remember, in one week we will do this all over again. She should heal by then, if she doesn't die. I've never seen one of your kind like this before, so? And I will get to tell her how much her brother loves her by leaving her with me. But I wouldn't waste too much time. I don't know how much more of this we can do before she really does die . . . eh?"

Behind him in the video, Dianna defiantly did her best to pick her head up and screamed, "GO FUCK YOURSELF!" Then one of the faceless cowards walked up and crushed her skull with a steel pipe.

Mac wiped the tears off his face, and in the coldest voice Lauren had ever heard from her boy, he said, "I'm just getting started." Then he shot the TV.

They stood in the hall, not saying a word for what must have been ten minutes. Duncan looked up and said, "I'm going to rip their heads off and while they are still looking around, piss in their faces, and shit down their necks!"

Then Erick picked his head up, and looking at his friends, calmly said, "I've got a much better idea." Duncan, Mac and Lauren looked at that calm face, then Lauren felt a chill go right down to her bones.

When they exited, they did so cautiously, in case whoever watched them go in was still there. This was the time when they had to worry. It was an old trick: you let your enemy in, then you kill him when he came out. Erick would watch while the others spread out and made their way back to the steps. If he saw anything, he would go and take care of it. He told Hawk and Mac to try to keep Duncan between whoever was watching and them, but they didn't know where the watcher was. They were most vulnerable in those first few seconds. Duncan, Hawk, Mac, and Lauren left together, spread in a line with Mac and Hawk between them.

The first bullet soundlessly grazed Duncan's shoulder but missed everyone else. Erick saw the flash of light about 300 yards away and popped out of view. He didn't stop the second shot in time. This bullet was already traveling when Erick arrived suddenly on the roof next to the shooter and smashed his fist into the side of the man's head, immediately rendering him unconscious. When he and the sniper popped back over at the museum, Hawk was lying on the concrete with a hole in his side.

"Sorry, Gramps, I forgot to duck," he wheezed.

Erick felt a chill go through him. He had thought that by giving the sniper so many targets he would hit Duncan or Lauren, they would heal, but Hawk? He wasn't fast enough, and the sniper got his grandson. He was wrong. The sniper either knew what he was looking for or was just lucky. They had shot his grandson! Hell was coming and bringing eternity with him.

The bullet had struck Hawk on the upper right side. It went through the arm missing the bone and went through the triceps, exited out the arm, striking him just under the armpit in the area doctor's call the right hypochondriac region between the fifth and sixth ribs. There wasn't much blood, leading Erick and Lauren to believe it had missed his liver. But his wheezing and the fact it was hard for him to breathe made Lauren think it had pierced the right lung. There was no exit wound. When Lauren asked if he could stand, Hawk said he didn't think so, he couldn't feel his legs.

"We need to get him in the car and get him to a hospital." Lauren was moving and thinking professionally. Mac interrupted her. "If we take him to a hospital, there may be too many questions. If we take him to Doc at the office, he can do everything, even surgery, there. But can we move him without back support?"

"Won't have to. Call Doc. Tell him what's coming his way. We will be in the X-ray room as that's the one room I know well enough that I won't risk appearing in the middle of the wall. Can you get this piece of shit to the mansion?" Erick said, pointing at the sniper.

"No problem," Duncan said. "I might be driving on the wrong side of the road here and there, but maybe I'll get lucky and kill this fuck!"

"Keep him alive. We have to chat."

With that, he placed his hand on Hawk's shoulder, and they vanished.

While Mac was trying to get Doc on the phone, Duncan whistled, "I don't know a one of us that can take another."

"And you have no idea how far," Lauren said before she left, following Erick.

Doc was in bed having a nightmare. Thrashing around on the bed, he had the top sheet tangled around him. The first chime of his cell phone on the nightstand snapped him awake. He picked it up before the third chime, and seeing it was Mac, answered, "What's happened!"

Mac didn't even take the time to wonder how Doc knew something was wrong. "Hawk's in the X-ray room with Erick and Mom. He has a .308 round in his chest with possible spinal damage."

"Got it!" Scrambling from his bed, emergency mode, as Doc called it, took over.

Erick came into the X-ray room on the floor next to the table as the automatic lights came on, startling him. Lauren showed up a few seconds after.

"I'm going to get some gauze and some towels," she said, going through the door, leaving it open. She looked across the lab and headed toward a cabinet by the exam table, just as Doc came through the door from the hall, slamming it behind him in his haste.

"How is he?" he asked, rushing past Lauren.

"Don't really know. We had no way to take vitals, but his pulse is ninety-six and steady, has no feeling in his legs." Opening the cabinet, she grabbed two sheets, a handful of towels, and a box of six-inch gauze pads. Doc veered over to the wall, and taking a backboard off it, headed straight to the X-ray room.

Raven and Elliot were still in her office working when they heard the commotion in the hall of someone running from the elevator. Then they heard a door slam in the hallway. Raven, not more than a few minutes ago, had gotten a severe pain in her chest that was bad enough that Elliot was about to call Doc. when it suddenly turned into a dull ache. They were discussing this when the commotion started. "Hawk," she breathed as all color left her face. She stood and ran past Elliot through the door into the hall, running the short distance to the medical office. Swiping her ID card in the lock next to the door. She heard the click and entered, followed by Elliot.

As they entered, she saw Doc ducking into the X-ray room and ran that direction. When she got to the doorway, she saw Hawk on the floor. There was a small pool of blood under him. Her breath caught and she covered her mouth so she wouldn't scream. Doc saw her and Elliot at the door. He knew the best way to keep her from not being overwhelmed and going into shock was to make them work. "Elliot." No response. "ELLIOT!" That did it, he saw the man shake his head and look at him.

"Yes."

"Next to the exam table, there are two large bags, red with a yellow stripe, get them." Without saying a word, Elliot turned and ran to comply. "Raven," she looked at him. "Take Lauren to the locker room next to the sterile lab and help her scrub up." Lauren stood and left for the locker room with Raven, just as Elliot came back with the two bags. "Okay, get in here!" Elliot suddenly looked calmer, Erick noted.

"What do you need me to do?" Elliot said, as he crouched down.

"This is the way this is going to go. You are the gofer, under-stood?" Elliot nodded. "I'll tell you what to do, just follow my instructions to the letter. Can you do that?" Another nod. "Okay, what you just brought are two trauma bags. Unzip both and open them wide. Inside bag one, you will see a blood pressure cuff and stethoscope, hand them to me. In bag two, you will see a pouch with what looks like a bag of water with a coil of tubing in it, give that to Erick. Good. Now reach over here and keep this gauze I'm holding tight against Hawk's side so I can let go." After Elliot did as instructed, Doc removed his hand and grabbed the cuff and stethoscope. He began to take Hawk's vitals, paying close atten-tion to his breathing, while Erick started an IV. When this was done, Doc reached in the first bag and pulled out a sealed, loaded syringe, which he promptly injected into the IV.

Hawk, who had been conscious through all of this, looked at Elliot as the morphine started to hit him and smiled, "Thanks, watch my sister for me, because she's going to freak. I got to go to lala land for a bit." With this, he shut his eyes and went to sleep.

"Good job, Elliot," Doc said.

"Yes, Elliot. Thank you." Erick looked tired and sat back for a moment.

Doc let him rest while he did a full examination on Hawk. When he was done, he looked at Erick and Elliot, "Think the three of us can get him on the backboard without moving his spine?" Both nodded. Doc laid the board next to Hawk. Erick, being the strongest, grabbed Hawk's upper body and shoulders, cupping his head in the crook of his elbow so it wouldn't move. He placed a cervical collar on Hawk while Doc moved the backboard. The biggest problem was keeping Hawk's upper body in its current position. Doc took the center and the hips. Elliot took Hawk's legs, keeping them in the position they were already in as instructed. Doc said, "On three. One . . . two . . . three! Perfect, guys. Let's pick him up and get him on the X-ray table so we can get an X-ray." Doc wished the new MRI machine was set up, but it was still in its crates.

Lauren poked her head around the corner shortly thereafter and asked how Hawk was. "Stable. He's got a bleed in the right lung and perhaps a pinched nerve, I don't think the spine is severed. But we need to move him to the other room and remove that bullet, can you set up for a few X-rays?"

"Yes. Erick, are you alright?"

He looked pale and very tired. "Transporting Hawk used the last of what reserves I had, I'll need to . . . eat to recover." He was trying to be careful what he said before Elliot.

Doc looked at him, "I thought so. I may be able to help there." Looking at Lauren with a smile on his face, he said, "Lauren, you want to bring what we cooked up?" She worriedly returned his smile and turned and ran away. Erick was puzzled somewhat. He knew Lauren had spent a lot of time in the lab with Doc. In the days after Eileen's death, he was taking care of arrangements for her funeral. He knew he wasn't the best person to be around then. After Johnathan came from Virginia, they had spent time with Raven on business matters. It helped to keep Raven, and him as well, he had to admit, focused and not so depressed.

Lauren spent her time in the lab to give Erick some space, but he thought they were working on the aging of Darrks and the abilities and processes they had shared with their mixed offspring. When she came back, she handed Doc a beaker of a rust colored fluid and a small glass. It looked familiar to Erick,

"I'll set up for the X-rays," she said, "you can explain what we found, Doc." Then she left the room to head to the X-ray booth to prepare the films.

Doc held the beaker up. "It wasn't as hard to find as I thought," he began, "using Lauren's blood, some samples I had of Mac and Hawk's blood, and a sample of my own, we broke it down and singled out what my blood had, then did the same for Hawk and Mac. When we did Lauren's, there was only one thing all our blood had, which hers did not. It was hidden in the hemoglobin." He poured some of the red fluid into a glass and handed it to Erick. "Try this. Lauren said it appeared right to her, as it took away that 'itch' she felt that told her she needed to feed. She also said she wouldn't know for sure until her body had become stressed and had burnt up her body's reserves. Then, if it worked and returned her strength, she would know for sure that we were on the right track. She has been waiting, but you may have just saved her from starving herself."

Erick looked at the fluid in the glass for a moment, it looked like the breakfast drink all Darrks used to have at the start of their day aboard ship, just a little darker. He took a small sip. It tasted like it as well, and almost immediately, his strength began to return. He drank about half the glass and found himself stronger—all the fatigue had left him. Something told him to stop though. He knew more would be too much and told Doc so. "If I drink any more, something tells me I might not like the result."

"Interesting. Lauren said the exact same thing."

Lauren returned with two X-ray panels a few moments later. She looked at Erick, "Well, what do you think?"

"I think you've found it." If it hadn't been for how worried they were about Hawk, Lauren would have thrown a party.

Doc and Lauren were examining the X-rays when Mac came in the lab, closing the door behind him slowly. He saw Raven in scrubs, standing behind them, with Erick's arms around her. "Well?"

"We will know in a moment." Erick looked at him, "And our guest?"

"Duncan found a nice comfortable room for him." He grinned, "In the walk-in freezer off the main kitchen."

"It isn't on."

"It is now," Mac replied with about the biggest smile Erick had ever seen on his face.

Erick let it go as Doc turned around, but he had to work hard not to smile himself.

Doc began, "I'd like to say everything is fine, but I can't. The bullet came in between the fifth and sixth ribs right under his armpit. The arm itself will be fine. In fact, it's already healing, and the wound closed itself without any stiches or cleaning. But the bullet is another matter. It appears to have grazed his lung with little damage and seems to have closed itself. The bullet missed the liver and traveled further in and buried itself against the sixth and seventh thoracic vertebrae—why he can't move his legs. I think it's just the swelling that is causing the paralysis. It has damaged the disk I think, but on the X-ray looks like it's just between the verte-brae against the disk although there is a crack in the seventh. The problem is removing it, I might do more damage than has been done already. But the bullet is intact and didn't fragment. It didn't hit bone until it hit the spine and had slowed considerably by then."

"Will he be alright with leaving the bullet in?" Mac asked this, as he'd known many guys who were around with a bullet in them.

"I don't think so. With all the nerves coming out of his spine there, it is sitting against a bundle of them, which can cause prob-lems. I'm not a neurologist. So, for the most part, I just don't know."

Erick thought for a moment before he spoke, "Remove the bullet. If he's healing like you said he is, his body will want to reject it and removing it will help him heal faster."

Lauren agreed, "If we leave it in, it will actually take longer for him to heal as his body will try and move it to the surface."

"Okay." He looked at Lauren, "Ready, my dear?"

Doc, Mac, and Erick scrubbed up and moved Hawk on the board into the sterile lab. Mac retreated to the observation room where Raven and Elliot were. They watched through the large window between them. Doc pulled in the ventilator and inserted the tube down Hawk's throat. He had Erick watching it and mon-itoring Hawk's vitals, while Lauren and he busied themselves set-ting up for surgery. It was time to begin.

An hour later, Doc finished closing Hawk up, and stripping off his gloves as he went, he walked into observation. "He's going to be fine. I've never seen anyone heal like that, except you," he said, looking at Mac. "I almost didn't put the stitches in, and the bullet all but popped out on its own. The lung is already almost healed. I looked at it while I was in there. Lauren's going to remove the tube and he should be able to breathe on his own already. You should be able to talk to him in the morning, well, later this morning." Looking at the clock, he realized it was 2:00 A.M. "I'm taking a nap," he said with a yawn. With that he walked off toward the locker room while Mac held a crying Raven.

Elliot breathed a sigh of relief, "Thank God."

"Thanks, Doc." Mac was almost crying himself.

Doc waved over his shoulder and kept going.

Erick walked up to Mac, "I'm going to change; then there's someone I need to talk to. I'll meet you at the house."

"Oh, yes." Mac looked at Elliot, knowing he couldn't stay, and Elliot's silent nod told him he would stay with Raven. "I got to go, hon." She nodded, saying she'd be okay, and Elliot gently put his arm around her as she leaned against him.

Then Lauren came up, and looking at Elliot said, "He's sleeping and is going to be fine. Will you stay with him? I have to go with them."

"Absolutely," Elliot answered.

"I'm going to stay with Hawk and Elliot." Raven looked at her brother asleep in the bed.

"Okay." Lauren gave her a hug, then she went to change.

Boyce Danton looked at one of his men in disbelief, "What do you mean you haven't heard from him? He hasn't come in?"

"No."

Boyce cursed in French, but the man had no idea what it meant; his native language was Italian. They always spoke in English. Both men were dressed in black fatigue pants, black sweaters, and combat boots, as were the other five men in the next room. Dianna was lying on a dirty mattress, gagged and chained to the floor in another small room off the main room.

"Take two of the others with you, go to where he was, and then check the old museum."

"Yes, sir."

Dianna heard them in the next room. They were going after the one with the orders to "shoot the youngest one when they come out" because he hadn't come in. Good. That meant they had caught or killed him. If he were alive, they might be able to get information out of him as to where this place was. But she couldn't count on that; she had to be realistic. As far as she was concerned, she hoped they found him with his balls stuffed in his ears. She was playing possum, lying still on the mattress with her back to the door. They were looking in at her every twenty minutes or so.

She was healing slowly, too much damage had been done and she was in a great deal of pain. But she damned sure wasn't going to let that sadistic fucking French Canadian know. She needed blood to heal. All her reserves were gone, and she was extremely low on her own blood. Without it, she could take hours to heal, if at all. Fact was, she admitted to herself, she was dying.

Erick removed the pin in the door to the walk-in freezer and opened it wide, letting a chill fog run out onto the floor. The man was in the corner. Duncan and Mac had stripped him to just his pants and socks, taking his sweater and boots. He was crunched up in a small a ball as he could manage, shivering. Erick looked at him, "Well, you seem quite comfortable. Nothing but the best for our guests." He stepped inside, the man sat there and just glared at him. "I see this going one of two ways. One, you tell me where my sister is and we decide what to do with you later, or two, you go through twice the pain you inflicted on my sister and tell me anyway. Which way do you want it?"

"You won't do that," he replied in a Russian accent. "You give me to police."

"You think so? Oh, pardon me."

The man shot off the floor like he had been shot out of a gun slamming into the roof of the freezer and bouncing off, then hung in the air between the roof and the floor. The wind had been knocked out of him, and his nose was dripping blood on the floor. Nothing touched him and yet he hung there, the fear in his eyes plain. "This is how this will go," Erick said as he slowly walked a circle around the man. A feeling of heat had started on the Russians cold skin, and soon it became a burning, steadily getting worse. "You see, my sister healed between your attacks on her body, and then more pain was inflicted. I can't do that to you because you will die, but I can do it in such a way as you will *wish you did*." He'd raised his voice the last three words. He wanted to let the Russian know he was serious, *dead* serious. The burning had become a searing pain all over his body, as if his skin was being roasted away. His breath came back and he started to scream, when suddenly the burning stopped and the pain was gone. Erick knew he could have touched him and got what he needed, but he wanted this one to know the pain he had helped put his sister through. He stared at Erick with hatred and yelled in Russian for Erick to do something that was anatomically impossible.

The burning started again, then the searing, and he began to scream again and again, then the pain stopped. "Die, Yankee pig!"

"Oh, you first please, I insist."

It started as a small headache, it soon became a migraine, and then he thought his head was going to explode. Then it eased back to just a headache, then the migraine, in Russian, he screamed, "Stop, stop!"

"Where is she?"

The headache stopped suddenly, and he fell to the floor. In Russian, he then began to give Erick an address in Lynnwood, just north of Seattle, then repeated it twice more in English. Erick grabbed him by the shoulder digging his fingernails in an inch deep and looked into his eyes. All the Russian saw was his death in those two blue orbs. "If you believe in God, I recommend you start praying she is still alive." He spun on his heel and stormed out of the freezer and shut the door. Putting the pin back in, he turned toward Duncan as Mac walked in.

"You were right," Duncan began, "you did have a better idea."

Lauren was understandably upset, as was Mac. Duncan wasn't saying anything. After what he'd seen Erick do in the freezer, he knew the last thing he needed to do was worry about Erick. Erick wanted to go alone, and he knew he could do it. They wouldn't be able to take him by surprise. If anything, they would be surprised by him. He knew this had to be done quickly. He could see it in the Russian's mind, and if his assessment was right, his sister was dying. He needed to get to her fast. A compromise was quickly made. Lauren and Duncan would give Erick five minutes before they followed. Mac would take the Escalade and meet them there. Soon as they said they agreed, Mac was running out the door, and Erick left just as fast.

Getting the layout of the house from the mind of the Russian, he took a risk and transported himself right into the living room of the small house. Three men were playing cards at a table in the corner. They didn't even have time to react, all three fell unconscious suddenly, one sliding off his chair onto the floor with a thud.

"What's going on out there?" A voice in accented French came from the kitchen through a door. As it opened, a white-haired man saw Erick and began to reach for a 9mm under his left arm, but he stopped halfway there with his hand across his chest. He tried to move and found he couldn't. It was as if he had been frozen in a block of ice, he could breathe but not speak. He could move his eyes but not turn his head.

"I'll deal with you soon enough." Erick's look of fury at the man was frightening, but knowing what he had done to Dianna left him terrified for his immediate future.

Erick went to the hallway and opened the first door, the room next to the kitchen. His sister was lying naked on a filthy mattress, her back to the door. Her wounds were half healed, and her body was almost spent. He barely heard her heart. The locks on the chains that were bolted to the floor suddenly fell away, and he moved closer, "Sis." He couldn't speak more than that, he couldn't even cry, he felt a sudden pang of fear that he was too late. It was as if his heart had left him.

"Rahm? Are you really here?" Dianna couldn't see, her eyes were still swollen shut. He barely heard her through the shattered lips—she was so weak. He moved closer, and putting his arm under her shoulders, he gently turned her over.

"Yes, Isisi, it's me."

She began to cry, large sobs came from her, and she tried to wrap her broken arms with so many holes in the bones around him, but they wouldn't work. He removed a large water bottle from inside his coat. It was full of the rust colored liquid from Doc. He removed the top and held it to her shattered lips, "Drink this." She took a gulp from the bottle, then threw up half of it. "Slowly! Slowly . . . just sip a little at a time." As soon Dianna could grab the bottle on her own, he let her take it. She kept sipping a little at a time and soon sat up on her own. Erick removed his long wool coat and draped it over her shoulders. She finished the bottle and just sat there for a moment, leaning on her brother, crying. As Erick watched, the swelling in her face and lips went down. Soon, he could see her eyes again, and he saw new teeth begin to replace the ones that were missing, and her lips healed. He heard the snapping and popping of her bones moving back into place and healing. Grimacing through the pain, she began to take deeper breaths as her ribs healed. What had looked like pulp at the ends of her arms became hands, the fingers straightening. She had far to go, but she wasn't in as much pain anymore, the relief on her face clear.

He saw Dianna looking over his shoulder and turned. He already knew who was there. He'd felt them arrive. Lauren and Duncan were standing in the doorway. There were tears rolling down Lauren's cheeks. They had seen Dianna before she had begun to heal. Erick had been right—five more minutes and she would have been dead. The look on Duncan's face mirrored his own. Con would pay for this. He'd released an animal on Dianna. Erick thought, *hell was coming. Fuck eternity. The devil was coming for you, Con, and you've let him loose!*

Erick, Duncan, and Mac were sitting on the chairs at the table when the other three men came in after looking for their missing man. They were smart enough to stop when they saw the other four, bound with coaxial cable and electric cords, piled on top of each other in the middle of the living room floor. The guns under their coats flew out into the corner. Eight Mac 10s with sound suppressors were on the table, having been taken from the back bedroom. The dark haired one with the white hair on the sides sat in the middle and looked at them coldly, "Let me see your hands." They looked at each other, puzzled. "Last chance, *your hands!*" They held out their hands, palms up. "The other side." As they turned their hands over, bruised knuckles on two of the men on the right of Erick gave them away. They suddenly screamed and fell to the floor, twisted in agony, until after a few moments, they died, the pain etched on their faces.

The one that was left opened his eyes wide as he looked at the two on the floor with blood coming out of nose and ears. "It's okay," Erick said in a calm voice as he looked at him, "the brains in their heads? They thought it best to explode and won't be needed anymore. They weren't using them anyway." He paused. The man got scared; the try at dark humor from this man was not good.

"Ah, I have your attention." Erick stood, "You're the lucky one, you may have been there. Although I think if you were, you would have joined these two," he pointed at the floor. "Lucky you." He looked the man straight in the eye, the man looked down at the floor; he didn't feel so lucky. "Head up." He kept looking at the floor. "HEAD UP!" his voice booming in the small room. "You want to run with these animals, then by God, own what you do!" The man picked his head up but still wouldn't look Erick in the eye. Good enough.

"You truly are the lucky one this morning. I have a message I want you to deliver. I have a message for Con. You listening to me?" He nodded. "Answer me! Are you listening!"

"Yes!"

"I give the same time he gave me, one week. He must answer by then. These are the terms. He can't hide from me, and it won't matter how many of you thugs he throws at me. It won't matter how many Nightwalkers he has. It won't even matter how many Darrks. Tell him he started this. He started this pain. If he wishes to feel this pain, so be it. I'll tear his place here on this world apart and teach him the meaning of pain. And in the end, as he bleeds on the floor, he'll know he is never going home. Or, I'll give him the precious key he desires so much and the ship. He can take whatever whining Darrks he has left and go on his merry way; with nothing. But if he harms one more of my family or friends ever again, I'll burn that cardboard world of his down to the ground with him in it. If he leaves my family alone, I'll fix the ship and give him the key. *That* is my message. *Those* are my terms. Go." The man looked at him like he was kidding him and didn't move. "I said go!" He turned and bolted out the door.

"You can't give him the key!" Dianna cried, standing in the hallway entrance, a blanket wrapped around her. "That's what he wants! You know this!" Tears came down her face. "He'll go back to Darrk and bring back the fleet! They'll destroy this world. We can't let him do that!" Erick went to her and wrapped his arms around her.

"It's okay. I have no intention of letting him get to Darrk," he whispered. Her crying stopped, and she looked at him, puzzled. "I'm going to let him have something much worse."

As they were leaving, Dianna looked at the Frenchman on the floor. "I want to bring this one." He was looking up at her defiantly.

"Why? Leave him here to die, lass." Duncan said.

"No, he has a much worse fate coming."

Duncan looked at Erick, "Bring him." Erick looked down at the Frenchman, then squatted next to him and said, "You . . . are fucked."

Erick looked around the room as Mac carried the Frenchman out the door, then he came back and gently carried Dianna to the car. The wires and cables had been removed from the three who were still alive. Paralyzed, they lay on the floor next to the two that were dead. They had found two dead in one of the back bedrooms, apparently victims of the assault on the museum. They were left there. Their eyes open, they stared at Erick in fear. "Sorry, boys, but the party's over. You have been found guilty." He watched the Escalade pull away in the predawn stillness. Erick's eyes looked at something in the air. In the basement, the gas line on the furnace suddenly came undone and gas started to fill the house. In the bedroom down the hall, a candle burned behind a closed door. Mac had assured him the neighbors would lose a few windows and have the shit scared out of them, but no one would get hurt. With a last look at the men, he gave them a small, lopsided salute, and vanished back to the mansion.

Moments later, there was an explosion, killing the three men and burning up the house. The investigator of the fire would say, several days later, a gas main had failed and a scented candle in the bedroom had set off the gas, killing the seven occupants inside.

Erick arrived on the back lawn by the bench and instantly felt the Nightwalker. The sun would be up in a few minutes, why was it out?

"Erick, Erick Scott!"

He spun around, looking around the yard, and he saw Brandon lying under the bushes. He went over to him and looked down at him. His right arm was missing from the elbow down. There was a bullet hole in the side of his head and several more bullet holes in his hoodie. "You have to help her, I couldn't. You have to help my mistress! They'll kill her! Please don't let them kill her, not my mistress." He was crying, which was rare for a vampire. Tears of blood rolled down his face, and it looked as if he didn't have any to spare. *There has been too much crying lately,* Erick thought. And it all was because of one Darrk. The sun started to come up and Brandon began to smoke. Erick went to pick him up, and he fought him, "No, go help Dianna! Please! Go help her." Then his strength left him. Erick gently picked him up and quickly carried him smoking down the hill to the guesthouse, the door opened for him as he approached. As he entered the living room, the bookshelf opened, and he went into the hidden tunnel. There he gently lay Brandon on the floor; going back to the bedroom, he grabbed a pillow and pulled the sheet off the bed. Running back to Brandon, he placed the pillow under his head, then tore the sheet in strips, wrapping the stump of his missing arm and his head. He suddenly opened his eyes. "No! Please! Go help my mistress . . ."

"It's okay. Brandon. She's safe, she's safe. Go to sleep now, go to sleep and heal."

He stared at Brandon for a moment, "I'll be damned," was all he could say. Brandon must have walked all the way from the museum in Ballard. With his arm missing and all the holes in him, he would have been too weak to fly, too drained to heal. He had walked to the only place he knew of that would help Dianna. "I'll be damned."

When they arrived at the mansion, Dianna was asleep. Mac picked up Dianna, and at Erick's suggestion, carried her to the guesthouse and placed her on the bed Erick had just remade with clean bedding. She would know when she woke that Brandon was there, and that Erick had left the door to the passage open. He would be easy to find. When Mac returned, Erick and Duncan had already put the Frenchman in the freezer with his sniper. They had turned off the freezer after interrogating him, but it was still cold in the eight-by-ten foot space. Erick didn't want them to get comfortable. So he turned it back on and set the thermostat for twenty degrees. Looking at Mac, he said, "a summer day in Siberia." Duncan said he would keep an eye on them and not to worry. He might even feed them occasionally and give them a bucket for a bathroom.

Erick called the pilot who had been waiting for them and said they were going to be late and wouldn't start out until the afternoon. Then he went upstairs and knocked on Johnathan's door, and telling him they were not going to leave until two in the afternoon, he told him of the events of the night before. Johnathan said he was going to take a cab to the office and see how Raven and Hawk were doing, and asked Erick to meet them there. Erick said to call Mac; he was leaving in a few minutes to be with Raven and Hawk, too.

Lauren had already gone upstairs for a shower, and Erick went down the hall to the bedroom. Opening the door, he saw her sprawled on the bed still dressed. He went to the bed, kicked off his shoes and lay down next to her. He was asleep in seconds.

At noon, Erick woke and looked around the room. Lauren wasn't there but hadn't been gone too long; there was still moisture on the mirror in the bathroom from her shower, and water on the floor. He showered and dressed. Almost taking a suit out of the closet, he stopped himself, grabbing blue jeans and a button-down long-sleeved plaid shirt, instead; thinking that maybe Lauren is right, that he did need to change his wardrobe choices. The casual clothes certainly were more comfortable. He wasn't a banker anymore anyway; he was the last engineer. As he headed downstairs, he felt the presence of another Darrk. He stopped on the top of the stairs. There were two suitcases in front of one of the empty rooms with Canadian flag decals of the maple leaf on the sides. He started down the stairs and was heading for the freezer on the ground floor to check on his "guests," but he decided to go to the rec room instead.

As he entered the rec room, he saw a case of Scotch sitting on the bar. Duncan, and a man who looked familiar, were tasting some out of an open bottle on the bar. Lauren was standing there with that look he knew all too well, her "you guys are crazy" look. He soon found out why. "You drink a whole bottle and walk to the patio from the bar on your hands and I will give you a case!" Duncan laughed. Then he saw Erick. "Hey!" It became obvious they had had more than one when he saw that the bottle they were drinking from was close to the bottom. "Me scotch finally cleared Customs!"

"I see that," he laughed and said, "Erick Scott," introducing himself, and holding out his hand.

"Robert Hamm, but call me Bobby, please."

They shook hands when it dawned on Erick who the lanky man was. Dressed in jeans and a snap down, long-sleeved western shirt; he also was wearing a brown leather vest and matching cowboy boots. There was also a tan cowboy hat on the bar. "Regin?"

"Was, yes. Your name back then was Rahm, wasn't it? The only engineer who made it here."

"Yes." He looked at Lauren, a bit puzzled, "Do you know why you're here?"

"Yes and no. I came when I got the message it was time and an address. That's all I needed."

Lauren answered with what Erick genuinely wanted to know. "No details are sent. It was decided the last time we all met together that the call to come would be a simple one. It would simply be 'it was time' and an address of where to meet. Bobby's cab dropped him here an hour ago. Duncan has already taken his bags upstairs. Details would be filled in at a meeting when all had arrived."

"I'm on your side," Bobby said. "None of us that show up here in the next few days want to see that ship return to Darrk. We all call earth our home now, for however long we live. And if by chance we must give up our lives to keep that ship here, we'll do it. Eighty-six hundred years is enough anyway, far as I'm concerned. I know you can't destroy the key; we all know what that would do. We may as well let them have the key and the ship, because the destruction would still kill this planet just as if we brought the fleet ourselves. We can't count on them not training another engineer, no matter how difficult that task may be; a lucky break is all they would need. I know the manuals for the ship were removed when we left, but someone must have them. I had hoped it was you, but from what I hear it was someone else. The tech has gotten good enough now; even I see how easy it would be to piece the parts together, although I wouldn't know where to start. And with metal 3-D printers? I don't think there's a part that can't be made. All that's required is a suitable metal. No. We are here to stop them."

Erick could not dispute the resolve this man had. He was telling the truth. He may still be a Darrk genetically, but he also was more human than Darrk. Earth was his home now, and he would defend it until his death.

Duncan ran into the room; he had gone to check on the two in the cooler while Erick and Bobby spoke. "Erick, I'm sorry. I screwed up."

"What happened?"

"They're gone." Erick ran for the walk-in.

After a brief study of the cooler, Erick started to blame himself for not crawling inside the Frenchman's mind. What little he did see he didn't want to go further. But there was something he remembered, someone pushing an air gun against his shoulder and firing it. He had been tagged; a tracking chip put in him. While he was asleep, someone had removed the bricks on the side on the house, went through the wall of the cooler and rescued him. Things just got harder.

"I'm sorry, Erick, really, I . . ."

"It's okay, Duncan, we didn't know, and you surely didn't know he would have a rescue team somewhere."

"But how did they find him?" Lauren asked.

"Tracker chip," Bobby sighed. "Same thing I put in my cows now so I can make sure they're in before a bad storm. Technology."

Erick and Lauren were packed and headed toward the door when Erick told her he wanted to check on Dianna before he left. Upon entering the guesthouse, he noticed the doorway to the tunnel was wide open. Going inside, he went in the short way to where he had laid Brandon on the floor. Dianna was leaning against the wall asleep, and Brandon's head was on her lap. He hoped Doc's elixir would restore Brandon as well, and Dianna needed more. He would see to it before he left.

Erick drove the Escalade to the office. They had given Duncan the task of making everyone comfortable until they returned. He would brief everyone on the situation and his plan when they returned, if he had the plan all worked out by then, he thought.

Raven, Elliot, and Johnathan were ready to go, they would meet in the lab, as he wanted to see Hawk before they left. When he entered the lab, he got one of the surprises of his life—Hawk was standing next to the bed; Doc steadying him on one side and Mac on the other.

"How does that feel?" Doc asked.

"A little painful, but good. My toes itch."

"Good! But I'm not scratching them for you." Doc looked at Erick, "He apparently is healing at an even faster pace than I thought. The pain he just mentioned is coming from the area of his back the bullet was against. It appears the disk is almost healed, and I can barely find the crack on the X-ray. He won't take pain meds as he said it slows healing."

Lauren was over at the light table, looking at the X-rays. "Erick, look at the difference between the ones from last night and this afternoon. He's healing at an alarming rate for a human."

Hawk almost said something, but Mac stopped him. "She doesn't mean anything; it's the doctor in her."

Erick pulled Doc to the side. "How fast can you make the drink you gave me for Dianna last night?"

"Quickly, it's not hard if I have all the ingredients. Did the quart I gave you last night work?" He had been pulled off the cot in the dressing room before they left to get it.

"A quart almost fully restored her, but she needs more. Do you think it will work on a Nightwalker?"

"I don't know. Could try, I guess, why?"

He explained Brandon was at the guesthouse and described the shape he was in, then he added that he was going to have a dozen Darrks who were going to need it as well.

"Then I'd best get started."

A L

Mac thought of staying, but it was determined there really wasn't much for him to do at the mansion. He really needed to clear up what was going on in Virginia, and Erick said he would need him if his plan was to work. Mac went forward and sat in the second seat for the takeoff, leaving Elliot and Raven talking with Johnathan about an approach on the lawsuits. Lauren was reading a book and watching Erick out of the corner of her eye. They hadn't taken off until after four, so that wouldn't put them in Virginia until late, and she had become concerned with how quiet and withdrawn Erick had become.

He was sitting in the seat directly across from her, facing the rear of the plane. She faced forward, with Elliot right behind her and Johnathan across from him. Raven was across the aisle with an empty seat in front of her that Mac would occupy when he wasn't up in the co-pilot's seat. The two seats across from Eric and Lauren were empty except for two boxes that held folders and other paperwork for Raven. Erick just sat there staring out the window, but she knew he wasn't seeing anything, at least not out there. Erick would get this way when he was doing large problem solving from repairing a drive engine to building a pyramid. She didn't know for sure what his focus was, but she could guess. Con had been ahead of him every step of the way; even the two that escaped seemed to have been preplanned. They had to have had a team in place long before they went to rescue them. They also would have needed the plans to the house. She went back to her book, knowing he would talk to her when the time was right.

Erick sat playing everything back in his mind, from the time he showed at the house in Virginia: the thugs coming into the house, the police showing up almost half an hour after they called, to the detective who couldn't find the bullets Mac said were as plain as day.

Then there was Dianna. She had told him Con had called and told her he was there at the mansion. She didn't inform the den because she thought it wasn't necessary. She had really come to talk to him. If she could get just the key, that would pacify Con for a time while she tried to think of a way to get Erick to fix the ship. Con was applying pressure on her and wanted her to take Raven or Hawk or both if she could, to force him to fix the ship.

She knew this wouldn't work. After she had come and found Erick and Hawk were caught in a transfer, she was trying to think of a way to get the key when Hathor/Lauren showed up. When she arrived, she didn't know it was Lauren. Brandon had been watching and just said it was a Darrk female. When she heard Lauren's howl, she knew trying anything else that night was futile. She sent the Nightwalkers away and went back to her home to think. Later that evening, Thorm came pounding through her office door demanding to know why he hadn't been told about Erick's arrival. She had told him it wasn't necessary to tell him, and he wanted to know if she'd gotten the key. When she said no, he stormed out the door, saying they weren't going to like that, talking like it was the others at the den that wouldn't like that.

In truth, Thorm's stupidity proved that Con was already talking to him, which she already suspected. There was no other way he would have known. So, she devised a plan to rid herself of Thorm and make it look like she was none the wiser about his relationship with Con. When Con called later and asked if she had the key, she told him the truth. She also told him the den was starting to give her problems, so she was going to let them "catch her" after the next night and let them attack Erick and assess the outcome. After all, she had said, they might get lucky. She didn't expect Thorm to tie her up the very next night.

This proved to Erick that Con was playing a game on three fronts. One, Dianna. Two, using the den to watch her and be prepared for an attack when he showed up, and three; that was the big one. Erick was running right into the problem. Con had already known about the house in Virginia and was having it watched. The three thugs were supposed to watch, not act. That's why it took the police so long to get there; they had to ask Con for instructions. The detective had left the two bullets so he could get back in the house. If it hadn't been that, it would have been something else. But Johnathan personally was the one that let them in, so they couldn't search the house. Dianna had never told Con that Erick wore the key around his neck, just that it was where he could get it. Dianna didn't trust Con, and rightfully so. So, they filed the lawsuits and told everyone the house has priceless art in it. When someone breaks in, they have a good reason to inventory and search the *entire house*. Erick guessed that the only reason they didn't find him while he slept, was he was in *Johnathan's* tomb! His father, grandfather, grandmother, and mother were in the tomb next door to the one he had slept in.

Erick wondered how many more of his places and properties Con knew about. His wealth estimate was off by about a billion dollars, so he had missed some, or he hadn't told Dianna the truth. For now, he would stick to the plan he had outlined in his mind and see what Con's next move was. But here in Virginia, he was going to burn his playhouse down. He needed Con to feel loss, and he would clean up a corrupt police force at the same time. And he desperately needed to cut off Con's escape route. He sat up, startling Lauren, "Sorry. Hey, Mac! Can you come back here?" It was time to start getting ahead of Con.

Mac came back to see Erick smiling and leaning on the backs of Raven and Johnathan's seats, Lauren had moved to the seat across from Raven, and was excited to see the change in Erick. Mac put his elbows on the backs of the seats of Elliot and Lauren. Like Erick, he had to hunch over a bit, which was fine by him. The co-pilot's seat was not made for a man who was six feet, six inches tall. Erick's smile was infectious and soon they were all smiling. And the smiles got even bigger when Erick laid out what he called Phase 1.

An hour later, they stopped for fuel and then took off again without even opening the door to the plane. This leg of the flight was two hours, and Johnathan called to have them picked up. Later, it was decided he would stay at the house with everyone else. Erick didn't want anyone separated from the others until the next afternoon, when the plan was put in action. As he and Lauren returned to their seats, Mac sat across from Raven for a while before he went forward for landing.

"Do you think it will work?" Raven asked Mac.

"I don't see how it will miss. Bad cops are greedy, that's how they become bad cops in the first place."

"We just need to make sure," Johnathan added, "we don't catch a good cop with a bad one. If he's on the level, he'll be on our side when this all goes down. If he isn't, we will sweep him up with the others. Then maybe we will get some real answers."

It was after two when they arrived at the house. The two guards in the house quickly helped them carry the bags inside, saying the less time outside the better at this time of night. Once inside, introductions were made. "Safer here than outside. This neighborhood has been giving this place all kinds of hell the last few days. I'm Walter; my partner here is Brandon. And we know Johnathan and Mac."

"I'm Erick Scott," holding out his hand. "This is Lauren, Raven, and Elliot." After handshakes all around were completed, the two guards said they would carry the bags upstairs and left them. The library doors opened, and a tall thin man stepped out.

About six foot three, he had a mass of curly brown hair on his head that looked all tangled, his brown eyes squinted, "Aw, they'll let anyone in this place!" His Southern drawl and the smile on his face said much.

"Albert Riggs, as I live and breathe!" Mac rushed over and gave him a bear hug.

"Hey! I'm spoken for!" he said, and hugged Mac back. "Nice to see you, Chief."

"What are you doing here?" Mac stepped back to look at him. In blue jeans, tennis shoes, and a Hawaiian shirt, he looked like he was on vacation. "Skip called me and said you guys might need a little help. He's worried the cops will railroad you and wanted back up."

"Everyone, this is Albert Riggs. He is a detective from New Orleans."

A memory tugged at Erick's mind. "God."

Al's eyes widened, "Excuse me?"

Mac realized what happened and covered, "Yeah, Doc and Hawk and I got a little slack-eyed and silly, started telling a few war stories one night. Yes, Al was assigned to Hawk's and my team."

"I'm sorry," Al blushed. "Just caught me off guard."

"No, I'm sorry. I'm Erick Scott, this is Raven, Elliot, Lauren, and Johnathan."

"Pleased to meet you. Hey, where you guys been?" he said to Mac, "I been cooling my heels since noon!" As they wandered off to talk, Erick saw Raven looking up at Maria's picture.

He walked over behind her, resting his hands on her shoulders.

"This picture could be me. I can see why you looked at me the way you did when I saw you for the first time after you got back. Were we really that much alike?"

"Yes. You even think a lot alike. Your sense of humor is about the same too."

"God, that must be terrible for you! Every time you see me, I would remind you of her."

"At first, yes. But, not now; in fact, when I see you now, I don't even think of her." Erick realized how bad that sounded and tried to correct it. "Not to say I don't think of her anymore, because I do. You are you. Maria was Maria. You may be a whole bunch alike, but you're also a whole bunch different." He gave her a hug, and noticed Lauren looking on, smiling.

"She was beautiful, Erick." Lauren looked at the signature at the bottom of the painting. Her eyes got wide, "is that a Vermeer?"

"Why does everyone ask that?" He then said, "Yes, she was. But so are you. I owe her my life, as I owe you my life. I am happy you found me."

Lauren giggled, "I didn't find you, blame him!" She pointed at Mac, who was still talking to Al. "Hey! Bruiser! You going to leave a lady by herself all night."

"He better not! Too many single guys around here!" Raven yelled, smiling.

Elliot had been walking around the house, looking at paintings and statues. He looked at Erick, "Priceless art they said. My God! This has been sitting here all this time? It's a good thing it will start to be moved tomorrow. It needs to go where it can be enjoyed."

"I agree. But wait till you see the attic and the basement." Looking at Lauren opening the doors to the living room he said, "And the living room, I think I'm in trouble."

Erick watched as Lauren looked inside, then promptly sat on the floor. "Oh . . . my . . . God," she breathed. Elliot wandered over to see what had gotten her attention. The light was dim, just coming from behind him, so he reached in the doorway. Fumbling for a switch, he found it, and turned on the lights.

He was speechless.

"You guys will be up awhile I think, I'm going to bed." And with that, Johnathan bid goodnight, but he didn't think anyone, but Erick heard him.

Sunshine came in through the window of the living room. The curtains hadn't been opened in years, and when Lauren tried to open one, it shredded and fell to the floor. The windows were mirror tinted to block UV rays she noticed; and stop prying eyes. She had spent a great deal of time cataloging the room and was far from finished. To her surprise, it wasn't dusty. The cleaning company dusted every month and that made what she had seen even more amazing.

Erick came in carrying a small tray with a coffee pot and two cups and set it on the small table by the door. Pouring two cups, he walked over to Lauren and handed one to her. "Oh, thank you." Taking a sip, she surveyed the room. It was supposed to be a living room, but it had no sofas, no chairs, and the only table was the one by the door. The pocket doors leading to the dining room were open and had been since the home was new. A dining room table had never been placed in it, and the doors to the kitchen were locked shut. The hardwood floors were clean and finely polished and showed almost no wear. Standing on it were several rows of glass cases, reaching to the high ceilings. On the ends of each cabinet was a suit of armor—Japanese Samurai armor, European armor from many periods, Chinese, Indian, African; it all seemed to be represented. Complete with weapons, she had never seen such a collection. Then there were the cases themselves. They were filled with sculptures. Some she guessed were Sumerian, others she knew to be Egyptian, North American, South American, Central American; all statues, pottery and carvings from all periods of the history of mankind—Inca, African, European, Chinese, Japanese, Aztec, Aleut, Thai, Anasazi, the list went on and on. Some sculptures were in wood, some in stone, copper, ivory, bronze, jade, silver, gold. Some were as small as a walnut, others as large as a man. An Aleut totem pole was in a corner. Everywhere you looked not an inch of space was wasted. One more item in the room would have blocked the view of something else, but right now? You could easily see everything in the room; it was so beautifully arranged.

And in the center of the room there was a mummy still in his sarcophagus, in an upright position, with its lid standing next to it, in solid gold, in a thick glass case.

"I think I'm going to need help." Lauren looked around the room for the hundredth time and pointed at the mummy. "That isn't who I think it is?"

"Yes, it is."

"Well, now I know why when they found his tomb, he wasn't in it." It was King Tutankhamen's high priest, the one who ordered the deaths of the Darrks in Egypt and the one responsible for the death of their sons. "You do know a good portion of what you have here is illegal."

"Not when I found it."

Another hour found Elliot, Mac, and Raven wandering between the cases. When Al came around the corner, he whistled and said, "Good lord!" He was dressed differently this morning. He had traded in the Hawaiian shirt for a long-sleeved flannel and a black Carhart vest, blue jeans and tennis shoes.

Johnathan came in and announced the car was here to take them to the office. Raven looked at Erick, "We are going to look at what was dug up on the two police detectives, the thugs, and the other law firm. This should prove to be an interesting morning. Don't talk to the police without Johnathan or me present. We will set up appointments for you and Mac for later today or tomorrow morning." Then she and Elliot followed Johnathan out the door.

Erick looked at Mac and Al, "Can we talk?"

At ten fifteen, twenty students from the archaeology and history departments of Georgetown University showed up in a large van, followed by a semi-truck with a fifty-foot trailer. They unloaded a full truck's worth of crates of various sizes. Coordinated by Lauren and one of their professors, the students began to pack and catalog the attic with sheer amazement apparent on their faces. Erick directed where things were to be shipped. He was spending part of his time in the upstairs hall and some down in the foyer with the security guards. They used the upstairs hall to pack after rolling up the rug and had stacked the crates carefully in the foyer. When they had cleared enough room in the attic, they began to pack there. Two of the students in white gloves began to crate paintings under Erick's direction.

The security guards numbered each crate and labeled them for shipment according to their contents and Erick's directions. Some went to the Smithsonian, some to Georgetown University, some to the mansion in Seattle. Some were going to be sent to a warehouse in New York for an antique shop Erick owned there, and others were going to another warehouse in Seattle. Everyone was amazed at how much there was in the attic, but after all, it was a very large house. Lauren and Erick didn't mention the basement yet, they didn't want to scare them off, and they kept the doors to the living room closed and locked.

At two o'clock on the button, thirty pizzas and two cases of pop and two of water showed up. Everyone seemed to eat fast so they could get back to work. Lauren and the other professor, Dr. Moss, spent a lot of time explaining to the students what the things were and where some of the pieces were from. Erick did the same when Dr. Moss or Lauren got stumped. After all, he'd put it there, not that he could say it.

The students left at six and said they would be back the next day. The professor asked if they could bring another class, as what they were seeing were things these students would probably never be able to touch in their lives ever again. Erick told him he was welcome to; he knew there was a lot of history in the house as a good portion came from a family home in Boston, and some of that predated the American Revolution. Lauren thought the man was going to start drooling. After they'd left, Lauren, Mac, Al, and Erick went to the basement. With them, they took eight heavy canvas bags. It was time to set a trap.

Raven, Elliot, and Johnathan came to the door and asked where Erick and Mac were. "Last I saw of them they were going into the basement," the guard answered, "about ten minutes ago." They went into the kitchen and sat at the table to wait for them to come up.

It wasn't long when the four of them came up with eight sacks that looked heavy. Setting them on the table, Erick asked when they were going to talk to the detectives. "They are going to be stopping by tonight after they talk to the family of the one that fell down the stairs. They saw all the activity over here and called. Seems they were upset that you might be skipping out."

"Good. Do you know who took the call?"

"I took the call from a Detective Moyer. But here is the information on our two detectives, one of them being Moyer." She laid out several sheets of paper, the bank and financial statements on both and the results of the property searches for them. Erick began to go over them. It seemed the older of the two, Larry Wallace, was barely making it. His pay was put in his account and was gone before the next payday. Someone else was a regular depositor, his wife. She put in an amount that went up and down. It ranged from three to five hundred dollars every two weeks. He, or rather the bank, owned a home in a suburb of Washington. He had taken a second mortgage on his house, and was making two payments a month, one for his first mortgage and another for his second. He had twenty years to go on the first mortgage, and with the payments on the second there was about eight months left.

He had been with the police force for fifteen years and had an excellent record with several decorations. There were two dings on his record, both dealt with child abuse. One was for slapping a man at the hospital when his son was brought in with a broken arm. This was when he was still in uniform. The other was for a man who had been caught abusing little girls. This one occurred after he'd made detective. The man had taken a swing at him and he apparently beat the man so badly he'd been suspended for a month without pay. It was interesting to note that there was money taken up at the station to pay his bills while he was suspended. Another item of note, he and his wife had adopted the boy from the hospital that had the broken arm when his father had been sent to prison for killing the boy's mother. Erick also noticed there was a check written every month to a church. It was always ten percent of their combined income, and it was made out to the Church of Jesus Christ of Latter-day Saints. It was written every month for as long as the statements went back, about three years. He saw no other income and no other property.

The other detective, Tim Moyer, had his pay directly deposited like Wallace, but that was where the similarities ended. He apparently made a car payment on a late model Chevy Tahoe SUV and a payment for a condo in Georgetown. His bank account had over fifteen thousand dollars in it. He couldn't have saved it either, as his payments on the Tahoe and the condo accounted for more than half his pay. There were also charges to eat out almost daily, and charges to bars that sometimes exceeded 300 dollars in one night. He was living way beyond what he was making. Looking further back on his statement, Erick saw a ten-thousand-dollar deposit, then a few weeks afterward, there was another ten. There were also deposits of five hundred dollars sporadically and another of eight hundred twice a month. He was having over two thousand dollars a month on average put in his bank account extra. Looking through the paperwork, Erick found the deposits of eight hundred were made from a company called Agave Limited. The twenty thousand also came from Agave Limited. Although he may be jumping the gun, Erick would bet that Agave Limited was somehow tied to Con.

Erick thought Wallace seemed to be an honest man, while Moyer clearly wasn't. It was time to turn up the heat.

About a quarter after eight, the doorbell rang and was answered by a guard. He let Wallace and Moyer in after they showed their identification and told them Mr. Scott and Mr. McGregor would be right with them. Then he resumed his post next to the door.

Moments later, Erick and Mac walked into the entrance, each carrying two very heavy canvas bags. Mac dropped one and about a dozen gold coins spilled out. He quickly scooped them up and put them back in the bag. One had rolled under the edge of crate and he had missed it. Moyer took note as to where the coin had fallen. Wallace was looking at a painting while Mac picked up what he had dropped. They continued over to a table by the doors of the library, setting the heavy bags on the table next to the other four bags carried up from the basement. The sound of coins ringing off each other was echoing in the long narrow room like a bell of a bicycle.

Erick and Mac turned toward the two detectives, "Wallace, wasn't it?" Erick said this as he walked over, holding out his hand to the older detective. Raven opened the door to the library and stepped out as Erick shook his hand, "I think we can talk in the library,"

Raven had left the doorway and was proceeding to the hall, heading for the kitchen, as Moyer watched her ass move back and forth in her tight skirt. Mac turned to him and said, "If you'll excuse me for a moment, nature calls. I'll be right back." Moyer nodded, and Mac began to run upstairs. Moyer looked at all the crates stacked in the room with shipping labels on then. Then he took a few steps toward the table and looked down at the eight bags. All were tied shut except the one Mac dropped, breaking the tie. Open at the top, he peaked inside. They were all gold coins; each one was stamped off center like it had been hit with a hammer. It appeared to have a cross on one side and looking at another coin a shield on the other side.

"1715 Spanish gold," said the guard. "A shitload of it!"

"Really?" Moyer looked at him, the guard smiled.

"Yeah, really. Mr. Scott showed one to me. Said his family got them from a shipwreck over a hundred years ago off Florida." The guard shook his head. "Just one of the damn things would pay my salary for the month! Makes me wish I had about half a sack of them."

"What's he doing with them?"

"I don't begin to know what rich people do with things like that. But he's sending them to Seattle. One batch left about an hour ago and this one leaves tomorrow."

"Batch huh. Tomorrow?" He pointed at the bags, the guard nodded.

Mac had started down the stairs. "Sorry about that. We can talk in the kitchen. Your name was . . ."

"Moyer, Detective Tim Moyer." Mac held his arm out, pointing toward the hall for the kitchen. "You look like you're packing everything here up."

"Yes, he is. After the incident here he feels it's time, I guess."

"Where's it all going?"

"I'm just a bodyguard. You'll have to ask him."

As they came into the kitchen, Raven was seated at the table with a small tape recorder and a file in front of her. She stood as Mac made introductions. "This is Raven Scott, an attorney for Raven-Hawk, my employer."

She held out her hand and Moyer shook it. "Yes, we spoke on the phone this afternoon. Any relation to Mr. Scott?"

"He's my uncle. I'd like to inform you I will be recording this interview so my partner can listen to it. It will become a permanent record once transcribed and placed in the file of this incident. Do you have any questions about anything not pertaining to this case?"

"None except are you single?"

She ignored the question. "Then let's begin," Raven sat as she turned on the recorder.

For the next hour, Moyer asked questions, some were the same questions just reworded. When it came to the questions about the two living suspects' story and the differences, Mac flatly said they were lying. No matter how you reworded it and sugarcoated it, they were lying, period. When asked about the one that died in the basement, he said he was dead when he got there. He had come to the top of the stairs, looked down, turned the light on, and went down to check on him, finding him unresponsive. Then

Moyer said that they said the "old man" asked them to come in and move something for him. At this, Mac shook his head.

"Really, do you think a man would ask three complete strangers to come in his house, past midnight, to move something? As I had told you before and will tell you again, they were standing across the street staring at the house when I pulled away. If he wanted something moved, he would have asked me."

"Then why did you come back?"

"It's like I told you, Detective, I had a feeling something was wrong." Mac paused, "I'm a bodyguard. I make my living by keeping people safe. You must trust your instincts, or some bastard someday will make sure you don't have any, forever. You may be wrong every now and then. But if you keep that feeling to yourself and don't act upon it until there is a clear and present danger, no harm, no foul. Those boys were here to do harm that night, and that is what I am paid for, to make sure it doesn't happen to the client or the people the client is with. It just sometimes does not work out well for the 'suspects' as you call them. If one fell down the stairs in the dark and broke his neck, so be it. Now is there anything else that we haven't gone over a thousand times in my previous statement? You had me fly all the way back here from Seattle to ask me the same questions after listening to a bunch of things you yourself know are lies. You're not stupid, Detective, so stop wasting my time and money like I am now and get the truth out of those two thugs. Whose side are you on?"

"I'm just trying to get the truth."

"Bullshit. You're just trying to hang this in such a way these people can get money out of my client. How about a few questions of my own? I know about those ambulance chasers these boys have for lawyers. They kicking a buck or two back at you for twisting the story, enough so it can go in front of some bought-off judge who will award damages? What's the deal here? The lawyers will take seventy percent, give you ten percent, and the judge takes ten percent and gives the thugs the rest to keep them quiet?"

"Now look, Mister . . ."

"Don't 'Mister' me, asshole," Mac was getting frustrated, "I've had enough of this shit."

Raven stood, "Detective, I think this interview is over."

"Very well, then. We'll contact you when we conclude our investigation."

"Contact her, I'm done with your spineless bullshit."

Without another word, Moyer got up and left the kitchen. Headed for the entrance, he casually stopped next to the crate where the coin was, and bending over as if to tie his shoe, he reached under the edge, retrieved the coin, and stood up while slipping it into his pocket. He thought about how close the bodyguard was to having it figured out. This was starting to not be worth what he was being paid. About the only thing the big guy had wrong was the money; he only got five percent.

As he had entered, he noticed Larry hadn't come out of the library yet, so he went by the front door and sat on a chair that by his estimation was probably worth a couple thousand dollars. What did this fucker care? He obviously had more money than he needed. If Larry would get on board, he could make more, but the guy was so honest he could have been friends with Abe Lincoln. Moyer's gaze wandered over to the table, and its bags of coins. He was still staring at them when the guard behind him said, "Sure is a lot of money there. I overheard them say about two million in gold alone, more if you sell it as Spanish coin."

Moyer turned in his seat and looked at him. "What do you mean?"

"If you melt it down and sell it, about two million. If you keep it as 1715 Spanish coins, it's worth twice that."

"Really?"

"Oh yeah. Collectors. Stuff like that comes around and they pay high dollar for it and don't say a word. What the hell, it's leaving here tomorrow but it sure is fun to think about."

Moyer found himself doing more than think about it. "When is it being picked up?"

"Oh, no. I may be from the South but ain't that stupid. It disappears, they crawl up my ass with bird dogs, and I get nothing out of it."

The door to the library opened, and the two men stopped talking for a moment.

"There's a bar about a mile away called the Rolling Dice, know of it?" Moyer said quietly as Erick and Larry spoke a little longer.

"Yeah."

"Can you meet me there at midnight? I'll buy you a drink."

"I get off at eleven, so I guess so."

"It may be the best stop you'll ever make." Moyer stood as the older detective walked over. Erick shook hands with each of them and bid them goodnight. As they left, Moyer winked at the guard before he shut the door.

Erick could not believe what he saw when he shook hands with Detective Moyer. This one needed to be removed in the worst way possible. He walked back as Johnathan came out of the library, and Raven and Mac came out of the hall from the kitchen. "Did he buy it?" she asked the guard.

"I'll find out at midnight," Al said, walking over from the door. "I'm meeting him at a bar called the Rolling Dice."

"Good. He bought it. Wallace is on board, too. I'll have to call him and tell him about your meeting. He has suspected his partner in the past but couldn't prove it," Erick replied.

"How do you know he bought it?" Al asked.

"Call it, intuition," Erick said with a smile.

"Is everything okay? I may have overdone it," Mac said. "I got a little frustrated with the smug bastard."

"You're kidding me," Raven began, "we need to put you on a stage!"

Elliot came running down the stairs. "Got it! The recording was good and clear. The mike by the door was perfect."

"So, I guess we wait for midnight," Al said. "Just one question." Everyone looked at him. "Where the hell is the Rolling Dice?"

The Rolling Dice was an old, run-down place that had seen better days. The white paint was peeling and two of the letters in the sign on the building were burnt out. The parking lot was almost empty. There were just three other cars in it; one was the gray Tahoe he parked next to. He was early, about ten minutes till midnight, and he didn't want to seem too eager. But, then again, he did get off at eleven he had said. Al got out of the pickup from the Raven-Hawk motor pool and walked to the door. He knew this was the toughest part. In sting operations, it was called "setting the hook," and while he could have worn a wire, it would not be the time to do so. If he were caught at this stage, they would never get another chance. Pulling open the door, he entered the bar.

Moyer was sitting at the bar, staring at the coin he had gotten off the floor. He had gone to see a friend who owned a coin shop and showed it to him. From what his friend said, it was worth much more than the guard told him. The dealer had valued the coin at between five and ten thousand dollars in good condition. The coin he had would be graded MS 64 or better. Moyer said all the ones he saw were at least this good. Each of the bags were marked one thousand coins, that would put each sack at about five to ten million each or about forty to eighty million dollars in all. He saw the guard walk in and put the coin away.

The inside was not well lit. Al wished he had a dollar for every time he had walked into a bar just like this one. The place probably hadn't been painted in years, and there was a faint smell of cigarettes, even though smoking in public places had been banned in this state for several years. Al saw Moyer sitting at the bar with a bottle of beer in front of him and a bored expression on his face. Another two men were sitting at a table at the other end of the bar and the bartender was talking with them. When he saw Al, the bartender walked over, asking him what he wanted.

He pointed to Moyer's beer, "How about one of those?" The bartender reached into the cooler below, twisted off the top and set the bottle on the bar as Al threw a twenty on the bar. After the bartender gave him change, he turned, and walking down the bar, returned to his conversation with the two men at the end. "Well, I'm here."

Moyer looked at him, "You ever do more than think about stuff?"

"Yeah, but I'm too close to this one. I would be one of the first they looked at."

"Perhaps." He looked away; he was sure now he would get this guy on board. "What if I told you all you would need to do is give me a little information and a piece of those little bags would be yours."

Al looked at him. "How would and when would I get it? All you have to do is take the info I give you and leave me hanging. Just another sap taken advantage of."

"The thought had crossed my mind." Moyer glanced at him, then took a swallow of beer. "But I would be too easy to find. It's enough to take it, but disappearing would raise suspicions, and I'm not going anywhere. By the time everyone in the crew got paid, it splits up well, but I like where I live, and I like my job. It gives me opportunities. And if you didn't want to hide or spend the rest of your life looking over your shoulder . . ." He let that sink in for a moment.

When the guard didn't reply, he went on. "Besides, it might just lead to a good partnership if you get around that kind of thing often. I checked around with a few people I know, your estimate was a little off. It's worth about five million a sack or more than forty million dollars in all, if I guessed the amount that was sitting there right. After the loss from having to sell it to someone who must hang onto it for a while so the market isn't flooded, my guy said we can get around twenty to twenty five million for it. Your cut, depending what it was sold for, would be two to four million. You going to work there tomorrow?" He saw the guard's eyes widen.

"Yeah."

"Even better. You can't ask for a better alibi than to be at work when it goes down, especially there. All I need is the pickup time and where it's going, for that you get a full share of the take. It will take about a week, maybe two, to unload it. Then I'll drop it wherever you say."

Al gave him a greedy look, "You serious? You're a cop."

"And you are a security guard. Doesn't mean we're not human." He slid Al his card. "That's my phone number so you can get ahold of me in two weeks. But we must move on this, time is short, and I still have to set this up."

Al seemed to think a bit, taking a long pull off his beer. "It's being picked up tomorrow at six in the evening. They are taking it to the private airport just out of town; eight small heavy cardboard boxes, each weighing about sixty to sixty-five pounds. It will be picked up by a courier service in an unmarked black minivan. If you don't get it by the time it's on that plane, it will be on its way to Seattle."

"They aren't sending it in an armored truck?"

"No, they don't want to draw attention to it in the neighborhood. It will be one person in a black minivan."

"This is going to be easier than I thought," Moyer said with a smile.

Al looked at him, "You owe me a beer."

"I owe you several!"

By the time Al got back to the house, the canvas bags had been packed into eight small heavy cardboard boxes and addressed to Raven-Hawk in Seattle. Al entered and looked at Erick and Detective Wallace. "We're good to go."

Thirty minutes later the detective looked at Erick, "You know you won't get these back until he's in prison with all the men he has working for him. Evidence is held until then."

"I'm aware of that. My family has had them for over one hundred years; having them missing from us for a year or so won't matter."

"Why are you doing this?"

"I would be lying if I didn't say I wanted the lawsuits to go away. But the plain truth is I detest dishonest people. Humanity can do better, and to be dishonest and a police officer in my book is inexcusable. Your partner is preying on the very people you are sworn to protect and serve. No, I'm happy to do it. Now go home to your family, you have spent enough time here today. You're going to have a long day tomorrow."

Just by looking at the man's face told him everything this man had just said was the truth. Wallace thanked Erick and turned to go home to get some sleep. It was going to be a long night tomorrow, even longer with the fact he was going to have to arrest his own partner.

Just then Lauren came in the door, holding a digital camera with a telephoto lens attached. She had followed Moyer from the police station to a coin shop. She had taken several pictures of him at the coin shop, even got one of Moyer handing the shop owner one of the coins. After that, she had gone to a grocery store across from the Rolling Dice and parked in a dark corner in full view of the bar. At eleven o'clock she got pictures of Moyer entering the bar, then of Al entering the bar shortly before midnight and leaving an hour later.

About ten minutes after he'd left. A sedan pulled in and four men got out. One went in the bar and came out with Moyer. They talked for about fifteen minutes, then the four men got in the sedan, and Moyer got in the Tahoe and left. She waited for a while to make sure she wasn't caught or seen, then came back to the house.

Wallace was looking at the pictures on the camera when he got Mac and Erick's attention. "Look at this." He showed them a picture of two of the men Moyer was talking to.

"Well, well." Erick looked amused.

"What is it?" Lauren asked, puzzled looking at Mac and Erick. Each had a small smile on them.

"It's our friends," Wallace said. "Our friends from the night Erick and I met." Wallace looked at the pictures sadly, then said, "I'm going home. I'll see you tomorrow." Handing the camera to Lauren said. "Goodnight," walking out the door. When he left it looked as if he had the world on his shoulders.

At eight the next morning, five grad students, the twenty students from the day before, and fifteen history majors showed up from Georgetown with the chubby Dr. Moss and another professor, a Dr. Foreman. Thin and short with graying hair, she was amazed at what was still in the attic, but when they started in the basement after lunch, she was speechless.

Mac, Al, and Erick had gone down in the morning and moved the trunk to the kitchen. It was still very heavy, Erick having only taken half the coins out of it. They were Spanish doubloons from the 1715 wreck and fifty-dollar Confederate gold pieces. Al commented that he didn't know the Confederacy had made fifty-dollar pieces, to which Erick said with a straight face, "They didn't?"

They spent the next two hours making sure all the firearms in the basement were unloaded. Erick was sure they were but felt they should be checked. They were, and when Mac came across two crates of ammunition for a Gatling gun, they took them upstairs and put them in a closet. Then he told Lauren the basement was "clear," and the students could start anytime. Walking up to Erick, he jokingly asked, "The Gatling gun isn't down there, I take it?"

Erick looked up from a box he was packing and said, "Oh yeah," and went right back to packing.

A large moving truck showed up at the curb with ten Raven-Hawk guards and ten movers, and the movers began to load the truck with items and crates going to New York. Four of the movers started packing the library.

About noon, six men from Raven-Hawk started moving equipment into the house and going upstairs. As it had been finished being packed and the last crates moved to the entry, everyone stayed out of each other's way.

The day was moving along smoothly. Then a crowd started to gather on the sidewalk on the opposite side of the street making Lauren, not to mention the movers, nervous. Erick stood in the middle of the entry hall, oblivious to the din going on around him, his eyes closed. After a few minutes, he opened his eyes and running into one of the students, excused himself, and said, "I needed that break." The student laughed and said he needed to teach him that trick, as it would work great studying for finals.

Soon after, Lauren noticed the crowd start to disperse, just wander away. When Lauren looked at him, he said, "They were wondering what they were doing, I just gave them help finding something else to do." The more she was around him, a man she thought she knew, the more she realized how much he had changed, and how powerful he had become. Thinking about it scared her a little, but she was glad that if it was in anyone's hands, it was in his.

By 5:30 that evening, most of the students had gone and the movers had finished loading the first truck to New York. Tomorrow, the first truck to Seattle would arrive and begin to load. Eric had decided to start an antique store in the area and would sort what was going where. His store and warehouse in New York was going to be full. The warehouse in Seattle was being set up and should be ready by the time the truck got there. When he got back, he would look for a location when he had time, or send scouts out like he did in New York, to narrow down the locations he would have to look at.

About that time, Detective Wallace came in with two other men he introduced, saying they were from Internal Affairs. They started to question him about his motives, and it didn't take long before Erick just said, "Okay." Pulling the cell phone out of his pocket, he dialed a number. "Yes, Elliot? Could you put Raven on the phone, please?" The two officers began to look at each other, wondering what he was doing, until they heard. "Raven cancel the van; we are shutting it down. Turn what we have over to that FBI agent; we will let them work on it from here."

"Now, wait a minute!" one officer began.

"No, you wait a minute." Erick looked at them coldly. "I don't give a damn about whether or not you care about corruption in your own department. I will not be manipulated and belittled by a law firm that preys on people, and I will not support a police department that manipulates me either, just to sweep that corruption under the rug so they can save face and stay out of the evening news, while still letting those corrupt officers continue to work in that department. Your job is to protect and serve the people, not harass and investigate after the fact."

"I have spent a great deal of time and money trying to help you, that time and money is a gift I've handed to you. If you don't want it, fine. I'll give it to someone else to take care of, which I could have done in the first place. In fairness, I'm trying to let you clean up your own mess. If all you want to do is grill me, the door's that way," he pointed. "If you genuinely want to catch your bad officer and the men he works with, improving the health of your department and the public's view of it, then I would suggest you shut up, let me proceed, and help the community like you are supposed to. So, let me finish this. Raven, you still there?" He paused, listening, then looked at the two men. "Well?"

The men looked at him sheepishly, it was one thing to be dressed down by another officer, but from a civilian and have him be right. It made one feel ashamed. "Okay, do it."

"Raven, send the van on time, please."

One of the Internal Affairs officers pulled out his cell phone and dialed someone. Then, pulling the phone away from his ear, he looked at it. Swearing he had charged it the night before, he slid it into his pocket, and walked back over to the other officer.

Erick and Detective Wallace were standing by the Vermeer, looking up and talking about the painting to pass time.

Then Wallace turned toward him and said quietly, "You were pretty hard on them."

"Sorry, I'm not much for jackasses."

"Oh no, don't take it that way. I've gone to those two before and got what they were giving you. They deserved what they got. No need to apologize." Then returning to the subject, "I looked it up, this Vermeer is unregistered, are you sure it's authentic?"

"One hundred percent."

Mac started down the stairs, "There's a black sedan pulled up down the street, two men. I think it's the chase car." When he hit the bottom, he grabbed a radio out of his pocket, "Al, you got eyes on them?"

"Yes, I do, I also have eyes on a white, late model Suburban, one occupant."

Erick turned to Wallace, "It's about to start, let's go." He started up the stairs as Mac headed for the back door. Wallace looked at the two of them, wondering who he was to follow, then started to follow Erick up the stairs, leaving the two Internal Affairs officers wondering where they went. Erick went across the hall to an open door and started up another flight of stairs. They came to the attic and he just kept going, so Wallace followed him around the corner of a chimney. There was another flight of stairs. He was breathing heavily when he reached the top, noting Erick wasn't even breathing hard.

What he saw amazed him. On a small deck, a canopy had been put up, between the two chimneys, and the gables of the roof, it would be unseen from the street. There was a row of several monitors, and three men wearing headsets with mikes on them, watching those monitors. Elliot and Raven were sitting on two chairs behind them, eyes glued to the screens. They were looking through the cameras on the whole street the house was on. Two of the monitors kept flipping through the images. He recognized some of them. They had the whole route to the airport. Every camera of every business all along the way was here. But the two main images on the two screens in the center were from drones.

"How are you accessing all the cameras?" He wasn't just surprised; he was dumbfounded.

Raven turned, "Our company put them in, we monitor the security in these businesses."

It was like he saw Raven for the first time, "He called you . . . what?"

"It was a bluff," Erick said simply.

"Remind me never to upset you guys or play poker with you."

Erick handed him a set of headphones. Putting them on, he could hear what was going on.

"Be advised, the van has turned the corner, two blocks from door."

"Copy that."

Wallace noted the three men at the front of the monitors; one was acting as a dispatcher and had control over what all the monitors showed, except two. Those were for the drones being flown by the other two at the table. One drone was looking down at the front of the house as the van pulled up.

Dispatcher: "Courier has arrived." Then the front door opened, and two security guards came out with a hand truck, went down the four steps and loaded the eight small boxes in the back of the van. When they were finished, they shut the doors. The van took off immediately.

Dispatcher: "Courier on the move."

The dash camera of a car caught the black van as it went by. Wallace saw no markings on the van, and he could see a black sedan parked about six cars ahead of the car with the dash cam. He noticed all the monitors had a piece of white tape at the bottom: car one, car two, drone one, drone two. The other monitors were labeled: roving one, roving two, roving three. Drone one followed the van.

Car one: "Courier has passed me. Chase car pulling out behind courier . . . now. Suburban pulling out . . . now. Moving in five . . . four . . . three . . . two . . . one."

Dispatcher: "Be advised, we are still missing two men, could be in two vehicles or one vehicle with two."

Car two: "Van has passed my location." Wallace saw the dash camera on monitor two and saw the van go by.

Car one: "Car two, be advised, I caught a light!" A red light showed on the monitor.

Car two: "Copy that. Chase car just went by. Suburban has gone by, moving in five . . . four . . . three . . . two . . . one."

Drone two: "I see trouble, guys; garbage truck on side street, revving the engine."

Dispatcher: "How do you know he's revving the engine?"

Drone two: "Smoke coming out of the stack."

Dispatcher: "Copy that."

Drone two: "Van, you are two blocks from truck."

Van: "Copy that." Wallace noted it was a woman's voice. It sounded strangely calm.

Drone two: "Silver sedan, coming up street toward truck." The camera on the drone zoomed in. "Be advised, there are two men in the sedan."

Dispatcher: "Guys, we have a party crasher."

Car one: "On the move, have cut down to alley. Be there twenty seconds." Whoever was driving that thing was really moving. Wallace saw it flying down the alley, dodging dumpsters.

Drone two: "Truck's pulling out!"

Drone one: "Look out! He means to ram you!"

Lauren saw the garbage truck and tried to avoid it but parked cars got in the way, she did the only thing she could do, she put her foot all the way down and the van shot forward, making the truck hit her rear corner, spinning her around into a parked car. Glass broke and pieces of glass and plastic started to fly all over the van. Her air bag deployed and one of the boxes broke open, spilling its contents and flew all around the van.

The man in the garbage truck hopped out of the cab with a sawed off shotgun. He put three rounds in the van to keep the driver's head down. The silver sedan pulled up at the front of the van, the two men jumping out, both with sawed off shotguns, each put a round in the van as the black sedan and the Suburban pulled up. The driver got out and ran around the back, opened the rear door of the Suburban just as the garbage truck driver got there and threw two boxes in the back from the black van.

The two from the silver car got to the back of the van, each got two boxes and lumbered back to the Suburban, struggling under the weight as the two from the black sedan ran up to the van. One grabbed a box while the other looked at the torn box and started to grab coins, "Leave it!" shouted the driver as he started to pull away. A Ford pickup truck slammed into the driver side at the rear passenger door of the Suburban, injuring the man sitting there. The driver took off, leaving the last two men that didn't make it inside. One pulled out a 9mm and started to shoot at the man in the pickup, who got out and returned fire, striking the man in the chest three times. The other one threw up his hands, giving up, just as a Trailblazer roared by after the Suburban. Six Raven-Hawk security cars suddenly showed up, surrounding the scene, and twelve men jumped out. The man from the pickup yelled, "Cuff him!" and ran over to the driver's side of the van. "You alright?" Al asked.

"I'm fine," said Lauren. "Go help Mac!"

Al ran over and jumped into one of the Raven-Hawk cars, it was a Charger used for interceptions and the fastest car there. Then he went squealing after Mac, leaving a cloud of smoke behind. He yelled into the mike button on his shirt, "Where are they?"

Drone One: "I'm on them, take a left on Chestnut."

"I'm not from here, dumbass! Right, left, how far? Give me directions that way!"

"Sorry, one block up, take a left."

Mac was right on the ass of the Suburban and he rammed the back end. It swerved and regained control, speeding up. Mac was driving a Trailblazer with a grill guard on it. An unmarked vehicle from Raven-Hawk, he had the lights and siren on, but when he rammed the Suburban, the siren started a funny wail. He heard the exchange between Al and the drone pilot. "You coming to join the party, Al!"

"Wouldn't miss it, Chief!"

Drone 1: "Turn right, next corner."

Al drifted sideways in the corner but kept control, shooting down the street at eighty-five miles an hour. "Get me ahead of them before they hurt someone!"

Drone 1: "Yes, sir. Two blocks up make a left and put your foot in it, light traffic. You're running parallel to their track and should be able to get ahead of them."

"Now we're talking!"

He squealed around the corner and floored it.

Drone 1: "Local police have joined the party; they are blocking traffic at your next light."

"Thanks!"

One block over, Mac saw the guns come out, "Oh shit!" the man fired four shotgun rounds, taking the hood off the SUV and the one next to him emptied a magazine of 9mm. Mac backed off with steam coming out of the radiator. "Be advised they are shooting out the back of the vehicle, I've had to back off a little." Mac began to wonder how long it would be until he overheated.

Drone 1: "Sir, you are almost even with him. One more block. He's turning right! He's turning right! Slow down for a second I'll tell you when to floor it!"

"On it!"

Drone 1: "Okay, floor it! Floor it!"

Al felt the seat belt go click and braced himself. He had gotten lucky at the approaching corner, the building was all the way to the sidewalk, and they wouldn't see him until it was too late. "Ramming speed!" he yelled, just as he saw the Suburban.

Mac saw the Raven-Hawk Charger, just before it hit the Suburban; he figured it was doing about eighty. When he saw the Charger, the driver of the Suburban Moyer was doing seventy-five. At the last second, he tried to turn away from him. Al struck the Suburban forward of the passenger door and on the front wheel. It snapped off and folded over the side of the engine, which deflected the Charger upward. As fast as he was going, the car would have been crunched into the side had that not happened, but the men in the Suburban were not as lucky. The angle of the Charger made the rear of the car, hit the roof and front windshield on the Suburban. Ripping the oversized gas tank of the Charger open and dumping the remaining twenty-one gallons of fuel from the car into the SUV through the missing front windshield and all over its side. As a spark ignited the fuel, and a large fireball went into the sky. The Charger finished going over the top, and when it hit the street, it barrel-rolled five times before it ended up in a Tux shop. It had left all the flames behind it.

The man in the tux shop was closing for the day, and when he saw the flying car coming right for him, he did the only thing he could do; he ducked behind the counter. Later in his statement, he said as soon as everything was quiet, he heard someone yell in a Southern accent, "Woo hoo! Holy shit!"

Back on the roof, Detective Wallace turned to talk to Erick; he was gone. He asked Raven, "Where did he go?"

"He had one more thing that needed clearing up," Raven answered calmly, even though her heart was pounding pretty fast; Erick had to finish Phase 1 alone. "He will talk to you soon as he gets this one more thing done."

Detective Wallace found he might not want to know what the "one more thing" was and didn't ask.

Erick stood on the sidewalk, looking at the plain building in D.C., and felt the Darrk inside. He knew the Darrk would feel him as well, and Erick could sense his panic. Walking up to the entrance, he unlocked the doors with a wave of his hand and entered the building. This lawyer was going to disappear just like he had appeared here ten years ago. No one would find him, may not even look for him. When he shook Detective Moyer's hand, he saw him and knew what he had been doing the last ten years, his last ten years.

Some days later, the house was packed up. The last moving van had begun to pull away from the curb, leaving a few pieces of paper blowing on the street. It was on its way to Seattle. Four SUVs went with it, even though it was just a normal looking moving truck, the cargo was not. The fourteen guards would have a rough few days, but they were being compensated well for the inconvenience of guarding a truck going non-stop to Seattle. Al, with a crutch under one arm and a ninety-degree cast on the other, fresh from the hospital that morning, was arguing with Mac, "I'm telling you it was six times!"

"No, it was five!" It had been going like that for the last two days. "I don't care what the tux shop owner said, he was behind the counter. I saw it!" Mac picked up the one crate that was still there and carefully loaded it in the van that was taking them to the airport. The three-foot by four-foot crate was unmarked. It was in good hands.

Raven and Elliot wandered in from the kitchen. Raven looked at the two men, arguing on the sidewalk in the spring sun. "Maybe we shouldn't have offered him a job. All they been doing the last two days is argue."

"It's going to be six to nine weeks before they remove the casts. He may not even like Seattle," Erick volunteered.

"He's a whole bunch easier on the eyes than Mac," Elliot laughed.

"You're getting as bad as Doc!" With that, she kissed Erick on the cheek. "See you at home, Grandpa."

Erick stood on the porch and watched them drive away, then he sat down on the top step and was still enjoying the spring sun, when a limo pulled up, and Johnathan exited it before the driver came around the car. Over the last of month, he had dropped a noticeable amount of weight and was getting a spring back in his step. "Well, I see you are enjoying this lovely day."

"Sometimes one must recharge the batteries."

Johnathan chuckled. "When is he supposed to get here?"

"He said they would come soon as they get out of church. He's in the first ward, so it should be any time."

Johnathan sat on the top step next to him. "You could have at least left some brandy." Erick produced a flask from under his jacket sitting on the step. "Ah, I knew you wouldn't forget."

A short time later, a minivan pulled up behind the limo. Detective Wallace, a pretty woman in a dress, and five boys from thirteen on down to five, got out of the van.

"Wow, this place is cool!" the eldest stared up at the house.

"You can go ahead and go in if it's okay with your dad."

The children looked at him in anticipation, "Okay, but no running around!" The children bolted into the house, and naturally did not listen to their father.

"Sorry, they have energy to burn after sitting in church." Wallace turned and introduced his wife, "Mr. Scott, Mr. Marks, this is my wife, Eileen."

Erick knew this already, but Johnathan did not. But the detective in him saw it. "Something wrong?"

"Oh no, Detective. I recently had my aunt pass away; her name was Eileen," Johnathan replied sadly.

"I'm sorry, and please, call me Larry."

"Very well, and please, call me Johnathan."

"And to make things a little less formal, please call me Erick."

"I don't hear the boys anymore, hon. I think we better go check on them."

"I'll get it, you take care of what you need to do." Eileen then looked at Johnathan, "I'm sorry to hear about your aunt."

"Thank you," Johnathan bowed slightly. As she went inside to see what the boys were up to, Erick turned to Larry, "So, what happened?"

"Seems you started a brush fire, spreading all over. The Bar Association shut that law firm you were having trouble with on Friday, or at least what was left of it, pending review of some of their practices. When we searched Moyer's condo, we found about thirty thousand in cash and a book. It listed the cases he threw, and the payments received from that law firm that was shut down, as well as the name of a judge he was delivering payments to. It also listed all the cases he hadn't been paid for yet, as most are pending. Internal Affairs is starting a review of everything."

"The names of the other two officers found in the Suburban were in the book, as well as four others, and one of the Internal Affairs officers that was here that evening, as well. The department has a lot to answer for, too. There was a reference to an Agave Limited out of Mexico City that paid Moyer twenty thousand, for what, we do not know, probably never will. They were also paying him eight hundred dollars twice a month for who knows what. We are never going to find out. Seems Agave Limited packed up this week and disappeared into thin air. The last one in the Suburban was the one we hauled out of here the first night we met. The two back at the site of the robbery were not cops, but both were known felons. One is your buddy from that night. He is the one who gave up. The other one was just a known thug. I think that covers it all, unless you have any questions?"

"No, I don't, but that is not the whole reason I called you here. Johnathan?"

Johnathan opened his case and pulled a legal sized file out of it. He handed this to Erick who opened it, and signed something inside, and then handed it to Larry. Baffled, Larry opened the file. As he read through it, his eyes got bigger and bigger. "I can't accept this!"

"Why not? It was your old neighborhood, your first uniformed patrol was here, and besides, I have been told someone bought up all the housing and is moving everyone to better buildings. They're redoing the whole neighborhood. Take it! That little house you live in is a three-bedroom and you have five boys; you have outgrown it and can't afford another right now. Here they would have their own rooms with plenty to spare, and in the lease, I'm responsible for all the maintenance."

Eileen was saying the bedrooms were still furnished as she walked out of the house, then seeing the blank look on her husband's face, asked him what was wrong. He handed her the folder. As she began to read it, her hand went to her mouth, she looked at Erick, "Are you serious?"

"Yes, quite. You have been working part-time cleaning motel rooms so you can be with your boys, and this way you won't have to. But this is a big house; it will be hard to keep up."

"Larry, a lease to own, for a dollar a month? In twenty years, it's ours?" She looked at Erick, "Why?"

"It isn't often I see a couple work so hard to raise their children right anymore. It is not very often I find a man as honest as your husband with morals and convictions, and above all, a love for his family embedded in his heart and a prayer for the good of our nation and all mankind uttered every night on his knees. You deserve this house, and it deserves a family that will love it back. I don't need this home anymore, and I certainly don't need the money from selling it. Sign the lease," Erick said, holding out the pen. "Sign it."

With shaking hands, they signed the lease and handed it back to Johnathan. He said he would get a copy back to them Monday. Handing them the keys and one of his cards with the alarm code on it, he told them to call if there were any problems. He then retreated down the steps and got into the limo. "By the way," Erick said, before climbing in the back of the limo with Johnathan, "the study of the furniture at Georgetown should be done next Thursday. They are supposed to bring some back on Friday. Good day." He got in the limo, shut the door, and it moved away from the curb.

As they watched them drive up the street, Eileen asked "When did you tell him about your prayer?"

"I didn't, that's why I went ahead and signed the lease. Only God could have told him that." He put his arm around her as they turned and went inside to tell the boys. As he entered, something caught his eye. The Picasso still hung on the wall across from the library.

Johnathan and Erick were walking in the park. Soon they came up behind a grove of trees out of sight from the rest of the park. "Are you sure you just want them rebuilt? That will cost a lot more money than leveling them and starting over."

"Yes, just have them rebuilt and turned into duplexes; they will be large, but they will be for families." Then he looked around, and a thought occurred to him. "And that modern monstrosity of an apartment complex they built next door, tear it down and put in a park, with a ball field, I think. Send me the plans, and I'll approve or modify them."

"Be seeing you, my friend." Johnathan wrapped his arms around him in a big hug.

"So ends Phase I. I don't think he is going to take my advice. He wouldn't have left his offices and disappeared. Ever-vigilant. Take care of yourself my friend, see you in a couple months." Erick waved, and vanished.

Johnathan looked down at the ground and started to slowly walk back to the limo. He had tears in his eyes, suddenly feeling very alone.

Erick arrived in the back of the mansion by the bench, hearing many heartbeats around the home, mostly Darrk. He stood and looked out at the Sound, enjoying the moment, then walked through the patio to the rec room.

As he entered, he saw a man with silver hair sitting with his back to the door next to Dianna, who looked fantastic. Lauren, on the other side of him, stood and walked over to Erick, smiling. His scent was familiar, but he couldn't place it. Dianna swiveled her barstool around, smiling as well. He guessed this would happen a lot today as all the Darrks Lauren and Duncan had called had arrived, so not placing the scent of the Darrk didn't bother him too much. His back still to Erick, the Darrk on the stool spoke in Italian, "I'd know that scent anywhere, you still smell like grease, Engineer."

He watched the stool spin around, and an older man sat before him. As Erick had only seen him briefly in this form before they buried him, it took a moment. He had looked much younger. "Commander Nantes!"

In perfect English, Nantes spoke, "Nate now." Hooking a thumb at himself, "Meet the old boss, same as the new boss." He smiled, pointing at Erick.

Erick walked up and embraced the Darrk he thought was dead, almost 9000 years before.

EPILOGUE

The two men got out of the pickup and looked across a field of alfalfa in the darkness. Then two women got out of the back seat of the Silverado and stood next to the men. "You sure this is it?" The tall blond next to him was looking out over the field, trying to find what they were looking for.

The man next to her said, "It's here." They were standing on a remote highway, eyes looking into the darkness, but what they saw was far from dark. They had driven out from Miles City after midnight, on Montana Route 59 toward Broadus, where the driver had slowed and pulled over onto the shoulder. There was no traffic or lights except for a light at a house a half-mile away, clearly showing a barn behind a house in silhouette. A dog was barking in the distance, coming from the farmhouse. There was no moon, but the stars made the field bright to the eyes of the four, almost like looking at daytime on a cloudy day.

The driver was looking across the field at a sloped hill; in his mind, he was seeing ten men standing on the top of the slope. Memories of a time long past. He turned around and looked at the steep mound behind them, about sixty feet away. The men who'd built the highway had almost found it, but they curved the road, going around it.

"The natives had buried it. They couldn't move it, couldn't destroy it, and couldn't burn it. In the end, they buried it, and did their best to forget the terrible thing that happened here," the man said. Triangular-shaped, the mound rose above the highway about forty feet. As the others turned around, looking in that same direction, he began to concentrate, tuning the others out. The ground began to rumble as small rocks began to roll down the sides of the mound. The rumbling increased, and then the mound started to rise. The earth and rocks were falling away, revealing a black pyramid, rising in the night. It drifted over to the highway, setting down on the road. Forty feet tall with a surface as smooth as glass, a green light blinked on the side of it, near the base. The silver-haired man had stripped down to his underwear and began to get taller, hair as silver as his head started to grow out all over his body leaving a large wolf with long ears in his place. Its green eyes looked back at the man standing there, and a series of growls came from it.

"That's a long time to not fly one of these things. Be careful."

More growls followed, then what almost sounded like a laugh. Its lips stretched over its jaws, exposing long sharp teeth. It touched its seven-toed paw to the side where the green light was, and a door opened on the side. With a long howl and a last look at the three of them, he entered, turned around, facing them, and sat. As a lift carried him up into the structure, the door hissed shut.

"Very funny, Nate, very funny," the man said.

Half a mile away, Ross woke up to his dog barking. Normally Shelia's bark was a sign of trouble, so he swung his feet out of the bed, onto the cold floor. Grabbing his jeans and sliding them on, he pulled a hoodie over his head and stuffed his feet into a pair of worn cowboy boots. "Mmm, what is it?" Mary, his wife, asked.

"It's okay hon, go back to sleep." With that, he stood, and quietly as possible, went out the back door, grabbing a .223 off the rack over the door and a strong flashlight off the counter. He was careful not to let the screen door slam and wake the children. Then he was looking at Shelia. The black, silver, and fawn-colored cattle dog was absolutely going berserk, staring off into the field behind the house. He peered, trying to see into the darkness, not wanting to use the flashlight and ruin his night vision. "Quiet, girl!" The dog stopped barking immediately, but still pranced around and whined, looking into the field. Ross had never seen her like this. Normally, she would stare down the largest coyote.

Then he felt it, a rumbling through the ground, earthquake? It didn't increase and wasn't as bad as a truck going by. Soon it started to recede, and he saw a dim light in the distance by the highway, then it went out. Looking into the darkness, he began to feel uneasy. Shelia jumping up and down didn't help. Then a long howl rang in the night like a wolf's, answered by Shelia, and soon howls were echoing off the walls of the valley as every dog, coyote, and wolf joined in. Suddenly, bright lights came on, and he saw a triangular shape sitting on the highway. As he watched, it lifted off the ground and most of the lights went out, then moving faster than anything he had ever seen, it streaked off into the night sky. He stood with his mouth gaping open, looking in the direction of the highway as the howling stopped. Shelia had calmed down and was sitting, looking in the same direction. He turned on his heel, retraced his steps to the house and opened the back door. Carefully putting the rifle back in its place and the flashlight on the counter, he went back to the bedroom. There, he undressed and went back to bed.

"What was it?" his wife asked sleepily.

"Ah, nothing." He lay in bed with his eyes open, until the dawn.

Erick watched the fighter disappear as the howls quieted. "Old dog."

Dianna looked at Erick, "He'll be fine. He was a fighter pilot long before he became a ship commander." Her mate was probably having the ride of his life.

Lauren put her arm around Erick's waist and said, "Let's go home."